a COWBOY FIREFIGHTER for Christmas

D0030084

KIM REDFORD

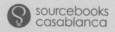

sourcebooks
casablanca

Published by Sourcebooks Casablanca, an imprint of Sourcebooks, Inc.
P.O. Box 4410, Naperville, Illinois 60567-4410
(630) 961-3900
Fax: (630) 961-2168
www.sourcebooks.com

Printed and bound in Canada.
MBP 10 9 8 7 6 5 4 3 2 1

Chapter 1

ON WILDCAT ROAD, A HALF-NAKED MAN BURST OUT of a pasture and ran onto the two-lane highway. He stopped on the white centerline and waved a bright red shirt back and forth high over his head.

Misty Reynolds slammed on the brakes of her SUV, caught searching for a radio station that wasn't playing Christmas music.

She gripped the steering wheel with both hands as she screeched to a stop, managing to narrowly avoid hitting the guy. She felt her heart thump hard with the burst of adrenaline and slumped against her seat in relief, grateful she'd been able to stop in time. She forced her breath to a slower, calmer pace.

As the adrenaline rush drained away, and she was able to focus, she got a better look at the stranger and licked her lower lip. This guy was all ripped jeans, cowboy boots, and big belt buckle over buff, bronze, sweaty body. His broad, muscular shoulders tapered to a narrow waist, and his long legs looked as if they belonged straddling a horse. He reminded her of her all-time favorite candy, Texas Millionaires.

It'd been a long time since a man had set her senses on spin cycle. And she'd nearly run him over. She wasn't sure whether to be annoyed or frightened. She felt a little shaky. Here and now was not a good time or place. Life was shaking her up enough already. She didn't need this problem.

She was headed toward a wide place in the road called Wildcat Bluff. The Dallas and Fort Worth Metroplex—as in big-city civilization—sprawled a couple of hours south. She had gladly left it and all the Christmas hubbub behind her. She was far away from everything now, except cattle, grass, trees. And the tantalizing stranger. But what was going on here?

Everything about the guy looked like trouble. In the 1880s, Wildcat Bluff had been notorious as a Wild West town that catered to cowboys and outlaws. Cowboys drove cattle herds north with dust in their eyes and returned with gold in their pockets. Desperadoes crossed the Red River from Indian Territory to get liquor by the drink and love by the night. Could this be the modern equivalent of a Texas horse thief? A carjacker? She glanced around as the hair on the backs of her arms prickled in alarm. Fortunately, the stranger appeared to be alone.

Still, she wouldn't take a chance. She hit the buttons on her door and heard the satisfying click of engaged locks and closed windows. She picked up her phone from the center console and checked for coverage. No bars. She couldn't call for help. She flipped open her glove box and looked for something big enough to use as a weapon. Nothing but a small flashlight. She wasn't completely without defense. She unclipped the small pepper spray canister off the metal link on her oversized aqua purse. She'd never used the spray before, but how hard could it be? She hoped that, if necessary, all she'd have to do was point and shoot. Still, it looked small and inadequate.

She mostly worked in the city and hadn't thought she needed to carry anything more than pepper spray. Now she wasn't so sure. Her BFF Cindi Lou had completed the training and paperwork for a carry permit and toted around at least a small .22 handgun, if not something with more stopping power. Cindi Lou, with her big hair and perfect makeup, was fond of reminding Misty that folks in Texas had a proud heritage of relying on personal self-defense in case of trouble since the days of the Republic of Texas when there was no other option. She'd been alarmed to hear that Misty was going into the countryside without a sidearm. Misty shook her head and felt herself tensing up. If worse came to worst, she would simply put her SUV in reverse or outmaneuver the stranger.

He ran the last few steps to her car, pulled on the door handle, and then hit the window with the flat of his hand.

She jerked back, gripping the pepper spray, as she kept him in sight. His belt was embossed with prancing reindeer, and the big buckle sported a Santa Claus face. If she included the holiday-happy red shirt in his hand, she'd assume Christmas, not carjacking, was on his mind. But he could also mean to disarm her with his fashion statement.

This close, he appeared wild. Hazel eyes flicked back and forth, resting on nothing or on everything. Dust peppered his tousled dark brown hair. His broad bare chest was coated with dirt and sweat. He looked good in the rough and rugged kind of way that set a gal's thermostat on "too hot to handle." She quickly flicked her AC to a higher setting and relished the burst of cold air.

"Help me!" he said in a deep voice muted by the closed windows.

"Do you have a medical emergency?" She held up her phone. "No coverage."

"Look over there!" He pointed toward the pasture.

All she saw was a little dust in the air. No telling what was going on. She'd play it safe. Once she put distance between them and could use her cell, she'd call to get him help.

"Do you have a blanket? Water?"

She felt his voice weave a spell around her like the finest of Texas male singers, an unmistakable quality of deep and sultry with a hot chili back-burn that left you wanting more. Classic singers like Willie Nelson, Roy Orbison, and George Strait came to mind.

She shook her head, breaking his spell. "Are you hungry?" Maybe he was homeless. "I have energy bars."

He frowned, drawing his dark, straight eyebrows together, as he shook his shirt at her. "There's a grass fire!"

Too late, she realized his red shirt was blackened and burned in spots. If she hadn't been so busy ogling his glistening sooty body and comparing him to outlaws, she might have noticed sooner. He'd obviously been using his shirt to beat out a fire.

"Only minutes to stop it." He glanced at her backseat, and his face lit up with happiness. "You've got towels!" He dropped his tattered shirt.

"Always. Just in case." Even as the words left her mouth, panic started to seize control. Breath caught in her throat. Chills turned her cold. And she felt pressure on her chest as if from a great weight.

She was terrified of fires.

They ranked as even more nightmarish than Christmas, ever since that early morning when she was twelve. She stopped that thought in its tracks. No good ever came from reliving the past. Right now, she had to get out of there before a panic attack overwhelmed her.

She threw her car in reverse.

"Stop! I'm Fire-Rescue." He hit her window with the flat of his hand again.

She was startled out of backing up and transfixed by his intense gaze, pinning her in place.

"I'm deputizing you as a Wildcat Bluff volunteer firefighter. Open your doors and help me."

Although his voice was muffled coming through the glass, she heard every word he said in that crystal clarity that precedes a full-on, foot-stomping, heart-stopping crisis.

She tried to focus on the fact that he was one of the good guys. Unfortunately, the knowledge didn't help her. She didn't have panic attacks often, but when she did, they were as scary as whatever had set them off. She took a deep breath and worked to stay focused. Breathe and focus, breathe and focus. It wasn't going to do anybody—least of all herself, and certainly not the stranger banging on her car window—any good for her to lose it now. She could get a grip. She had to get a grip.

She carefully set the pepper spray down beside her phone and wrapped her fingers around the solid surface of the steering wheel to ground her body while she fought her fear with a reassuring repetition of words in her mind. "Be here now. Safe and sound. Be here now."

"If that fire gets loose, it'll burn across these pastures

and kill cattle, horses, and wild animals. Timber will
go up fast and furious. Wildcat Bluff won't stand a
chance," the stranger shouted, pounding his fist on the
roof of her car. Obviously he was close to losing it, too.

She felt his words start to override her panic. She
gripped the steering wheel harder. She needed to help
him. She wanted to help him. She couldn't let her weakness stop her from saving others. She was safe in the
here and now. She swallowed down her response, took
a deep breath, then released the locks and opened her
door. The scent of burning grass hit her and she reeled
back against the seat. She put one hand across her nose
to reduce the smell of smoke and another across her
chest as if in protection.

"Thank you!" He jerked open the back door. He
grabbed three towels and slammed the door shut.
"Name's Trey."

"Misty," she mumbled, prepared to do—well, whatever this hot, strong guy thought she could do. He tossed
a blue towel onto her lap, and flashed a quick but genuine smile that filled her with tingly energy from the tips
of her hair right down to her toes. It was a good kind of
warmth, like sunbathing in the summer without a care
in the world.

"Well, come on then, Misty!" he called over his
shoulder. He took off toward the smoke and a break in
the fence line.

She immediately felt the loss of his radiant energy.
The sight of him in all his muscular glory running like
all get-out didn't hurt her illogical desire to follow
him, either. That thought made her smile and set back
her panic a bit. If she wasn't careful, she was going to

start writing poetry to honor him. She felt her breath come a little easier. Something about this guy made her feel braver.

Yet, did he actually expect her to fight the fire with him? Did he think she would run toward that horrible smell of burning grass instead of fleeing it? Did he imagine she would fight the flames with nothing more than a single, solitary towel in her very vulnerable hands? He must see something in her that she was pretty sure simply wasn't there.

Fear and safety aside, she wasn't dressed to fight a fire. North Texas was experiencing a December heat wave, and she was wearing capris and flip-flops. She could get hurt. She lowered her hands to her lap and gripped the towel. But if she didn't help, how many more might be hurt? People. Animals. Property. Timber.

She had to help. She glanced down and noticed stains on the towel from some long-ago picnic. She couldn't ever have imagined using her towels to put out a fire. But if ratty towels and her shaky courage were all that stood between death and destruction, they would have to do.

Mindful of possible traffic, she put her SUV in drive, pulled to the side of the road, and turned off the engine. She stepped outside. Ninety degrees wasn't a miserable one hundred, but still plenty hot, particularly for the holiday season. Christmas was bad enough. Christmas and a heat wave together was—well, it was like hell on Earth. Complete with fire. How about some brimstone next?

She slammed the door shut, blocking retreat, and forced one foot in front of the other as she edged around the front fender. The scent of burning grass grew stronger. And just like that, she felt the sharp edge of a flashback threaten to overwhelm her. She clenched her empty fist, driving fingernails into her palm. She used the pain to ground her in the here and now. And in her mind, she employed her safe words. "Be here now. Safe and sound. Be here now."

She looked across the fence and took a deep breath, despite the stench. Not a wall of fire. Instead, a line of red-orange flames ate up the dry grass, leaving black stubble behind as the blaze sent up plumes of smoke. She watched Trey beat at the conflagration with a towel in each hand. He was making progress. She felt hope that her towels could actually make a difference. But he couldn't completely stop the flames. The fire line was too wide. Without her help, he was going to lose the battle.

He glanced over his shoulder at her. She felt his gaze as an almost physical sensation, willing her to help, giving her strength, sharing his courage. She felt a surge of determination. She wouldn't let him fight alone.

When she reached the sagging barbwire fence, she carefully stepped over it and quickly walked to Trey. "What do you want me to do?"

"Can't let the fire cross the road or it'll be hell and gone." He pointed toward the other side of the fire line. "You take that end. Beat out the flames as fast as you can. We're ahead of the blaze, and we've got to stay that way."

"Okay." With one simple word, she knew she'd turned her world upside down, but she wouldn't back down.

As she moved into position, she saw that fire consumed the dry grass at an unbelievably fast rate. They were in the middle of a bad drought. Add unseasonably warm temperatures to the mix and everything was vulnerable. Up close, intensity ruled. Heat. Smoke. Smell. Fortunately, the fire hadn't spread too far. She raised her towel over her head and whipped down hard, smothering the flames. Brief elation filled her. Maybe she—they— could fight this fire. And win.

Trey was slapping at the flames with everything he had, and she followed suit. Quickly they had a rhythm going—*slap, lift, slap, lift, slap, lift*—and with each slap a little bit of the fire gave way.

"Good thing I brush-hogged around here, so the grass is short," Trey called out, without losing a beat.

"It could be worse?"

"You bet."

"I can't imagine."

"Watch your feet!"

She felt heat sear her toes and jerked back. Black soot streaked her tangerine toenail polish and the crystal stones on her sandals. She suddenly felt dizzy and off balance.

"Are you okay?" Trey quickly stomped out the flames near her feet with his scuffed cowboy boots.

"Yes." And strangely enough, she did feel better with him so close by her side.

"I'm buying you a real pair of shoes."

"You don't have to do that. These are fine," Misty said, although she didn't know why she suddenly felt defensive about her footwear. Maybe it was because she prided herself on being practical—usually—not one of those women who dressed in a way that made them appear absolutely helpless.

"Not out here," Trey said as he looked at her in a way that made her suddenly self-conscious.

"I wouldn't be here if not for your fire."

"It's *our* fire." He moved back to his end of the line and beat fast and hard at the flames.

She simply shook her head as she struck the ground again with her towel while she carefully kept her feet back from the flames.

"You'll need boots next time."

"Next time!" She looked over at him in horror. *Mistake*. She felt her mouth go dry. The sun spotlighted him as he raised blackened towels and struck downward. Powerful muscles in his back, shoulders, and arms gleamed with sweat and rippled with exertion. As if he'd been swimming, his faded jeans were plastered to his taut butt and long legs. She shook her head to dispel his image, but nothing helped put out the fire that now burned inside her.

"There's always a next time." He tossed a slightly crooked smile her way as he lifted towels to extinguish more flames.

"Oh no." She hadn't come all this way to get distracted by the first hot guy who literally crossed her path—even if he did flag her down with his shirt. She particularly didn't need to get involved with one who was into Christmas and dragged her into fighting a grass fire in the middle of nowhere. She didn't want to ever put out another fire. This was a onetime deal to help out a man in an emergency and stop a prairie fire from eating up acres instead of one grassy swath. In the future, she would leave firefighting to the experts.

Besides, she was here on business. Texas Timber

had hired her as an independent troubleshooter to find out who had burned down one of the company's Christmas tree farms, and possibly caused other problems. She'd been warned not to trust anybody in Wildcat Bluff County. Now, first thing, she was involved with a local. A really hot local. She couldn't hold back a soulful sigh. At least she might excuse her interest in Trey as simply business since he might be helpful in her investigation.

"You're a deputized firefighter now," he said.

"That can't be legal." She attacked the grass with renewed energy. They were actually making good headway now.

"If there's trouble, everybody pitches in."

"Police? 9-1-1?"

"We're the first responders." He struck hard at the ground with his towels.

"There must be a county sheriff. Highway patrol."

"And the Wildcat Bluff Police Department." He stomped at the blackened grass. "How long do you think it'd take help to get here?"

"Good point."

"We all depend on the Wildcat Bluff County Volunteer Fire-Rescue."

"That's why you deputized me? I'm a total stranger! I could have been—well, big trouble. I actually thought you were, at first."

"But you aren't," he said with another charming grin.

She couldn't resist cracking a smile back, even despite the circumstances. She shrugged, beginning to understand that life out here was different than in the city.

Sweat trickled down her body. Soot tasted bitter in her mouth. Sunlight beat down on her head. If she came out of this with nothing more than sunburn, she'd be lucky. Yet, that didn't matter. She was helping stop a fire. She was saving lives and property. She was taking a step toward recovery.

As the flames dwindled in size and scope, she edged toward him. Soon they worked side by side, putting out the remaining hot spots. He loomed well over six feet and made her feel diminutive, even at her perfectly respectable five seven.

Finally, he stopped and stretched his back.

"Fire's out?" She wanted him to confirm what she saw with her own eyes.

"Yep. Looks good." He scuffed his boots across the crusty grass. "Can't thank you enough. If you hadn't come along when you did—"

"You'd have thought of something." She interrupted to keep him from saying another word. His melodic voice with the deep Texas drawl couldn't help but put her in mind of hot, sweaty bodies sliding across cool, satin sheets.

"I needed a miracle and prayed for one the minute I saw the fire." He walked over to her. "I heard my answer in your car coming down the highway. I headed back to the road, running flat out. And there you were in your pure white SUV, looking so cool and unafraid of the wild man pounding on your window. You had a miracle in your car. Towels. Not many people would have had them just waiting on a backseat."

She didn't feel so cool and unafraid. Who had this guy been looking at? Still, his words made her swell with an unusual type of pride. "Like I said, I always do. Just in case."

He clasped both towels in one hand, and held out the other. "Thank you. You're my Christmas angel."

"Just plain Misty Reynolds." She shook his hand, feeling his strength, his heat, his calluses.

"Pleased to meet you." He rubbed the back of her hand with his rough thumb, and then slowly released her. "Like I said, I'm Trey…Trey Duval."

For a moment, she couldn't remember the polite response required of her. She was caught in the magic of his touch, the mesmerizing sound of his voice, and the unusual color of his eyes, circles of gold, green, and brown. She glanced away to release his spell. "Good to meet you, too."

"Are you going to be around long?"

"A bit. I'm on vacation." She hoped her cover story would ring true to everyone she met in Wildcat Bluff.

"Where are you staying?"

Misty hesitated, but Trey really did seem like a good guy. Besides, he'd learn it soon enough from the locals. She decided to trust the instinct that was telling her to trust him.

"Twin Oaks B&B. No website, but I caught a couple of good reviews online."

"Ruby's got more customers than she can shake a stick at. No need to promote. That natural spring draws folks."

"Guess a lot of business is the best promotion."

He nodded. "It's usually pretty quiet in Wildcat Bluff. But we'll get plenty of folks out here for our Christmas in the Country festivities."

"I'm not here for anything Christmas. I've been working hard and need a quiet place to get away." She didn't like the sound of festivities. They could complicate her investigation. Still, she doubted a few candles in windows and plastic lighted displays in front yards would draw much of a crowd.

"I'd imagine fighting a wild fire isn't the best way to start your vacation."

"True. But how do you think it got started?" Now that the blaze was out, her mind kicked into gear. Did this fire connect with her investigation? It'd be quite a coincidence if it did, but she couldn't rule out natural causes from the heat and drought. Still, she'd checked topographical maps before she'd arrived in the county. If she remembered correctly, the flames were burning a path straight toward a Texas Timber Christmas tree farm. On the other hand, the blaze had started on a ranch, so maybe it had nothing to do with Texas Timber. Plenty to ponder here.

"Good question." He squeezed the burned towels between his fists. "I'll be following up on it."

"If I can be of help, let me know."

"Think on it. Maybe you saw something."

"Or somebody?" she prodded, sensing his implication.

He nodded as he glanced with narrowed eyes around the area.

"Arson?"

"Possibility."

"I didn't notice anything unusual, but maybe something will come to me." She pushed sweat-dampened hair back from her forehead, shelving her questions for the moment. "You must be thirsty. I've got bottles of water in the car." She wished she'd had enough water to help fight the fire, but at least she had enough to ease their dry throats.

"Thanks. I owe you a big, thick, sizzling steak."

"I thought it was a pair of boots," she teased before she realized she was flirting with him. She pressed her lips together to stop any other wayward words from escaping her mouth.

He smiled as his eyes crinkled invitingly at the corners. "That too."

"I'm glad I was able to help." She spoke as primly as possible.

He held up the towels. "If you don't mind, I'd like to keep these."

She handed over her scorched towel. "Keep mine, too."

"Guess I owe you three towels."

"Not at all. Like I said—"

"You don't need anything from me." He cocked his head. "But if you'd like dinner, I can grill a mean steak." Another killer grin.

"I bet you can." Misty wondered if he meant a date. She felt excited at the idea. She stepped back. If she didn't get farther away from him, she felt as if she might spontaneously combust.

He took her cue and changed the subject. "Would you mind giving me a ride?"

"A ride?" No excuse for it, but her mind skittered sideways to an image of his big empty bed. So much for changing the subject.

He took a step toward her. "To Wildcat Bluff."

She couldn't help but notice his voice held a huskiness

that hadn't been there before. "I see. You need a ride to town."

"I sent off my horse."

"You ride horses?"

"That's what cowboys do."

"You're a cowboy firefighter?"

He tipped an imaginary hat.

Chapter 2

TREY EVALUATED THE BLACKENED SECTION OF THE pasture. Might still be hot spots, but for now, he'd been damn lucky. He glanced at his luck. He'd crossed paths with a hot gal on a hot day. What were the odds? He wasn't one to look a gift horse in the mouth, but too many coincidences always made him uneasy. Still, she'd been a trouper. He couldn't ask for more.

"I'm parched," Misty said. "Bet you are, too."

"You offered water, didn't you?"

She grinned, revealing pretty teeth that'd make any orthodontist proud. "I haven't got just any old water. I've got bottles of East Texas Ozarka on ice in a cooler."

"Be still my heart." He joined her tinkling laughter as he placed a hand over his heart. And realized he wasn't wearing a shirt. Where the hell was it? He glanced around as he thought back. Oh yeah, he'd thrown it down on the road. He wasn't just shirtless. He was dirty and sweaty, too, meaning he was about as far off a gal's radar as he could get. Guess bad luck had to balance out good luck. But it hardly seemed fair.

No walking this one back. He might as well play the hand he'd been dealt. All he could do was try a distraction. "We've done all we can here. You ready for that drink?"

"Absolutely!" She smiled in delight.

He turned away from the depths of her pale green

eyes, too much like the lure of a cool, clear pool on a hot summer day. Talk about distraction.

He stomped over to the fence. He held the barbwire down with his boot so she could cross with less trouble. The last thing he wanted was for her to get an injury. He watched as she stepped over the fence with long legs. Leggy trouble. He followed the sway of her narrow hips as she walked away. Bigger trouble. The situation was shaping up to leave him tossing and turning at night on his too-empty king-size bed. But there was always a price to pay for the good things in life.

He held the three towels with one hand while he stepped over the barbwire. He kicked the fence post back in line with his boot so the wire didn't sag as much. Not perfect, but good enough to hold till he had a chance to fix it right. He had other fence to repair today, too, but nothing critical. It'd all still be there tomorrow. For now, he wanted to know a little more about the stranger with the perfect timing. And he never minded time spent in the company of an interesting woman.

While Misty walked back to her SUV, he checked the highway for his shirt. Sure enough, it was still where he'd dropped it. He grabbed the mess of torn, burned, smelly fabric. Shame, too. He'd had the shirt long enough that it was broken in just right. That meant soft with no holes, faded color, or style that made gals cringe. Not easy to meet the challenge, but the shirt had done it. Maybe he ought to bury it back home and put up an "RIP Good Shirt" sign.

"What are you going to do about your shirt?" Misty walked over with a black garbage bag in her hand.

"It's a favorite."

"I understand. But—" She snapped open the bag.

He took her meaning. "Guess I'd better say good-bye." With a dramatic sigh, he dropped the shirt and towels into the trash bag. Misty rolled her eyes, but Trey noticed she was also fighting an amused smile. The smile tickled him in a way he couldn't put his finger on, and that made him a little uneasy.

As he walked with her back to the SUV, he scanned the area. He didn't see anything out of the ordinary. No smoke on the horizon. No loose cattle out of pastures. No sounds indicating trouble. A hawk's dark shadow passed over the highway. Trey glanced up. The raptor lazily circled in the big blue sky overhead, trolling for supper while rodents no doubt scurried for cover on the wide expanse of the golden prairie below.

He relaxed a bit, feeling hunger, thirst, and tiredness creep up on him. No surprise after all the activity. For now, all was as it should be in his world, so life was good.

Back at the SUV, Misty opened a door, leaned in, and tossed the garbage onto a floorboard.

He watched, not even attempting to be a gentleman. She wasn't nearly as pristine as he'd thought, because she was running him a close second in the sweaty, dirty department. He wondered if, underneath her pretty blue capris, she wore nothing but a bit of lace and silk. Snow white, if he didn't miss his guess, although he'd like to find out for sure. White suited his Christmas angel.

He heard the sound of ice clinking in the cooler before she stood up and turned around. She held three bottles with water dripping down their sides. Looked like heaven to him. She set a bottle on the ground before she held one out to him. He wrapped his hand around her cold, wet fingers. A hot spark arced between them. Her green eyes widened in surprise.

She jerked her hand away, unscrewed the cap off her own bottle, tilted it up to her lips, and took a long drink of water.

He wrenched the top off his own bottle and slugged back half the liquid, spilling water down his chin to his bare chest. He had to cool off before he said or did something he'd regret later. He poured the last of the water over his head to wash away some of the sweat, the stink of the fire, and the heat she'd built in him.

"Need more water?" She picked up the other full bottle and tossed it to him.

What he wanted was a taste of her. He grinned as he dropped the empty and caught the new bottle. "Thank you. Nothing better than cold water after a hot fire." He cracked the top on the bottle, took a long swig, and chuckled under his breath. "Well, almost nothing."

He could still hardly believe his good luck. First, he'd gotten to the fire in time to put it out without much damage. Then, help had come in the form of his own personal Christmas angel. Blond-haired. Green-eyed. Red-lipped. Misty would make the perfect stocking stuffer.

Maybe now that she was here, the holiday season would finally kick into gear. What with the drought and heat, it'd been hell getting in the mood. Not just for him, but for the whole area. No matter how many decorations they put out, no matter how many parties they planned, no matter how many holiday clothes they wore, a pall hung over Wildcat Bluff County.

He'd even put a Christmas wish list on his refrigerator door under a Frosty the Snowman magnet. He'd written one item and one item only on the list. *Snow*. If they could get a thick blanket of snow across the county, their heat and drought problems would be over. Plus, they'd celebrate Christmas in style. 'Course, chances of getting snow were slim to none. He was just whistling in the wind. Still, he'd settle for a good gully washer.

But that was before his Christmas angel had descended on Wildcat Bluff County. She might carry some weight in high places. She'd definitely add cheer to his personal life. As soon as he got home, he'd add her to his list. *Item #1: Snow. Item #2: Misty Reynolds.* On second thought, he'd better reverse the order. Chances of achieving Item #1 were none. Cuddling with Item #2 was in the realm of possibility. You couldn't tell him angels didn't need loving as much as the next person. He just hoped angels were fond of snow.

That was the upside of the situation. The downside lurked like a rattlesnake in a woodpile. He got the itchy feeling there was more to Misty's story than she was telling. He had trouble believing she'd vacation in Wildcat Bluff or Wildcat Bluff County. Drive a four-wheeler on back roads? Cast a fishing line in a lake? Hunt deer or turkey in season? Throw a leg over a horse to barrel race? He couldn't picture it.

He couldn't see her as an Old West tourist either. Maybe relax at Ruby's Twin Oaks B&B with its amenities and natural spring. But Hot Springs, Arkansas, won hands-down as the place to go for pampered getaways, what with all the legendary spas, nightspots, and racetrack. Sure, she'd said she was here for peace, quiet, and relaxation, but he just had trouble believing it.

Then again, he was on high alert after so many unexplained fires, downed fences, and cattle let loose. All that, plus the heat and drought, made him edgy and distrustful of strangers. He could be dead wrong about Misty. He'd sure like to be. She'd created an itch that begged to be scratched. Too bad he held the short end of the stick on time and trust.

Any which way he sliced it, he feared his Christmas angel had singed wings. Not that it meant he shouldn't get close to her. What was that old saying? Keep your friends close and your enemies closer. He'd keep her as close as he could get her. She was holding something back. Might be important. Might be nothing. Folks had lots of secrets they preferred not to share. He had a few of his own. In this case, he had a feeling her secret involved Wildcat Bluff County. And that was his concern.

Not that his body gave a damn. More than one leggy blond had led him around by his nose like a prize bull. He'd sworn off the breed. No blonds. No cowgirls. No city gals. 'Course, that left slim pickings. If he had good sense, he'd cross Misty off his wish list. Still, no point being hasty. She was real fine. Anyway, Christmas angels were as rare as hen's teeth. And he hadn't sworn off *them*. Maybe, if necessary, he'd find a way to burnish this one's wings bright and shiny again.

"Do you think it's safe to leave now?" Misty gestured toward the pasture's blackened area.

"Figured we'd wait a bit." Someone needed to stay and watch till there was no chance the fire might reignite.

"I need to check in at the B&B."

"Ruby won't mind if you're late."

"You could stay here. I'd send somebody out to get you." She finished off her bottle of water and picked up his empty one.

"Someone ought to be here soon. Like I said, I sent my horse back to the barn. A ranch hand will get the word out that I need help once he sees my mount."

"They'll know where to find you?"

"General area." He glanced down the road, but it was empty. "Might take time till somebody spots my horse."

He might as well admit, at least to himself, that he didn't want to let her go yet. He should though. She'd already helped more than he had any right to expect. But he felt possessive. If he was right, he'd seen yearning in her eyes that matched his own. If he was wrong, he wanted to be the one who put yearning there.

He was getting in bigger trouble by the minute. He could blame it on being out in the sun too long without his hat. But it wasn't brain fever that was tormenting him. It was another fever altogether.

As he finished the water, he made his decision. "Best not wait. If you'll tell Ruby at the B&B I'm here, she'll contact the fire station."

"But *where* exactly are we?" She held out her hand for his empty bottle.

"Wildcat Ranch fence line on Wildcat Road." For some crazy reason, he felt like she belonged in Wildcat Bluff County and ought to know the landmarks. He handed his bottle to her and watched her walk over to her SUV and toss all three empties onto the floorboard. He liked the fact that she was cautious about littering the countryside. Showed she cared about nature.

She turned back to him, smiling. "Water hasn't tasted that good in a long time."

"Nothing better after fighting a fire." He heard the whine of tires on asphalt. Maybe help was finally here.

"Somebody's coming!" She pointed at the road toward Wildcat Bluff.

He turned to look. Sure enough. Must be a local. They were traveling like a bat out of hell.

A dark blue pickup with a Texas Firefighter license plate and a green wreath tied to its silver grille squealed to a stop behind Misty's SUV. A tall man leaped out. He carried a large fire extinguisher as he ran up to them.

"Too little, too late," Trey called. "But you're still a sight for sore eyes."

"Who's she?"

"Misty Reynolds, I'd like you to meet my cousin, Kent Duval, second-best cowboy firefighter in the county."

"Don't believe a word of it." Kent grinned, revealing dimples in both cheeks. "He's the second-best, but the biggest liar, bar none."

"No point listening to him," Trey teased. "His mama dropped him on his head when he was a toddler."

"At least she didn't inflate my head to the burstin' point."

"Guess you two *are* related," Misty said.

"Only when it suits." Kent chuckled, a deep, rumbling sound. He lifted his straw cowboy hat with a sprig of green mistletoe tucked in the rattlesnake band to reveal thick sable hair.

"Take it you got my message," Trey said.

"Yep." Kent frowned, settling his Stetson back in place. "Cuz, try not to do that again. I stopped by your barn to borrow the saddle we talked about. Took a year off my life when I saw your singed hat tied to Samson's saddle horn."

"Glad you were there."

"And good thing I knew where you were mending fence today."

Trey nodded as he gestured at the burned area of the pasture. "Caught the fire just in time. And Misty happened along with towels in her backseat."

"In her backseat?" Kent made the words sound suggestive. "She had just what you needed when you needed it. What are the odds? You always were a lucky cuss." Kent winked at Misty.

Trey knew his cousin only too well. He had a well-deserved reputation with the ladies. "Now you're here, you can watch for hot spots. Misty's taking me to town." And he'd get that ride with her after all.

"You staying at Ruby's place?" Kent asked.

"Twin Oaks B&B," Misty said.

"How long?"

She rolled her eyes. "As if it's anybody's business."

Kent chuckled. "You better believe you're everybody's business now you're in Wildcat Bluff County."

"We'll see," she said.

"How about we leave Trey out here to watch for flare-ups? I'll follow you to the Bluff, see you get settled in okay, and show you around town. Christmas decorations aren't to be missed."

Trey moved in close to Misty and put a hand on her shoulder. He felt her stiffen, but she didn't shrug him off. "We're going to town. You're staying here."

Kent raised an eyebrow. "That the way of it?"

"You damn well better believe it." Trey hadn't felt so possessive of a woman in a coon's age, or maybe *never* was a better word for it. She was *his* Christmas angel.

Kent raised his hands as if in self-defense and stepped back. "Got you." He smiled at Misty. "Darlin', this big galoot gives you any trouble, let me know. I'm at your service, day or night."

"How kind," Misty said. "But I'm used to taking care of myself."

"Wouldn't have our ladies any other way." Kent tipped his hat. "I'll check out the damage." He gave Trey a nod before he walked toward the fence.

"I'll stop by the station and report," Trey called to his cousin's retreating back.

Kent raised a hand in reply.

"Intense guy," Misty said.

"You *like* him?" Trey turned toward her.

"He's your cousin, not mine." She shrugged. "No opinion one way or another."

And it dawned on him. He was acting jealous as all get-out. Item #1 on his Christmas list was getting way out of hand. If he was as smart as the average bear, he'd be able to control his reaction. 'Course, he might already be up a tree and reaching for honey that was way out of his reach. That thought made him grumpy.

"Let's get out of here."

Chapter 3

As Misty drove toward Wildcat Bluff, she wanted to ask Trey a million questions, business and personal. She might never have a better opportunity than with him in her passenger seat. However, Texans didn't take kindly to questions, particularly ones from strangers. Invasive questions were considered rude, at the very least.

Cindi Lou was a proud member of the Daughters of the Republic of Texas, and she insisted the cautious trait of Texans harkened back to the old days when people arrived in the Republic from all over. Many were on the run from the law, creditors, or family. Others simply wanted a fresh start. In any case, folks quickly learned— often at the wrong end of a six-shooter—not to ask name, former location, or business.

With that in mind, Misty couldn't afford to become known as a "Nosy Nellie" or she'd never complete her job. If she were in Dallas, she'd have an easier time of it. Folks with lots of different backgrounds were moving into the Lone Star State for jobs and many of them didn't mind answering questions. Southern Californians were only too happy to talk, even to giving their last therapy session in detail. But she was going to a small Texas town where everybody knew everything about each other. She'd have to slide in sideways to get answers.

But that's what she did best. She wasn't there for a

hard investigation—nuts and bolts or forensic accounting. She'd been hired for a soft investigation—ferreting out secrets or concealed facts. To do that, she needed to make friends, elicit trust, and conduct research. She liked people, so this type of troubleshooting came naturally to her.

If it weren't for Cindi Lou, she probably wouldn't even be a troubleshooter. When she'd met Cindi Lou, Misty had been a hardworking gal from North Dallas with a master's degree in library science, but with college debts and three jobs, she was still losing ground because she couldn't find local work in her field. Cindi Lou had advertised for a librarian to organize her family's library in their mansion on Turtle Creek in Highland Park. When Misty had applied for the part-time job, Cindi Lou had hired her on the spot.

Turned out Cindi Lou was the descendent of big oil money. Her great-granddaddy had been a wildcatter in East Texas in the 1930s and struck it rich with black gold. That meant Cindi Lou was a Hockaday, SMU, and Neiman Marcus graduate, but she always said she was in recovery because she'd inherited her great-granddaddy's wildcatter streak.

Cindi Lou sat at the hub of an information network, rubbing elbows with everyone from street folks to movers and shakers. She saw patterns in life, so she put together folks who had problems with folks who had solutions. Right away, she'd suggested Misty become an independent troubleshooter because she had the research skills and personality traits to be helpful to those in need.

Five years later, Misty was glad she'd taken the suggestion and changed her life. She'd helped many individuals and businesses. Cindi Lou had built on her calling, too. She'd expanded her network into a quirky hexagonal 1950s Midcentury Modern one-story office building in Dallas. She'd named herself Hub Mistress when she'd set up her office in the center of the building. Misty had her office there, along with several other young women whom Cindi Lou had befriended and encouraged to take chances in cutting-edge or thinking-out-of-the-box work. And Cindi Lou efficiently managed all their businesses.

Even though Misty's background was different than Cindi Lou's, they had a lot of other things in common. Cindi Lou hadn't felt as if she'd belonged with her family once her beloved great-granddaddy had passed away. Misty had no family, not since she'd lost her wonderful aunt who'd raised her in a warm and loving home in Dallas. Friendships were important to them both, but Cindi Lou was pushing Misty to reach out and experience more of life.

Aunt Camilla, who was Misty's father's sister, had always encouraged Misty to do the same thing. She'd bought season tickets to the Dallas Summer Musicals for them every year. Misty had loved going to the big old theater in Fair Park, where they'd also gone to the Texas State Fair. That was where Misty had first really noticed the differences in architecture. She'd asked her aunt about the beautiful buildings and learned they were Art Deco style. At that time, it had seemed to Misty that Aunt Cami knew everything because she taught history in high school and took Misty on driving tours and to museums, libraries, and parks.

Now that Misty thought about it, maybe she'd turned

to library science as a way of cataloging all that knowledge stuffed into her head at an early age. She smiled warmly at the thought. Aunt Cami had also stuffed her with tasty treats. She still smelled gingerbread and brownies when she thought of her aunt. She sighed. Cancer had taken her way too soon—just like all her family had been lost to her too soon.

Now that she was older, she appreciated her aunt even more. Misty's parents had died on Christmas morning when Misty was just twelve. She'd been consumed with grief when Aunt Cami had taken her home. Her aunt had been a single parent on a teacher's limited salary, but she'd raised Misty and helped her through college. In all those years, they'd never celebrated Christmas. Neither wanted to remember or relive that terrible Christmas that had changed their lives forever. And Misty had lost or intentionally stuffed away most of her cherished memories so she could go forward in life and not live in the past. Instead of Christmas, Aunt Cami and Misty had given each other gifts and goodies on Winter Solstice.

Misty had always been cautious after losing her parents, so Aunt Camilla had encouraged her to experience more of life. Now Cindi Lou was doing the same thing. Maybe they were both right.

She glanced sideways at Trey. The big, handsome, shirtless cowboy firefighter sat there in her front seat, filling the air with enough testosterone to make a gal feel giddy. He was certainly full of life. But she needed answers, not a hunky guy. There were lots of ways to make small talk to learn important facts. Weather and locale were good ways to start.

She'd like to trust Trey, but trust wasn't something she could afford in Wildcat Bluff County. Fire had destroyed a Texas Timber Christmas tree farm before the harvest. Another fire on an adjacent tree farm had been caught and extinguished before too much damage was done. Heat and drought could be a factor, but arson was the main consideration. Fortunately, the Christmas cutting and hauling season was over, but that still left other Texas Timber tree farms in various stages of growth.

Normally, she didn't get calls or referrals during the holidays, but Texas Timber had been insistent that they needed a troubleshooter in Wildcat Bluff County now. She'd get a bonus if she could find the culprit or figure out what was causing the fires by Christmas. She wanted to be away from the holiday madness in Dallas anyway, so she took the job.

Only she sure hadn't counted on a cowboy firefighter upping her own internal heat. She quickly turned the AC higher.

"Think you may never get cool again?"

Not with him so close. But she didn't say that. "Temperature on my gauge reads eighty-nine outside. Will winter ever get here?"

"Heat lets up at night."

"I wonder if the B&B lures many people into the warm spring right now."

"It's a good way to ease sore muscles." He chuckled, a low, intimate sound. "Lots of ways to get those. Some better than others."

"I'd just like some sweater weather." She decided his voice ought to be outlawed as unfair to the state of a woman's thoughts. She could almost feel vibrations from his deep, resonant voice twining deeper inside her mind.

"With this weather, it doesn't seem much like the holidays, does it?"

"Not hardly."

"On the plus side, I bet Ruby'd want us to use the spring after we saved the town with our heroics." He leaned toward her. "What do you say? Beer and barbeque later out at the pool?"

"It's a tempting offer." She kept her eyes steady on the road, not about to give in to the impulse to ogle him again. "But I haven't even checked in yet and—"

"I'll bring the fixings over after the sun goes down."

"But—"

"Least I can do after your help today."

Obviously he wasn't a man to take no lightly, or any other way. She didn't want to make any waves, at least not yet. Plus, he had to be a font of information. She'd just take advantage of that fact.

"I don't know much about this area of Texas." She had in mind what her Aunt Cami had taught her and what she'd researched online for updated facts before she left Dallas, but a local's viewpoint was bound to be different and more beneficial.

"You want me to be your tour guide?"

"Please, would you?"

"Sure thing. We get enough tourists around here that we've all got our spiel down pretty good."

"Perfect."

"This highway was once Wildcat Trail. It leads to Wildcat Bluff, where the town looks out over the Red River Valley. The Bluff was originally founded as a ferry terminus so folks could cross the Red River between Texas and Indian Territory, or Oklahoma now. Delaware Bend and Preston Bend were wild ferry towns, too, but they got flooded to make Lake Texoma."

"That's a huge, popular lake. Too bad towns had to be lost to create it."

"They were already pretty much ghost towns."

"Wildcat Bluff got lucky, didn't it?"

"We've got more than luck going for us." He gestured toward the front window with a pointed finger. "Wildcat Bluff County is special. We're situated in the Cross Timbers."

"I've heard the Timbers are mostly gone."

"Not here. We've got thousands of acres we've been riding herd on since the eighteen hundreds."

"Your family?" She was learning more than he realized he was telling her. He was proud of this land and the fact that they'd saved this section of the Cross Timbers. She admired him and those who'd had the foresight to save a unique land. Aunt Cami would've loved knowing about this, too.

"Several clans. Plus, newcomers."

"I don't see the Cross Timbers."

"Over there." He pointed again. "We're driving up the north-south corridor of prairie. Up here it's about ten miles wide. Other places it can be as narrow as three miles or as wide as thirty miles. It's bordered on both sides by dense trees and shrubs."

"I see the line on the east side. What is all that growth?"

"Post oak, cedar elm, bois d'arc, dogwood, Virginia creeper, blackberry, and a bunch of other stuff."

She nodded, taking in as much as she could while she drove. She'd never seen this section of the Cross Timbers before.

"In the old days, there'd be a brush fire every year, and the tree line grew back so dense nobody could ride through it. The Comanche used the Cross Timbers as a secret route through *Numunuu Sookobitu*."

"You speak Comanche?" She glanced at him in surprise.

"Most folks around here know a little bit."

"What does that mean?" she asked, beginning to enjoy herself, as if she really was on vacation. Trey was a good tour guide. He seemed to know a lot.

"Comanche Earth." He looked over at her. "Comancheria is another name for the Comanche Empire that stretched from Central Kansas all the way down to Mexico."

"Are you a history buff in addition to all your other pursuits?"

He grinned. "I guess you could call me that. I like to read about this area and listen to tales from the old-timers. I can't get too excited about the kings of England or European royalty."

Misty laughed. "I like history, too. But give me the Alamo any day." She liked Trey even more now that she knew he had so much in common with her and Aunt Cami. Only her aunt would've brought him up to speed on British, Scottish, German, and other history, too. And she'd have taught him to like it.

"Right." He pointed toward the prairie. "See over there? That's a handy trail between the two lines of dense growth. Nobody could see the warriors or get to them through the timber. But we keep the wild fires under control now so it doesn't grow as thick."

A twist of trees marched down the east side of the road, but Misty saw only plains on the west side. Yet she could imagine a long line of colorful Comanche warriors on horseback wearing breechclouts and carrying bows and arrows as they rode down the prairie to protect their people and homeland. She blinked, chasing away shadows of the past. No shadows. No ghosts. No sign of fire.

"Beautiful country," she murmured, but her mind had fixated on the Comanche. Now that she thought about it, Trey had the high cheekbones, bronzed skin, and unusual eyes that could mean he was part Native American. Plus, his family had been here a long time, maybe from the beginning. Now he was even more exotic, more exciting to her. She wanted to ask him directly about his heritage, but that wouldn't do. Still, she was learning a lot.

"We're situated between the dry West and the wet East, so we get the best of both worlds. And our timber keeps rainwater deep in the soil."

"Are there buffalo?"

"I run a small herd out on the prairie." He chuckled as he tapped his fingertips on the dashboard. "More for pleasure than anything else."

"What do you mean?"

"I like having them on the ranch. I like looking at them. And I like knowing they're safe."

She nodded, understanding him more all the time. "You really love this land, don't you?"

"Can't imagine living anywhere else."

"I feel that way about Dallas. So much to do and so much fun."

"City born and bred?"

"You know it." She laughed. "And when there's a fire, a big screaming truck full of hoses and firefighters comes to the rescue, not some stray motorist with towels."

He chuckled. "Don't count us out here. We've got rigs and firefighters that fit the bill."

She smiled even as she acknowledged that they were worlds apart. Country guy versus city gal. They were too different to ever bridge the gap. Still, she could enjoy the beauty of North Texas. And her cowboy firefighter.

As she followed the road, golden prairie dotted with black and red cattle spread out around her. Clumps of trees—mostly green live oak—provided shade for animals. A couple of pickups passed them, drivers raising a forefinger in acknowledgment. Soon she saw the bluff up ahead, an imposing chunk that dominated the land below it.

As she started the drive upward, she passed gnarled trees, dense shrubs, and sandstone outcrops. She felt a sense of danger, as if she were driving back in time. Trey made her feel reckless. She could almost imagine throwing her usual caution to the wind and running wild by the side of a cowboy or Indian.

As the road continued to wind upward, the land grew increasingly untamed around her. A large bird launched into the air from the side and struggled to gain altitude right in front of her windshield. She stomped on her brakes and swerved to avoid hitting it.

"What was that?" She started forward again, heart beating fast. "I've never seen anything like it."

"Wild turkey."

"Really?" She watched the massive brown-feathered bird settle into a gully and then disappear with a shuffling strut into tall, sheltering grass with the unmistakable gobbling of a turkey.

"Slow as molasses. Guess I should've warned you to look out for them. Deer, too. You don't want to damage your vehicle."

"What about the animals?"

"Collision doesn't do them any good either."

"I'd think not." She drove more cautiously as she peered from side to side. "You just introduced me to a whole new issue. And I thought Dallas drivers were dangerous."

He chuckled. "Give me a few critters to tussle with any day."

Up ahead, the road dead-ended in front of a dense growth of twisted trees and entwined undergrowth. Green, brown, thorny. Surely it was much like the original, impenetrable Cross Timbers.

She stopped and looked from right to left. "Did I make a wrong turn?"

"Independent cusses settled Wildcat Bluff. They wanted safety and privacy. They got it."

"Do you mean we walk in from here?" She imagined carting her belongings up a narrow trail to a dusty cabin. Despite rave reviews, the spring might be a muddy hole in the ground. Who knew what wild animals shared the water? She sighed. Her day kept getting more complicated the closer she got to Wildcat Bluff.

"Dogleg right, then back left."

She looked at him in exasperation. "If you hadn't noticed, there's an impenetrable wall in front of us, and the road ends here."

"Trust me."

Not much other choice. She turned sharply to the right, looked left, and saw a gap wide enough for trucks or campers, two or three abreast. Nobody would ever guess there was an entrance here.

"Go on." He pointed forward. "Plenty of room to drive horses and wagons through there back in the day."

She followed the wide road upward. As she reached the summit, the sun bathed Wildcat Bluff in a golden glow. She gasped. Christmas had come to the Bluff, and the town was awash in red and green, gold and silver, white and blue. Multicolored lights blinked on and off where they had been strung from building to building along the town's rooflines. Country Christmas songs filled the air. She'd really fooled herself into thinking she could get away from all the Christmas folderol. If Dallas had been holiday mad, Wildcat Bluff was outrageous.

She braked and shut her eyes. First, fire. Now, Christmas. She didn't know how she was going to survive the emotional onslaught. When tears burned behind her eyelids, she sniffed to keep back the moisture.

"I know," Trey said. "It can catch you by surprise and bring back all your wonderful childhood memories."

She swallowed hard, unable to respond. She absolutely would not be overwhelmed by her emotions. She'd had sixteen years of practice at putting those feelings in a closet and slamming the door shut. She was a grown, professional woman and she could handle anything Wildcat Bluff threw at her. She'd simply focus on the present and whatever lay beneath shiny tinsel and country charm. And do her job.

A long row of one- and two-story buildings built of rock and brick nestled behind a white portico that covered a long boardwalk. Sunlight glinted off shop windows. Once more, she felt as if she'd stepped back in time into a Western town like the ones she'd seen in old tintype photos that Aunt Cami had shared with her. Yet everything appeared as fresh as if it'd been constructed yesterday.

"Wildcat Bluff spreads out from Old Town in streets named after trees and cats. We've got architecture from Victorian to Art Deco to Midcentury Modern to Ranch Hacienda. Modular housing, too. Offices are in homes or in the business and warehouse district to the south. You name it, we've probably got it."

"Sounds eclectic."

He chuckled. "More like a lot of hard-headed mavericks built across the centuries to suit their own whims."

"I like it."

"Glad you do. I'm right partial myself."

"Are these original structures?" She was proud of her steady voice and clear thoughts.

"Here on Main Street, yes."

"They're beautiful. And the buildings are so perfectly maintained. But how did they get built here? I mean, who had those skills?"

"Italian masons."

She looked harder at the buildings, trying to reconcile skilled masons with the old West. She noticed more details. "Saloon" was painted in tall yellow letters near the roofline of a brick two-story building. Next door was the Wildcat Hotel with a second-floor balcony enclosed with a stone balustrade supported by five fancy columns.

"I don't understand." She pointed from one building to another. "Back then, this town would have been on the frontier of Texas. Where would they have found European masons?"

"I guess most people don't know the history anymore. Back then, there were coal mines over to the west of here. And the Choctaw Nation had coal mines in Indian Territory near McAlester. Those old train engines were hungry beasts—ate coal by the ton load. Italian miners came over to work the mines with locals. Some of those guys were masons."

"Wildcat Bluff must be quite the tourist attraction."

"Sometimes. Like at Christmas. But we're not set up to be a resort destination."

"Still mostly undiscovered by outsiders?" Misty found herself authentically interested in what Trey was telling her about Wildcat Bluff. She hadn't had much in the way of expectations of the place coming up here. Of course, she could have listened to Trey's smooth baritone all day—and well into the night.

"Impossible to stay undiscovered," Trey said as he sighed and shook his head. "With all our natural resources it's impossible to stay under the radar. Water. Timber. Coal, gas, oil. Cattle. Not to mention our soil's so fertile it'll grow most anything."

"Wonderful." Misty was impressed.

"Yeah. On the other hand, somebody or other is always after what we've got."

"Like Dallas and Fort Worth?"

"We're on the Red River. You know how fast those cities are growing and needing water. The state and feds are looking at us, too."

"I know the drought's bad, but we've got lots of lakes in Texas."

"They're already tapped into, so folks are eyeballing the rivers. The Colorado River in Arizona and the Rio Grande down in South Texas used to be big rivers not so long ago. Not now. Water's siphoned off to the farms, towns, you name it."

"But the Red River's not that big to begin with. Won't they just leave it alone?"

He shrugged as he made a sweeping gesture toward Main Street. "We're protecting the land like we've always done, so we're good so far."

"I'm glad." She imagined an unbroken line of brave warriors watching over and taking care of the Comancheria.

He had set her mind to spinning. Could a fight over water rights affect Texas Timber? If the water table dropped too much, tree seedlings might not be able to take root. That'd have a major impact on business. If someone else wanted the water, they might want to get rid of Texas Timber. Other natural resources could also be at the root of the company's problems. After she checked in at the B&B, she'd jump on her computer and see what else she could find out, now that she had a new lead to follow.

Trey had just proved his worth. He was a lot more than a handsome face and a hot body. He had a steel-trap mind to go with all his other assets.

Chapter 4

"WHY DON'T YOU PARK ON MAIN STREET AND TAKE A gander at Old Town?" Trey was genuinely having a good time with Misty. It wasn't often he got such pleasure from delivering his tourist spiel. Misty already seemed like more than just a tourist to him. He had things to do, but he wanted to keep her with him a while longer.

"Are you still my guide?"

"You know it." He pointed toward the Wildcat Bluff Hotel, where fresh fir wreaths with huge red bows decorated each window in the redbrick two-story building.

"What a lovely place. Maybe I should've stayed here." She parked in front of the hotel's grand entrance of cream brick keystones and brass planters with Christmas-tree-shaped rosemary bushes.

"Ruby'll do right by you." He noticed two ladies stop and pointedly look in the window at him before they scurried on down the boardwalk. What was that about? And then he remembered. He was still shirtless. Not only that, but he was sitting in a vehicle with a good-looking woman in front of a hotel. He could just imagine how this story was going to develop as it spread around Wildcat Bluff. He chuckled at small-town life. At least it wouldn't hurt his reputation.

"Is that really a saloon?" Misty gestured next door as she leaned forward for a better look.

The sound of boot-scooting country music floated

through old batwing-style doors. Strings of blinking Christmas lights and star-shaped ornaments festooned a row of plate-glass windows with the words "Lone Star Saloon" painted in gold in old-fashioned curlicue script. A wooden cigar store Indian at one side of the doors had been irreverently adorned with a bright red Santa hat.

"Yep. Old Town hasn't changed much since the 1880s. The Lone Star Saloon still serves the same function. Food. Drinks. Dance hall. Live country bands on weekends."

"Sounds like fun."

"We get a lot of tourists looking for a taste of the Old West like they do in Tombstone, Arizona." He glanced at Misty, wanting her to like everything about Wildcat Bluff and wondering again why it was so important to him. He hadn't known her an hour and he was acting like it was his first rodeo—first win, first buckle, first gal. There was something about her that he flat-out liked. She was courageous, he'd give her that. She was also comfortable to talk to and sexy as hell.

"I've been to Tombstone. It's great."

"We're wall-to-wall folks during Wild West Days over Labor Day weekend." He still couldn't stop bragging about his town. "They like to see our reenactment of the shoot-out between the Hellions and the Ruffians for control of the town."

"Sounds like the shoot-out at the OK Corral in Tombstone." Misty smiled.

"Yep. Sometimes those old-time outlaws fought the law. Sometimes they were just fighting each other for turf."

"Where does the shoot-out take place?"

"Right here in front of the Lone Star." He pointed at the batwing doors.

"Aren't you going to tell me who won back in the day?"

"Why don't you come back for Wild West Days? You could see the reenactment and find out." Now he was proposing she come back in nine months when she'd hardly been in town nine minutes. Still, she might like it. He watched her reaction, hoping she liked the Bluff, or him, well enough and wondering at his own sense of insecurity. He felt like a teenager all of a sudden, with no experience with girls—or women. Misty was definitely all woman. She was soft, curvy, and sweet smelling, in spite of a little sweat and soot.

"How about I ask somebody?" She gave him a play-ful look with her pale green eyes.

"Bet we could find you a part to play. Dance-hall dar-lings in their white pinafores turned the tide. You'd look good all dolled up like that." He couldn't resist teasing her to see what kind of a response he'd get.

"You're trying to lure me back with irresistible ideas like that."

"If you think that's tempting, I've got some even better suggestions." He leaned toward her, feeling the cold of the AC against the rising heat of his bare skin.

"No more! I'm not made of stone." She turned from him and pointed down the row of buildings. "Adelia's Delights. I love the name. What's there?"

He knew she'd used the distraction to cool things back down, and it wasn't a bad idea. "Gifts. Tearoom."

Inside one window, a life-size Santa Claus dressed in bright red velvet with a wide black belt and matching black cowboy hat waved back and forth. A pretty tortoiseshell cat snuggled up to Santa's cowboy boot. She was a cat so perfect she looked like a stuffed animal until she turned her head to look in their direction.

"I see Miss Kitty's in town," Misty said with a mischievous lilt to her voice. "Is the town marshal named Dillon?"

Trey laughed. "That's Rosie, Queen of Adelia's. She's one of the best Hemingway mousers in town."

"And literary, too?"

He laughed harder. "Wildcat Bluff has a long history with cats. Store cats take care of bugs and rodents. Companionship, too."

"And they guard the books?"

He shook his head, knowing she was teasing him now. He was enjoying every minute of it. She was almost too sharp for her own good. "If you get a chance, you'll notice Rosie and other cats here have an extra dewclaw on one or more paws."

"Like the polydactyl cats at the Hemingway House?"

"Hah! You've heard of the polydactyls."

"I've seen them in Key West. Bought the T-shirt, too."

"Even better." He couldn't help but like a gal who liked cats, especially one who knew about Hemingway's.

"Somebody must have brought cats out west over a hundred years ago," she said thoughtfully.

"They were worth their weight in gold in lots of places. They kept out vermin." He chuckled. "Lots of fights over cat-stealing."

"Hard to imagine now."

"Not so hard here in the Bluff. Folks still prize their cats."

"I'd like to go in just to meet the cat. And then shop, of course."

"Plenty of time later. I need to stop by the fire station and check in."

"I'm yours to command." She tossed him a mischievous glance.

"Best not promise something you don't mean." He gave her a teasing look in return. He knew exactly what he'd command her given the opportunity.

"Directions, please."

"That's not any better. Gets a guy's hopes up."

"You're being obtuse on purpose, Mr. Firefighter." She arched one eyebrow, a sparkle in her big green eyes.

"I've been called thickheaded before. Don't bother me a bit." He leaned toward her, looked deep into her eyes, and saw the same heat there that he was feeling. He slowly kissed the tip of one finger and placed it against her lips. "A little bit of soot there. A devil's kiss on an angel's lips."

She pushed his hand away, but she also licked her lower lip as if unable to resist tasting him. "Now you're just trouble."

He felt that little lick go straight to his belly. "You look like a gal who could use some trouble."

"And you're the guy to give it to me?"

"If it's my kind of trouble, I'd be happy to help." Right about now, he'd be happy to take a good long while to quench the fire they were building between them.

"No doubt. You're such a helpful guy."

"Anything to please a lady."

"How about those directions?"

"Which ones?" He grinned, feeling hot enough to grill steaks on his bare flesh.

She tossed him a sharp-eyed glance, as if shutting down the fun. "No more talk about—well, you know what."

"Okay, for now." He didn't mean that either, but he'd play by her rules till he found a way to persuade her to substitute his for hers.

"How 'bout those directions?"

"Coming right up."

With Trey navigating, Misty backed out of her parking space and drove down Main Street to the end of Old Town.

He pointed right. "Take Cougar Lane. You'll see the fire station on the left."

She drove a short distance, and then parked in front of the large silver building with a bright red roof, five bay doors, and one regular door. Festive white lights twinkled along the edge of the roofline. "It's modular."

"We get most of our funds from donations, fundraisers, and grants. That means we put our money in rigs, not bricking the outside for curb appeal."

"It's a sturdy-looking structure."

"New, too. Took us five years to put together enough dough to build it. We still use the original station for the older rigs, but it's at a separate location."

"Impressive."

"All volunteer staff." He opened his door.

"Including the mouser?" She pointed toward the front

of the station at a gray cat with gold eyes sporting a red bow around his neck. "Is he a Hemingway, too?"

Trey chuckled. "That's Ash. He's got the regular number of toes. Still, nothing gets past him even when he's duded up with a red bow around his neck." Trey watched the fire station cat stretch, give their vehicle a slit-eyed look, and saunter around the side of the building and out of sight.

"He's gorgeous. I adore cats. They're so beautiful and intelligent. I'm really impressed Ash hasn't torn off that ribbon."

"Wouldn't dare. Hedy's word is law. Ash proudly wears costumes for all the holidays."

"Maybe I can see Ash up close later."

"Sure." He opened his door. "Hedy's most likely in the office. Wait here. I'll be right back."

"You don't need to go with me to the B&B."

"I want to introduce you to Ruby." He stepped outside, opened the back door, and picked up the bag of evidence. Not that he thought it'd help much, but there might be some type of residue on the fabric.

As he started toward the office, the door banged open. Hedy zoomed outside in her power wheelchair. She wore her steel-gray hair in a single plait down her back. Her sharp brown eyes missed nothing.

"Not hurt, are you?" she called.

"No. Caught the fire in time. Kent's watching the pasture for possible flare-ups."

"Good." She quickly motored over to him. Rudolph the Reindeer's red nose blinked on and off in her earrings and necklace. She held up a bright yellow T-shirt. "Sakes alive, put this on and cover up your nakedness. A lady could happen by."

"You're more than enough lady for me." He grinned as he exchanged the garbage bag for the Wildcat Bluff Fire-Rescue T-shirt with a crimson Firefighter-EMT logo. "My shirt's in that bag. I used it and those towels to put out the fire. Consider it evidence."

"Fat lot of good that'll do."

"You never know." He quickly pulled the T-shirt over his head, smoothed it over his chest, and tucked it into his jeans. Guess it made him halfway respectable.

"Who's the gal?"

"Come over and meet our latest hero."

When they reached Misty's side of the SUV, she opened her door and stepped out.

"Misty Reynolds, this is Hedy Murray. She owns the store you admired in Old Town."

"I'm so pleased to meet you," Misty said. "I can't wait to see inside Adelia's Delights."

Hedy chuckled. "Hope you like the store. Fact of the matter, I like to stay busy. Keeps me out of mischief. I'm glad to make your acquaintance, too."

"I deputized Misty as a Wildcat Bluff Volunteer Firefighter."

"Deputized! Ain't no such animal." Hedy snorted, rolling her eyes. "But we can use all the volunteers we can get."

"She'll be helping out while she's in town."

"Staying long?" Hedy asked.

"Not too long. I'm here on vacation," Misty said.

"Where are you staying?"

"Twin Oaks B&B."

"Good choice. Not that the hotel isn't prime territory. Lots of folks stay there, too."

"It looks wonderful."

"Darn tootin'." Hedy backed up. "Pleasure. Got to get back to the phone lines. See you two later."

Trey watched her zoom inside the station before he and Misty got back into the vehicle.

He glanced at Misty. "Before you ask, Hedy was a hell of a horsewoman. Champion barrel racer. Now, she never misses a local rodeo. She's been confined to a wheelchair since her favorite palomino threw her. She cursed her bad riding, not her horse."

"What a shame."

"Nope. That's what comes from riding horses. You're going to get stove up one way or another."

"Worth it?"

"You bet." He chuckled. "Now she pretty much uses her skills to train cats and firefighters, too." He figured a city gal like Misty probably couldn't understand the love of horses. Not yet anyway. Start her out on something smaller, if not easier, like cats. "Head on down Cougar Lane."

"Are you sure you don't want to stay here?"

"I'll catch a ride at Ruby's back to my place."

"Do you want me to take you?"

"Thanks. But it's too far out of your way. I'm finally going to give you a chance to check in and catch your breath."

"A shower is at the top of my list."

He laughed, running a hand through his hair. "Mine, too."

She joined his laughter. "I bet anybody we meet will agree about our showers."

"Let 'em complain. We're heroes."

He held up his hand for a high five. When she responded, he felt her touch like fuel to a flame.

Chapter 5

"Twin Oaks Bed & Breakfast is up on Cougar Knoll." Trey gestured down Cougar Lane. "Just keep going and you'll get there."

"I see what you mean about the houses." Misty drove slowly to take in the view. Most of the large homes were set back from the road on an acre or perhaps two. She admired a Spanish hacienda with a red-tile roof, a pink brick single-story ranch with a silver metal roof, a white antebellum with wide columns soaring from the portico up to the second story, and a multicolored pastel Victorian. All were beautiful. They also had Christmas decorations prominently displayed so people driving by could enjoy the designs from country-style painted wood to city-bright plastic and neon. She couldn't help but think how much Aunt Cami would have enjoyed seeing these houses.

"Twin Oaks is special," Trey said. "Nobody much wanted to deal with those ten acres on the outskirts of town. Rocky ground with little natural beauty except for two ancient oak trees. The natural spring was there, but it had been boarded over and people had mostly forgotten about it."

"I liked the look of the hotel in town."

"You won't be disappointed in Twin Oaks, not now."

"Why's that?" Misty didn't say it, but she couldn't be disappointed at the moment. All she had to do was glance Trey's way and see the twinkle in his eyes as he held back the details of what she was going to experience. She tried not to smile too much or he'd get the idea she was much more interested in him than she should be on such short acquaintance. Yet she wondered if she had already given herself away.

"Jake Jobson is why. He moved here and married Gladys Sundown of a local clan. Jake had been a Seabee—U.S. Navy Construction Battalion—in the Pacific Theater in World War II. He was crazy about designing and building stuff. In the eighties and nineties, he spent his retirement years creating Twin Oaks for Gladys, the love of his life."

"Will I get to meet Jake and Gladys?"

"It's a shame, but no. They passed on a few years ago. I don't know what they'd think about Ruby—that's their daughter—turning the place into a B&B. They were private folks. But everybody is sure glad she did. It's a great setting for weddings, reunions, getaways."

"Now I can't wait to see it."

At every turn, Misty kept being surprised. She also felt a little embarrassed at her earlier attitude. She'd arrived without much expectation for the area and the people. She should've known better. Texas was big enough that there was a huge variety of terrain and residents. Cindi Lou was right. She needed to get out of the city more and start living life to its fullest. She glanced at Trey again. She bet he lived his life to the fullest every single day. Maybe she could learn from him.

"We're coming up on the property. Wait till you see what Jake did with all those pesky rocks."

She gasped in surprise. "That fence is a work of art."

She drove past an amazing rock fence scalloped from rock post to rock post with a rope of twinkling blue lights strung along the top.

"Jake washed and sized every one of those rocks before he cemented them together."

"Beautiful. Did he plant all those trees, too?" Misty pointed at the neat, orderly rows of green pine trees on the property.

"Sure did. He told me he liked the peace. He built a brick-and-wood bench beside the pond just so he could sit and listen to the wind whisper through the pines."

"He sounds like a romantic."

Trey chuckled. "Maybe he was. He was tough, but he had a soft side, too. He always called Twin Oaks his little love nest."

Misty laughed in delight. "What a great guy."

As she drove up to the B&B's entrance, she saw an arched black metal sign overhead that read "Twin Oaks" entwined with the silhouettes of two oak trees. Another long rope of twinkling blue lights highlighted the sign. She turned in past twin rock buttresses that curved outward from the fence on either side of the entry and drove onto the estate.

"Plenty to do here in season. Basketball. Tennis. Swimming. Golf." Trey pointed ahead. "You can park by the white board fence that encloses the horse pasture behind that red barn."

She drove across dry grass, pulled up to the fence, and stopped her SUV. She sat still for a long moment as she listened to the wind whisper through the trees. She gazed at the imposing house that rose in planes, angles, and sharp roof lines. Red brick. Green trim. Slate-gray shingles. Three-car garage. Extra parking for guests by the tennis court. Beautiful in its stark simplicity and welcoming ambiance.

"Looks like Jake built a multilevel Midcentury Modern house in the eighties." She turned to look at Trey in astonishment.

"Sure did. He was a young man based in California during World War II when he first saw that style. Remained his favorite architecture."

"I can't wait to see inside."

"Not disappointed?"

She glanced into his bright hazel eyes. "Impossible. You're right. This is a special place. I'm glad I'm staying here."

"Good. Come on. Let's get you settled in."

She got out, picked up her laptop in its case from the backseat, and slid the strap of her large handbag over her shoulder as she walked to the rear of her SUV. Trey was already there waiting for her. When she opened the back and started to pick up her bags, he grabbed the heaviest right out from under her hands.

"Let me do like my mama taught me and act the gentleman." Trey easily lifted her two cases. "It's enough for you to handle your laptop and whatever else is in that giant bag."

"Thanks. Always the question for men, isn't it? What do women put in their handbags?"

"Scary thought. Don't want to know."

She joined his laughter and locked her SUV. They were some distance from the house. She walked beside him across dry grass to a two-story pergola outlined by twinkling blue lights with a green picnic table on each level. The redbrick pergola appeared to be the viewing stand for the tennis court enclosed by a high chain-link fence.

"Jake really was a visionary, wasn't he?" She gestured around as she walked across the cement court.

"And he did the work himself. Bit by bit."

"Even more impressive."

At the front of the house, she noticed sliding glass doors under a covered entry porch. A silver-and-blue wreath hung on each door. White poinsettias with green leaves brightened a redbrick planter. A huge oak tree, with the trunk wrapped in silver and blue tinsel and lights, cast the area in shadow.

Misty heard a meow and glanced up. Bright blue eyes in a white face with a black mark across the nose stared down at her. She smiled at the cat on the roof. Another beauty. She might as well start taking lots of cats in Wildcat Bluff for granted like everybody else.

Trey walked over, patted the oak's trunk, and looked up. "Meet Big John. Big Bertha is on the other side of the house. Jake built between them so if lightning struck, it'd hit the trees."

She followed his gaze upward. High above, the center trunk was gray, lightning blasted, but the tree was a survivor. New branches had grown tall and strong around the storm damage.

In Wildcat Bluff, everything appeared intensely alive, even in winter. Creativity, happiness, and love of life were obviously nurtured here. Misty felt a little like Big John, damaged by life's storms but still strong—and still growing—just like Aunt Cami had always wanted for her.

"Welcome to Twin Oaks Bed & Breakfast!" The sliding glass doors snapped open. A lithe woman in jeans, a red top, and black cowboy boots stepped outside. She wore her dark hair straight and blunt-cut at her shoulders. She'd tucked a white poinsettia bloom behind one ear.

"Hey, Ruby." Trey patted the tree again. "Just introduced your new guest to your favorite guy."

"Did you now?" Ruby said in a husky, alto voice. "All I ask is that you don't whisper sweet nothings to Big John so he runs off and leaves me lonely."

Misty laughed. "I'll do my best not to lure him away."

"Thanks." She held out a sun-browned hand. "Ruby Jobson, chief cook and bottle washer. You must be Misty Reynolds."

"Pleased to meet you." Misty shook Ruby's firm hand. She knew right away that Ruby was Country Texas by her brisk walk, humorous talk, and strong handshake. She might meet a few women like her in Dallas, but here in the countryside, most of the women would be like Ruby. Straight talkers. Hard workers. Salt of the Earth. They had a generosity of spirit that never turned anyone hungry away from the table. Misty knew she couldn't be in better hands.

"Heard Trey's had you busy," Ruby said in a typical Texas understatement.

"All in a day's work. Put out a fire with a towel. Drive to Wildcat Bluff with a half-naked man who has my vehicle smelling like a campfire. Meet a six-toed cat. And listen to the seductive whispers of Big John."

Ruby guffawed. "Sounds like you're my kind of gal."

Misty appreciated the compliment. She wasn't

usually so clever with words. Wildcat Bluff was apparently having a positive impact on her. She felt more alive than she had in a long time.

"Come on inside and make yourself at home. Trey, you too."

Misty stepped onto the terra-cotta tile of an enclosed breezeway. Pots of red poinsettia plants added vibrant color. The garden room extended across the house to another wall of glass with sliding doors. She could see a brick gazebo with one side built around the trunk of an ancient oak. Big Bertha. Now she could see how Twin Oaks got its name.

In typical Midcentury Modern fashion, organic outdoors moved indoors with red brick halfway up the walls to meet bright white above and green plants in terra-cotta pots below. A ceiling fan circulated air across a colorful poster of a woman on horseback framed in gray barn wood that read, "National Cowgirl Hall of Fame, Fort Worth, Texas."

"Wildcat Bluff cowgirls make quite a showing there," Ruby said, sounding quietly boastful.

"I've never been to the cowgirl museum."

"Ought to go." Ruby swiveled toward Trey. "Got to bring this gal up to speed. You up for a trip to Fort Worth?"

"Ask the cows." He set down Misty's luggage.

"Hah! Ornery critters. They keep you hog-tied. You got to bust loose every now and again."

"Thought I'd bring barbeque over tonight with a mess of curly fries and fried jalapeños," Trey said in a dry tone. "Wild enough for you?"

"Take my pickup and go home, mouthy cuss."

"Need me to bring anything back from town?" Trey gave Ruby an aw-shucks look as if he were completely innocent.

Misty wanted to laugh out loud, but instead she just shook her head at their friendly banter.

"Thanks, but I'm all set." Ruby put her hands on her narrow hips. "Only two other folks are staying here. Real nice couple from Houston. They own a string of antique stores in Texas, so they're scouting around for merchandise."

"Nobody's asking about water rights? Gas? Coal? Timber?" Trey asked.

"So far, all's quiet on that front."

Misty cringed. She'd met nothing but nice people in Wildcat Bluff. She wished she wasn't with them on false pretenses. Still, she'd been warned not to trust anybody, so she wouldn't. Besides, nice and polite could cover up a lot of sins. She'd just have to make sure they never learned about her association with Texas Timber, or at least not till after she'd completed her investigation.

"Misty, glad you could join us," Ruby said. "Vacationers are always good company."

"I'll try not to get in your way."

"Not a word of it. You're my guest and I want you to enjoy the place. Daddy built it for fun, so see if you can get stodgy Trey to let loose."

"I've been called a lot of things, but never stodgy." Trey put his large hand across his heart as if hurt. "Just for that crack, I'm only bringing tasty barbeque for two."

"At least you like to live dangerously." Ruby snorted, obviously trying to hold in her laughter.

Trey glanced at Misty, something hot glimmering in

his eyes, then quickly snapped the sliding doors shut behind him.

"Wonder who put a burr under his saddle?" Ruby cocked her head at Misty. "Doubt it was me."

Chapter 6

MISTY TOOK A DEEP BREATH AS SHE WATCHED TREY walk away. With a backside like that, he hardly needed anything else going for him. Instead, he had plenty of everything that could set a gal ablaze.

When he reached the dark green pickup with TOB&B painted in white on its side, he turned and started back.

Misty opened the sliding door, wondering what he wanted to say.

Ruby leaned out. "Keys are on the driver's side floorboard!"

"Thanks. I'll get them," he said when he reached the open door. "Now, ladies, don't go starting fires—of any kind—without me." He mischievously winked. "Misty, your half-naked firefighter will be back with grub real soon."

"What about me?" Ruby asked, humor bubbling in her voice.

"What do naughty gals get?" He tried to look stern, but his eyes were twinkling too much for it to be effective.

"Naughty guys, I hope. And a rack of ribs."

Trey laughed hard, shook his head, then sauntered back to the truck, got inside, and drove away.

"Hot, ain't he?" Ruby said in her raspy voice. "That Duval clan and their cousins, the Steele family, are notorious for attracting more fire than they can put out."

"No opinion, one way or the other." Misty tried to sound businesslike, or at least prim and proper.

"Hah!" Ruby pointed at the tail end of the pickup as it sped down the road. "No point fooling yourself right off the bat. Love 'em or hate 'em, there's not a woman ever lived who didn't have an opinion on the Duval and Steele males."

"I met his cousin Kent."

"Now there's a heartbreaker if ever there was one."

"Do any of them actually get married?"

"Guess you mean, why settle for one cow when you can milk the herd?"

"That's not what I meant."

"'Course it is." Ruby leaned near and lowered her voice. "Truth is, when those guys fall, they fall hard. It takes a real special woman to bring them to their knees with a diamond ring in their hands."

Misty sighed as she closed the door, realizing she'd appeared too interested in the local cowboys.

"Kent and Trey haven't been roped and hog-tied."

Misty chuckled at the image. "Maybe they ought to be."

"If you held the rope, I doubt they'd complain."

Misty refused to go down that dangerous road. "I'm just here for a peaceful getaway. I doubt those guys are what you might call peaceful."

Ruby gave a big guffaw that filled the breezeway. "Just the opposite."

Misty adjusted her shoulder bag, more than ready to end this conversation. She glanced down at her luggage.

"Here I am jawing while you're wanting your room and a bath, aren't you?"

"That'd be lovely. I'm afraid I'm a little smoky and smelly after the fire."

"I can tell you right now the folks of Wildcat Bluff County appreciate you pitching in to stop that grass fire."

"Glad to be of assistance."

"Some people would've gone on by. You showed a big spirit, particularly a generous Christmas spirit."

"You really like Christmas around here, don't you?"

"Nothing better." Ruby sighed, rubbing her forehead as if in pain. "But this year? It's not easy getting in the right frame of mind, what with the heat and drought and fires."

"Can't last forever."

Ruby cocked her head, giving Misty the once-over. "That's the spirit. And there's a pretty Christmas angel for some Christmas spirit in your suite."

"Did Trey suggest it?"

"Trey?"

"He called me his Christmas angel for stopping to help."

"Did he now?" Ruby's eyes glinted with interest. "Guess he's got Christmas on his mind."

"Suppose so." Misty reached down to pick up a bag.

"Let's go upstairs." As Ruby started to get Misty's other piece of luggage, the front sliding doors snapped open.

At the sound, Misty turned around to look, expecting Trey or Kent. Instead, she saw a woman with platinum-blond hair and a big white smile to go with her tall, slim, well-maintained body. Right behind her was a man just as finely put together who obviously worked out to stay in shape. They looked to be in their forties. The woman wore a charcoal pencil skirt with a red silk blouse and black high heels. He wore creased jeans, a burgundy shirt, and brown leather boots.

"I'd like you to meet J.P. and Charlene Gladstone. They're antique dealers." Ruby gestured toward Misty. "And this is Misty Reynolds. She's here on vacation."

J.P. tipped his cowboy hat. "Pleased to meet you. You sure do brighten up the place."

"Absolutely," Charlene agreed. "And I'm happy to have another lady's company."

"Good to meet you both," Misty said as she evaluated the couple. She bet J.P.'s expensive cowboy boots had never seen stirrups or muddy pastures and Charlene's heels would never stand up to the challenge either. City folks, no doubt about it.

"Any luck finding antiques?" Ruby asked.

"We found a few things on our want list." Charlene glanced east. "Sherman, Denison, and Bonham are always good places to look."

"Sounds like a fun way to make a living." Misty decided the two appeared to be successful and savvy businesspeople.

"Twenty years of fun," Charlene agreed. "You just never know what nuggets of Texas history you'll run across."

J.P. chuckled. "And we're always on the lookout for the latest popular kitsch."

"Always," Charlene said. "Right now we're searching for antique Christmas angels."

Angels again. Misty had to smile. "Perfect season for your hunt."

Ruby's gaze met Misty's. "This time of year everybody seems to be looking for an angel."

J.P. shrugged. "A greenback's a greenback, no matter how you slice it. Angels or flying pigs. We'll search it out." J.P chuckled as he glanced down at Misty's luggage. "But don't let us keep you from settling into your room. Plenty of time to chat later."

"I'll look forward to it." Charlene patted her sleek, shiny hair.

Ruby grabbed Misty's bag, then quickly opened the door into the house. "Right this way."

Misty gave the couple a polite smile, picked up her luggage, and followed Ruby into a house that smelled of cedar and cinnamon.

Ruby closed the door behind them. "That's my suite to the left. The other three suites are on the top floor. Glad Daddy had the idea of giving everybody their own bathroom. It saved me a lot of work when I decided to open a B&B."

Misty passed the closed door to Ruby's suite and entered a large living room. She caught her breath at the beauty. The ceiling soared to the roof in an A-line with a balcony behind them overlooking the area. To the right, a half-brick wall opened up to a bright, yellow kitchen that was reached by three brick steps. A redbrick fireplace cut across one corner and extended to the ceiling. Contemporary furniture with a geometric pattern on the upholstery completed the room. Yet everything was overshadowed by a huge Christmas tree that dominated the corner of the room opposite the fireplace.

A colorful peacock with spread tail feathers perched on top of the tree in place of an angel. Ornaments in the shape of peacocks, feathers, and glass balls in turquoise, lapis, hot pink, and gold festooned the tree. Aqua and pink bulbs glowed warmly against the green of the cedar tree.

"That's stunning!" Misty walked over to get a closer look. Brightly wrapped packages and colorful sacks were tucked around the tree's base.

"Glad you like my creation. I'm right proud. First year for it. We're doing weddings and birthdays in the peacock theme, so why not a Christmas tree?"

"Gorgeous." And best of all, it didn't remind her of traditional Christmas decorations, so Misty could enjoy it.

"Not everybody agrees. Some folks like classic red and green. And angels." Ruby chuckled as she waved a hand toward the mantel, where a green garland draped down the length with colorful peacocks tucked here and there.

"Did you decorate all this yourself?"

"When I've got big, brawny cowboy firefighters to come in here and help? Not likely!"

"Looks neatly done."

Ruby laughed. "Not that it didn't require a little repositioning after I shooed them out the door, but they did the hard part."

"I have to admit I'm having a little trouble imagining Trey and Kent hanging Christmas tree ornaments."

"Big tree to get in here and get set up. I needed the muscle." Ruby adjusted a peacock ornament. "And don't let anybody kid you. Those guys can be gentle with their hands when the occasion calls for it."

"Hmmm." Misty's mind wandered as she imagined gentle hands in all the right places.

"You'll see. They're good guys. You should see them handle horses." Ruby winked at her. "Now, let's get you upstairs and into your room."

Misty followed Ruby up the steps to the expansive kitchen with light wood cabinets, white laminate countertops, and a vintage dining table and matching chairs that fit perfectly with the Mid-Century Modern architecture. She hurried to catch up as Ruby ascended a short flight of stairs to the top level.

"I put you in the Sun Suite." Ruby opened a door and threw it wide. "Hope you like it."

Misty stepped into a room with peach walls and white trim. Sunlight streamed in through two windows to cast a warm glow over everything. A bright orange spread covered the queen bed, with purple and green throw pillows added for more color. Minimalist furniture with straight lines in cherrywood made up the headboard, dresser, desk, chair, and settee. A blond-haired angel dressed in a long, white satin gown with a harp in her hands was positioned prominently on top of the desk.

Ruby walked over and punched a button on the base of the Christmas angel. The angel's arms moved up and down as if strumming the harp to a tinny rendition of "Hark! The Herald Angels Sing."

Misty felt dizzy, as if all the air in the room had suddenly been sucked out. She set down her luggage, laptop, and handbag. She quickly walked over to the settee and sat down, feeling as if she might cry. She put her hand to her mouth to stop the tears, the memories. She hadn't been this overcome in a long time. She absolutely could not let a Christmas song thrust her back in time to the moment when her life had been turned upside down. She overrode the song in her mind with her safe words, "Be here now. Safe and sound. Be here now."

Ruby smiled fondly at the Christmas angel. "That song was written in 1739, if you can believe it. Now that's the power and endurance of Christmas." Ruby turned away from the angel. "Honey, what's the matter?" She hurried over to Misty and put a hand on her shoulder.

"Tired. I just need a shower—to rest."

"No wonder. And here I am prattling on to beat the band." Ruby backed up. "Your closet's behind that door. Bathroom's behind the other. Key's on the desk. You need anything, just holler."

"Thanks." Misty glanced up in time to see Ruby shut the door behind her.

As the song came to a blessed end, she let out a sigh of relief. There was simply too much Christmas at Twin Oaks, but she didn't have to put up with it in her own room.

She hurried into the bathroom and picked up a large white towel. She stalked over to the angel, grabbed the square base, and hauled the offending object to the closet. She shoved the angel into a back corner of the top shelf and carefully covered it with the towel, not leaving a bit to be seen.

She closed the closet door with a snap and glanced around the room. No more Christmas in sight. Perfect.

What a crazy day. She'd unpack, get a bath, and maybe take a nap. But first, she'd check in with Cindi Lou. She needed a heavy dose of the reality of her real day-to-day life in Dallas.

Cindi Lou picked up on the first ring. "Darlin', tell me you're safe in Wildcat Bluff."

"I'm here in my room at Twin Oaks. It's a beautiful place."

"Good. Took you longer to get there than I expected. Is everything fine?"

"Yes. But—" Misty dropped onto the comfortable settee. "Are you sitting down? Have you got a Dr Pepper in hand?"

"Always. Now, give."

"I put out a fire."

"You what?" Cindi Lou's shock rang out loud and clear. "Are you really okay?"

"I faced my fear and used my towels to help this cowboy firefighter put out a grass fire on my way into town." Misty felt proud to tell her friend how strong she'd been earlier.

"Wait. Back up. Did you say cowboy firefighter?"

Misty chuckled, knowing her BFF only too well. "You skipped over the important stuff and went straight to the guy, didn't you?"

"He's hunky, isn't he? I can tell by the sound of your voice. Does he have a brother, cousins, friends?"

Misty laughed harder. "I met his cousin."

"And?"

Misty sighed, thinking back to the two cowboys standing side by side and looking like the poster boys for hotness.

"Oh, you've got it bad," Cindi Lou chortled in her booming voice. "They're that good, huh?"

"I don't have it bad," Misty said in her best prim and proper voice. "But I admit they're eye candy on steroids."

"Photos. Snap a selfie with the hunks and send it to me."

"I doubt they're into selfies."

"Now that sets my mind ablaze. What are they into? Ropes? Spurs? Big long fire hoses?"

Misty couldn't keep from laughing at her friend's wonderful outrageousness. "Maybe you'd better come up here and ask them."

"And leave the Hub? Sure as I did, a major crisis would descend out of the blue. But thanks for the thought." Cindi Lou loudly slurped her drink.

"Everybody so far has been really nice and friendly."

"The Texas way. You know that can mean little to nothing."

"Or everything. At least it makes life easier."

"Now, remember to take care."

"I'll be careful." Misty glanced around the room, calculating safety. She was on the top floor at the far end of the hall. In case of fire, she wasn't in an optimal position to escape. That made her feel a little uneasy, but not enough to demand another room and chance calling attention to herself and endangering her investigation.

Cindi Lou huffed into the phone. "You heard me, didn't you?"

"Yes. I was thinking. Tomorrow I'll try to find a fire extinguisher and keep it in my room."

"Good idea. You can't be too careful. Now, was that grass fire arson or simply natural from the heat and drought?"

"Don't know yet, but it allowed me to meet Trey, Kent, and Hedy, who are all Wildcat Bluff Fire-Rescue volunteers."

"That's a good start on your investigation."

"Anything going on there I should know about?"

"A few nibbles, nothing more. It's mostly quiet during the holidays, so nothing to write home about."

"Good." Misty didn't want any other distractions.

"Remember to stay in touch with your Texas Timber VP contact."

"I will. Audrey wants an update anytime, day or night, if there's something new to report."

"So do I." Cindi Lou's voice changed to one of concern. "If you want out of this project, just say the word. I'm serious."

"And miss out on cowboy firefighter selfies?"

Cindi Lou chuckled. "I admit that's hard to pass up."

"Another thing. Christmas is this town's favorite holiday."

"What do you mean?"

"Outrageous decorations, music, you name it, are all over the place." She thought how Aunt Cami would love everything about Twin Oaks except the holiday decorations.

Cindi Lou groaned. "Are you sure you don't want to come home right this minute?"

Misty snorted in disdain. "Surely you jest. I'm a professional troubleshooter. I live for fires and Christmas."

"I get it. You're the Lone Ranger righting wrongs. Pick up Tonto and go for it."

Misty chuckled. "You and your old Westerns. As a matter of fact, my Tonto is named Trey."

"You're kidding me."

"I'm in Comanche country."

Cindi Lou smacked her lips loudly over the phone. "One word. Photos. Got it?"

"I'll see what I can do."

"And stay safe."

"Will do, Hub Mistress."

Misty clicked off, stood up, and set her phone on the desk. She already missed Cindi Lou's vibrant presence. But she had a job to do and she was going to do it. She already felt a connection to Wildcat Bluff and she didn't want to see its residents or property hurt by a dangerous predator.

Once she had a bath, she'd set up her laptop, write up first impression notes, and start files on everyone she'd met who could have connections to the fires. Later, she'd research online. She particularly wanted to find out about local water rights. She was looking for what didn't fit or what fit too well. She also wanted to see the fire scene at the burned Christmas tree farm and chat with folks around town. She'd adjust her investigation as information came to her, but for now, she was pleased with her start.

As she tugged her top over her head, her thoughts roamed to a cowboy firefighter named Trey. Shirtless, what a hunk. But she had to be practical. He was simply part of the investigation. Maybe even a suspect.

Even so, a smart gal never turned down good barbeque or the chance to ogle eye candy. And she prided herself on having at least a modicum of functioning brain cells.

Chapter 7

Trey drove up to Twin Oaks, parked, and cut his pickup's rumbling engine. He'd already corralled Kent and Slade, a Steele cousin, into returning Ruby's truck. He could see it parked beside the barn. His cousins might still be here, so he hoped he'd brought enough barbeque.

He took a deep breath and felt his mouth water at the smell of the grub he'd bought in Old Town. After ranch chores, plus this morning's firefighting, he was mighty hungry. He glanced around the area, like he always did, looking for trouble. All the firefighters kept an eye out for Ruby and her place since she lived alone. She knew to call one of them if she had a water pipe break or other problem, but sometimes pride got in the way of common sense. At the moment, everything on the property looked mowed, edged, caulked, and painted.

He grabbed the sacks of food and stepped outside. Sun was almost down, so the air was cooler, but not by much. He checked the sky in all directions for traces of smoke. He took a deep breath. No smell of smoke either, now that he'd washed it out of his hair with a shower and changed clothes. After the grass fire, he still felt on edge. That'd been way too close for comfort. If his Christmas angel hadn't arrived in time, there'd be no barbeque or spring tonight. Volunteers would still be out there trying to put out the prairie, or Dudley's ranch house, or maybe the Texas Timber Christmas tree farm. The blaze had been headed that way.

A white van was nosed up beside Misty's SUV. He figured the vehicle belonged to the antique dealers Ruby had mentioned were staying at her place. He gave the vehicle a closer look. A lot of dust clung to the tires and turned the white paint a dingy gray. Odd. The vehicle looked more like it'd been driven on backcountry roads or pasture instead of pavement. Who knew where dealers went to find old stuff?

As he crunched across the dry grass, he thought about his Christmas list. He'd rewritten it with Misty's name in the number one spot and snow as number two. He'd put the sticky note back under his Frosty the Snowman refrigerator magnet. Maybe like would beget like. He'd even settle for a good gully washer, they needed water so bad. Right now the area was a tinderbox just waiting for a carelessly thrown cigarette butt on Wildcat Road or any back road.

As Trey walked around to the front of the house, a white cat jumped down from Big John's lower limb and headed at a trot toward him. No doubt Temple could smell the meat, but Trey liked to think the cat liked him and felt safe around him. Cats, dogs, and horses tended to like him. They knew he was a critter-friendly guy. He set the paper bags down on a corner of the brick flower bed, opened one sack, and selected a sliver of beef. Temple leaped up on the brick, blue eyes bright with impatience.

"Don't ever tell me I didn't give you a Christmas present." He set down the meat and picked up the bags.

Temple meowed before he delicately began to eat,

particularly meticulous about keeping his bright white fur clean.

"You're welcome." Trey patted the cat on his head, received a loud purr in response, and then stepped inside the garden room. "Hey folks, supper's on!"

When there was no reply, he moved into the living room. Ruby stood with two strangers near the peacock tree. No Misty. He felt a stab of annoyance. Had Kent gone behind his back and taken his Christmas angel out for dinner? If he had, there'd be hell to pay.

Ruby glanced over. "Hey, Trey. Smells good. Come on in. Meet my guests, J.P. and Charlene Gladstone. They're scouting around for antiques." She motioned in his direction. "Trey Duval is a local rancher."

"Pleased to meet you." He held up the sacks. "Anybody interested in the best piping-hot barbeque in town with curly fries and jack-cheese-stuffed jalapeños? I even got some peach turnover fried pies."

Ruby rubbed her tummy. "Took you long enough. Is that Lula Mae's?"

"Yep. Chuckwagon Café at its finest."

"I saw that quaint little place in Old Town and wanted to try it," Charlene said.

"Now's your chance."

"Good food. Good company. Nothing better." J.P. shook Trey's hand. "I'm so hungry I could eat a horse and chase the rider."

Trey joined the laughter at the old joke as he eyed the newcomers. Good-looking, put-together city folks. Not quite comfortable here. Charlene was giving him the once-over like she wasn't real committed to her marriage. Sure raised his hackles. He ought to keep an eye on them since they were sharing the upper floor with Misty and living in Ruby's home.

He took the three steps up to the kitchen and plopped the sacks on the countertop.

Ruby joined him. "Barbeque still hot?"

"You bet." He glanced upstairs. "Misty in her room?"

"Nope."

He frowned as the irritation surged back. "Kent didn't—"

"Simmer down." She tugged containers out of the sacks and took a deep breath. "Kent brought my truck by and left."

"Slade?" He pulled the sack containing two rib dinners toward him.

"Left too."

"Good." He couldn't help the smile that tugged at his lips. "That's real good."

"'Course, Dudley—"

"Dudley! He can't corral his cats, much less a woman."

Ruby shook her head. "I was funning you just to see how the wind blew."

"Blows hot."

"Want a cold beer to cool off?"

"Yep."

"Want the location of my newest guest?"

"Yep."

Ruby leaned in close. "Now take it easy on her. She may not be used to alpha males."

"What do you mean?"

She rolled her eyes. "If the gal's here on vacation, she's tired, stressed, and looking for relaxation."

He grinned, feeling a rush of heat in his belly. "I can handle all that. Easy as peach turnover pie."

"That's not what I meant and you know it." She pulled open a drawer and set out flatware.

"No need to run the dishwasher. I picked up those little packages of plastic forks and napkins."

"Don't even go there. I have pretty poinsettia Christmas plates for my guests and holiday napkins."

He held up his hands. "Just trying to help."

"That's what I mean." She leaned closer to whisper. "You can come on strong and not know it."

He put a hand over his heart. "Ruby, you wound me. I've been with a woman or two in my life. They didn't tell me I stank in that department."

"I'm sure you don't."

"Okay. If you think a city gal prefers roses to barbeque and beer, I'll run out and get a couple dozen. Anyway, I owe her for all the help today."

Ruby sighed and rubbed her forehead. "Get beer out of the fridge, pick up your barbeque, and get those plastic utensils out of my sight."

"No roses?"

"She's relaxing out by the spring. Take her food and she'll probably follow you anywhere."

"So, you're saying that like a man, the way to a woman's—"

"Heart?"

He grinned. "I wasn't thinking 'heart,' but guess it'll do."

She shook her head. "Not another word. Get your grub and go."

"Yes, ma'am."

He quickly snagged four beers, rolled off a handful of paper towels, and stuck them in the sack with two rib dinners and plastic forks. As he headed down the steps, he nodded at the Gladstone couple.

"Won't you be joining us for dinner?" Charlene asked in a suggestive tone, smiling with rosy red lips.

"Not tonight."

"Another time?"

"Could be."

"I'll hold you to it."

He nodded again, wondering at her persistence. He had more important matters on his mind. Misty made a guy want to rush back to her. He stretched out his long legs and was out the door and into the garden room.

He didn't know why, but it seemed like some women had a way of complicating the simplest things. Come to think of it, maybe all women had that trait.

Chapter 8

MISTY SAT ON THE EDGE OF A TERRA-COTTA-TILED pool in the shadow of an open-air gazebo, amazingly and beautifully built of red brick in a Roman bath style. She wished she could have met the man who had designed Twin Oaks, so she could have thanked him for creating such beauty.

She listened to water bubble up from the natural spring and flow into the lower pool where it swirled around her calves. The water's warm temperature felt perfect to ease tension and relax muscles. She stretched her toes, feeling the pull of muscles in her calves that had been tested by her firefighting that morning. She'd thought about changing into a bathing suit, but she'd opted instead to simply wear a change of capris and knit top with another pair of flip-flops because she didn't really want to swim.

As she relaxed in the peaceful setting, she listened to the sound of trickling water and wind in the pines. Even the heat of the day had cooled to a comfortable level that evening. She sighed in contentment.

Dramatic arches enclosed a large gathering area along with the spring and pool. Black wrought-iron out-door furniture sported plush aqua cushions for comfort. An open fire pit nestled between two luxurious lounge chairs. The black barrel smoker looked big enough to handle food for a large group. She could easily imagine enjoying a party out here, smelling hamburgers and hot dogs sizzling on the grill and listening to the splashes and giggles of kids in the pool.

She glanced upward. White fairy lights illuminated the gazebo ceiling above, adding a soothing touch to the twilight. A gentle breeze carried the scent of pine from the rows of green trees not far away. An owl hooted, an eerie sound followed by the whoosh of wings as the bird flew deeper into the pine forest. After such a surprisingly strenuous day, Misty relaxed deeper into the serenity of the moment, letting her cares melt away.

She could almost imagine a positive Christmas. *Peace*. Here in this beautiful, restful place. *Goodwill*. Here with kind, generous people.

Instantly, those thoughts bought back the old horror of Christmas when she was so young. Her body tightened with anxiety, and her breath caught in her throat. She couldn't breathe. She felt choked by thick smoke. She coughed, trying to ease the constriction, but she could hardly catch her breath. She panted, taking short, shallow breaths as she felt her heart rev up hard and fast. She heard her painful gasps grow louder than the sound of the spring. She called on her safe words, mentally repeating, "Be here now. Safe and sound. Be here now."

Too much. That was her current problem. Too much Christmas. Too much fire. Too much emotion. She always walked a fine line, not allowing herself to have too much of anything. She couldn't afford to get too tired, too hungry, too cold, too hot, too happy, too sad. All things in moderation kept her stable.

But Wildcat Bluff, Trey Duval, and the fire had pushed Christmas into bright neon, flashing on and off in her mind. She'd started to feel too much, and obviously she couldn't afford to do it. She took deep, calming breaths. She mustn't think about Christmas, not here, not now. *Not ever.*

Normally, all the stability tricks she'd learned in recovery worked to ease her panic attacks. But not now. She gasped harder, feeling her chest contract as if a band squeezed tighter and tighter. Anxiety became fear. What if she needed medical help? How far away was a hospital or doctors? And even worse, what if she appeared weak in front of these capable people when she wanted them to view her as she truly was, strong and capable?

Somehow, she had to overcome this rare panic episode. She wasn't willing to do it with mind-numbing drugs. She'd done the zombie routine for one week and vowed never again. She looked outward to try and relax her mind, but night had fallen. The stately pines now appeared dark and dangerous. Anything could lurk in their shadows. A carpet of fallen pine needles was particularly susceptible to fire, and the ground was covered in dry grass and fallen leaves. Everything combustible. Fortunately, if worse came to worst, she could leap into the pool and be surrounded by water. Yet flames could turn the spring into a boiling cauldron.

She desperately needed to get back to the house and into her bathroom for her inhaler. She'd be safe. She'd have a chance to recover, to do her deep-breathing exercises and yoga positions with no one the wiser. But she felt frozen, unable to move in any direction. She gasped harder as she watched for the telltale sign of yellow-orange flames to flare up among the trees to signal an out-of-control fire.

If she stayed here, she could give an early warning of fire. If she stayed here, she wouldn't be seen in distress. If she stayed here, she might overcome her anxiety by sheer force of will.

But she couldn't stay here. She had to move and help herself. There was no one else to lend assistance, even if she'd wanted it.

Still gasping for breath, she pulled one foot out of the water and swiveled toward the house. A tall, dark shape stepped into the gazebo. Shocked, she slid backward and hit the water, sending waves cascading over the tile floor. Now her panic came from water, not fire, as it closed over her head. She came gasping to the surface, drenched from head to toe, as she found solid footing on the bottom of the pool.

"Misty!" Trey dropped the sack he carried on a table and knelt beside her. "Are you having an asthma attack?"

Horrified and embarrassed, she shook her head, water dribbling down her cheeks, unable to speak. She felt her knit shirt cling like a second skin, revealing everything. She tried to pull it away from her bra, realized the water offered better cover, and ducked down, still wheezing.

"Let me get you out of here and to the house."

She backed away. The water now covered her shoulders. She only needed a little longer to regain control. Trey was bringing back all her earlier emotions. He loomed so big and strong, so powerful and confident, so ridiculously handsome, while she was drenched, with her hair and makeup ruined, that she felt her heart beat even faster. She was no longer sure if she was reacting to the past or to the present. He made her want to be brave, strong, beautiful, not tingling all over with emotions best kept suppressed so that she could breathe.

"It's okay." He sank down to sit on his boot heels by the edge of the pool. "I'm an EMT. All our volunteer firefighters are trained as emergency medical technicians or paramedics."

She wanted to scream that she wasn't a medical emergency. She just needed a moment to catch her breath. But she couldn't get the words out. She held up a hand, shaking her dripping head.

"I can call an ambulance. My cell is in my truck since I'm not on duty, but I can run up to the house and use Ruby's phone." He was on one knee now, thigh muscles tensed as if he was ready to jump into action in an instant.

"No!" She dragged air into her lungs. "Please, give me a moment."

"Panic attack?" he asked in a gentle, quiet, calm voice.

She simply nodded, hating to admit what felt like a weakness. Yet she saw no censure in his gaze. Only concern.

"Still damn serious. I could hear you struggling for breath back up the path." He leaned toward her. "Scared the hell out of me. If something happened to you, I'd never forgive myself. And neither would anybody else."

"Not your fault," she whispered. For some reason, her breath came a little easier.

"We need our Christmas angel."

She rolled her eyes. Just what she didn't want to hear. She couldn't seem to get away from angels in this town.

"Do you have an inhaler in your room?"

She nodded, pulling a deeper breath into her lungs.

She felt a little better. Maybe her symptoms were receding as quickly as they'd come.

"I'll get it."

"No!" She felt her chest tighten again. "Dark. Alone." She reached out to him, feeling unreasoning fear begin to take root again. "Smoke."

"Smoke?" He went down on both knees to clasp her hand. "Okay. I understand. I won't leave you."

She moved closer to him, coming up out of the water a bit, never mind her wet clothes. She covered her mouth with the palm of one hand, as if to silence her harsh breath or reassure her body, while she held on to him with the other. Somehow he comforted her. Maybe that was one of the important things that firefighters learned to do, along with putting out flames. Often there were victims. Too often innocent people never made it out of fires alive. She shivered hard all over.

"Listen to me," he said. "Focus on my voice. You're safe. No fires are anywhere near here. You're safe."

She nodded as she felt her breath come easier and her heart rate slow down. He was right. She knew it, but she still needed to hear it, particularly from a firefighter.

"You sound better."

"Yes." She took a deeper breath, feeling strength and clarity start to return so that she felt more normal.

"I'm going to let go of your hand, but I'm not leaving you." He sat down on the edge of the pool, jerked off his socks and boots, tossed them aside, and put his feet in the water. "Come here."

She wanted the comfort of his arms, but if she gave in to her weakness now, how did she go forward when she was alone again?

"Misty, I understand. We've all had moments when we needed somebody to be there for us. It's okay to reach out for help." He dropped his hands to his knees. "Please don't be afraid of me. I got you into this situation, so it's my fault. But if you hadn't been there when and where you were, we'd have lost a lot." He took a deep breath. "Come here, Christmas angel."

"No angel."

"Yes, you are. Today you saved our town and much of our county. Saved lives. Saved Dudley's ranch house. Probably saved a Christmas tree farm. In my book that means you saved Christmas for hundreds of little kids this Christmas, next Christmas, and the Christmas after that."

She shook her head at his reasoning.

"I know what it's like since it happens every time I fight a fire. After it's all over, after the adrenaline winds down, after everybody's gone home, that's when the fear or exhausting fatigue can hit. I'm so sorry. I wouldn't have put you through this for the world."

"And you?" She reached out, reacting to a surprising need to comfort him. He clasped her hand and rubbed his rough thumb across her palm.

He smiled as he jerked his head toward the table. "I brought beer and barbeque, didn't I? Best comfort food I know."

She nodded while tension unraveled in her chest. She took a deep breath as her heart slowed to an almost normal level. He understood. He'd been on the front line of fires. He'd felt the surge of conflicting emotions. He knew what it was like to win and lose in the fight for life.

"I'm here for you, trained and everything." He

chuckled, a deep, reassuring sound. "Why don't you give me the chance to use what I spent all that time learning to do?"

She smiled, even as she realized he was intentionally trying to reassure her and lighten the situation.

"That's better."

She acknowledged that his training was working for her. She did feel stronger, like a computer overriding its programming. Yet maybe he wasn't the answer. Maybe anybody would've done in his place. Maybe she just needed not to be alone. Still, she couldn't help but doubt herself. He was here, not anybody else. And he understood.

"Much better." He squeezed her fingers.

She took a deeper breath as her heart rate ratcheted down another notch. She had to admit he'd affected her strongly from the first. He'd awakened emotions long dormant. She could blame him for her panic attack. She wanted to blame him. But when he gently tugged her toward him, she didn't.

"You're safe." He slipped into the water, pressed jeans, crisp fresh shirt, leather belt and all, and enclosed her in his arms.

He sounded good, the deep vibration of his voice spiraling throughout her. He felt good, all hard, smooth muscles wrapped around her. He smelled good, like spicy barbeque and fresh-baked bread. She took a deep breath, drinking him in as the ache in her chest receded and another took its place. Only this hot ache was much lower down. Her stomach growled, but she'd lost her hunger for food. Trey dominated all her senses.

Chapter 9

WHAT WAS IT ABOUT MISTY THAT BROUGHT OUT TREY'S protective instincts? He held her gently when he wanted to crush her against his chest. He'd seen her savvy, sassy self. Now he'd glimpsed her vulnerable, inner self. Simply made him like her all the more. Panic attack. Over fire? There was a story there. He'd like to ask her, but it'd be rude and invasive and she'd probably resist sharing it. Maybe she'd tell him in time. She'd obviously overcome a lot of fear to fight that fire with him. It made her strong in his book. It gave him a bit of a mystery to solve. And it made her more delectable than ever.

He didn't want to like and admire somebody who'd be leaving in a week or two. She might reel him in like a fish on a line before she tossed him back for being too country, too cowboy. He wasn't used to being tossed back. And he didn't figure he was going to get used to it, not now or ever. He'd take what he could get while he could get it. Dallas wasn't all that far away. Bottom line, he'd find a way to keep her in Wildcat Bluff till Christmas. Sure was the right thing to do, her being his Christmas angel and all.

For now, he had her in his arms, and that was exactly where he wanted her. He could feel the sleek, soft wetness of her hair against his chin. Even wet as she was, he caught the scent of cinnamon and spice that reminded him of Christmas. Shampoo, perfume, or clothes, he

didn't know or care. Suited her fine. Just like her body
fit him to a T. He'd known she'd be perfect for him from
the first and now he'd proved it.

He still had a niggling doubt in the back of his mind
about why she was in Wildcat Bluff. But he didn't want
to go there, so he thrust that thought into the cellar and
slammed the door shut. He'd deal with her possible
deception later, when the stars weren't bright in the sky
and she wasn't warm in his arms.

He stroked down her back and felt the smallness of
her waist as he pulled her closer. He heard her sigh, a
soft escape of breath. He understood. He had the same
feeling of rightness. When she clasped his shoulders to
hold him tighter, he felt her damp, plump breasts warm
against the solid muscles of his chest. Wet fabric didn't
leave much to the imagination. Now he wanted a hell of
a lot more than a hug from her.

They might as well be naked. Warm water swirled
around them, plastering their clothes to their bodies from
the waist down. She was all delicious curves and val-
leys. He was getting hotter and harder by the moment.
If he didn't move away, he was going to reveal exactly
how much he wanted her. Yet he couldn't resist placing
a kiss against her temple, a promise to keep when he
wouldn't feel like a heel for taking advantage.

She leaned back and touched a fingertip to her lips
before pressing her kiss to his mouth as she mimicked
his earlier touch. He kissed her fingertip, gentle when
he wanted to be savage. Yet he understood the necessity
of leashing physical needs to address emotional ones.

"Thank you." She stepped back. "You came to
my rescue."

"Turnabout's fair play. You came to my rescue earlier."

"I'm not usually so needy."

"It can happen." He gestured toward the sack on the table. "That's why I brought food for us."

"It's cold now."

"Won't matter."

"True."

"Want to eat at the table?" He gestured toward the round picnic table with comfortable chairs around it.

"We're wet."

"The night's warm."

He stepped out of the pool, dripping water from his jeans, and held out his hand. She hesitated before clasping his fingers and allowing him to help her out of the water. Her slight hesitation alerted him that she didn't quite trust him. Not too surprising since she hadn't known him long, but he wanted to change that fact. He wanted her to completely trust him.

She tried to shake out her capris, but they clung to her like a second skin. She glanced up at him. "Now that you've landed me, you aren't going to toss me back as too scrawny, are you?"

Funny how she'd had the same thought he'd had earlier. "If you're hooked, good and proper, I know how to reel you in." He'd meant to be glib, but his words had come out with a ring of truth. "I have barbeque as bait." He grinned to make light of his words, but still felt the seriousness underneath them.

She gave him an inquiring look and chuckled to ease the sudden tension. "Better be wary of what you hook. Might be more than you bargained for."

"Bet I can handle it."

"I wouldn't bet against a cowboy firefighter EMT." She motioned toward the sack. "But right now, I'm going for your bait."

"That I can deliver." He grinned, feeling his world slide back into place.

"You'd better," she said with a lilting tease in her voice.

"I might even do you one better. I bet Ruby's got some towels stashed around here."

"I wouldn't mind getting some of the water out of my hair."

He walked over to a cabinet where he knew Ruby kept paper towels, napkins, and other such kitchen stuff. He opened a door, found kitchen towels, shook his head in disappointment, then tried another door and hit pay dirt. He pulled out three white bath towels and headed back to Misty where she stood by the table, dripping water down the length of her.

"Want me to dry you?" he asked with a suggestive tone in his voice.

"No thanks." She chuckled as she held out her hands. "I believe I still know how to do it."

"But where's the fun in that?" He couldn't resist teasing her, but his words held a kernel of truth, too.

She simply shook her head at him as she accepted two towels. She blotted her face, smearing her makeup a bit, before she wrapped a towel around her hair. She quickly patted down her body before she folded the towel, set it on a chair, sat down, and sighed in contentment.

He dropped his folded towel on the seat next to her. He wasn't about to try and sluice off his jeans. Wouldn't help much and he'd look like a wimp. Besides, they'd both air-dry pretty quick in the dry heat. He sat down, feeling a sense of satisfaction. Long, hard day followed by tasty barbeque and fine companionship made life right. He ripped open the food sack, pulled out beers, set them out, and then placed a white, square container of food in front of each of them. Last, he tossed her a bag with a fork and napkin.

"Don't say a word about the utensils." He grinned. "Ruby already raked me over the coals for improper table settings."

"Reminds me, where are the tablecloth and candles?"

"Don't even go there."

She chuckled as she pulled the towel from her head, set it in a crumpled heap on the table, and fluffed out her damp hair. She tore open the cellophane package and took out her fork and napkin. "I doubt this flimsy napkin will be enough. I like my barbeque messy."

"That's why I brought the paper towels."

"Good thing." She grabbed a handful and slid the rest toward him.

He flipped open the plastic lid to his barbeque.

"Smells wonderful." She opened her container, too. "You brought ribs?"

"Don't you like them?" He glanced at her in surprise.

"You brought a lady the messiest food you could order."

"Can't fool me. That's just the way you like it."

"Right." She pointed a rib at him. "I'm so hungry I could eat a horse—"

"And chase the rider."

"Spoilsport."

"Already heard that one today."

"Aren't we sensitive?"

"What I am is hungry." And he started in on his ribs, a tender, tasty treat if ever there was one.

As they scarfed up curly fries, jalapeños, potato salad, coleslaw, ribs, and beer, they were silently intent on their food.

Trey heard nothing except the trickling of the spring until a coyote howled an eerie cry in the distance. Soon the animal was joined by a chorus of other coyotes.

Misty tossed down her rib bone. "What is that noise?"

"Coyote pack."

"Sounds dangerous. Are they allowed to roam free?"

"How are you going to stop them? They were here first. Besides, they're good rodent hunters, so they help balance the ecosystem."

"I've heard they go after small dogs in towns."

"Only if their territory has been overrun and they're starving with no place to go. It's a shame for coyotes and dogs."

"I guess Dallas spreading out onto farms and pastures could do it."

"Yep."

"But we're safe?"

"Coyotes are basically shy creatures." He gave her a mischievous glance, raising one eyebrow. "But if you'd like to sit on my lap, I'd be happy to protect you from any dangerous critters that might happen by. Warm you up, too, since you must be chilled, wet and all."

She tossed a rib bone at him. "You're just looking for trouble."

"If you'd like to give me some, I wouldn't complain."

"I'm dripping-dry just fine without your lap."

"Shame about that." He shook his head in disappointment.

She laughed. "You're just bad."

"And that's good?"

She tossed another rib bone at him, laughing harder.

"Hey, I'm going to be wearing more barbeque sauce than I'm eating if you keep that up."

"But that's good, isn't it?"

"Now you're the one who's looking for trouble."

"Think I've found it?"

He leaned toward her and wiped barbeque sauce from the corner of her mouth with his fingertip. He put his finger to the tip of his tongue. "Sweetest sauce I ever tasted."

"Hah! What's good for the gander is good for the goose." She leaned in close to him and quickly licked the corner of his mouth. She sat back, looking quite pleased, obviously expecting him to go on teasing her.

But he felt her touch like a punch to the gut. If that was a sample of what she could do to him, he wanted her tongue all over him, licking and stroking and tormenting until he returned the favor. She was playing with fire and didn't know it. Pretty quick, he wasn't going to be able to control the inferno she was building in him.

"Trey?" She raised her eyebrows in obvious concern. "Was I out of line?"

"Hell no!"

He leaned over, grasped the back of her neck, and planted his lips on hers. She tasted like beer, barbeque, and a sweetness that could only be her own. He felt a growl lock in his throat as something feral threatened to bust loose. Yet he remained gentle, not about to spook her, as he nibbled from one corner of her mouth to the other, then probed slightly with his tongue.

When she parted her lips, his groan broke free as he pushed into her soft, warm depths. He heard her sigh, a soft, husky sound, as she returned his kiss, grasping his shoulders and pulling him closer.

"Howdy out there! Where are you two?" a woman's voice called, breaking the stillness of the night.

Misty gasped and jerked back. "Is that the Gladstones?"

"If it is, I'm going to sic the coyotes on them."

He heard footsteps on the brick walkway that led to the spring. He cursed under his breath at the lousy timing. He couldn't even get up, not in his wet jeans, or he'd reveal exactly what they'd been up to out here.

Misty put a hand over her mouth, eyes wide with surprise and wonder, as she stared at him. "I guess that kinda got out of control. But we've been under a lot of stress."

"Not out of control at all." He tugged her hand toward him and kissed her soft palm. "I've wanted to kiss you since the first moment I saw you."

She gently cradled his face with her hand. "We've been a little busy for you to follow up on that plan till now."

"I didn't know if you'd be so inclined."

"Guess I am, or was, but we'd better leave it here."

"You sure?" If he had time, he'd change her mind, but the footsteps were drawing close.

She nodded as she pulled her hand away and placed it in her lap.

"There you are!" Charlene stepped into the gazebo.

"We brought more to drink." J.P. followed her, holding a tray of beers.

Trey leaned close to Misty. "You're my Christmas angel."

She shook her head in denial.

"Won't let you forget it."

J.P. set the tray on the table, seated Charlene beside Misty, and eased down in a chair. "Pretty place, isn't it?"

"Yes," Misty agreed.

Charlene winked at Trey. "So, what have you two been doing?" She patted Misty's hand, her fingers sporting red-tipped nails and sparkling rings. "Sugar, your hair is all wet, and your makeup's a mess. Maybe you ought to check a mirror."

Misty pulled her hand away, surprised at Charlene's rudeness. Maybe she'd been struck by the green-eyed-jealousy monster despite being married to a nice-looking man like J.P. and didn't want another gal hanging out with Trey. Whatever the case, Misty knew her makeup wasn't in the best shape, but she didn't much care. And Trey didn't appear to either.

But she'd learned something important about Charlene for her file. The perfectly put-together antique hunter liked to think she was the only woman on-site who could turn a man's head.

Chapter 10

MISTY CAUGHT TREY'S GLANCE, BUT ALL HE DID WAS shrug and appear amused at Charlene's comment.

"That'll happen when you take a spontaneous dip in the spring," Misty said, throwing Charlene's words back at her. "Feels wonderful. You ought to give it a try while you're here. Washes away all your troubles."

Charlene clicked her long nails together as she smiled with crimson-tinted lips. "Skinny-dipping? Naughty girl."

J.P. sat up straighter and gave Misty a closer look.

"Not at all." Trey jumped into the conversation. "Clothes and all. Looked like so much fun I had to join her. We're sitting here letting our clothes dry, enjoying the night and shooting the breeze."

"He's been telling me about his work as an EMT." Misty decided to get the discussion away from her wet clothes and messy makeup.

"You're an emergency medical technician?" Charlene's big eyes widened in surprise and interest.

"Let me answer that." Ruby stepped into the gazebo, carrying two battery-powered hurricane lanterns. She set them on the table before she took a seat across from Misty.

"Cozy." Misty liked the soft illumination, but she hoped it didn't reveal more makeup smears or too much about what she and Trey had been doing alone. She touched her lips, felt the puffiness, and wondered if they were swollen. If so, maybe nobody would notice. When she heard Trey's soft chuckle, she knew he knew what was on her mind.

"Trey is one of our volunteer firefighters," Ruby explained. "They also assist our community as paramedics."

"We noticed your fire station." J.P. popped the top of a beer as he gave Ruby a sidelong glance. "Place looks new."

"It is," Ruby agreed with enthusiasm. "The Wildcat Bluff County Volunteer Fire-Rescue Station is our pride and joy. Everybody pitched in, and we held benefits to raise funds for the new building. We're all working hard to be able to afford to update and upgrade our old station, as well as get training for our volunteers."

"Our town and county need the services, so we make the extra effort," Trey said. "The big cities have the money to pay full-time employees, but we're all-volunteer. Folks from every walk of life in our county help when there's trouble. There's a lot of hometown spirit here. Our young men and women volunteer right out of high school and keep right on helping others all through their lives."

"That's impressive," Charlene said with a smile.

"When a local home or business or ranch catches fire, we take it personally because it's one of our neighbors," Ruby explained. "And make no mistake, our fire station and apparatus would be nothing without the folks who serve faithfully whenever called to duty. They're our greatest asset."

"We all just do what needs to be done," Trey said as he glanced around the table.

"Hogwash!" Ruby pointed at him. "Without you, Kent, Slade, Sydney, and all the other volunteers, we'd be up a creek without a paddle."

"You're fairly near bigger towns like Sherman with far greater resources, so why don't you rely on them?" Charlene asked.

"Sherman and Denison are good for hospitals or other services, but they're too far away for emergencies," Trey explained. "Our folks live here in the Bluff or out on farms and ranches. If there's a fire or medical emergency, they need help right away. In town, we try to arrive in less than three minutes. Farther out in the county, we get there as fast as we can make it."

Charlene nodded. "Do you get many fires?"

"Lately, we've been getting more than our share," Ruby said.

"Guess that's on account of the heat and drought." J.P. took a swig of beer.

"It's on account of something." Trey finished his beer and set it down with a sharp snap.

"Misty helped him put out a grass fire on her way to the Bluff," Ruby added with warmth in her voice.

"Without her, we wouldn't be sitting here tonight." Trey gave Misty a warm look. "She's our Christmas angel."

"Is that so?" J.P said. "Guess we all owe her something for her involvement."

Misty caught a look that passed between J.P. and Charlene. They must think she expected something. "Oh no, I'm not owed anything. I was happy to help out."

"Do you often help strangers?" Charlene clicked her nails against the top of the table.

"I was just in the right place at the right time." Misty avoided answering Charlene's odd question, not wanting to make any reference to her business.

"I'm thinking you might want to be more cautious in the future." Charlene cocked her head to one side. "This appears to be a safe community, but life can be dangerous."

"Now, Charlene, don't be putting your own worries on to somebody else." J.P. spread his arms wide to include those at the table. "My dearest tends to be a little worrywart."

"She's right to be cautious," Trey said. "But in this case, Misty saved the day."

"She certainly did," Ruby agreed.

Charlene turned to Trey with a big smile. "Now that you've impressed us with talk of your big new fire station, I hope I'll get a tour."

"That'd be a real pleasure to see," J.P. agreed.

"Do you have time while you're looking for collectibles?" Ruby asked.

"For something this interesting, we'll make time." Charlene glanced at J.P. "Won't we, dear?"

"Anything you want, my little buttercup."

Misty blinked at the endearments. They seemed out of place. But perhaps not. If Trey kissed her again, maybe she'd be calling him "buttercup," too. Somehow she didn't think so. Cindi Lou had warned her not to trust locals in conducting an investigation, and that advice had served her well in other cases. Now she was adding out-of-towners to that list of those not to trust, even if they did appear perfectly innocent.

She glanced at Trey. He raised an eyebrow. So he

didn't get the "buttercup" endearment either. He also hadn't invited the Gladstones for a tour of the station. She shrugged in response. Shockingly, she realized they were communicating without words. That couldn't possibly be a good sign for noninvolvement, but it did sort of tickle her fancy.

"Trey, thanks again for bringing barbeque tonight," Ruby said.

"You're welcome."

"Yes, we do thank you," Charlene added. "When we head home, I'm going to stop by the Chuckwagon Café and get barbeque to go."

"I enjoyed it, too. Thanks." Misty smiled at Trey, remembering the spicy taste when she'd licked the barbeque sauce from his lips. From his pleased expression, he remembered, too.

As Ruby started to pick up their trash and leftovers, a white streak of a cat leaped up on the table, grabbed a rib, and disappeared into the darkness.

"Temple!" Ruby scolded.

Trey laughed. "You know the best food is stolen food."

Ruby joined his laughter. "You're right. And don't try to tell a cat any different."

"If he gets sauce on his fur, he'll be a red and white cat tomorrow." Misty chuckled at the thought of that sight.

"Oh no, you'd never see a messy Temple," Ruby said, "He wouldn't allow his dignity to take such a blow in public."

"Smart guy," Trey said.

As everybody laughed, Misty looked out into the night for bright white fur, but she saw only darkness.

She liked the idea of Temple enjoying his stolen treat. She glanced at Trey. Was he a stolen treat, one she couldn't resist snatching for her own? She shook her head, knowing she had to get control of her thoughts and actions. She was here to do a job—an important job that paid her well and came first—that might mean putting off certain temptations, at least till the job was complete.

Ruby piled the remains of the barbeque dinners on the tray and added the empty beer cans. "Folks, I've got big doings tomorrow, so I'm headed to bed. Don't let me spoil your fun if you want to stay out here."

Trey stood and picked up the lanterns. "I need to go, too. Early morning. I've still got fence to fix."

"I'm done, too." Misty checked to make sure nothing had fallen under the table, picked up her wet towels, and then got to her feet.

"We're ready to pack it in as well," J.P. said. "We're shopping tomorrow to see if we can find a cache of vintage owls."

"They're popular again, so collectors are asking for them," Charlene explained.

"What type?" Misty asked.

"Anything. Everything. Ceramic. Plastic. Macramé."

"Macramé?" Misty wondered out loud, finding it hard to imagine.

"Don't ask." Charlene shivered. "It was a seventies phenomenon. Back to the Earth type of thing. Everybody must have been making it. Necklaces. Bracelets. Wall hangings."

"Beautiful work, for the most part," J.P. said.

"If you like that kind of thing," Charlene added.

"We found a windup owl about six inches tall yesterday. Late sixties. Its eyes go round and round in a psychedelic pattern." J.P. laughed. "You've got to say 'groovy' when you look at it."

Misty laughed as she accepted the wet towel Trey handed her. She was in a mellow mood as she walked with everyone back to the house. Out of the darkness, Temple leaped onto the walkway and led them with his tail held high.

When they entered the garden room, she started to follow the others and Temple inside the house. She felt a hand on her arm holding her back. Trey gestured with his head toward the front sliding doors.

"Good night," he called.

Ruby picked up Temple and glanced back, smiling. "Now be good and don't keep my guest up late. And Misty, just put those wet towels down on the tile. I'll get them later."

"Thanks," she said as she set down the towels. "I'll be right up."

"See you tomorrow." Charlene fluttered a hand at Misty. "Don't do anything I wouldn't do."

J.P. laughed as he put an arm around his wife's waist. "Come on, honey, time's a-wastin'."

Misty waited till the others were inside and the door shut behind them before she turned to Trey with a shiver that had less to do with her damp clothes and more to do with the cowboy. "Don't you have to be up early milking cows or something?"

He chuckled. "Feeding and watering steers. Mucking out horse stalls. Want to help?"

"Sounds like loads of fun, but I believe I'll pass."

"Over here." He pointed at the wooden swing that hung on metal chains from the ceiling across from a softly glowing floor lamp between two plush chairs.

She sat down on a soft white cushion and looked up at him in inquiry. He eased down beside her, so close their thighs brushed together. They were both still damp. She felt the coolness of her capris contrast with the heat of his thigh against hers. He smelled like barbeque and the great outdoors, fresh, clean, and woodsy. The fabric of his jeans stretched taut across the muscles of his legs. She could see the veins on the backs of his hands and his thick, muscular wrists from handling animals. She swallowed hard. Every single thing about him put her nerve endings on alert.

He set the swing to moving back and forth. "I've always liked to swing. My grandparents had one on their front porch. For spooning, my grandpa used to say."

"I like to swing, too." And her wayward thoughts led her down the path to a naked Trey pleasuring her as the swing swayed and squeaked to his lusty thrusts. *Oh my*. If he knew her thoughts, he'd definitely think his Christmas angel was naughty, not nice.

He picked up her hand and cradled it in his bigger, stronger one. He stroked back and forth across her palm with his rough thumb. "I want to make sure you're okay before I leave."

"I'm fine." She shivered at his touch, despite the way he made her temperature rise.

"For now. But when I'm gone?"

"I'll still be fine."

"Maybe I won't."

"I don't know what you mean."

He raised her hand to his lips. He pressed a soft kiss to her palm before he traced a pattern across her soft flesh with his tongue.

She caught her breath at the tingling burn his touch created in her. How could one man make her feel so intensely needy with so little effort? Her clothes were cool and damp, but heat blossomed and blazed in the deepest, most sensitive part of her.

"I want you to think about me tonight when you're in bed."

"No. I'll be asleep."

He pressed a kiss to each of her fingertips. "Even if you know I'll be thinking of you?"

"No. You'll be asleep, too, after a day like today, putting out fires, doing ranch chores."

He kissed the pulse point of her wrist. "Are you calling me a fibber or should I question your truth?"

She knew her fast heart rate was giving her away. She snatched back her hand and leaped to her feet.

He lazily stood up. "Seriously, I'm concerned about you. You might wake up with something worrying at you, something you need, another panic attack."

"I told you I won't."

"I'm going out to my truck to get my phone. When I get back, let's program your number into my cell." He grinned at her before he walked to the sliding doors.

She didn't know how he'd done it, but he'd made getting her phone number sound like a sensual act. Maybe he had phone sex on his mind. Maybe he thought they could share selfies. She abruptly stopped those thoughts before she went farther down that dangerous path.

He slid open the door, then stepped back. "Wait right here. I'll be back in a jiffy."

"And if I refuse?" She decided to put up some resistance to his dominant stance for her own moral rectitude, if nothing else. "I hardly know you."

"I aim to change that." He grinned again, revealing strong, white teeth. "After all, I'm your personal paramedic. Doctor's orders."

When he stepped outside and shut the doors behind him, she watched his long legs eat up the ground. His silhouette was familiar to her already and every bit of it was easy on the eyes. Did he really expect her to obey him? He acted like they were already a done deal. She felt a little frisson of excitement. Maybe it'd depend on the deal. Or was he just a flirt who felt some concern about her health? She was the one who'd let her thoughts stray, or stampede, down a forbidden path.

She wrenched her mind back to business. He was the insider here. She was the outsider. He was a firefighter, so he knew about fires in the area. She couldn't access those records or that knowledge without sending up red flags about her true intentions.

Bottom line, she needed his information. Worse, she wanted him. Even more dangerous, he appeared to know it and was more than ready to let on that he wanted her.

She flipped her hair back from her face in the universal action of a determined woman. She was a professional troubleshooter. She could certainly give her phone number to a cowboy firefighter and not lose any sleep over it.

And before she had a chance to ponder him any longer, he was back. He must have jogged to and from his truck because he was suddenly sliding the door open, striding to her side, and holding out his phone.

"I'd take it kindly if you'd program your number into my phone," he said in a low, melodic voice.

She didn't know quite how he did it, but just the sound of his voice put her in mind of big, soft beds and long, hot nights. She took his phone, quickly tapped in her number, and handed it back, being careful not to touch the heat of his hand.

"Thanks." He leaned down, pressed a quick kiss to her lips, then turned and strode to the open door. He glanced back. "See you tomorrow." And he was gone into the night.

She stood there a moment, feeling the heat of his kiss linger on her lips, and then shook her head. She was not going to moon over a man. She had a job to do.

She checked to make sure the door was locked before she went inside, up the stairs, and to her suite. She heard her cell chirping inside. She quickly unlocked the door and stepped inside.

She grabbed her phone. "Hello."

"Now you've got my number, too," Trey said. "Sweet dreams."

And then she was alone with her phone, his number, and the prospect of extremely sweet dreams.

Chapter 11

MISTY UNLOCKED HER SUV DOOR EARLY THE NEXT morning. The Gladstones' van was already gone. She guessed they were driving pretty far afield in search of vintage keepsakes. Interesting couple. Not quite her cup of tea, but she supposed others would be impressed with them, as well as their business.

She set her to-go cup of Ruby's delicious-smelling coffee in the cup holder and a blueberry muffin on the center console. She plopped her handbag down on the passenger seat and set her phone beside the muffin, almost expecting it to ring. But that was just her wanting to hear Trey's seductive voice again, and who knew when he might call, if ever. He certainly hadn't contacted her during the night or this morning.

Anyway, today he wasn't on her agenda. She wore comfortable jeans, a knit top, and running shoes since she had her sights set on reconnoitering the county and talking with folks in town. She particularly wanted to see what was left of the burned Texas Timber Christmas tree farm. Trey had been a big help as a tour guide when she'd driven him into town, and now she had better background knowledge from a local viewpoint.

She glanced around at the beautiful estate, morning sunlight bathing the pine trees and buildings in a golden glow. Still hot and dry with no letup in sight. If somebody had their sights set on causing trouble, between the weather and holiday distraction, there was no better time than the present. Texas Timber obviously understood that fact only too well.

As she ate her delicious muffin, she thought about her research. She'd been too tired the night before to follow up on her plan, so she'd looked into water issues this morning. She'd found several interesting articles online. Turned out North Texas cities, as well as Oklahoma City and Southwest Oklahoma, all wanted the Kiamichi River Basin water in Southeast Oklahoma. That happened to be the homeland of the Choctaw Nation and the Chickasaw Nation, so they were now involved in trying to preserve their water rights. Lawsuits had been filed. Studies were being done. But as far as Misty could tell, that situation didn't affect Wildcat Bluff County. What might affect the county was the feds blustering about taking more private ranchland along the Red River with access to that water. But for the moment, she didn't see how any of those issues could affect Texas Timber, although she'd keep them on a list as potential problems.

She took several sips of coffee and felt good to go. She backed up, drove out under the Twin Oaks sign, and made a right turn. She'd already programmed the GPS in her vehicle, so she simply punched the screen to call up the directions for her location. She pretty much had in mind where she was going, but she didn't want to take a chance on getting lost on backcountry lanes.

Soon she turned onto Wildcat Road and headed south back toward Dallas. She passed ranches and farms with cattle or horses grazing in pastures and big, round rolls of golden, baled hay baking in the sun. She could see where streams, maybe dried up now, meandered across the landscape by the trees that grew along their low banks. A pickup came hurtling toward her on the other side of the road and the driver raised the first finger of his right hand on the steering wheel in a neighborly greeting. She returned the favor, being reminded that good manners were vitally important in the countryside.

She turned onto a two-lane road that had well-maintained barbwire fence running along either side. She looked out over sun-bleached grasses and leafless trees. Everything looked as dry as a tinderbox just waiting to be set off by accident or intention. Small groups of red cattle congregated under big green live oaks, already getting under shade from the glaring sun overhead.

She came to a cross lane and turned left down the smaller but still good asphalt road. Up ahead she could see blackened land. She felt a tightening in her chest and her breath caught in her throat. Not now, surely not now. At least she had her inhaler with her. Why had she ever thought it'd be a good idea to investigate a fire? But she hadn't thought she'd be dealing with live fires, only the aftermath of a fire. And she hadn't had trouble with her phobia in years, so she couldn't have anticipated the extent of her reaction.

She turned up the AC and took a deep breath, feeling her anxiety slowly settle down. That's right. This fire was long over and had nothing to do with her. In her mind, she repeated her special words, "Be here now. Safe and sound. Be here now," and she felt better, reminding herself that she had fought a blazing fire yesterday and won. This was nothing compared to that.

She drove on down the road, pulled off the side into a ditch, and cut the engine. She got out and glanced around, smelling an acrid scent. On either side of the lane stretched blackened land with tall tree stumps rising up like ghostly sentinels. Complete devastation as far as the eye could see. Instead of fear, she felt a deep sense of loss. All those vibrant green cedars grown over countless years had been waiting to be harvested and sent out into the world to adorn living rooms and make people, particularly children, happy at Christmas.

It was simply a flat-out horrible shame. How many innocent birds and animals had died in the flames? What if the fire had swept over ranch houses and into town to kill people? Hot indignation welled up in her. Now she was particularly glad she'd taken the job. She couldn't right this terrible wrong, but she'd do her best to find the culprits and see they never did anything this devastating again.

She walked down the road, looking from left to right along the ground. She hoped to see something, anything that might be a clue. But of course, too much time had passed and not much could have been left in the wake of the fire. Still, she looked from ground to sky and back again. She'd read the fire investigation report. Arson by accelerant was suspected, but accidental conflagration by a tossed cigarette or campfire in the current intense heat and drought conditions could not be ruled out either.

It'd be easy for anyone to set a fire on the edge of the property or walk deep into the trees and start a blaze because there were no fences to keep people out. And there was no one around to see the culprits because no local folks were hired to work the Christmas tree farms. Crews were brought in from out of town to plant seedlings that were left to grow.

Crews returned to harvest and haul the trees to market at the right time of year when the cedars were the correct size. The business was lucrative, growing, and competitive. Texas Timber owned other tree farms in East Texas. None of those had burned, so this fire could have been an accident.

But Texas Timber executives didn't think so. And now that she was here, she didn't think so either. Maybe she was having a flight of fancy, but something about this fire felt sinister. She walked farther down the road, wishing something, anything would speak to her. A black crow cawed loudly and flew over her head toward Wildcat Bluff. Now she understood the bad feeling. All vibrant life was gone. She shivered at the thought.

She'd seen enough. She walked back to her SUV and sat down inside. She realized that she felt no anxiety and had no breathing issues. Instead, she felt deep determination to take on this problem and win.

She drove back out to Wildcat Road and headed toward another of Texas Timber's Christmas tree farms. She wished she'd learned more at the fire site, but at least she'd taken the first steps.

After a few miles, she turned down another good asphalt road. On the left she saw small green cedars growing in long rows into the distance. She felt a great sense of relief that these trees looked so alive and well. She glanced to the right. A barbwire fence enclosed ranchland with black cattle grazing on hay on the other side. Here peace and serenity and life reigned in contrast to the burned-out tree farm.

Once more, she'd seen enough. She swung her SUV around, turned left onto Wildcat Road, and headed north for Wildcat Bluff. She wanted to get a better sense of the town and its residents. Adelia's Delights would be a good place to start since she'd already met Hedy at the fire station. And Hedy'd probably know where to get a high-grade fire extinguisher.

When Misty drove into town, she found a parking place in front of the Lone Star Saloon. She sat there a moment as she looked around Old Town. Lots of folks walked up and down the boardwalk, carrying packages in their hands. They laughed and talked with each other as they went in and out of stores. She could hear Christmas music playing on the outdoor sound system. All in all, nothing looked amiss. In fact, everyone appeared extremely happy.

She drank more coffee as she checked her phone for messages. Cindi Lou had texted a smiley face, so she returned it since there was nothing noteworthy to report. No calls from Trey, so he was probably doing whatever kept ranchers busy with cattle. She might as well get on with her day.

She put her phone in her purse, slung it over her shoulder, and stepped outside. Hot already. She could smell the enticing scent of cinnamon, apples, and caramel. Somebody down the block was luring customers into their store with the irresistible aroma of holiday food. Instead of following her nose, she headed toward Adelia's Delights.

She entered the store to the sound of chimes, and then quickly closed the door behind her to keep out the heat. She smiled in delight, for she felt as if she'd been transported back in time, particularly after she read "Established 1883" on a sign on the wall. She admired the mellow oak floor to the high ceiling of pressed tin tile in an intricate design to the tall glass containers of old-fashioned hard candy on the checkout counter near the ancient black and gold cash register in back.

She could easily understand why Hedy loved this store. Knickknacks in all shapes, sizes, colors, and prices filled deep shelves and glass cabinets. One section contained country pickles, jams, and other edible items in canning jars. A prominent display of the Bluebird of Happiness, sky-blue glass birds in all sizes made in Arkansas, gleamed in the front window.

A tearoom area had small, round ice cream tables with matching chairs tucked into a quiet corner near a front window. A tall cedar tree decorated in red and green antique ornaments with a Christmas angel in a white satin gown on top graced that section of the store.

Misty quickly decided the tearoom was a likely spot for a quiet conversation with Hedy, who was bound to know everything going on around town, and particularly at the fire station. She just hoped Hedy was at work today. She headed for the back of the store.

"Misty, you're just in time!" Hedy zoomed around the checkout desk in her wheelchair.

"For what?"

"Watch the place for me, will you?"

"Sell merchandise?" She blinked in surprise.

"Station's gone quiet. Sure to be the new computer system acting up again. We'll get the glitch solved, but so far I'm the only one who can fix it." She glanced out at the street, then back.

"Do you want me to drive you? You could close the store."

"Right before Christmas? Not on your life."

"But how will you—"

"I've got a wheelchair van and I drive with hand controls. I get around fine and dandy."

"I'll be happy to help, but I don't know how to deal with sales."

"No need. Morning Glory'll be over to do that."

"Morning Glory?"

Hedy chuckled. "She's got the store next door. Didn't you notice it? *Morning's Glory*. Too clever by half, I say."

"What does she sell?"

"My point exactly." Hedy rolled her eyes. "Far as I'm concerned, she's still stuck in the sixties. And proud of it. She's a flower child, if you know what I mean."

"Not exactly."

"You'll see." Hedy pointed to one side. "Our stores are connected by that open archway. If folks want to buy something, call her."

"Okay. I'll do my best. How long will you be gone?"

"Not long. And thanks." Hedy waved a hand as she headed toward the back of the store. "Morning Glory'll be over to introduce herself pretty quick."

Left alone, Misty stood in the middle of Adelia's Delights. She kept getting surprised in Wildcat Bluff, not only by the situations but by the people, too. Hedy obviously trusted her, a stranger, enough to leave her in charge of her store. That would never happen in Dallas.

"There you are!"

Misty glanced around. A tall, slim woman with a riot of long, curly ginger hair wore a lapis-blue shirt, long, swirling skirt in many colors, and burgundy cowboy boots. At least half a dozen necklaces hung down to her small waist.

"You must be Misty. I'm Morning Glory." She clasped Misty's hand in a strong shake.

"Pleased to meet you."

"Heard you have a good vibe."

"I just got to town yesterday."

"Good news travels fast." Morning Glory grinned and small lines radiated out from the corners of her eyes to give her a warm and friendly appearance.

Misty smiled, not knowing quite what to say.

"Anybody who'll take on a grass fire with nothing more than a towel is on the side of the angels." Morning Glory glanced up at the top of the Christmas tree. "Heard you're our Christmas angel."

"Trey again? I just helped out."

"Like today." Morning Glory tapped the toe of one boot. "It's quiet now. Later, you could get a stampede."

"Christmas shoppers?"

"You know it."

"What do you sell?"

"Oh, this and that." She clutched her necklaces. "Candles, oils, herbs, vitamins. That type of thing."

"I'll enjoy seeing your merchandise."

"Anytime." Morning Glory held up two fingers in the peace sign. "We'd better put on our business faces."

"I'll call if I need you."

Morning Glory fumbled with the jewelry around her neck, selected a necklace, pulled it over her head, and held it out to Misty. "This one's obviously for you."

"Thank you." Misty hesitantly took the necklace, not wanting to be rude. "Is this macramé?"

"Made it myself. Beautiful, isn't it? I'm thinking I ought to buy some supplies and teach a class before it's a lost art. What do you think?"

"Looks like a lot of work."

"Thing is, as I'm sure you know, when it's art, it's not work."

Misty simply nodded.

"Now there's an idea. Maybe I'll teach macramé during Wild West Days over Labor Day." Morning Glory looked Misty up and down. "Put on your necklace and let's groove on it."

Misty attempted to remember what Trey had said about the original Wildcat Bluff settlers. Independent cusses or something like that. Now she believed it. She slipped the smooth, knotted macramé over her head. She stroked the pendant that dangled from it.

"In case you don't know, that brass piece is horse harness hardware. The hardware works perfectly for pendants since it comes in all sorts of designs like swans, animals, and such. Back in the day, a shiny row of those sewed on leather looked pretty on horses pulling conveyances."

"I had no idea." She didn't say it, but she wasn't even surprised that folks in Wildcat Bluff would wear horse harness hardware around their necks. Somehow it suited the place. And oddly enough, she thought the necklace pretty.

"That's your guardian angel. Everybody needs one, particularly a Christmas angel. I knew there was a special reason I wore that necklace this morning."

Misty stroked the wide wings, long gown, and bare feet of her angel. More Christmas. As soon as she got to her room, she'd better stow the necklace with the harp-playing angel in her closet.

"Now, you'll do fine to teach macramé classes."

"Teach? I'm sure others around here are better suited to help you. Besides, I'll be back in Dallas."

"Never try to predict your own future."

Misty nodded again. Maybe she could make headway in her investigation. "Thank you. I just might need this guardian angel. I understand there've been a number of fires around here."

"Bad mojo."

"Have they all been grass and tree fires, like the one I helped with?"

"No. Buildings, too."

"Good thing you've got such good fire-rescue volunteers."

"That's the truth of it. Great bunch." Morning Glory whirled away. "I'm off to mix up a little of this and a little of that."

As Morning Glory sashayed away, Misty wondered if the pretty woman had ventured a little too far on the wild side in her early years or if she was simply a creative personality. Either way, Misty couldn't help but like her.

She glanced down at the necklace. She appreciated the thoughtfulness. The pendant didn't look too overbearingly like an angel. Artfully avant-garde. She'd wear it a little while so as not to offend Morning Glory, but she didn't need any extra reminders of Christmas.

Maybe she'd sit in the tearoom and wait for customers. Now that she thought about it, this situation could be a blessing in disguise. She'd have a great opportunity to start up conversations about local fires with shoppers as they looked around at merchandise.

She admired the bluebirds again, then sat down and looked out the front window at folks hurrying to and fro. Suddenly, a loud Klaxon sounded in the store and outside, above the boardwalk. She stood up in alarm.

"Misty, quick!" Morning Glory called from the back of the store. "Come on."

She glanced around. Morning Glory wore a fire-fighter jacket over her shirt and a helmet on her head. She held similar bright yellow items in her hands.

Shocked, Misty looked from Morning Glory toward all the noise outside. Folks were streaming out of the stores, pulling on firefighter gear as they ran toward their vehicles. Hedy must have gotten the system back online and was testing to make sure it worked correctly.

"You can wear Hedy's gear." Morning Glory ran to the front door and quickly locked it.

"This is a fire drill, right?"

"No! We've got ourselves a real fire. A big one based on the number of blasts. And everybody helps out on a big fire. My pickup's out back. We'll take it."

"Another fire?" Misty hated the thought. She pushed back the threatening edge of darkness as she clutched her new guardian angel. She'd fought a fire once for this town. Surely with all these people and something more than three towels, she could do it again.

"Quick. I've got a bad vibe about this fire." Morning

Glory tossed the extra firefighter helmet and jacket toward Misty.

She caught the gear and took deep breaths as she followed in Morning Glory's wake.

Chapter 12

TREY POUNDED A U-NAIL INTO THE WOODEN FENCE post and eyed his handiwork. He liked this section of old fence line. No telling how far back in time it went, since the posts were made of bois d'arc. That was the French name, but the trees were also known as iron wood or Osage orange because Osage hunters, like Comanche hunters, often made their bows out the extremely hard wood. He figured the fence would probably outlast him. Up through the Midwest, the trees were called hedge apple. Farmers had planted hedgerows of bois d'arc back during the bad old Dust Bowl days as barriers to stop the vicious winds from lifting the topsoil and carrying it to the Gulf of Mexico. They'd also put the green hedge apples that grew on the trees in cabinets to keep out bugs.

He eased his hammer into his back pocket. Not much breeze today, so not much to keep him from baking in the sun. But it felt good, cleansing even, after the AC in the house. He took off his hat, pulled a blue bandanna out of his pocket, and wiped the sweat out of his eyes. He took a deep breath of the warm, dusty air that smelled like dry grass as he glanced around the pasture. Samson stomped a hoof under the shade of a live oak tree, patiently waiting to get back to the barn. Trey had already set out hay and made sure the stock tanks were full of water for the cattle. Ranch hands were taking care of work in other pastures.

All was as it should be. He could see it plain as day. But he still felt like a horse with a burr under his saddle. Fire, heat, and drought could be the irritating culprits, but most likely his feelings were due to his Christmas angel. He'd tossed and turned all night. One kiss. A few smiles. A bit of banter. And he was getting in deep. With a city gal, no less.

A little hard, sweaty work fixing fence was just what the doctor ordered to get his mind off Misty. He'd ridden Samson out at dawn with supplies and water. He could've taken one of the ATVs, but he'd wanted the ride to get the kinks out of his body. Besides, Samson was an old friend, and he needed that kind of easy company right now.

But nothing put his mind to rest. Samson would turn thirty pretty soon. And so would Trey. Made a guy think about his life and where he was going with it. Samson wouldn't always be around. That was the way of life. Trey was still living in his folks' guesthouse. He liked the simple and easy comfort. He also liked being near his parents, but they were slowly getting up there, even if he didn't want to think about that fact, and change was in the wind.

He stuck his hat back on his head, tied his bandanna around his neck, and eyeballed the post. Not strong enough. He plopped another u-nail into position over a strand of barbwire, held it with forefinger and thumb, and struck down hard with his hammer to pound the nail into place. At least barbwire and u-nails didn't change.

Truth be told, he wanted more in life. After Cuz Sydney had brought Storm into the world on a wild and stormy night, he'd enjoyed the hell out of the sassy little girl. Made him want one of his own to teach how to ride a horse, rope a steer, barrel race, give big hugs, and take to rodeos. But he couldn't do it on his own. He needed a gal to help, but not just anyone would do. He wanted the kind of long-term love his parents had managed to hang on to through thick and thin.

So far he hadn't met the special woman who'd turn his life upside down in the best way possible. Well, he hadn't until—Katie, bar the door—yesterday. An image of blond hair, green eyes, and a knockout body came to mind. Smart as a trick pony, too. But that fine gal was on one side of the fence and he was on the other. Not what you'd call an ideal situation, but he'd yet to quit a rodeo before he was out of the chute.

He looked down the line of fence and was satisfied with what he'd done. He'd already fixed the fence on Wildcat Road. Lucky break for them all, Misty coming along at just the right time the day before. Then again, it was about time the county got a break. And a Christmas angel to put it into play.

He'd done enough work out here for the day. He'd take Samson back to the barn and see what needed to be done there. He walked over to the shade of the live oak, rubbed Samson down his long nose, and put his hammer and u-nails in the saddlebag. He pulled out his cell. Sometimes he could get coverage out here. No new messages. He'd check again at the barn.

He put his left foot in the stirrup and swung his right leg up and over the saddle. He heard leather creak as he settled comfortably into the saddle. He picked up the reins, clicked to Samson, and headed for the barn at a leisurely pace. As he rode, he looked around to make sure all was in order. Place was a tinderbox. What he wouldn't give for snow, so it'd slowly seep into the ground, but he'd take a rainstorm even if the water mostly ran down into the streams.

By the time he reached the barn, he was feeling relaxed about life. He'd see Misty later. Any time spent with her couldn't be anything but good. He dismounted and led Samson into the cool shade of the barn. Other horses nickered to him from their stalls. He checked on them. A ranch hand had already mucked stalls and filled water tubs.

He removed Samson's saddle, blanket, bridle, and saddlebags, then set them to dry in the tack room. He curried Samson's russet coat to get rid of the sweat and dirt before giving the horse a big hug and fresh oats in his stall. All done, Trey pulled his bottle of water out of his saddlebag, took a long drink, then got out his phone.

He saw he'd missed a text and a message. He checked the text and got a jolt. Fire alert! He felt his heart rate speed up. If he hadn't meandered across the pasture, he'd have been here to get the alarm first thing. As it stood now, he'd be late, but he knew other volunteers would already be in place and putting out the fire. He'd get there as fast as possible and help any way he could once he saw the situation. On his way out of the barn, he grabbed a couple of stained but clean towels just in case he needed them.

As he jogged to his truck, he listened to a message from Hedy. There'd been a computer glitch, so the fire alarm was late going out. Slim Norton lived on the farm adjoining the fire. He'd noticed the smoke first, but when he'd called 9-1-1 he'd gotten no answer. He'd driven to the fire station and arrived about the same time as Hedy, who'd fixed the problem and notified volunteers. As luck would have it, Kent and Sydney had been in town, so they'd piled into two rigs and headed for the blaze.

Trey was relieved to hear his cousins were on the job. He jerked open the door of his pickup, tossed the towels on the shotgun seat, and grabbed the keys from the floorboard. He set his phone on the center console, inserted the key in the ignition, backed out, and made for Wildcat Road.

Soon he joined a line of trucks heading hell-bent for leather to the fire. He wasn't the only one in the county who'd just gotten the alert. He watched a plume of white smoke rise into the western sky. From its location, the conflagration looked to be at the Winston farmhouse or nearby pasture. If the blaze got loose and turned into a widespread brush fire, they'd have a major disaster on their hands.

When Ole Man Winston had died a few years back, his Dallas family had stripped the house's furnishings and sold the acreage to a local businessman. Bertram Holloway had let the house turn into a dried-out husk, more firetrap than anything. Good thing the place was uninhabited, so there was no chance for loss of life—as far as he knew. Trey's greatest concern was fire containment.

He turned onto a gravel road and bumped along behind the other pickups. They sent up a line of dust in their wake. He strained to see ahead so he'd know what they were up against, but the fire area was on a rise and he was down below it. Still, he could already smell smoke.

When he reached the top of the rise, he saw the fire and felt his belly unclench. House, not pasture. The blaze would be more containable. Better yet, Sydney and Kent were on the scene in full gear and had help from four other firefighters. They were dousing the house with water from the engine and the booster.

Volunteers ahead of Trey parked their vehicles and raced toward the fire. They carried fire extinguishers, axes, and shovels. Some had thrown on protective firefighter helmets and jackets. Others wore cowboy hats and jean jackets. They wouldn't enter the house, so they didn't need full turnout gear.

He stopped his truck behind the other pickups and jumped out. Smoke and heat lashed his face. And damn it all, he could smell accelerant. Somebody had set this fire with gasoline. He jerked open his back door, reached inside, and pulled out a high-visibility orange and yellow firefighter parka. He shucked on the jacket and tucked leather gloves into his pocket.

He jogged toward the fire, knowing all the bake sales and benefits had been worth it. Their new red engine had a two-thousand-GPM pump capacity and one thousand gallons of water with thirty gallons of Class A Foam. Their smaller red booster truck had a three-hundred-GPM pump capacity and a two-hundred-gallon water tank. He figured they had enough water so they wouldn't need to pump from a pond or stock tank because there were no fire hydrants in the country.

He watched Sydney expertly wave the nozzle of the engine's large-diameter hose and expel high-velocity water on the house. Two firefighters wrestled with the hose to keep it stable, so it didn't twist, turn, and buck like a wild rodeo bull. Kent kept up a steady flow with the line from the booster's water tank. Smoke and steam rose upward from the house as the streams of water fought to bring the fire under control.

Suddenly the windows exploded outward in self-ventilation, sending out shards of glass and other debris. Kent and Sydney staggered backward and went to their knees. Trey sped up to go to their rescue, thinking of little Storm's pain if her mother was hurt. But Kent and Sydney got back on their feet and kept the water barrage going on the house.

With the glass in the windows gone, the fire quickly expanded in size as it ate up the extra oxygen. Soon the wooden structure was fully engaged and pumping smoke from every crevice and open window. Flames and smoke surged high into the blue sky. There wouldn't be any saving the structure.

Trey caught up with the other volunteers as they spread out around the house to control stray sparks while Kent and Sydney kept up the water barrage. Firefighters were beating back the fire, despite the orange and yellow flames spitting and licking and clawing to take back what they gave up. Every fire had its own personality. This one reminded Trey of an angry cat.

At the moment, he wasn't essential to fighting the fire, so he took a bigger view. He checked the wind. They had a slight breeze from the south that was pushing flames northward. As bad luck would have it, Slim's farmhouse was to the north and on an elevation in the land. Fire rose because heat rose, so if the fire got loose, it'd make a beeline for Slim's home. Containment was vital.

Trey wondered if anybody had notified Bertram

Holloway. Not that it'd matter. Bert wouldn't be around. He never was when one of his decrepit, insured buildings went up in flames. They'd find him fishing or some such thing up in Southeast Oklahoma, innocent as the day is long but richer by the end of it. Bert insisted somebody had a vendetta against him. That was possible, since it was rumored he'd made enemies by the way he did business. Still, nobody'd been caught setting fires or leaving incriminating evidence, so there was no way to prove either theory.

Bert's building fires didn't explain the sudden rash of grass and tree fires. High temperatures and prolonged drought seemed the logical explanation, but that idea didn't sit well with Trey. Maybe it was too easy an answer or maybe he had a gut feeling there was something more sinister at work.

He glanced around to see where he'd be most useful. He caught his breath in surprise. Misty stood beside Morning Glory's pickup. She held a firefighter helmet and jacket limply in her hands, but she'd made no use of them. Instead, she watched the blazing house with horror etched on her face.

What was she doing here? If she had a panic attack, he'd get her out of here as fast as possible. At least his pickup was last in line so he could get out. He probably ought to take her away anyway. But why was she with Morning Glory? He'd thought she was safely tucked away at Twin Oaks and enjoying her vacation.

Misty suddenly threw down the firefighter gear and ran toward the fire. Shocked, he rushed after her, caught up with her, grabbed her around the waist, and pulled her tight against his chest.

"What in tarnation are you doing?" He fought to hold her against him. She suddenly had the strength of somebody three times her size.

"Look!" She pointed toward a clump of bushes set away from the house. "We've got to save those babies."

"What babies?"

And then he saw a mother cat with her teeth clamped in a kitten's fur on the back of the neck. She struggled to drag her baby to safety in the bushes, even though the fur on her back had been singed away.

"Let me go!" Misty kicked back at him, trying to get free.

"Not on your life. It's too dangerous." He tightened his grip around her as he glanced back at the house. Nobody else had noticed the cats because their attention was focused on the fire.

Mama Cat deposited her kitten in the bushes, and then she ran back to the burning house. She slipped into the open crawl space underneath the floorboards of the house and disappeared into the darkness.

"I'm going after her." Misty panted, gasping for breath, even as she struggled to get free.

"No!" Trey turned her around so he could look into her face. "Stay here. I'll do my best to get the cats."

"Please don't endanger yourself."

"I'm a first responder. That's what we do." He gave her a quick kiss on her soft lips, more comfort than anything.

As he ran to the house, he zipped up his firefighter parka, pulled up the hood to protect his head, and tugged on his gloves. He dropped to his stomach and looked under the house. He couldn't see anything in the dark, but he could feel the heat and steam, smell the acrid smoke. He had seconds to rescue the cats. If Mama Cat had her kittens near the entry, he could snatch them.

When he heard the sharp demand of Mama Cat's yowl and the plaintive mewling of kittens, he knew they were close. He dug his elbows into the mud and slithered into the crawl space underneath the burning house. He took short, shallow breaths to avoid the heat that could sear his lungs. He saw the gleam of cat eyes and counted three or four kittens nestled in an old towel. Mama Cat hissed at him. He tossed the towel over the kittens. He backed out, dragging the litter of babies with him while Mama Cat raced out ahead of him.

He took a deep breath of clean air as he got to his feet. He glanced down at the squirming bundle. And smiled. He'd saved lives. He couldn't ask for a better outcome.

"Are they okay?" Misty hurried over to him.

"Think so. Let's go have a look."

He walked away from the heat, steam, crackling fire, and firefighters hollering to each other as they brought the fire under control. He gently laid his bundle on the ground. He flung back the hood of his parka and noticed Mama Cat intently watching him. He pulled apart the raggedy, dirty towel to reveal the kittens. Three small, furry faces—bright eyes slit in the sunlight—turned up to him. They looked none the worse for wear. He felt a surge of happiness that they appeared okay.

Unfortunately, the fourth kitten, a black and white tuxedo, lay unmoving on his side. Trey's heart sank at the sight of the runt of the litter. The kitten was obviously in distress due to smoke inhalation, a situation that was regrettably much too common with birds, cats, dogs, and other animals in house fires.

Mama Cat butted Trey's leg with her head, then gently picked up a kitten by the back of the neck with her mouth and headed for her nest in the bushes.

"Should we let her take them?" Misty asked, looking back and forth between the kittens and Mama Cat.

"There'll be less stress on them if they're with their mother. And I'm thinking she's still nursing them." He nudged the runt with the tip of his finger and got no response. "This one needs our help now."

Misty carefully lifted the kitten and held him in the palm of one hand. "He's not breathing well."

Trey took off his bulky leather gloves and dropped them on the ground. He gently lifted the kitten from Misty's hand. He placed two fingers on the kitten's left side behind the front leg and shoulder. "He still has a heartbeat."

"That means a chance to live."

"I'll do what I can for the little one, but—"

"Let me help."

"Will you run to my pickup? There's an unopened bottle of water in the cup holder and clean towels on the front seat. We need the water and a towel." He gestured toward his bright red truck.

She took off toward his pickup.

Chapter 13

TREY GLANCED AROUND TO CHECK ON THE FIRE. Thankfully, they'd caught the blaze in time so it wouldn't spread. He wanted to cheer, but he didn't want to alarm the kitten he held or Mama Cat, who was moving the last of her healthy babies to shelter. He'd let Slim Norton know where his barn cats were and about the injured kitten. Who knew why the mother had decided to nest under the old house instead of in Slim's barn, but there was no arguing with a cat's logic. They did what they did for their own reasons. Even if Mama Cat moved her kittens again, she'd go to Slim for food and he could follow her to the kittens. All would be well there.

He nodded to several of his friends who'd backed away from the fire and were drinking from bottles as they watched the dwindling blaze. Water hissed as it hit the smoldering remains of what had once been a family's home. Pops and cracks and groans and crashes filled the area as the house slowly collapsed in a blackened heap of debris, leaving one corner starkly upright. All in all, as a firefighter would say, it was a good stop.

He caught Kent's curious look and held up the kitten. His cousin nodded in response. They all hated to lose vulnerable animals to fire, so folks would be glad Trey was doing his best to save the kitten while others kept the fire contained to the house.

He checked the little one's breathing by holding his finger in front of the tiny nostrils. Not much breath at all. But the heartbeat was still strong.

Misty ran up to him and held out a bottle of water and a towel. "I got it all! What now?"

"Thanks. Need you to wet the kitten."

"Just pour water over him? You're sure that won't hurt him?"

"Got to cool him down quick as we can. Then dry him."

She sprinkled water over the kitten's small body, and then gently blotted off the excess liquid.

"Thanks. I'm going to try AR. That's artificial respiration."

"You can do that with a cat?"

He nodded. "As soon as I get a good response, I want you to drive us to the vet's clinic."

"Me drive your big hulking truck?"

"Keys are in the ignition."

"Okay. You keep the kitty alive, I'll drive Godzilla."

Trey chuckled as he glanced up at her. He was glad to see she was handling the fire so well. Her breathing might be a little ragged, but that was her only physical issue as far as he could tell. She'd bucked up here just like she had at the grass fire. Strong gal with a big heart.

He set the tiny kitten in the center of his big firefighter glove. The sight reminded him of King Kong holding tiny Ann Darrow in the palm of his hand. Could Trey save this little one? He'd never performed AR on a cat before, but he had watched training videos and he had to try. He wiped the sweat from his brow with a corner of his towel, unzipped his jacket, and knelt down with his bright parka flaring out around him.

He positioned the kitten so he lay on his side with his four legs extended on top of the glove. First, he opened the kitten's mouth and tugged the tongue to the front of the mouth. Second, he gently closed and held the mouth shut. Third, he made sure the kitten's neck was straight so the airway was open. Fourth, he stood up, lifting the kitty on his glove. He bent forward and sent a soft puff of air into the kitten's nose, one breath every four to five seconds.

Now was the time for a Christmas miracle.

Morning Glory ran up to them, necklaces jingling around her neck. She leaned in close to the kitten. "Blessings on this sweet baby. Let the spiritual forces of this magical season of renewal and rebirth help this kitten find the strength to recover."

"Thank you," Misty said.

Morning Glory turned to Misty and gave her a quick hug.

Trey kept up the puffs of air, about the same strength as he would for a human baby, hoping against hope that it'd be enough. Soon he saw the kitten's chest rise with his breath, then relax after his breath.

He gave Misty and Morning Glory a big smile before he went back to giving air to the kitten. At the same time, he experienced everything around him with the keen clarity that came in a crisis or emergency. He glanced up. Now that the house fire was under control, the firefighters had turned their attention to the kitten. He knew they were rooting for him to keep the little one alive.

"Vet now?" Misty asked as she picked up Trey's extra glove.

"He's breathing, so let's go."

"Blessings." Morning Glory held up two fingers in the peace sign.

As Trey headed for his truck, holding the kitten in his glove, Misty raced ahead of him. He continued the AR as he followed her. She flung open the passenger door to his pickup and he eased onto the leather seat. She shut the door, and then ran around to the other side. She sat down inside, tossed his glove in the backseat, and started the engine.

"Where to?" she asked.

"Left on Wildcat Road."

She headed downhill, obviously driving quickly but cautiously so as not to jostle the kitten.

He held the little one steady and kept up the puffs of air, grateful and amazed the kitty kept responding to him. Maybe Wildcat Bluff would get a Christmas miracle as well as a Christmas angel. He glanced over at Misty. Maybe the two came together.

When Misty turned onto the main road, he pointed toward a one-story, white cinder-block building in the distance.

"That the vet?"

"Yes."

She gripped the steering wheel with both hands as she sped down the road well over the speed limit.

"How's our boy?"

"Hangin' in there."

Misty covered the last distance, wheeled into the empty parking lot, scattering gravel, and pulled up close to the front door. She leaped from the truck, ran around the front end, and jerked open Trey's door.

He dropped the glove so he could cradle the kitten in both hands. As he stepped down, he continued the AR. He quickly strode up to the building painted with bright murals of large and small animals—horses, cows, goats, dogs, cats, birds—in pinks, blues, yellows and other vibrant colors. A string of horse-shaped lights in green and red outlined the edge of the roof. A large silver-and-green wreath with a crimson cardinal in a shiny nest hung on the front door.

Misty opened the door for Trey, anticipating his every need, and he stepped inside. He heard her follow closely behind him.

"Trey, what've you got?" a tall woman with short steel-gray hair called from behind the counter as she jumped to her feet. She wore jeans and a T-shirt with a photo of a laughing horse, all big white teeth and flapping lips. "I heard about the fire."

"Male kitten. Smoke inhalation." He felt relief at the sight of Sue Ann Bridges, their large and small animal veterinarian. He'd feared she might be out on a call. Her assistants were well trained, but he wanted her for this kitten. Sue Ann was totally dependable and wonderful at saving animals.

"AR?"

"Yes."

"Good for you." Sue Ann quickly left the desk, disappeared from sight, and then opened the inner door. "I'll say it again. You need to get animal oxygen mask kits for all the volunteers."

"No money yet." He followed her down the wide hall with Misty right behind him.

"Put them on your fire-rescue Christmas list." Sue

Ann opened a door off the hall and gestured inside. "Quick. Get that baby in my consultation room."

Trey laid the kitten gently down on the examination table and stepped back. He bumped into Misty. He put an arm around her shoulders and tucked her against his side. She clutched his waist and squeezed in response. Felt right as rain.

Sue Ann expertly placed a small mask over the kitten's nose and mouth, stroking his soft fur in comfort. "These kits come with three mask sizes to fit dogs, cats, ferrets, rabbits, guinea pigs, birds, and whatever other critter you might run across. Raccoon. Possum. Skunk. Folks save the lives of wild ones all the time and keep them at home."

"Skunks?" Misty asked.

Sue Ann chuckled. "Good friends. Best if you take out their scent glands."

"I'd think so," Misty agreed. "They are pretty."

"Sure are," Sue Ann said. "But back to those animal oxygen mask kits."

"They're on our to-do list," Trey said.

"Not high enough on it. Oxygen masks save lives. Animals are part of our families and deserve the same type of help we give humans."

"I agree. But we're tapped out of funds after the new station, apparatus, and computer system."

"What about organizing a benefit for animal oxygen kits?" Misty asked. "I'd be happy to donate to the cause."

"Who's she?" Sue Ann glanced from the kitten to Misty and back again.

"Misty Reynolds," Trey said. "And this is Sue Ann Bridges."

Sue Ann looked up again. "You're our Christmas angel?"

"I'm just here on vacation."

"Good thing you showed up." Sue Ann lifted the mask from the kitten's face and set it aside. "You must've sprinkled angel dust over this baby, because he's breathing on his own now."

"Not me," Misty said. "Morning Glory blessed him. You and Trey saved his life."

"He's not out of the woods." Sue Ann cuddled the kitten in the crook of her arm and was rewarded with soft meows.

"What do you mean?" Misty asked.

"I can't tell yet about the extent of his injuries."

"But he's breathing and he's talking to you."

"I know," Sue Ann said in a soft, gentle tone as she stroked the kitten's small head. "But it's simply too soon to tell if he'll make it."

"You mean, don't get our hopes up?" Trey asked.

"He'll get the best of care. That's all I can promise."

"Thank you," Misty said. "I'll pay his expenses."

"No, you won't." Trey glanced down at her with what he hoped she recognized as his no-compromise stare.

"It's Christmas," Sue Ann interrupted them. "This kitten's health is on me."

"Thanks," Trey said. "I owe you one."

"Now, who's missing this baby?" Sue Ann asked.

"Slim Norton's barn cat had a litter and hid them under Ole Man Winston's house. That's the building that caught fire." Trey stroked a finger down the kitty's soft back. "I'll let Slim know one of his kittens is here."

"She's the mother who has fine polydactyl kittens,

isn't she?" Sue Ann checked the kitten's paws. "Look at this baby. He's got an extra dewclaw on every single paw. Special kitty."

Misty reached out and tentatively touched one of the kitten's oversized paws. "He's gorgeous."

Trey squeezed Misty's shoulder, liking her better all the time. He had a soft place in his heart for a woman who loved animals.

"So Bert had another property burn?" Sue Ann shook her head as she stroked the kitten.

"Yep. But we kept the fire from spreading to the pasture or up to Slim's house."

"Good job." Sue Ann turned to Misty. "You— Angel—see if you can finagle the powers that be to help us come up with those animal oxygen kits."

"Stop right there," Trey said. "Misty's here on vacation. She doesn't have time for that. I'll see what I can do about a benefit."

Sue Ann winked at Misty. "You gonna ride herd on him to get that benefit going?"

Misty chuckled. "Think it's possible?"

"Right woman with wings?" Sue Ann laughed. "Might be at that."

"Ladies, I'm still here, so don't go talking about me behind my back." Trey joined their laughter. "I said I'd see what I could do and I will."

"When can we see this kitten again?" Misty asked.

"You just leave him in my hands. He doesn't need to be stressed with folks looking at him and wanting to handle him."

"You'll let us know how he's doing, won't you?" Misty asked.

"Call the front desk or come by for an update."

"Thanks." Misty reached out and stroked the soft fur between the kitten's eyes. The kitty looked up and licked Misty's finger with his long pink tongue.

"Looks like you made a friend," Sue Ann said with warmth in her voice.

"He'll be fine." Misty glanced at Trey. "Don't you agree?"

"That kitten will do his best for you." Trey knew it'd hit her hard if the kitty didn't make it, but he had no power over life or death. He was just a cowboy firefighter who got lucky sometimes.

"And we'll do our best for him," Sue Ann said.

"Come on, let's allow the little tyke to get some rest." Trey steered Misty toward the door.

"We'll know more in twenty-four hours," Sue Ann called after them.

Trey glanced over his shoulder. "I've got you on speed dial."

"And he's got animal pet oxygen kits on his mind," Misty added.

Trey chuckled, squeezing Misty's shoulder. Christmas was shaping up to be quite the doozy. But if they could find a way to save kittens and other animals, nothing could be finer.

Chapter 14

MISTY STEPPED OUT OF THE CLINIC WITH TREY RIGHT behind her. She looked in the direction of the house fire, but no longer saw smoke spiraling into the sky. That'd been close. If not for the quick work of volunteer fire-fighters like Hedy, Morning Glory, and others, the blaze would have spread and left behind a swath of charred land like the Christmas tree farm. She shuddered. She never wanted to see that kind of devastation again.

Now she could only hope the kitten would heal and live a good, long life. She already felt a strong connection to the kitty, even if the little one belonged to somebody else. She glanced at Trey, who was dirty, sweaty, and smelling of smoke. He was her hero. He'd saved the kitten with his quick thinking and AR knowledge. He didn't avoid difficult situations. He charged right into the middle of them. And came out a winner.

In contrast, she'd been avoiding painful memories and situations for much of her life. She did fine in her professional life, but she hung back in her personal life. That'd all changed the moment she'd met Trey. Suddenly she was fighting fires, rescuing kittens, driving a pickup, and smooching with a cowboy. She didn't know if she was empowered, inspired, or simply exhilarated, but all of it brought a smile to her lips. She'd had no idea life could be so breathtakingly remarkable. She chuckled at the idea of bringing Cindi Lou up to speed.

She took a deep breath to check her lungs. She felt fine. Maybe she was okay because she was away from the fire, but she'd been fairly good there, too. She'd had a little trouble breathing, but not much. Could confronting her fears actually help overcome them? She didn't know, but she had a feeling she was going to find out in Wildcat Bluff.

Trey clasped her hand and threaded their fingers together as they walked to his truck. She felt the rightness of being with him as so natural that she found it hard to believe she'd known him such a short time. And yet, she also felt as if she'd known him forever.

Trey opened the door to his truck and looked down at her, concern in his hazel eyes. "Please don't get your hopes up."

"I know." She realized he didn't want her to be hurt. "But I won't get them down either."

"It's just that I've seen this kind of injury before, folks and animals. Smoke inhalation is dangerous."

"If right's right, that kitten will live." She rubbed a smudge of soot off Trey's lean cheek, feeling as if it were the most natural thing in the world to touch him, but quickly stayed her hand. What was she thinking? She hardly knew him. She stepped up on the running board, picked up the towel lying there, and sat down in the passenger seat.

He put a hand on the door frame and leaned down toward her. "I wish right was always right, but you never know for sure."

"Please, let's just hope for the best." She felt tears sting her eyes, realizing the kitten's plight was causing too many old feelings to resurface.

He put a finger under her chin and lifted her face toward him. "Sorry. I just don't want you to be disappointed."

"Thanks." She blinked back tears. She didn't want him to see her weak again, not when he was so strong. And normally, she was strong, too. But here—in this time and place—she felt as if she were coming undone, and the situation simply wasn't acceptable. She had a job to do, one that was vitally important to the welfare of others. She took a deep breath and shoved down her thoughts and emotions.

He closed the door, walked around the front of the truck, opened the back door, and tossed his parka on the floorboard. He sat down beside her and grabbed the towel from her hands. "Sorry I'm so dirty. I was mending fence and came straight to the fire." He hurriedly used the towel to wipe over his face and hair, then down his neck and arms. He grinned as he glanced at her. "Best I can do till I get a shower."

"Nobody's going to hold it against you if you get dirty working and saving kittens."

"Good to hear."

"One thing is for sure. Towels come in handy around Wildcat Bluff."

He threw back his head and laughed a belly-deep chortle. "I guess that's an understatement, isn't it?"

"You might say that."

He laughed harder, then stopped and looked at her. "I needed a laugh, but I guess you knew. Pretty rough, wasn't it?"

"You saved the kitten. That's all that matters."

He nodded, just sitting there looking at her as if he

could drink her down like the finest wine, or beer, all day long every single day of the year.

Heady stuff. If she started down that path with him, she didn't know if she could ever return. "Guess you need to get back to the fire. I could use a lift to Old Town so I can get my SUV."

"Going back to Twin Oaks?"

"Not sure. Maybe I need to unwind first." She couldn't tell him, but she needed to get back on the job and finish what she'd started that morning. Still, Trey was a good source of information, as well as every other amazing thing.

He pulled his cell from his back pocket, checked it, and then set it on the center console. "Fire's winding down. They'll let me know if they need me."

"I'm sure you've got cattle to wash or something."

"Wash?" He laughed hard again.

"Something cowboyish." She loved to hear him laugh in his deep, melodic voice. If he got any hotter, she ought to hang up her spurs—if she'd had any—and go home where she was safe. Everything about him was so sensual that he bypassed her brain and went straight to her damp, hot core. And when he touched her, she was absolutely lost to her cowboy firefighter.

"How about I do something cowboyish like take you to lunch?"

As if to give her no chance to make an excuse not to accept his invitation, her stomach rumbled in loud need. She abruptly felt as if she hadn't eaten in a week.

"Guess that'd be a yes." He glanced at her and grinned, causing laugh lines to radiate from the corners of his eyes. "I'm so hungry I could eat a horse—"

"I thought we were done with that old joke," she teased.

"Never. It's a classic."

"True."

With his hand on the key to start the truck, he stopped and looked at her with a serious glint in his eyes. "You do real well in an emergency."

"If not for the aftermath, huh?"

"You're right there when it counts. You're the one who saw Mama Cat rescuing her kittens. I doubt if I'd have seen them. Like everybody else, I was focused on the fire."

"Thank you. Still, you're the one who crawled under the house and pulled the babies out. That was very brave."

"Thanks. Guess we make a good team."

She nodded, feeling warmth well up in her as she basked in his praise and appreciation. "But that doesn't mean I'm going to be roping cows with you."

"Never know." He grinned as he started his pickup, the big engine turning over with a loud growl. "Chuckwagon Café okay?"

"Perfect. I'd like to see the place where you got that great barbeque."

"And taste more of it?" He pulled out of the clinic parking lot and headed down Wildcat Road toward town.

"Or something just as good."

"No place better for pecan pie."

"Yum." She was being self-indulgent and knew it. Still, she deserved a little reward after such an arduous time in Wildcat Bluff. And—she had to admit—lunch would give her a perfect opportunity to extract more information from Trey. She simply had to keep her eye on the goal and not get distracted by extraneous male attributes. Well, maybe not extraneous, but definitely distracting.

In Old Town, Christmas lights twinkled in store windows, on street lamps, and amid green holly bushes with red berries in planters on the boardwalk. Waylon and Willie sang Christmas songs outdoors through a loud sound system. Cars filled most available parking spots and shoppers laughed as they hurried in and out of stores.

Misty could imagine Old Town looking much like a scene out of Charles Dickens's "A Christmas Carol" if there was a bit of snow. Even a drought and heat wave hadn't dispelled the allure of seasonal festivities. She couldn't explain it, but she felt more warmth for Christmas now than she had in a long time.

A spot opened up and Trey parked in front of Adelia's Delights. Misty noticed the "CLOSED" sign still hung on the door, as well as one on the door to Morning's Glory. She hoped they hadn't lost too much business because of the house fire.

Trey picked up his phone, got out, and started around the front of his truck, tucking his cell into his back pocket.

She realized he was going to open her door in his gentlemanly way again. She wasn't used to that type of behavior, but she was learning she wasn't used to the cowboy way. Still, she was much too accustomed to doing for herself to stop now. She opened her door as he drew near and stepped out. In her hurry, she forgot she was high off the ground and needed to use the running board. She touched nothing but empty air, lost her balance, and fell forward against his hard chest.

"Easy there." Trey wrapped his arms around her and let her slide down the long length of his body.

She couldn't have been more embarrassed about forgetting that extra step. She immediately tried to push back, but she ended up with her palms pressed against the hard muscles of his chest. He smelled of smoke, leather, and dry grass, almost as if he'd ridden straight out of an ancient Comanche camp.

"No need to rush." He stroked large hands up and down her back. "You okay?"

"I forgot the height." She felt superheated everywhere he touched her. To make matters worse, she had no desire to move. She wanted to stroke him just as he was stroking her. If this kept up, she'd need a fire extinguisher every time she was around him.

"Happens. You didn't twist an ankle, did you?"

"No. I'm fine." She pushed against his chest, but he didn't budge. She realized in surprise that she had no way to move him back if he didn't want to go. He was like a rock. "You can let me go now."

"You sure?"

"I'm hungry."

When he chuckled at her words, she felt the vibration up her hands, her arms, and into her own chest. Turned up the heat even more.

He leaned down so his lips were close to her ear. "Are you hungry for food or something else?"

"Food!"

He chuckled again, then let her go as he slowly stepped back. "You drive a hard bargain."

"You promised lunch."

"And I never break a promise." As if they were back in the 1880s, he held out his elbow for her to grasp.

She hesitated, but how could she resist the allure of the mischievous glint in his hazel eyes?

"When in Rome, or in this case, Wildcat Bluff—"

She tucked her fingers around his elbow. He drew her in so close that the curve of her breast pressed against him.

They walked down the boardwalk as if they were a lady and gentleman out for an afternoon promenade. She could easily imagine that horses and buggies filled the streets instead of noisy vehicles. Somehow the past seemed more peaceful, more manageable, more refined than the present. Then she remembered that they were in a town that had catered to the wildest of the wild. Shootouts, brawls, and Rebel yells had probably filled the air.

"Have you been in Morning's Glory?" Trey stopped in front of the store's colorfully decorated window.

"Not yet. I just met her earlier today."

"She's quite the character."

"In Wildcat Bluff, how can you tell?"

He laughed. "Guess you've got a point."

"Great people." She wiggled her fingers at the ginger cat that was taking a nap in the fake snow by the pointy-toed slippers of three elves dressed in red-and-green outfits with multiple strands of macramé necklaces around their necks. With their jaunty red hats with dangling white balls and overdone makeup with big red lips, the elves looked more naughty than nice as they waved at passersby with electronic arms tipped by white-gloved hands.

"Morning Glory does like to start a dialogue." Trey pointed at the display.

Misty smiled. "What do you suppose she'd like us to discuss?"

"Let's not even go there."

"Angels?" She chuckled as she touched the angel hanging from the macramé necklace around her own neck.

Trey cocked an eyebrow as he glanced down at her with darkened eyes. "Now I could talk about angels—all night long."

"Not me. I'd prefer to talk about—well, cowboys."

She didn't wait for his response or the gleam she knew she'd see in his eyes. Instead, she quickly turned and walked the few steps to the Chuckwagon Café. She focused on the carved wooden café sign painted in red and white that hung from hooks above the boardwalk. Red-and-white checked curtains filled the lower half of the windows. Someone had hand-painted colorful Christmas scenes on the upper half of the windows. Santa Claus and his gift-laden sleigh were pulled by brown-and-white painted ponies. Boisterous children wearing earmuffs and mittens tugged a green Christmas tree home from the forest.

"I wonder who painted these windows." Misty pointed at the artwork. "It's wonderful."

"Morning Glory'd be my guess. She's talented enough to do about anything creative."

"I like her." Misty fingered the harness hardware hanging around her neck. "Did you notice my necklace? She gave it to me."

He picked up the angel, rubbed a thumb over the face, and glanced up at Misty. "Suits you."

"You started this entire Christmas angel thing. I don't think I'll ever hear the last of it."

He smiled, eyes crinkling at the corners. "I didn't spread it far. Once something catches folks' fancy, it's hell and gone."

"I'm sort of embarrassed about it."

"Don't be. We needed something or someone to give us hope. You were at the right place at the right time."

"And you had the idea."

He let go of the angel, then brushed a strand of hair back from her face, lingering suggestively on the soft shell of her ear. "For sure, you're our Christmas angel."

Chapter 15

MISTY SIMPLY SMILED AT HIM, REALIZING THAT particular horse—or Christmas angel—had already left the barn and there was no bringing it back. She might as well make the best of the situation and use it to her advantage.

"You gotta admit it's got a certain charm." Trey tweaked her ear and grinned as he reached around her and pulled open the door to the Chuckwagon Café.

She stepped inside and heard sleigh bells jingle against the front door's glass window as the door closed behind them. A group of local folks seated at two tables glanced up, nodded in greeting, and went back to their meals.

"Hold your horses!" a man hollered in a deep, rough voice from the back of the café. "I'll be out in a minute."

Misty glanced around the long room, noting the high ceilings covered in pressed tin squares and the smooth oak floors like in Adelia's Delights. Wagon-wheel chandeliers—old lantern-type globes attached to the outer spokes of horizontally hanging wooden wheels—cast soft light over round tables covered in red-and-white checked tablecloths. A tiger oak bar with enough dings and scratches to look original stretched across the back of the room with battered oak bar stools in front and a cash register on one end. A window behind the bar revealed a kitchen updated with chrome appliances.

In one corner, a large cedar Christmas tree reached almost to the ceiling. Red-and-white candy canes, red-and-white plaid bows, and twinkling red-and-white lights decorated the deep green boughs. The scent of cedar battled with the tantalizing aroma of food for prominence.

"What a lovely place," Misty said. "I could almost believe we've stepped back over a hundred years in time."

"Bet the food's better now."

"No doubt."

"Let's sit at my favorite table." Trey indicated a table for two near a front window. He walked over and pulled out a spindle barrel-back captain's chair with a red-and-white checked seat cushion.

"Thanks," she said as he seated her at the table.

He sat down and eased the curtains apart. "Never know what you'll see on Main Street. That's why I like to sit here."

"Perfect view."

"Yeah," he quickly agreed as he turned his gaze from the street to her. "Couldn't be better."

She grabbed a two-sided, plastic-coated menu from between the salt and pepper shakers and big bottle of hot sauce, so she could look at anything but his teasing gaze. She'd never met a guy before who could so easily and comfortably and effectively flirt. He must have graduated top of his class. For that matter, his cousin Kent wasn't far behind in that graduate degree. No doubt Texans could be outrageous teases for the sheer fun of it, but Wildcat Bluff raised the art form to a new level.

She picked up the other menu and offered it to Trey, wanting him to look at something besides her. She might not have crawled under a burning house, but she wasn't as pristine as she'd started the day.

"No thanks. I don't need it."

"You know what you want to order?"

"I'm a creature of habit."

"Barbeque?"

He nodded, smiling with boyish charm. "Chopped beef sandwich. Curly fries. Coleslaw. Sweet tea."

"Sounds good. But I still want to check out my options."

"Be sure to find out the daily special before you make up your mind. That's always good, too."

Misty glanced down the list of down-home Texas favorites. "I bet their chicken-fried steak is delicious."

"And huge. Better save that order for a day after mending fence or busting a bronc."

"Then I'll be saving it forever."

Trey chuckled. "You never know."

She didn't say it, but she did know. Life for her didn't include falling off a huge animal like a horse or hitting her thumb with a hammer. At least it hadn't till she'd met Trey. Now she wasn't so sure. He might have her up on the back of a horse or hammering a fence before she quite realized what had happened to her. No two ways about it, Trey Duval was a dangerous man.

When she heard the uneven sound of boots thudding across the wooden floor in their direction, she glanced up. Now there was danger with a capital D. An enormous cowboy made his careful way toward them. He was six five easy, and solid muscle. A thick crop of ginger hair accented hazel eyes. A barbwire tattoo circled his right bicep—about as big around as her waist—while a lasso tattoo graced the other. Scuffed brown cowboy boots led to faded jeans with ripped-out knees that led to a tight white T-shirt. But the machismo stopped there. He'd tied a red-and-white checked and ruffled apron around his waist.

"Lula Mae," she read out loud from the pocket of his apron. "Pleased to meet you."

Trey snorted, but didn't say anything.

"Darlin', all the gals are pleased to meet me." The stranger stopped near the table, favoring his right leg.

Trey snorted louder.

"Just so you know, you can call me Lula, or you can call me Mae, or you can call me Lula Mae, just so long as you call me."

"And please call me Misty." She couldn't help but laugh at his ridiculous words.

"You think I jest?" He appeared wounded by her laughter.

"Slade Steele, you big goof," Trey said, sounding exasperated. "She's never calling you."

"I don't see a brand on her, but I'm not seeing nearly enough of this fine filly, am I?"

"You're seeing all you're ever gonna see of her." Trey drummed his fingertips on the tabletop.

"Will you two stop talking about me as if I'm not here?" Misty glanced from one to the other. "And for the record, I'm not a filly."

"I didn't say it." Trey crossed his heart with two fingers.

"Believe me, I spoke those words as the sincerest form of flattery," Slade said.

"I believe you." Trey smiled at Misty with a teasing

glint in his eyes. "My cousin knows how to appreciate fine horseflesh."

"Go ahead and keep this up," Misty said with mock annoyance. "I bet there are other places in town to eat."

Slade pasted a sincere look on his face. "I apologize if that's what you want. But please don't take your business elsewhere. Granny'll have me washing dishes for the rest of my life."

Misty laughed, shaking her head. She couldn't help but like the outrageous cowboy. Slade made three graduates of what she could only imagine was the Wildcat Bluff School of Flirts. If there were more, she didn't know how the cowgirls around here survived them. Unless, of course, the gals were just as ornery as the guys. Ruby might be a good example of that idea.

"Right now Granny's still at the fire so I'm safe." Slade drew his straight eyebrows together in a frown as he focused on Trey. "Granny and Mom keep treating me like a put-out-to-pasture gelding. I should've been fighting the fire instead of holding down the fort here."

"Doctor's orders. And you know it," Trey said without giving an inch.

Slade growled before he turned back to Misty. "Might as well get this show on the road." He changed to a sweet voice. "My name is Slade. I'll be your server today. What would you care to drink?"

"Sweet tea," Trey said, "for both of us."

"What do you recommend?" Misty couldn't resist needling Trey by playing up to the big guy.

Slade winked at her. "I've got a lot I could recommend, but maybe you'd better go with the tea."

"What's the special?" Trey interrupted the banter.

"Five-alarm chili. Made a batch myself this morning."

"Ouch. That'll take the lining off a gut."

"That's why I made the jalapeño cornbread. Cuts the fire."

"Nothing you make cuts the fire," Trey complained. "Don't have it in you. That's why you ride bulls."

"Dang it. Why'd you have to go and bring up rodeo? Are you orderin' a fist sandwich?"

"Sorry. Forgot." Trey managed to look contrite and unrepentant at the same time.

"I'll take the chili and cornbread." Misty hoped her choice would help ease the unhappy look on Slade's handsome face, but she also hoped supporting his cooking would ease him into opening up more about his life in Wildcat Bluff. If the cousins would sort of forget she was here, or accept that she was part of the group since she was with Trey, or continue showing off for her, she could learn a lot about folks in the town. She was in a perfect position to listen and learn.

"My usual," Trey said. "I saw Sydney at the fire."

"Bet she took that big whopping engine, hit the sirens and everything."

"You know it. Kent had to settle for the booster."

"Dang hothead." Slade rolled his eyes. "We should've gotten her in line when we were kids."

"Like we didn't try."

"What're you gonna do with a six-foot-tall strawberry-blond cowgirl with a mind like a steel trap?"

Misty couldn't help but chuckle at the image. She'd seen Sydney fighting the fire and the gal was impressive. She could tell how much the cousins loved Sydney by the way they talked about her. Misty hoped she'd get to meet the cowgirl soon.

"Or a six-foot-five cowboy?" Trey chuckled, gesturing toward Slade.

"Twins!" Slade complained. "You'd think I could've at least had a womb to myself. But no, I've had a banshee on my case my whole life."

"Valkyrie, not banshee," Trey corrected, "what with all that Viking blood."

"Sydney's slain enough hearts." Slade gave a big, heavy sigh. "But I doubt she's taken a single guy to Valhalla."

"I wouldn't bet on it." Trey laughed hard, giving Misty a glance to include her in the humor.

She chuckled, imagining all the tricks and pranks Sydney must have played on her cousins over the years.

"Stop it!" Slade held up a hand in protest. "Remember. No rodeo. No Sydney love life."

"My lips are sealed." Trey grinned before he turned serious. "Ole Man Winston's house bought it."

"Bert around?"

"Nope."

"Par for the course."

"Granny and Aunt Maybelline ought to be back from the fire soon. I bet they're making sure it doesn't reignite, or they could just be shooting the breeze," Trey said.

"All I can say is they better be back soon. I've got a hot date with a barrel racer."

"When don't you?"

Slade sighed, slumped, and rubbed his right hip.

"Sorry." Trey looked sincere. "Gals won't desert you."

"Yeah right."

"We saved a kitten." Misty decided to change the direction of the conversation that appeared headed downhill, even though she could've listened to their good-natured bickering all day. Trey had talked the same easy way with Kent. Even Ruby. What she wouldn't give to have that type of big, close-knit family and friends. An unshakable love had to be at the base of all their interactions. Of course, she had love and friendship, but not in so much abundance. She still missed Aunt Camilla every day, but now she enjoyed other friends and her BFF Cindi Lou, too.

"You saved a kitten?" Slade nodded at Misty before he gave Trey a questioning look.

"One of Slim's barn cat litters. We left the little tyke at the clinic."

Slade cocked his head at Misty. "Oh, now I get it. You're our Christmas angel."

"Trey's idea, not mine."

"In that case, bet the kitten makes it."

"I hope so."

"Now, darlin', if this cowboy gives you any trouble, feel free to call me. I may have a hitch in my get-a-long, but most bull riders do. We've never let it stop us—not for long anyway."

"There's always a first time." Trey gave Slade a warning stare.

"I'd better get you two some food before Trey gets the grouchies."

Misty watched as Slade limped away, feeling sympathy for the cowboy. "He's hurting, isn't he?"

"Took a big dive off a bad bull."

"And he cooks?"

"We all cook. We grew up helping out here." Trey chuckled. "Granny believes a man in the kitchen is worth two in the bedroom."

"And that means?"

"Guess they wanted us to have something to fall back on after rodeo and well—whatever." Trey cocked his head to one side, appearing thoughtful. "Nothing lasts forever."

She sighed, knowing too well what he meant. "But you've got a ranch, don't you?"

"Family ranch. And I rodeo."

"Bulls?"

"I'm not a glutton for that kind of punishment. I've been known to throw a leg over a horse or two. Rope steers, too." He slowly licked his lower lip as he looked at her. "I've got a special touch with leather lassos."

She caught her breath, unable to say a word. He looked very much as if he'd like to rope her, tie her up, and have his way with her. She felt liquid fire run through her body.

He cleared his throat. "Christmas in the Country is this Saturday. I wonder if—"

"Here you go." Slade plopped down two iced teas and silverware wrapped in napkins. "Food'll be right out."

"Thanks," Misty said, picking up her cold glass of tea.

"Trey, you hear any more from Texas Timber?" Slade took a wide-legged, defensive stance, and put his hands on his hips.

Misty almost dropped her glass. She turned a sharp look on Trey, hoping against hope he didn't turn out to be on the wrong end of her investigation.

Chapter 16

"TEXAS TIMBER." TREY GROANED AS HE CLENCHED HIS jaws so as not to say something he'd regret later, but just hearing the name made his gut burn with frustration and irritation.

"I just wondered if they were still pestering you," Slade said.

"When *don't* I hear from that company?"

"Aren't they the Christmas tree folks?" Misty leaned forward with an interested look on her face.

Trey stopped his thoughts and gazed at her. He'd fast come to expect to see her blond hair, green eyes, and pink lips. Felt right, too. When push came to shove, she wasn't part of the community, much less his own family. Not to mention, there was still the matter of what she was holding back. He hadn't forgotten it, even if he'd been trying hard at every turn to reason it away. Not that his body gave a hoot about anything except getting close to her.

"Yes, they are." Slade nodded at Misty in agreement. "Texas Timber wants to buy Wildcat Ranch's old-growth section of the Cross Timbers. But Trey and his folks put paid to that idea."

"We're trying to," Trey added. "Just wish we could get them to listen to reason."

"I can't imagine that tangled mess would make good Christmas trees." Misty quirked her eyebrows in confusion.

"Native exotic wood." Trey didn't want to get into it, but there was no stopping Slade once he'd set off down a trail like a bloodhound.

"Worth its weight in gold, I guess," Slade said. "It's supposed to be used for all sorts of inlay on furniture and the like."

"Trey, you don't want to sell?" Misty asked. "Couldn't you use the extra funds to enlarge cattle or buffalo herds? That type of thing."

"Not only no, but hell no." Trey paused, considering the bigger ramifications of the ongoing issue. "It's like the Red River's water we talked about. We're up against a tide that's set on obliterating our Texas heritage."

"Sometimes feels like we've got a choice of becoming Disneyland or Neutral-land. Don't much care for those options," Slade said. "'Course, I'm not a big fan of the state's idea of Six Flags Over Texas. At least the Comanche Nation and the Caddo Confederacy flags oughta be waving over Texas, too. This is our homeland. You'd think we could get as much respect as those who weren't even from here."

"Don't get him started on the flags." Trey shook his head, knowing his cousin was right but not wanting to get sidetracked down that impossible lane.

"Every time I go from Texas to Oklahoma and back again, I see those six flags waving pretty as you please high above the Texas Visitors Center." Slade stomped his boot in disgust. "I'd write a letter in protest if I thought it'd do any good."

"The State of Texas should consult historians and get their facts and flags straight," Misty said with sympathy.

"Thanks." Slade gave her a warm smile.

"I do know Dallas is fast losing its heritage," Misty added. "They're tearing down and rebuilding all the time."

"Guess they call it progress," Trey said thoughtfully, "or a moneymaker."

Misty nodded in agreement. "At least San Antonio retains its heritage. And Fort Worth, too."

"Tourists pay their bills." Trey picked up his tea and took a drink. "And it's a good thing folks are still interested in seeing the Old West. Helps pay our bills here, too."

"Isn't there other land or trees that'd be just as good for Texas Timber?" Misty asked.

"They'd buy out Wildcat Ranch—the whole kit and caboodle—if we'd sell." Trey set down his tea. "But this is family land. There's no price big enough to buy our heritage."

"Texas Timber got a toehold in Wildcat Bluff County when Bert sold acreage to them," Slade explained.

"At least Texas Timber didn't cut down old growth," Trey said. "They turned pasture into Christmas tree farms. Pine and cedar grow fast, so there's a good profit to be made in turnover."

"They're not bad neighbors," Slade admitted, adjusting his stance. "And they keep up their roads just fine."

"All true." Trey rubbed at the condensation on his glass.

"Then I don't understand the issue. You sell or you don't sell." Misty stared at Trey with a confused look in her green eyes.

Chairs scraped across the wood floor as a table of diners stood up and headed for the cash register.

"Got to get back to work," Slade said. "I'll be back with your grub."

Trey watched his cousin walk away. He didn't want to talk about Texas Timber. He didn't even want to think about the outfit. But maybe setting out the situation to a stranger would make the whole thing make more sense. Besides, Misty had a good head on her shoulders.

"Texas Timber?" Misty nudged in a soft voice.

"If Texas Timber would take no for an answer, I'd say fine and dandy. They'd move on. I'd move on."

"Why won't they accept your answer?"

"They think everything's for sale, I guess, including Wildcat Ranch."

"Maybe they're used to getting their way."

"No doubt." He rubbed his forehead in frustration. "They keep upping the deal like money makes a difference."

"It does to most folks."

"I figured at some point they'd give up and go away."

"They aren't?"

"Things took a turn for the worse." He looked out over Main Street, but didn't really see it. "Not long ago, problems started cropping up on the ranch. Cut fence and loose cattle here and there. We can handle that, but it adds to workloads and endangers animals."

"I can see that'd be a bad problem."

"And fire. You helped me tame that grass fire, but it almost got away. And it's not the first one we caught in the nick of time. But if this keeps up, one of these days we won't catch the fire and we won't find the cut fence till way too late to save lives and property."

"You think this has something to do with Texas Timber?"

"Well, yeah." He felt his frustration edge upward. Hadn't she been listening to him? "Who else stands to gain?"

"That guy whose house just burned down?"

"Not Bert Holloway's land or property."

"Maybe he wants to buy it. You said several of his properties have burned down."

"Sure, Bert'd snap it up cheap. That works when somebody's susceptible after a string of bad luck. So, I guess you're right. I can't completely cross him off my list of suspects."

"What about somebody else?"

"Texas Timber stands out."

"I can see why, but I wouldn't rule out some other culprit." She tapped her knuckles on the tabletop for emphasis. "I mean, what does Texas Timber stand to gain if they burn down the very thing they're trying to buy?"

"Yeah, I've thought of that too, but the fires haven't been near the Cross Timbers area." He took a big slug of tea to cool down. "One thing is for sure, with this heat and drought, the ranch is vulnerable."

"I'm sorry. Bet you hardly have time to enjoy the Christmas season."

He reached across the table and squeezed her fingers. "I'm not gonna let this deal ruin Christmas."

"Good." She clasped his hand in return. "Why don't you let me help? I've got some time on my hands."

"Thanks, but no thanks. You're here to enjoy yourself and that's what you ought to do."

"Remember, I'm your Christmas angel."

"How could I forget?" He felt the soft warmness of her hand and wanted to kiss each fingertip like he'd done at Twin Oaks. Truth be told, he wanted to do a whole lot more than that. But he was in public. Folks were blabbermouths, and he didn't want to embarrass her or cause talk.

"Come on, say you'll let me help or at least use me as a sounding board."

He gave her hand a final squeeze, then let go and leaned back in his chair. He wished he could completely trust her, but he did feel better telling her about his situation. One way or another, Texas Timber would eventually get the message and take a flying leap into the nearest lake. "How about I take you to Christmas in the Country on Saturday?"

"What's that about?"

"It's fun. Lots of folks will be in Old Town for the festivities."

"I won't need to dress up in old-time clothes, will I?"

"If you've got jeans, a shirt, and boots, you'll be fine."

"What if I don't?"

"Shop. You wouldn't pass up a chance for that type of fun, would you?"

She laughed and her green eyes sparkled. "But I won't know what to buy. Maybe you'd better help me."

He threw up his hands, joining her laughter. "Now we're getting into dangerous territory."

"I thought we were already there."

Something in the tone of her voice and the look in

her eyes alerted him to the fact they'd changed from talking about shopping to talking about what was building between them. They were headed into deeper water. And he was about ready to take the plunge.

He cleared his throat, figuring he'd better get them back on track. "I'll be working events part of the time, but we could have fun."

"I'd love to go. Just let me know when and where."

"Great." He thought about the hayride. Too bad the weather wasn't cooperating for snuggles under quilts. He'd just have to make do another way. He figured he could be creative if it meant getting close to Misty.

"Here you go!" Slade stepped up with a large tray balanced on the palm of one hand held high in the air. He set the tray on a nearby table, and then quickly arranged their orders in front of them.

"Thanks," Misty said. "Everything looks wonderful."

"Let me know how that chili suits your belly." Slade waggled his eyebrows. "That alone will tell me plenty about you."

"If it's too hot, she can share my food." Trey tilted his head toward the kitchen, hoping his cousin would get the message to vamoose.

"I doubt it'll be too much for me." Misty picked up her spoon, dipped it in the big bowl of chili, and glanced up at Trey. "I like it hot."

"Enjoy." Slade winked at Trey as he turned to leave. "Got work to do before the slave drivers get back. See you later."

"Nice meeting you," Misty said.

"Likewise."

Out of the corner of his eye, Trey saw his cousin

walk away, but his focus stayed on Misty as she raised a spoonful of dark red chili to her pale pink lips. The sight of her about to spoon that chili into her open mouth set off his own personal heat wave. "I like it hot, too."

Chapter 17

MISTY LOOKED DEEP INTO TREY'S EYES, WHICH HAD gone dark with desire. She felt the heat between them grow, causing a deep, damp burn in her sensitive core. She crossed her legs in an effort to relieve the itch and bumped him with the toe of her shoe.

He grinned, revealing white teeth in a predatory smile.

"Excuse me." She set down her spoon filled with chili without taking a bite and picked up her iced tea. She took a big slug and backed off her heat a bit.

"Kick me any time you want."

"I didn't mean to do that."

"Sure you don't want to play footsie under the table? I'm game."

"I want to try my chili." She crossed her feet at her ankles and tucked them under her chair. She didn't know how almost every encounter with Trey turned sexual, but there was no denying that it did exactly that.

She quickly spooned a bite of Slade's chili into her mouth. Wow. She felt her eyes water as the chili seared her palate, then her throat, and all the way down to her stomach. Delicious. Not just hot, but a symphony of pepper flavors.

"You like?" Trey pointed at the bowl of chili.

"Yum. Slade's a chili genius."

Trey chuckled. "Don't let him hear you say that or he'll get a big head."

"He deserves it." She took another bite, savored the taste, and swallowed the chili. "How's your sandwich?"

"Good like always."

She nodded but her mind had taken a detour. She imagined herself in the role of Lady Justice—a blind-folded woman holding out a scale—with chili balanced on one side and Trey on the other. Which was hotter? Misty's mouth burned with one, but her entire body burned with the other. No doubt, the scale tipped to Trey as the hottest of the hot.

And that fact just made her job harder now that she knew he had a beef with Texas Timber. Of all the bad luck with a guy, this was it.

She felt trapped in the middle. As far as she knew, Texas Timber was an upstanding company. Otherwise, Cindi Lou would never have recommended them and she wouldn't have accepted the job. But now? Could Texas Timber be using her not as a troubleshooter, but to get information that would ease their way into a buyout of Wildcat Ranch? Yet, that didn't make a lot of sense. A Texas Timber Christmas tree farm had burned before it could be harvested for the season. She'd seen the terrible aftermath with her own eyes. And she'd actually been there for a grass fire and a house fire.

If she set aside her attraction to Trey so she could think clearly, where did this new information leave her?

One: Local fires, including the one on the tree farm, were a natural by-product of the heat wave and drought. But that didn't explain the cut or loosened fence, if that was an actual fact.

Two: A local guy named Bert was behind the house

fires to make money. But that didn't explain the tree farm fire or grass fires or cut fence.

Three: An unknown person, or maybe persons, was setting the fires, or some of the fires, for unknown reasons, as well as messing with fences. But that had no basis in fact.

Four: Trey was igniting grass fires and cutting fence that he could catch without too much harm in order to up the price on Wildcat Ranch by scaring Texas Timber with possible loss of the timber they most wanted to buy. But that didn't explain the Christmas tree farm fire or house fires.

Five: Texas Timber was involved in the sabotage of Wildcat Ranch and their own tree farms to scare Trey into selling before he lost everything valuable. But that didn't explain the house fires or what would be the company's unusual willingness to lose major revenue.

She felt like scratching her head. None of the facts added up. But at least she had some facts now. Nothing fit together to make a cohesive whole. She was missing something, or a whole lot of somethings, so she simply needed more information. Hedy would be a good source. And Misty'd get back on her computer when she returned to Twin Oaks. She hoped she could find a way to put Trey in the plus column of her investigation instead of the negative—or questionable—column.

All in all, she had five possibilities, but none of them were particularly viable. She'd start the process of elimination and follow leads. She wasn't back to square one, but she wasn't much closer to closing her troubleshooting job and getting home by Christmas.

With her mind still on her problems, she shoveled

a big bite of chili into her mouth and swallowed hard. She felt the chili go the wrong way and blaze a trail downward. She grabbed her tea and chugged the last of it, but her throat still felt on fire. She coughed, patting her chest as if that'd help, while tears blurred her vision.

"Here, drink mine."

"Thanks." She felt Trey thrust his glass into her hand. She gratefully took several swallows and felt a little better. She realized they'd shared the tea almost lip to lip. She quickly thrust the glass back into his hands, wondering if she'd left lipstick on his glass.

"Looks like you left a little for me." He turned the glass so the pink telltale image of her lips faced him, and then he put his own mouth to that spot and drank the last of his tea. He set down the glass and smiled at her. "Sweeter than before."

She couldn't keep from chuckling at his audacity. "You're nothing but trouble."

"I do my best." He grinned, joining her laughter. "Come on." As he rose to his feet, he took money out of his billfold and tossed it on the table.

"I'll have to owe you for lunch. My purse is in my car."

"Lunch is on me." Trey gave her a meaningful look. "My Granny'd give me what-for if I let a lady pay for her own meal."

"But, Trey—"

"Not another word or you'll be impugning my cowboy manners."

"Guess I wouldn't want to do that." She smiled at his feigned—or she thought it was feigned—affront. "I'll do something nice for you in return."

"Now there's a happy thought." He smiled, then cast a quick glance around the café. "We better get out of here. If Slade thinks you can't handle his chili, you'll never hear the last of it."

"I swallowed wrong."

"No matter."

She stood up, still taking deep breaths to relieve the heat. Slade's five-alarm chili would be with her for some time.

"Bet you can hardly see with your eyes on fire." Trey grasped her around the waist and led her toward the front door.

"Won't Slade expect us to say good-bye?"

"I'll let him know his chili made you sick as a dog and he'd better not make any more."

"Don't you dare!"

Trey opened the front door, causing the bells to jingle, and then hurried her outside. "He probably put extra jalapeños or worse yet habaneros in your chili just to test your stomach."

"He wouldn't."

"Are you kidding me? That's Slade we're talking about. He rides bulls, or he used to ride them. What's a little five-alarm chili to him?"

"I guess not much." She inhaled deeply, feeling the burn lessen as chills replaced the heat.

"Anyway, he likes to test his own limits and everybody else's limits, too."

"Still, please don't insult him. He makes excellent chili."

Trey chuckled, tugging her closer. "I doubt anybody could insult him."

"True enough."

"Seriously, are you okay now?" He reached up and gently tucked a strand of hair behind her ear.

"Yes, I'm fine. Thanks for lunch. And everything."

"My pleasure." He glanced at the street, then back at her. "Gotta go. You need anything else, let me know."

"Will do."

She watched as he got into his pickup and started the engine. What a hunk of a guy. She sighed, wanting so much more from him, knowing she shouldn't want it, and yet wondering if she could resist. He was making no secret of his desire for her, but that knowledge simply added to her dilemma.

He lowered his window and held up a hand in good-bye as he drove away down Main Street.

She waved in response before she resolutely turned away. Now she must get back to the business at hand.

Chapter 18

MISTY QUICKLY PULLED THE KEYS OUT OF HER POCKET as she walked to her SUV. She punched the red button on the opener and heard the familiar beep to signal she'd unlocked her car. She pulled open the driver's side door, reached inside the console, and grabbed her handbag. She slung it over her shoulder and relocked her vehicle.

She stepped up on the boardwalk and glanced at Old Town. Country Christmas music filled the air, along with the delicious scent of kettle corn. Twinkling lights in blue and white outlined the edge of the portico. Shoppers thronged the boardwalk, hurrying in and out of stores. The holiday was in full swing.

Misty chuckled to think she'd once imagined avoiding much of Christmas in Wildcat Bluff. Not only was that idea way off the mark, but she was beginning to gain an ease with the season that she'd have thought impossible before arriving in town. She touched the Christmas angel around her neck. She'd even gotten used to wearing the lovely pendant. Not that she intended to wear it a lot, but the angel did have a certain charm.

With all the hustle and bustle in Old Town, Misty doubted now would be a good time to try and elicit information from harried shopkeepers. If Hedy wasn't too busy, she'd be the best place to start anyway.

Morning's Glory and Adelia's Delights both had

"OPEN" signs on their doors again. Misty assumed the house fire was completely under control, so volunteers had returned to their businesses. She couldn't help but be impressed with the local fire-rescue. She was glad she'd had a small part in saving lives and property since she'd arrived in the county, but she hoped she wouldn't be called upon to help again.

She opened the door to Adelia's Delights, heard the door chime, and stepped inside. She smelled chocolate and coffee. The wonderful scents reminded her that she could use a cold drink of water, or even a Dr Pepper, right about now to soothe her throat after Slade's chili. An icy beverage might cool her down after the heat outside and Trey's teasing ways. Surely she could get a drink with lots of ice in the tearoom.

Hedy was at the cash register in back taking care of customers, so Misty walked over to the Bluebird of Happiness display. Rosie had somehow climbed up on a shelf and wrapped her long-haired, lithe body around the delicate bluebirds for a quiet nap. She opened an amber eye, flipped her long tail, gave Misty a considering look, then tucked her head down and went back to sleep.

Misty smiled at the contented cat. She wouldn't mind a nap herself. It'd been quite a day so far. She picked up a bird and watched the blue glass capture the sparkle of sunlight that came in through the front window. Now that truly evoked happiness. She liked the idea. Maybe she'd buy a big one for Cindi Lou to set on her desk. Not a Christmas present, but a happiness gift. She set the small bird back in place on the display.

"Excuse me," Misty said as she moved Rosie's fluffy tail to one side so she could pick up the biggest bluebird.

Rosie replied with a big yawn, revealing sharp, white teeth, then she snapped her mouth shut, laid her head down, covered her pink nose with her tail, and went back to sleep.

Misty smiled at the cat's ability to relax so completely no matter what was going on around her. Not a bad trait to acquire.

She walked back to the counter where Hedy helped a woman while two men waited for service. She stroked the smooth contours of the bluebird while she watched the transaction. Maybe when these customers were gone she'd get a chance to chat with Hedy.

"Merry Christmas." Hedy handed a green shopping bag to the woman who hurriedly walked away.

Hedy gave Misty a quick smile and a nod before she focused on the two men. "Bert. And Bert Two. What brings you into Adelia's Delights? Shopping for the fairer sex?"

Both men guffawed with deep, booming voices while they held their cowboy hats in their hands.

Misty went on alert. Could this be the Bert whose building had burned down earlier? Surely there couldn't be two men with the same name in the community, so he must be. What a perfect opportunity to observe him.

"Howdy, Hedy. Just wanted to stop by and let you know I'm back in town."

"Glad to hear it." Hedy motioned behind them. "I'd like you to meet Misty Reynolds. She helped with the house fire today. Misty, this is the owner, Bert Holloway. And his son, Bert Two."

"Pleased to meet you," Misty said. "I'm sorry for your loss."

"You have my profound thanks for your kind help," Bert said as he turned to face her, holding out his hand.

Misty gave him a quick handshake as she looked him over. For some reason, she'd expected him to look rough around the edges. Instead, he was a tall, good-looking guy wearing a Western-cut suit with a bolo tie and expensive ostrich cowboy boots. He had thick, dark hair streaked with silver and tanned skin that suggested he spent much of his life outdoors. His son was a chip off the old block in looks and attire.

"Yes, thanks." Bert Two held out his hand, too.

She meant to give his hand a quick shake, but he caught her fingers and held tight as he smiled down at her.

"You're a lovely addition to our town. Hope you're gonna be here for some time," Bert Two said.

"Not long. I'm just enjoying a quick getaway." She returned his smile as she tugged her hand away. After everything she'd heard, she had no reason to trust these two men. Yet gossip didn't necessarily equate with truth, so she'd withhold judgment.

"Dad came back as soon as he heard the news," Bert Two said.

"Place went up fast," Hedy explained. "There wasn't anything Bert could've done even if he'd been here."

Bert shook his head, looking downcast. "I've been targeted, because the hits just keep on coming."

"There'll be an investigation," Hedy said with sympathy.

"For all the good it'll do." Bert turned a sad gaze on Misty. "Somebody's awful clever or somebody doesn't care to do his job."

"That's the truth of it," Bert Two agreed.

"Now you two don't need to get down on our fire or police or the county sheriff. They're doing their best." Hedy gripped the arms of her wheelchair as she leaned toward them.

"If so, why don't they go after the dad-burn reprobate that's got it in for me?" Bert asked with a plaintive tone in his voice.

"You don't know that to be a fact," Hedy said.

"Yes, I do," Bert insisted. "I'm not gonna name names in front of a stranger to our community. I've told the authorities the name of the culprit, but do they arrest him?"

"No," Bert Two said.

"Do they have proof?" Hedy asked.

"The proof is in the pudding," Bert said with finality.

"Bad blood doesn't necessarily mean somebody's out to hurt you." Hedy glanced at Misty and shook her head. "But maybe they'll find evidence this time."

"Good luck with that." Bert Two glanced around at the group. "What'll be left after all that fire, smoke, water, and folks tromping over the place? Not much, I'll wager."

"Volunteers tried to save your building." Misty defended those who'd gone to so much time and effort to save Bert's property. She wanted to hear more gratitude from these two men.

"Guess I don't sound like it, but I'm mighty appreciative of all their many efforts." Bert turned his hat round and round in his big hands. "I'm frustrated as all get-out."

"And that's the truth," Bert Two added.

"It's a shame," Hedy said. "But maybe this'll end it."

"I sure do hope so," Bert agreed.

Hedy gestured toward Misty's bluebird. "You want me to wrap that up for you?"

"Yes, thank you."

"Here I am jawing when you've got business to conduct," Bert said. "Thanks for listening. I needed to get that off my chest."

"He's been stewing about it," Bert Two explained.

"I can understand." Hedy took the bluebird from Misty.

"We'll be going now," Bert said. "If you hear anything that'll help catch the culprit, you'll let us know, won't you?"

"Sure will." Hedy glanced up. "You have as good a day as you can, now."

Bert Two turned toward Misty. "If you don't mind my asking, where are you staying in town?"

"Twin Oaks B&B." Misty wasn't surprised by the question anymore. He could easily find out, so she didn't hesitate to tell him.

"Good choice. You get lonely or bored, just give me a call." Bert Two whipped a business card out of his pocket and held it out to her. "I'm always ready to squire a pretty lady like you about town."

"You might want to ask Trey about that first," Hedy interrupted.

Bert Two frowned. "Trey? What does that cowboy have to do with the price of milk?"

"He's taking me to Christmas in the Country," Misty said, noticing the pride in her voice.

"That so?" Bert Two looked surprised, then he

shrugged. "If that doesn't happen to work out, I'd be happy to take you. We'd have a good time."

"Thank you. But I doubt my plans will change." She accepted his business card. He might be a helpful contact later.

"Just so you know, I'm a sensitive guy and I know how to treat a lady right," Bert Two said.

"Darn tootin'," Bert agreed. "We're that kind of men."

"Maybe you two had better head home before it gets any deeper in here," Hedy said, chuckling.

"Now, Hedy." Bert gave her a dazzling smile. "If you weren't so hardheaded, you'd have found out long ago how well I treat a lady."

"Bert, I'm pulling on my waders." She chuckled as she pointed toward the front door. "You best get back to business and let me do the same."

"I'm going, but you know my offer's always open," Bert said as he took a step away from the counter.

"Nice meeting you both." Misty smiled politely.

"Don't wait too long to call me," Bert Two said. "I'll be cooking up a big pot of chili soon."

Misty's stomach clenched at the thought, but she gave a little wave good-bye as the two men turned and sauntered toward the door. She didn't breathe a sigh of relief till the front door shut behind them.

"Don't know about you," Hedy said, "but they tend to wear on my last nerve."

Misty flipped Bert Two's business card on the counter. "Better drop that in the bag with my bluebird. I might get a hankering for chili."

"Guess it's not nice to make light of their trouble,

but those two are a magnet for it." Hedy touched the bluebird. "Pretty thing, isn't it? I'll carefully wrap your bird in tissue so there's no chance it'll break."

"Thanks. If you've got it, I'd also love a cold drink with lots of ice. I just ate a bowl of Slade's five-alarm chili."

Hedy laughed long and hard. "That Bert Two, he's got a way of steppin' in it that just won't quit."

Misty shared her laughter. "If you have time to chat, I'd like to help figure out how to put on a benefit to raise funds so all the fire-rescue volunteers have animal oxygen mask kits with them in case of an emergency."

"I heard about the kitten. You're observant, aren't you?"

"I just hope the kitty makes it."

"He's getting the best care." Hedy cocked her head as she looked closely at Misty. "No doubt we need the kits. You really want to help with this problem, don't you?"

"Sure I do."

"Tell you what, let's get a couple drinks and take a load off." Hedy pointed at a table in the tearoom. "You grab a seat while I get the drinks."

"First, let me pay for the bluebird and the drinks." Misty pulled her billfold out of her handbag and plunked down a credit card on the countertop.

"Thanks." Hedy picked up the credit card. "But the drinks are on the house. Least you deserve for saving that kitten."

"Trey takes all the credit for that feat."

Hedy quickly swiped the card. "Don't sell yourself short. Your sharp eye and quick action helped save the day." She set the receipt and credit card on the countertop.

As Misty signed the receipt, Hedy quickly wrapped the bluebird in red tissue paper, tucked it into a green paper bag, and set it on top of the counter. Misty picked up all her items and placed them in her purse. "Thank you."

"Anytime." Hedy motioned toward the tearoom. "Go on now. I'll join you in a minute."

"Let me help get the drinks."

"Not a bit of it. I've got a system all worked out."

When Hedy zoomed into the back room, Misty walked into the tearoom and moved a chair out of the way at a table to make space for Hedy's wheelchair. She sat down, leaned back, and relaxed, feeling the tension drain out of her. It felt really good to let go for a bit.

"Here you are." Hedy motored up to the table with two red plastic iced tea glasses that she set on the tabletop. "That's pineapple hibiscus tea over ice. Hope you like it."

Misty took a sip. "Oh, that's delicious."

"Glad you appreciate the taste. I'm right partial to the fruit and floral teas when it's hot outside."

"And it's certainly hot."

"Long day." Hedy sipped her tea and moaned in pleasure. "Just what the doctor ordered. But I guess we'd better talk quick before the next shoppers find their way through my front door."

"Odd about the fire." Misty hoped Hedy might open up and tell her more about the county's problems.

Hedy shook her head. "Odder about the new computer system going down. If I didn't know better, I'd think—"

Misty leaned forward. "What?"

"Oh, nothing. I'm just getting suspicious about everything. There've just been too many oddities around here."

"Trey told me about the grass fires and cut fence."

"Yeah, they aren't helping matters." Hedy looked closely at Misty. "He's come to trust you real fast."

"Guess putting out that grass fire together made trust between us a necessity."

Hedy cocked her head to one side. "I can see how it would do just that." She took a sip of tea as she leaned forward. "You're good for him, you know?"

Misty smiled, feeling pleased but also feeling like a fraud even if her actions were to help the county. "I like him."

"Good." Hedy leaned back. "I hope you like our community, too."

"I like everything about Wildcat Bluff. And the folks."

Hedy grinned. "That's real good."

"Guess I was thrust into the middle of the action from the get-go. Now I'm concerned about all these problems in the community. If I may be of help, please let me know."

Hedy nodded thoughtfully, as if considering her next words. "You're a natural to head up a benefit for animal oxygen kits."

"It'd have to be soon. And I've never done anything like that before."

"We're all overextended during Christmas in the Country, so we need somebody like you to ramrod it through."

"I'll be happy to try."

"Get Trey to be your partner. He knows the ropes around here."

"I'll ask him."

Hedy chuckled. "Don't ask. *Tell*. That's the only way to get a guy in line on a project."

Misty joined her laughter. "Okay, I'll give that a try, too."

"Trust me, it's a winner." Hedy glanced up at the sound of the chimes as a woman opened the front door, stepped inside, and glanced around with a look of delight on her face. "Appears our time's up. Tell you what, let me make some phone calls and set up a meeting of fire-rescue volunteers at Twin Oaks. Christmas in the Country would be the perfect time for a fund-raiser if we can squeeze in another event."

"When?"

"Tonight." Hedy set down her glass. "About eight suit you?"

"Sounds great."

"Got to take care of business."

"Thanks. I'll see you later."

Misty watched Hedy zoom away, feeling good about their conversation. She was making progress. She reached into her handbag and pulled out her cell phone. Cindi Lou had left several texts asking if Misty was okay. She quickly texted her BFF back to let her know all was well. She'd call later to bring her up to date, and she might even mention a cowboy firefighter named Trey.

Chapter 19

TREY DROVE UNDER THE TWIN OAKS SIGN ABOUT eight that evening. Hedy had texted him earlier to come to a fire-rescue meeting. They usually met at the B&B, but he hadn't figured they'd get together again till after Christmas in the Country. Something important must've come up.

He parked beside Kent's dinged-up blue pickup. Slade's shiny black Jeep was there. And Sydney's fancy yellow truck with the red and orange flames streaking down the sides stood out like a ray of sunshine. Hedy was most likely parked in front of the house so she could use the ramp up to the kitchen. He was glad to see Misty's SUV in place, so he might get a chance to talk with her later. Somehow or the other, she always left him wanting more.

When he got out, he put his cell phone in his back pocket and looked around the place under the mercury vapor light attached to a tall, creosote-painted pole like most people in the country used to cut back the night. Nothing out of the ordinary jumped out at him, so he walked past the Gladstones' van. He stopped and looked again. The van appeared dustier and dingier than ever. Were they driving to hell and gone? He guessed locating collectibles was tougher and harder work than he could imagine. Still, for his money, the van in no way suited the couple's impeccable image. Only thing he could figure was that they must leave their fancy vehicles at home when they were out hunting for stuff.

As he walked across the tennis court, he ran a hand through his still damp hair. It felt good to be clean. After the chores were done, he'd finally had a chance to shower, shave, and change into fresh clothes. It'd been another long day and another vicious fire. At least they'd saved a kitten. He'd called the vet earlier and the kitty was still holding his own.

Good thing the temperature was easing up now that dusk had set in. He couldn't help but wonder if the heat wave would ever break. He'd underlined "snow" on his Christmas list before he'd plopped the snowman magnet back in place on his refrigerator. So far, one and two on his Christmas list stayed out of reach, but he lived in hope of snow for Christmas and to snuggle, or more, with his Christmas angel.

When Trey reached the sliding glass doors in front of the house, Temple slipped out of the darkness. He looked up and meowed, obviously requesting more tender beef.

"Sorry, boy. I'm fresh out of your favorite food tonight." He reached down and stroked the soft white fur.

Temple yowled in displeasure as he walked up to the doors, sat down, and waited for entry.

"Maybe next time." Trey was well aware that cats never forgot something they liked to eat. For that matter, they never forgot any of their favorite things. Guess he didn't either.

He slid open the doors and Temple walked inside first, tail held high. He followed the cat and stopped when he saw J.P. and Charlene sitting in the swing.

Temple did no such thing. He tiptoed over, sniffed their shoes, shook his head in displeasure, and walked over to the front door to be let inside the house.

Trey chuckled at Temple's response to the couple. "Guess he didn't like where you've been."

"What does a cat know," Charlene said with disdain as she patted her perfect coiffure.

"I'd never bet against the olfactory abilities of a cat or dog." Trey had meant his first words as a joke, but he felt a need to defend Temple in light of Charlene's response.

"Trey's right, dearest," J.P. said as he stroked Charlene's red-nailed, long-fingered hand. "Our abilities in that area are puny in comparison to cats and dogs."

"At least they can't talk." She looked pleased with that idea.

"Mostly they don't need words to make their opinions clear." Trey didn't know how he'd gotten into this conversation. He just wanted to get inside to the meeting. He glanced over at Temple waiting by the door. It was never a bad idea to defend a four-legged friend.

"I'm sure you're right," Charlene quickly agreed, batting her long false eyelashes as she tapped the pointed toe of a red-and-black high-heel shoe. "How was your day?"

"Busy." Trey wasn't going to get into a serious discussion with them.

"Heard a house burned down," J.P. said. "Sad business."

"Yep," Trey agreed. "Derelict, so not much loss."

"That's good." Charlene smiled as she patted the spot beside her. "Why don't you join us?"

"Thanks, but I've got a meeting inside." He started

toward the door and stopped, remembering his manners. "You have a good day?"

"Oh, yes. We're quite pleased with our work. Aren't we, snookum?" Charlene squeezed J.P.'s hand.

"That's true," J.P. agreed.

"Great. Talk with y'all later." Trey quickly crossed the room to the inside front door.

"Anytime," Charlene called.

Trey opened the door for Temple, followed the cat inside, and shut the door behind him. He watched as Temple made a beeline for the peacock Christmas tree, carefully stepped in between packages, selected a soft spot, turned around several times, and settled down for a long nap.

"Up here," Ruby greeted Trey. "We're gathered around the table."

Trey took the three steps up to the large kitchen and dining area, smelling the rich aroma of hot apple cider. And stopped cold. Misty stood in the kitchen holding a mug and looking pretty as you please. She also looked as if she belonged exactly there. He felt his heart speed up at the sight of her. Hard to believe, but she'd only been in town a couple of days. And here she was at a fire-rescue meeting with his closest friends and kinfolks, if you didn't count his absentee parents, who'd decided to take a much wanted and even more needed Caribbean cruise for the holidays.

"Hey, Cuz." Kent chuckled from where he sat at the table. "Meeting's over here. Not in the kitchen."

Trey jerked around to look in that direction, not wanting to be considered smitten by the new gal in town. Hedy sat at one end of Ruby's 1940s enameled, tin-top pie table once used by women to roll pie dough upon the smooth surface with a rolling pin. This one had a Western-design top attached to a wood Art Deco–design base painted in faded yellow and orange. Ruby sat at the other end of the table. Kent, Slade, and Sydney sat on one side. Three chairs were left empty on the side facing him.

"Uncle Trey!" A pint-size urchin with wild ginger hair and big hazel eyes ran toward him. She wore a rhinestone-studded T-shirt in bright aqua with pressed jeans and turquoise cowgirl boots.

"Hey, Storm." He knelt down in time to catch her as she flung her small, wiry body into his arms.

"I won Little Wranglers All-Around Champion!"

"Gotta love youth rodeo in Texas." He looked with pleasure at her animated face.

"And I won a saddle, too."

"Good for you. Stiff competition?"

"Hah! You jest. Never for me."

"You sound like your mama." He glanced up at Sydney, who appeared like the proud mother hen she was since she'd brought Storm into the world five years ago.

"Glad you could make it." Sydney gave him a lazy smile that belied her high energy level and knock-out appearance.

"What's up?" Trey hugged Storm, got to his feet, pulled out a chair, and sat down at the table.

"We got important bidness." Storm wiggled into the chair beside him.

"Misty, do you want to start the meeting?" Hedy asked.

Trey blinked in surprise as he swiveled to take a good look at Misty. Like him, she'd had a chance to shower and change clothes. Unlike him, she'd opted to dress up a bit. He wore forgettable jeans and a T-shirt. She was unforgettable in a yellow sundress with spaghetti straps and a full skirt that ended above her knees. She also wore yellow sandals on her high-arched feet with pink painted toenails. She gave him a knowing little smile.

Misty held up her mug. "Drink?"

Oh yeah, she was a long, cool drink of water on a hot day. He nodded, about all he could do since his mouth had gone dry.

"Care for gingerbread?" Ruby asked. "I made it fresh today."

"Yum!" Storm patted her tummy as she grinned at Trey.

"We've already served ourselves," Ruby added. "Misty, you're up. Will you bring some for Trey?"

"Sure will." Misty busied herself in the kitchen, then walked over and set a full, red mug adorned with a Santa Claus face and a red matching plate with a slice of gingerbread on it in front of him. "Forks and napkins are already in the center of the table."

"Thanks." He took a sip of the tart cider. "Now, what's this meeting all about?"

"Ball's in your court." Hedy gestured at Misty.

Misty sat down on the other side of Storm. She wrapped her hands around her own Santa Claus mug on the table. "I just can't rest easy till the fire-rescue volunteers have animal oxygen kits."

Trey nodded in agreement and encouragement. He picked up a fork and took a bite of delicious gingerbread.

"I talked with Hedy this afternoon about a benefit to raise funds for the project," Misty added.

"Good idea," Trey said. "We've done benefits before. We can sure do another one. Are you thinking about sometime in the spring?"

Misty shook her head and glanced at Hedy. "I hate to wait that long. What do all of you think about a benefit during Christmas in the Country?"

"I like it," Hedy quickly agreed.

"Good. With all the fires in the area, I don't see how we can wait." Misty gestured around the table.

Slowly but surely, everyone began nodding in agreement.

Trey sat back in surprise as he looked at the others. "But wait, that's so soon. We're extra busy during the holidays. I don't know how we can fit in another event."

"I totally understand your concern." Misty tapped her fingertip against the metal tabletop. "I told Hedy I'd spearhead the event since everybody else is so busy."

"That's real generous," Ruby said. "Plus, what happened at the fire today with the kittens tells us all we need to know. We can't wait."

"I gave the benefit some thought this afternoon." Misty smiled at Slade. "I had chili for lunch at the Chuckwagon Café and got inspired."

"I'm not a bit surprised to hear that news." Slade grinned at her.

"On the other hand," Ruby joked, "if you didn't get heartburn, you were lucky."

Everybody at the table laughed as they turned to look at Slade.

"No need to malign my cooking just 'cause you're jealous of my culinary skills." Slade stood and took a small bow before he sat down again.

"That's exactly right!" Misty gestured around the table.

"Right?" Trey looked at her in confusion.

"What do you think about the Wildcat Bluff Chili Cook-Off?" Misty glanced hopefully at the group as they all went quiet in thought.

"Yeah!" Storm broke the silence. "Can we have giant trophies and everything?"

"The Wildcat Bluff Chili Cook-Off Benefit," Hedy said as she rolled the sound around in her mouth as if tasting it.

"I like it." Kent smiled at Misty. "Clever idea."

"I'll win." Storm thrust out her chest. "I want another trophy."

"Youth Division," Sydney said. "Moms will love it. The more inclusive, the more people will enter."

"We can sell tickets for all you can eat. That'll bring 'em in, too." Slade took a big sip from his Santa Claus mug.

Trey felt as if they'd steamrolled right over him. What with all the problems they were having in the county, plus Christmas in the Country, he didn't see how they could handle another event. "I don't mean to be a spoilsport, but how can we find the time to put on a chili cook-off?"

"Misty's our secret weapon," Hedy said. "She volunteered to head up the event or we couldn't do it."

Trey looked at Misty in concern. "It's not your problem, and I thought you were here to rest."

"I can't stop thinking about that little kitten struggling for his life right this very moment."

Trey smiled, admiring her commitment to animals. "I can't argue with that. Guess we'll find some way to do it."

"Just think," Ruby said. "Christmas in the Country is the perfect time for the Wildcat Bluff Chili Cook-Off 'cause so many folks will be in town. And they'll be feeling generous."

"Good point," Kent agreed. "And we've had those kits on our buy list from the start."

"I'll need help." Misty looked at Trey. "I don't know many folks around here."

"You've got me to help." Trey heard the words fall out of his mouth. What was he doing? He didn't have extra time. But he knew why he'd said it. He'd get to spend more time with Misty. And even more important, animals would benefit.

"I appreciate it." Misty gave him a warm smile.

"Perfect," Hedy said.

"Y'all work out the details." Sydney reached across the table and patted Misty's hand. "We're here for you. Just let us know whatever you need whenever you need it."

"Thanks." Misty smiled in reply. "I'm sure I'll be calling on all of you."

"Now that's settled, anybody need more cider?" Ruby asked.

"Not me." Storm pushed out her chair and stood up. "I need to practice."

"For what?" Trey swiveled to look at her.

Storm tugged on his chair, but it didn't move. "I need you to turn your chair out from the table."

Trey followed her instructions, enjoying watching her as he always did, particularly since he didn't know what she'd be up to next.

"Okay." Storm glanced around the group. "Now, I expect constructive criticism."

"What for?" Hedy asked.

"Mommy's taking me to Fort Worth to see Santa Claus."

"And so?" Ruby leaned forward to give Storm her complete attention.

"I've got a super Christmas wish to put to Santa Claus. I want to get it just right."

"And you need to practice?" Trey patted his lap.

"You got it." She plopped down on his lap, leaned her head against his chest, and looked up at him with sincere hazel eyes.

"What do you want for Christmas, little girl?" he asked, keeping a solemn expression on his face as he played Santa Claus.

"I want a goat-roping dummy."

Everyone around the table exploded in laughter.

Storm frowned at them. "This is serious business."

Trey bit his tongue to keep the laughter at bay.

"I don't need a goat-roping dummy this year. I'm too little." She put her hands on her hips. "But I'm growing fast. For sure, I'll need it next year."

"Wouldn't you want to wait till next year to get your dummy?" Trey gently squeezed her small shoulder.

"No! I want it in place. You just never know when you may need a goat-roping dummy."

"You've got a good point there," Trey solemnly agreed as he looked into her determined eyes. She always spread so much joy. He'd wished for a little girl of his own for some time. He glanced over Storm's head at Misty. For the first time, he could imagine a tiny girl with ginger hair and pale green eyes.

Misty smiled, reached out, and squeezed Storm's small hand. "You did just great. I'm sure Santa Claus will make sure you get your goat-roping dummy."

"You think so?"

"How could he not?"

Storm cocked her head. "You know, he's a grown-up. And they can turn foolish as fast as I can run barrels."

"Wish we could all be a smart little girl like you," Misty said.

"Tell you what." Storm reached up and patted Misty's cheek. "You stick with me and I'll see you get those oxygen kits for Christmas."

"Thanks."

Trey hugged Storm close and smelled the strawberry shampoo in her long, soft hair. She gave him a quick kiss on the cheek, then wiggled out of his lap and danced away.

Maybe he ought to add to his Christmas list.

Chapter 20

WHEN THE FIRE-RESCUE MEETING BROKE UP, TREY HELD the screen door open for Hedy so she could zoom down the ramp to her vehicle. He hugged Storm and watched her dance outside before she clattered down the brick stairs.

Sydney gave Trey a big hug and whispered in his ear. "Now don't do anything I wouldn't do." And she pointedly glanced at Misty.

Trey chuckled as he caught her meaning. "Wouldn't think of it."

"Bet there's plenty you could think of." Sydney joined his laughter before she hurried outside after her daughter.

Kent held up his hand and high-fived Trey. Slade gave him a wink. And then the two cousins were out the door, letting the screen door slam shut behind them. Quiet descended on the kitchen. Trey hooked the lock on the screen before he shut and locked the main door. He turned back to Misty.

She smiled. "Guess we've got our show on the road."

"Looks like it."

"If you two need me for anything, ask me tomorrow." Ruby covered a yawn with one hand. "I'm off to bed."

"It's been a long day," Trey agreed, "but we don't have time to lose if we're going to make this benefit work."

"Place is yours if you want to stay up and make plans." Ruby glanced in the direction of the gazebo. "Why don't you take cider down to the spring? Ease your feet in the water. Sure to feel good."

He glanced at Misty. "You up for that?"

"I'd enjoy it. But I don't want to keep you up."

He smiled as he clasped her hand, feeling that familiar surge of heat. "I think I can last a little longer."

Ruby cleared her throat. "Don't let me interrupt anything."

He chuckled as he looked at his friend, who was grinning at the hand-holding. "We'll just grab drinks and be on our way."

"No need to rush." Ruby waved good-bye as she headed down the stairs. "Nighty-night."

Trey watched as Temple got up, leisurely stretched, and ran ahead of Ruby so he could lead her into the suite. She quietly shut the door behind them.

He turned back to Misty. Finally, they were alone. It had taken all day, but they'd managed it.

She picked up their mugs from the table. "I'll pour us fresh cider and turn off the stove."

He glanced around to make sure all was in order. Everybody had pretty much cleaned up after themselves. He snatched the last bite of gingerbread, ate it, and set the Santa Claus plate in the sink. No doubt about it, Christmastime had the best goodies to eat.

"One last plate." She picked it up, rinsed it off, put it in the dishwasher, and started the wash cycle.

"I'm sure Ruby will appreciate all the cleanup in the morning."

"Least we can do for her wonderful hospitality."

Misty poured cider into their mugs, then handed him one and picked up the other.

"Need anything else?" He made one last glance around the kitchen and was satisfied nothing was left undone.

"I'll keep notes in my head." She turned out the lights except for the one over the stove. She walked down the stairs to the living room now lit only by the purple, fuchsia, and apple-green lights of the peacock tree.

"That's some tree, isn't it?" He joined her downstairs.

"Sure is. I heard you had a little something to do with getting it set up."

"Followed orders. Can't take credit for anything else."

She glanced up at him, almost glowing in the colorful lights of the tree. "I think you can take credit for a lot. That's a beautiful work of art."

He shrugged. "Ruby's the talented one."

She reached out and gently wrapped her fingers around his forearm. "Come on. Let's create something nobody'll ever forget."

He knew she meant the benefit, but his mind slipped back to Storm and an image of another little girl who had yet to be. He clasped Misty's soft, warm hand with his bigger one. "I'm ready when you are."

He led her out to the sunroom. Christmas lights illuminated the area. He checked to see if the Gladstones were still on the swing, but they were gone. Most likely they'd taken a drive to look at Christmas decorations around town. He hoped they weren't at the gazebo.

Misty tugged him over to the back sliding door, dropped his hand, and stepped outside.

He joined her. "Cooler this evening."

"Surely this heat wave will break soon." She started down the lighted brick path.

"Did you shop in Old Town today?" He wondered if she'd bought the dress there as he followed the seductive sway of her skirt.

"I drank tea with Hedy in her wonderful store."

"That's when y'all cooked up this benefit?"

"Right."

When they reached the gazebo, he checked around for the Gladstones, but he didn't see them anywhere nearby. He didn't hear them either. The only sounds that broke the silence of the night were the trickle of the spring and the wind in the pines. He smelled pine and dry grass, maybe a little dust from the drought, but that was about all.

"It's so pretty here." Misty set her mug of cider on the table, then reached into the pocket of her skirt and pulled out her phone. She set it on the table beside her mug.

"Yeah." But he was thinking about her, not the gazebo. He set his mug down across from hers. He didn't want his phone anywhere near the water, so he took it out of his back pocket and set it on the table.

"Before I leave Twin Oaks, I want to put on a swimsuit and take complete advantage of this pool." Misty kicked off her sandals and walked over to the water.

"Let me know when and I'll join you."

She chuckled as she pulled up her skirt, sat down on the edge of the pool, and put her feet in the water. "Feels wonderful. Come on and join me."

He just shook his head as he watched her. She had no idea how everything about her was affecting him. He didn't want to talk about the benefit. In fact, he didn't want to talk at all.

She moaned in delight as she kicked upward with one foot and a spray of water sparkled in the white fairy lights.

That did it. He toed off one boot, then the other. He stuffed his socks in his boots, rolled his jeans up to his knees, and sat down beside her—close enough to feel her body heat. He eased his feet into the warm water.

"Wonderful, isn't it?" She raised her foot and let water drip down from her toes.

"Nothing better, well—almost nothing." He glanced sideways at her. She was better, no two ways about it.

"So much happens around here. I feel as if I'm bouncing from one major crisis to another every day." She reached down and let water flow through her fingers. "Know what I mean?"

"A lot is going on. Christmas is a great time of year, but it's a tough time for some folks, too."

"Like strong emotions?"

"And loneliness."

She caught her breath on a slight hiccup and struck the water hard with the heel of one foot.

"Misty?"

"Nothing." She kicked the water harder. "I mean, you're right."

"I heard therapists are busy during the holidays."

She tossed him a strained smile. "But I bet not in Wildcat Bluff."

"Maybe you're right." He felt as if he was missing something important about her and the holiday, but he didn't know what.

She took a deep breath and quickly released it. "I'm not sure how to start planning the chili cook-off. But mostly I keep thinking about that kitten."

"I called the vet and he's doing okay so far."

She chuckled. "I called, too."

"But it's still too early to know if he'll make it."

"He's going to live. I just know it." She stood up and walked over to the spring where it bubbled up and cascaded down to the pool. She held her fingers under the running water. "Now, we need to make plans."

"Right." With the white fairy lights twinkling in Misty's blond hair and across her yellow dress, she looked like a golden goddess come to Earth. His Christmas angel.

"Date. Venue. Food."

"Let's see. We don't have too many options." He forced his mind back to business. "Christmas in the Country is this weekend. Christmas Eve is on Saturday this year. Best time to have the chili cook-off would be on Saturday before the hayride. I'm fairly confident we could work it into the schedule."

"That'd be perfect." She clapped her hands in delight. "Did you say a hayride?"

He chuckled at her excitement. "I'll be driving. You want to ride with me?"

"Absolutely." She flicked water toward him. "Venue? You know this town better than I do."

"School cafeteria is the best place."

"Is that possible?"

"As far as I know nobody else is using the space at that time, so I don't see why not."

"We could put the chili entries in a row, so folks

could walk down the line or mix it up." Misty mimed where she'd set up the entries.

"Good idea."

"We might include extras like corn chips, shredded cheese, and chopped onion to go with the chili."

"I like it." And he liked her enthusiasm, too.

"Do we want to invite local folks who benefit from fire-rescue or open it up to the general public?"

"What do you think?"

"I'd go with everybody. The more the merrier." She excitedly tossed a handful of water into the air. "How do we let people know about the chili cook-off?"

"We usually announce benefits by putting fliers in Old Town windows and in the newspaper. We can also put up an announcement on the town's website. The *Wildcat Bluff Sentinel* comes out once a week."

"Is there time to get information to the paper?"

"I'm pretty sure there is. I can write up a notice tonight and send it to Cuz Teddie for his weekly column."

"But don't we need approval for the date and venue?"

"Let's assume it's a go till we hear otherwise."

"Okay—if that's the way things are done around here." She rubbed the tip of her nose as if in thought. "What will Teddie need for his column?"

"Pretty much the usual thing." Trey considered it a moment. "Wildcat Bluff Chili Cook-Off. Saturday evening before the hayride. School cafeteria, unless otherwise notified. Benefit for Wildcat Bluff Volunteer Fire-Rescue animal oxygen mask kits. Something like that."

"I like it."

"News will spread fast by word of mouth."

"Even better."

He grinned at her. "Sounds like we've got a handle on your benefit."

"*Our* benefit." She walked over and looked at him. "We wouldn't be this far along without your help." She leaned down and placed a quick kiss on his lips. "Thanks."

"Is that all the thanks I get?"

"You want more?"

"Don't I deserve it?"

"Guess you do."

She sashayed over to a chaise lounge with plump aqua cushions. She glanced over her shoulder and gave him a compelling look before she sat down, stretched out her long legs, and leaned back. She beckoned him with her long fingers.

No words were necessary. He got up, stalked over, raised her long legs, and sat down. He gently set her ankles on his thighs and stroked her bare feet in widening circles. He massaged her soft, smooth skin—ever so slowly—up her ankles to her calves to her knees. He hesitated at the edge of her skirt before he continued upward with his strong fingers massaging the firm skin of her thighs that felt hotter with each touch of his hand. Soon he would reach the center of moist, hidden heat that beckoned him closer.

"Not fair," she said in a husky voice as she slowly sat up. "I'm getting all the thanks, not you."

"I'd have to disagree." He pushed her skirt up higher.

She leaned toward him, thrust her fingers into his thick hair, and placed a heated kiss on his lips, licking and nibbling across his sensitive flesh.

He groaned as he wrapped his arms around her and

pulled her closer. He deepened the kiss as he plunged into her mouth—tasting, teasing, tormenting—as he set them both ablaze.

She came up for breath, smiled at him, and spread her fingers across the hard muscles of his chest. She massaged him as he'd massaged her and he felt his nipples harden in response. He grasped her shoulders and eased her back against the chaise lounge as he nestled his lower body between her legs. He took a deep, shuddering breath as he cupped her breasts with both hands, feeling her soft roundness completely fill his palms.

Still he couldn't get enough of her. He kissed her swollen lips, then trailed kisses from the corner of her mouth across the edge of her jaw to her earlobe, where he nibbled the soft flesh with his teeth. He was rewarded with her quick shiver and intake of breath. He kissed down her throat as he eased the straps of her dress off her shoulders and slowly pulled down the bodice. He glanced downward to see her round breasts with rosy tips revealed to him.

He kissed her twin mounds while he moved one hand down her body. He eased up her dress and found her hot, moist center through sheer silk. He massaged and tweaked until she writhed up against his hand, panting with need. He caught her mouth with his own and plunged inside just as she shuddered with release.

"Oh," she gasped, breathing fast. "Let me thank you, too." She found the bulge in his jeans, grasped the zipper, and started a slow descent.

He groaned, knowing she was tormenting him on purpose, drawing out the suspense till he could feel her hand give him what he'd been aching for since the first moment he saw her.

And in that long moment between anticipation and fulfillment, he heard the loud chirping of a cricket.

She stiffened in his arms and pulled her hand away.

Puzzled, he looked into her green eyes.

"My phone."

"Call 'em back later."

"Might be an emergency."

"I'm an emergency."

"Won't take a minute."

He sat up, took a deep breath, and stalked over to the table. He grabbed her phone. As he handed it to her, he glanced down. Two words glowed in the night. "*Texas Timber*."

Chapter 21

TREY JERKED UP HIS ZIPPER THE INCH MISTY HAD lowered it as he watched her walk away to take her phone call from Texas Timber. He felt blindsided, but he should've known better. She was too perfect. She'd said all the right things at all the right times. Everybody liked her, trusted her, and wanted to be with her. She was even leading the charge to get animal oxygen kits.

And she had to be working for Texas Timber, the rattlesnake in his woodpile. How could he believe anything she'd said or done since the first moment he'd met her? Every sultry look. Every sweet kiss. Every hot touch. For that matter, maybe she didn't even have a fire phobia that led to panic attacks. Surely she couldn't have faked it all. But that thought might go to prove he still wanted to believe in her.

Why hadn't he at least looked her up online? That was a quick and easy check. But he'd been fighting fires, taking care of cattle, getting ready for Christmas in the Country. He hadn't had a free moment. But he should've made time. He'd involved his family, friends, and community. He sorely regretted inviting the fox into the henhouse. But he was on alert now, and all his protective instincts were in play.

One major question remained for consideration. How far was Misty willing to go to get a signature for Wildcat Ranch on a Texas Timber agreement? Start fires? Cut

fences? Crawl into his bed? The first two—he had to
stop. The second—well, why not? If she was willing
to take advantage of him, why couldn't he return the
favor? He knew how to slip a halter on a heifer. And that
wouldn't be one bit of imposition on his part. If she was
determined to get animal kits for volunteers, that was
all to the better. If she wanted to help with Christmas in
the Country, fine by him. If she wanted to snuggle, he
wouldn't kick her out of his bed. But he'd keep one eye
open all the time.

That brought him to his second round of reasoning
about his not-so-nice Christmas angel. Was she working
with somebody? And if so, whom? It could be an outsider, local, or just about anybody—except his friends
and family. He'd trust them to the ends of the Earth.
Still, he didn't see how she could be handling all the
problems on her own, particularly since she hadn't been
in town or she hadn't shown herself in town before now.

At least he knew why he'd had that uneasy feeling
about her from the first. He didn't want to accuse her if
she wasn't guilty, but he couldn't take a chance on her
innocence. Too much was at stake. At least now Texas
Timber had a face. *Misty Reynolds*. Devil or angel, he'd
make that final decision at some point. Sooner or later,
he'd find out why she was really in town. He hoped he
was mistaken about her, but he doubted it. Why else
would Texas Timber send her here?

Misty raised her voice. "Yes, Audrey. I understand
you're available 24/7. I am, too. I'll get you a detailed
report tomorrow morning. And I'll stay in touch. Good-
bye now." Misty disconnected and slipped the phone in
her pocket.

"Everything okay?" Trey pretended to know nothing about her call, but his mind was racing with everything he'd learned about her. Texas Timber must be keeping her on a short leash if she had to make herself available anytime day or night. Either that or what she was doing in Wildcat Bluff was vitally important to the company.

"Sorry. I had to take that call." She sat down at the table and took a sip of cider.

"Trouble?" He picked up his boots and socks before he sat down across from her.

"Not really. I'm on vacation, but some clients need to be reassured no matter what."

"Christmas can affect people that way." He rolled down the legs of his jeans. "You never said what you do for a living."

"Didn't I?"

"Is it stressful?"

"Not usually. I'm a troubleshooter. Corporate mostly."

"Sounds like interesting work." He pulled on his socks, not looking at her so he'd appear casual about his questions. But he jerked on his boots when he realized troubleshooter fit perfectly with a company harassing folks to get their land. That was the last thing he wanted to hear.

"It can be, but it's usually pretty boring." She drummed her fingertips on the tabletop. "Not interesting like your ranching or firefighting."

"Guess everything can get boring after a while."

"I apologize for—well, earlier. I'd like to make up for it another time."

"Sure. It's late anyway."

"Thanks. I really like your family and friends."

"They like you, too." He picked up his phone and slipped it into his back pocket.

"Storm is adorable."

"Stinker is what she is." He smiled fondly as he lifted his cup of cider to his mouth.

"Sydney is lovely, but sometimes she seems a little sad."

Trey took a drink, buying time. Misty was on a fishing expedition about his family. He'd give her what she could find out anywhere.

"Is it the holidays, do you think?"

"Partly, I guess. Sydney's husband died in Afghanistan. Several years ago now. Big loss for everybody."

"Oh, I'm so sorry. She must really miss him at Christmastime."

"She's got Storm to fill her life."

"I'm so glad." Misty smiled over the rim of her mug.

"Brock was one of a kind. Cowboy first. But he got a hankering to serve his country. He joined the U.S. Army and became a Ranger."

"Impressive."

Trey ran a hand through his hair. He missed Brock and felt it more than usual at Christmas. Misty had an angel's way of bringing out a man's pain and helping heal it. But she had a devil's way of using it to suit her own ends.

"Forgive me. I didn't mean to bring up sad memories." She reached out with her palm up.

He squeezed her hand, feeling the now familiar heat blaze a trail up his arm toward his heart, but he shut it down. He needed to know a whole lot more about her beside his physical response. "Why don't you come out to my ranch tomorrow?"

"Really?"

"We could make more plans for the benefit. And I'd like you to see how the other half lives."

"I've never seen a ranch. I'd enjoy it."

"Great." He could well imagine how much she'd like to see the ranch she was trying to hand over to Texas Timber.

"What time?"

"Will around eleven in the morning after my ranch work suit you?" First he'd boot up his laptop and find out more about her.

"That's fine."

"I'll cook a couple of buffalo steaks."

"Sounds delicious. I've never eaten bison. What do you want me to bring? Dessert?"

"Just your pretty self."

"I'm serious."

"So am I." He patted her hand before he got to his feet.

She stood up, too. "Really, I'm sorry about—"

"Don't be." He leaned down and pressed a quick kiss to her lips. "Gives me a good reason to get you out to the ranch."

"I'll need directions."

"Too tricky." He wanted her completely in his control tomorrow. By then, he might have a few questions to put to her. In any case, he wanted her to see what she was trying to destroy. "I'll pick you up."

"But—"

"No buts."

"All right. I wouldn't want to get lost."

"Not gonna happen."

She carried her mug in one hand as she walked over to the brick path. "Could we look around a little on your ranch? I'd like to see it."

"Sure." He shook his head at her request. She was digging her ditch a little deeper all the time. No doubt she wanted to reconnoiter for Texas Timber. Let her. She'd see Wildcat Ranch was getting along fine no matter how much was thrown at it. Maybe he could convince her—and Texas Timber—that he and his family would never sell their heritage.

"I'm excited about going to your ranch."

"I bet you'll like what you see."

She chuckled as she looked at him. "I already do."

Smiling, he joined her on the path. He tossed the dregs of his cider onto the dry grass as he considered Misty. She was good. He had to give her that. If he hadn't seen Texas Timber on her phone, he'd be about as far as he could get down the road she was leading him.

"Guess it's time to get some sleep before our big day tomorrow."

"Yeah." He caught her sweet scent and heard her soft breath before she turned and started up the path toward the house. Devil or angel?

He didn't give a damn. He still wanted her.

Chapter 22

MISTY SAT AT HER DESK IN TWIN OAKS THE NEXT DAY. She was open for business with her laptop ready, her cell phone nearby, and her mind in gear.

Sunlight warmed her suite, birds chirped outside, and soft quiet surrounded her. She reached to the side of her laptop and picked up the glass bluebird she'd bought at Adelia's Delights. She stroked the smooth contours, thinking about the warm and friendly and helpful people she'd met in Wildcat Bluff, before she set the bird back down on the desk.

She still felt a little high—truth be told, more than a little—from those exhilarating moments with Trey the night before.

She'd looked him up online. She'd learned as much from what wasn't there as what was there. No website for Wildcat Ranch. No Facebook. No Twitter. No anything else. He was mentioned in a few newspaper articles at benefits or other functions for Wildcat Bluff Fire-Rescue, but that was mostly it except for his string of impressive rodeo wins. He obviously didn't do social media, but she wasn't too surprised by that fact. He was a hands-on kind of guy.

And that thought set off a heat wave, earthquake, tsunami. She tingled all over with extreme body memory. She'd felt too hot since the moment he'd brought her to the brink, then nudged her over with masterful strokes. She wanted more, needed more, craved more. But she was a professional on a job and he was part of her investigation, so she was trying to be objective about him.

Yet she was feeling anything but objective with her thoughts swirling around him like a whirling dust devil. He was a package of pleasure waiting to be unwrapped for hours of decadent indulgence.

She needed to keep her mind on business. Cindi Lou was due a call and would definitely get her thoughts back in the right place. She picked up her cell and hit speed dial for her BFF.

"Misty, how is every little thing in your neck of the woods?" Cindi Lou asked when she answered the phone.

"Bumping along," Misty said automatically before she quickly put her thoughts in order. "Did Audrey call you?"

"You know it."

"She had bad timing last night. Interrupted me." Misty knew she sounded too abrupt, but couldn't seem to help it.

"Audrey's just getting antsy. What did she barge into?"

Misty felt a wave of heat roll over her as thoughts of Trey leaped to the surface. "Oh, well—"

"What's going on?"

"You saw my report, didn't you? I wrote and emailed it to Audrey this morning."

"Yep, I got my copy. Read it. Liked it. Filed it."

"Good."

"Audrey's a fine VP, but she's got Texas Timber brass breathing down her neck. They want an answer before the situation blows up in their faces."

"I'm only on my third day in Wildcat Bluff."

"She knows that. I know that. But do the big honchos care? They want their problem solved yesterday."

Misty sighed, knowing that was always the case. "I've gathered facts fast here because everyone is so kind and helpful."

"Not all. Somebody's a ringer."

"You're right. But I'll find that troublemaker."

"You always do. Now, Audrey said you sounded distracted or something. She'd waited to call at night when she thought you'd be free to talk longer."

"I wasn't free." Misty caught her breath on a sharp intake as little bursts of memory exploded in her mind— Trey's hot breath against her earlobe, soft kisses across her breasts, strong fingers raising her dress.

"Oh my." Cindi Lou's voice lowered intimately. "It's that hunky cowboy firefighter, isn't it?"

"He's helping me with my investigation." Misty tried to sound professional but knew she missed it by a long shot.

"Sure he is. Bet he's trying to discover if you buy your undies at Victoria's Secret or Walmart."

Misty couldn't help but chuckle. This was a good example of why she loved her BFF. Cindi Lou had a knack for getting quickly to the bottom line. "Honestly, he's like every dream guy you could ever imagine rolled into one big—"

"Orgasm?"

Misty laughed harder. "That's one way to put it."

"But is it the right way?"

"Yeah."

Cindi Lou chortled loudly over the phone. "This calls for a fresh Dr Pepper. Hang on a sec."

Misty heard her friend crack open a can and take a big swig.

Cindi Lou smacked her lips. "Darlin', I hate to be the one to break the news, but you've got it bad."

"Do not."

"This is Cindi Lou you're talking to. When did you ever let a guy get a peek at your undies in just a couple of days?"

"They've been intense days."

Cindi Lou laughed a big, booming sound of delight. "That makes a difference, how?"

"It just does."

"I knew it. First time you ever mentioned him, you had this kind of breathy tone to your voice that I've never heard you use before."

"I'd just fought a fire. I was having trouble breathing, if you must know."

Cindi Lou laughed harder. "Couldn't happen to a nicer gal."

"He could be involved in the fires. I mean, he is involved because Texas Timber is trying to buy his ranch."

"I read that in your report. You're trying to hang him with gossamer threads. I can't see it."

"I know it's a stretch to think he'd sabotage his own property to try and up the price, but I can't rule anybody out at this point."

"Take care not to throw the baby out with the bath." Cindi Lou slurped her drink. "I'm still waiting for that photo."

"Look him up online. There're some shots of him at rodeos."

"Yum." Cindi Lou smacked her lips. "Now, any chance he's a serial philanderer? I could do some in-depth research here."

"Not a chance. I'm seeing him on his home turf with his family and friends around him. He's true blue." Misty picked up the bluebird and held it up to the light, thinking of Trey. "Anyway, as soon as I nail the culprit, I'll be home and back to my real life."

"Misty, give it a chance. Remember, we talked about you enlarging your world." Cindi Lou grew quiet a moment. "You might actually be looking at love. Would that be so strange?"

"Trey and I were thrown together in dangerous situations, so we've experienced heightened emotions. That's all."

"My money's on love at first sight."

"That's a myth."

"Maybe. Maybe not."

Misty set down the bluebird. She needed to turn the page and move on. "You read about the animal oxygen kits benefit in my report, didn't you?"

"Great idea."

"Would you please go online, buy five kits, and overnight them anonymously to the Wildcat Bluff Fire-Rescue Station? I'll pay you back. This way they'll have a few oxygen kits in case of a fire between now and the benefit."

"You bet I'll do it. And you won't owe me a cent. It's my contribution to the cause."

"Thanks."

"How's the injured kitten?"

"I called the vet first thing this morning." Misty felt

sadness wash over her. "Sue Ann didn't sound too sure the kitty would make it."

"That's a crying shame."

"There's still plenty of hope."

"You better believe it." Cindi Lou grew quiet as if thinking. "When Trey picks you up later for that ranch tour, why don't you give him a break? Bless his heart, he's just a guy."

Misty chuckled, knowing folks never wanted to have "bless their heart" attached to their actions. But she took Cindi Lou's meaning, not simply for Trey but for herself, too. "Okay. I'll go easy on him."

"Atta gal! You go for it. Whoops, got a call on another line. Bidness beckons. Catch you later." And Cindi Lou clicked off.

Misty leaned back in her chair. She'd needed that talk. Cindi Lou always helped put life in perspective. But love? They both dealt in hard reality, so why had Cindi Lou taken off on this flight of fancy?

No way to know for sure. And Misty didn't want to explore that path. She simply needed to get her mind back on business.

After a sound night's sleep, she'd decided she'd better give the appearance of being on vacation to keep up her cover story. She'd taken a dip in the pool, breakfasted with Ruby, Charlene, and J.P., then she'd explained that she planned to nap and read in her room. They'd soon left to take care of business. Alone in the empty house, she'd quickly gotten down to her report and research.

She still wasn't done. She looked at the laptop screen, tapping the keys with a fingertip as she considered her next move. Clickety-clack and she found a website for

Wildcat Bluff. She scanned through basic information about the town and county with lists of Old Town businesses like Adelia's Delights. Christmas in the Country and Wild West Days each had their own page with colorful photos of folks having fun at various events. Wildcat Bluff Volunteer Fire-Rescue even had a website with a list of services, names of volunteers, and photos of the rigs.

Next she typed in "Wildcat Bluff Sentinel" and discovered a surprisingly good site. She scanned articles and read the most recent ones about the drought and fires, but she didn't learn much of anything new.

So far, her best information had come from meeting and talking with local folks and visiting actual sites. But she was still missing something important. She had to keep digging till she found the connecting thread that would pull her investigation together. And she had to do it soon, before another fire broke out.

She checked her sporty watch with the bright yellow band for the time. Trey would be here soon. She felt her heart rate speed up at just the thought of seeing him again. She didn't know how he could have such a strong effect on her. Cindi Lou's idea about love had to be the product of too many hours of reading her beloved romance novels. Despite her own denials, Misty wondered if Cindi Lou might be getting close to the truth.

For now, Misty was all dressed for her trip to Trey's ranch. When Ruby'd learned Misty was going there, she'd gotten excited and insisted Misty borrow a green-and-white striped Western-cut shirt with pearl-snap buttons and a hand-tooled leather belt. Misty had to admit those clothes paired with her own jeans looked just right for a ranch. She only had her athletic shoes to wear, but

they were better than flip-flops. She hoped Trey appreciated all the effort she and Ruby had put into Misty's visit
to his ranch.

She checked her watch again. Time to meet Trey
downstairs. She saved a file, closed her laptop, and
stood up. She didn't want to take a purse with her, but
she didn't want to leave her laptop or handbag easily
accessible either. Not that she expected trouble, but it
never hurt to be cautious on a job. She tucked her cell
and a lip gloss into her front pocket.

She walked over and pulled her smallest piece of
luggage out of the closet. She slid her laptop and purse
inside, and then locked the bag. She pushed it back in
the closet behind the bigger piece of luggage and below
the angel still under a towel. Not a perfect solution,
but definitely a deterrent. Finally she slipped the luggage key and her room key into her other front pocket.
A little bulky, but it was still better than toting around
a handbag.

Now she was all ready to meet Trey. She closed and
locked the door behind her. The house was still empty
except for her. She hoped Ruby was having a good day
and the Gladstones were finding lots of collectibles.
She walked downstairs, then into the breezeway. She
looked out the front sliding doors at the beautiful day.
Trey would most likely park in front of the garages, so
she'd wait for him on the swing where she could see him
drive up to the house.

She sat down and heard the swing squeak as she
settled down on the soft cotton cushion. She loved the
idea of the indoor swing and enjoyed pushing back and
forth with one foot as the swing swayed beneath her.

She glanced up and saw that Ruby had twined silver tinsel with a string of silk white poinsettias through the two chains that held the swing to the ceiling. Another Christmas touch that struck Misty—for the first time in so very long—as a beautiful reminder of the season. She didn't understand how it was possible, but Wildcat Bluff was having a healing effect on her in so many ways.

As she sat there, she looked out and saw Temple watching her from one of Big John's long branches. Temple closed his eyes in acknowledgment, so she did the same with him. He made her think of the injured kitten again. She wondered if Slim ever sold his barn cats. If the kitty made it, she could imagine taking him back to Dallas to share her apartment. He'd be a wonderful reminder of Wildcat Bluff. And he'd be a wonderful companion, too.

A movement on the road caused her to glance in that direction. She felt a little catch in her throat at the sight of Trey's pickup turning in and pulling up to the house. He opened the door and stepped down, looking spiffy in pressed jeans, a green shirt, and cowboy boots.

As he walked up to the house, she noticed he moved a little stiffly, as if his muscles were sore or he was controlling his actions or he was holding something back. If she hadn't been with him so much, she doubted she would have been aware of the difference. Maybe he'd taken a spill from his horse or strained his muscles. She hoped he was okay.

She quickly stood up, opened the sliding glass doors, and beckoned him inside.

When he walked up to her, he smiled with warmth in his eyes. "Did you go shopping? You look great."

"Thanks. Ruby loaned me the shirt and belt. I wanted to fit in at the ranch."

He gave a low whistle. "You look good enough to put under my Christmas tree."

She laughed, feeling happy. "Glad you approve."

"You missed one thing." He looked down at her shoes.

"Best I could do."

"I think we can do a little better for the ranch."

"Really?"

"I got you an early Christmas present."

"You didn't need to do that." She felt truly surprised and not sure how to respond to a gift from him.

"Come on." He gestured toward his truck. "I promised you a pair of boots, didn't I?"

"I thought that was a joke about my flip-flops."

"I keep my promises."

"You don't even know my size."

He glanced down at her feet. "We'll see if I guessed right."

She felt uncomfortable at the idea of him buying her such an expensive present. "I'll pay you back for the boots."

"Nope." He shook his head in denial. "If you need a reason, look on them as payment for helping stop that grass fire."

"I was happy to help."

He stepped close to her and lifted her chin with the tip of one finger. "Now, are you gonna accept those boots or get into deeper trouble with me?"

She felt as if she might drown in the depths of his hazel eyes. "What kind of trouble?" Those words fell out of her mouth in a kind of breathy wonder. She was shocked at the way he could bypass her brain. She quickly snapped her teeth together to stop any more wayward words from escaping her mouth. Yet she couldn't stop the heat that was once more engulfing her body.

He gently rubbed his thumb back and forth across her lower lip. "You want me to give that some thought or wing it?"

She quickly stepped back. "Tell you what, I bet I'll love those boots, but I want to give you a gift in return."

"If you don't like the style, you can exchange them at Gene's Boot Hospital."

"I saw that store in Old Town. It looked like shoe repair."

"That, too. Gene's has been around since the cattle drive days. Cowboys ordered new boots on the way up to Kansas and picked them up on their way back when they had money from the drive."

"But hospital?"

"If you were a hard-driving cowboy, you'd want the best repair you could get for boots that cost a season's wages, wouldn't you? Hospital sounds like the ticket to me."

"Makes sense when you put it that way." She glanced upstairs. "Hang on a minute. I've got something that just might suit you."

"We're burning daylight."

"I'll be quick."

She went back into the house and up the stairs into the kitchen that still smelled like delicious gingerbread. Later, she'd have fun helping Ruby bake cookies and hearing Charlene and J.P. tell funny tales about another day of hunting for the collectibles they'd managed to find in out-of-the-way places. She'd enjoy all of that, but she doubted it'd compare to spending time with Trey.

Misty unlocked the door to her suite, went inside, walked over to her desk, and picked up the Bluebird of Happiness. She hesitated, thinking about Cindi Lou. Maybe she shouldn't give the bluebird to Trey since she'd originally bought it for her BFF. But no, Cindi Lou would want her to give Trey a gift. Misty would simply buy another one at Adelia's Delights before she went back to Dallas. Now if the bluebird had been a case of Heritage Dr Pepper made with original cane sugar and bought at the Dr Pepper Museum in Waco, Cindi Lou would've put her foot down fast about sharing that gift. Misty chuckled at the idea. Nothing got between Cindi Lou and her Dr Pepper.

Misty wrapped the beautiful bluebird in tissue paper and tucked it back inside the Adelia's Delights holiday bag. It wasn't a gift with nearly the same value as cowboy boots, but the sentiment was worth a lot, and she would find Trey something else later.

She turned to leave, then glanced at the top of the dresser where she'd left the macramé necklace. Suddenly she didn't want to leave the Christmas angel lying there. Felt like bad luck. She quickly pulled the necklace over her head and headed downstairs.

When she stepped into the garden room, she saw Trey waiting for her near the sliding doors. She hesitated a moment to take him in. Tall, broad-shouldered, long-legged, muscular, smart, funny, tender—the list could go on and on.

"Ready to go?"

She nodded, feeling a little tingle of excitement.

"You just want your boots, don't you?" he teased with a mischievous glint in his eyes.

"What else?"

He chuckled as he slid open the doors and stepped back so she could leave before him. "I can think of better things."

She didn't say it, but he made her think of better things, too.

Chapter 23

MISTY PAUSED TO WAVE GOOD-BYE TO TEMPLE, WHO was surveying his domain from one of Big John's far-reaching limbs. When she looked around, Trey had already opened the door to his truck for her. She quickly walked over, settled onto the front seat, and set the blue-bird sack on the floor.

Trey moved around the front of the pickup and got inside. "You ready for your boots?" He started the engine and upped the AC.

She nodded in anticipation.

He reached behind his seat, picked up a big paper sack, and grinned at her as he set the bag on her lap.

She read "Gene's Boot Hospital" in an old-style Western typeface on the sack before she pulled out a large box. An illustration on the lid showed a rattle-snake biting a snake boot with the brand, "Nocona," in fancy letters.

"Go ahead and open." He chuckled. "It won't bite."

She laughed at his snake reference as she raised the lid and saw bright red boots with a turquoise wing design stitched across the toes and tops. "They're beautiful!"

"Thought they suited you."

She leaned over and gave him a quick kiss on his cheek. "Thank you. But they're much too expensive."

"Not for you." He pointed at the boots. "Nocona is a good old Texas brand. Enid Justin got the idea to start herself a cowboy boot company about 1925 in Nocona. That's a town not far from here."

"Clever lady." Misty stroked down the toe of one boot, feeling the smooth, taut leather.

"Cowgirls wear boots like those for rodeos."

"Think I'll just keep my feet on the ground."

He chuckled. "That'll work, too."

"Why are cowboy boots made like this?"

"Think stirrups." He pointed at the boot. "High heels won't slip. Leather soles won't snag. Pointed toes ease in and out. And a high shaft protects legs from brush and thorns."

"They look good, too."

He laughed. "Ranks right up there."

She joined his laughter.

"Why don't you see how they fit?"

She checked the size on the box. "You've got a fine eye. These are in my size range."

"Good start."

She set down the box and took off her athletic shoes. She tried to slide her right foot into a boot, but it didn't work. "Something's not right."

"Try putting your fingers through the loops on the top sides. Pull up on the boot at the same time you push down with your foot. You want it snug across the instep."

When she felt her foot slide home, she laughed out loud in triumph.

"Maybe we should've done this in the house where there's more room."

"It's perfect in a pickup." She pulled on the other boot, tossed her shoes in the box, and put it behind the seat.

"How do they feel?"

"Wonderful."

"Glad to hear it."

She picked up her sack from the floor and handed it to him. "And here's a gift for you."

He hefted the sack. "Kinda heavy." He put one hand in the bag, fiddled with tissue paper, and pulled out the bluebird. "Real fine." He held the bird up to the window so sunlight glimmered in the blue glass.

"Bluebird of Happiness," she said. "It's a symbol of good luck."

"Thanks." He gave her a lingering kiss on her lips. "I can use all the luck I can get."

She could tell he liked the bluebird, so she was pleased with both their gifts. Truth be told, she was more than pleased with her Nocona boots. They were absolutely stunning. She glanced down at her feet and admired the boots.

He carefully rewrapped the bluebird and set it inside the center console. "You all set for a cookout?"

"Can't wait to see your ranch."

He backed away from Twin Oaks, turned down the lane, and headed toward Wildcat Road.

Misty clasped her hands in her lap. Despite everything—the gift, the kiss, the words—something about Trey was different today. She'd noticed it when he'd first walked toward her today. Nothing obvious. Yet she'd become so attuned to him in such a short time that she couldn't help but be aware of it. She was also highly alert when she worked as a troubleshooter, so she focused on the smallest details. All in all, she felt a little uneasy.

She wished she'd driven her own car. She liked to

be able to come and go as she needed so she was completely independent. But this was Trey's show today and that meant she needed to accommodate him.

She didn't say anything. He was quiet, too. Normally their silences were comfortable, but not today. She felt a building tension and couldn't understand it. Maybe he didn't really want to buy her the boots but felt obligated to keep his word. Maybe he regretted inviting her to his ranch. Maybe he was simply too busy to take time for her. She stopped her thoughts. She could think of a million reasons not to be in this place at this moment. Bottom line, she needed and wanted to see the ranch and learn more from him.

From her high perch in the truck, she watched the countryside as Trey turned onto Wildcat Road. He drove south away from town. She pretended interest in the view, but she stayed vitally aware of him as she watched him handle the big truck with ease.

And he still remained quiet. Maybe he was turning into the strong, silent type. But she knew better. He had something on his mind.

He turned off onto a wide asphalt road with gravel shoulders. She recognized the area. She'd driven down this road when she'd been scouting Texas Timber's Christmas tree farms. Why would he bring her here?

On the right side of the road, barbwire fence enclosed open pasture where black cattle grazed on dried-out grass or stood in the shade of live oak trees. Everything looked as dry and dusty as ever. On the left side of the road, neat rows of cedar trees in size from seedlings to knee-high rose into the air.

"Came this way for a reason." Trey broke the silence

as he pointed to the left. "Christmas tree farm. Seen one before?"

"Not until the other day when I drove around this area."

"Texas Timber already harvested the bigger trees for the Christmas season."

"That's the company?"

He gave her a sidelong glance. "Ever hear of them?"

She hesitated, wanting to tell him everything. She couldn't completely trust him, so she remained silent.

"Christmas trees are big business, big money."

"I read an article about it online."

"Thirty-four million Christmas trees sold last year," he said.

"That's a lot."

"Takes a lot of land to grow them."

"Guess Texas makes sense for that business." She felt as if her new red boots were tightening every time he took her another step down this path.

"That's my land on the right."

"Beautiful."

"You can see the difference, can't you?"

"Yes." She took a deep breath. "But isn't there room for both types of use on all this land?"

"Sure is. But Texas Timber wants to buy my family's ranch and turn it from what you see on the right to what you see on the left."

"That'd be a shame."

"Glad you agree." He pointed right again. "Wildcat Ranch has been in my family for generations. Some of the land is still pristine, and it'll stay that way come hell or high water."

"I take it you don't plan to sell."

"Not in this lifetime."

"Makes sense. Why sell if you don't want or need to do it? Like you say, there's other land for tree farms."

"You sure?"

She felt a chill run through her body. Now they were getting down to what was bothering him. "Why wouldn't I be sure?"

"You've never heard of Texas Timber?"

She shrugged, not willing to commit to anything.

"I saw your website." He flicked his eyes toward her as he slowed his truck on the road. "Troubleshooter. Vague kind of business."

Now she really wished she'd driven her SUV. She felt her unease explode. He had her alone in his truck on a lonely road headed to his isolated ranch. And now she understood he was going to give her the third degree. But why his sudden distrust?

She felt her mind spin backward, desperately searching for something, anything that'd explain his abrupt change. And then her memory hooked, spun, and caught. In the gazebo, he'd reached her phone first and handed it to her. Could he have read "Texas Timber" in the millisecond before she'd grabbed her cell? Oh, yes. That'd explain why he was different today.

"Are you sure you're on vacation?" He stopped the truck and turned to focus on her. "I wouldn't want my family and friends upset or hurt."

"What are you trying to say?"

"I'm not beating about the bush."

"Do you think I'd deliberately hurt your friends and family?" She hated the idea that he'd even consider it.

"No, I don't." He ran a hand through his hair in frustration. "But somebody's causing trouble around here."

"Well, it's not me."

"But you're not what you seem, are you?"

She turned away from him, not wanting to see the accusation in his gaze. It'd all blown up in her face. She needed to come clean, but could she trust him enough to do it?

"Misty, help me out here. I need answers."

She took a deep breath and turned back to him. "I would never—not in a million years—do anything to jeopardize your loved ones."

He nodded, still searching her face as if trying to read deep into her very soul.

"If you won't believe me then—" She reached down and tried to tug off a cowboy boot. It stuck like glue.

"You're not giving back the boots."

"Trey, I'm not in a position to discuss—"

"What are you? And don't give me that vacation malarkey. I wasn't born yesterday."

She took a deep breath. She either trusted him or she didn't. She couldn't stay stuck on the fence. She glanced out the front window.

Smoke spiraled into the sky.

Chapter 24

"Smoke!" Misty pointed over Trey's shoulder, feeling her hand shake slightly from the strong emotions that were flooding her.

He frowned at her as he shook his head. "I'm not falling for that. We're going to get to the root of why you're here."

"I'm serious." She slipped her phone out of her pocket and hit speed dial for 9-1-1. Nothing. She tried again. No bars.

He gave her a narrow-eyed look before he whipped his head around to look out the window. "Oh, hell!"

"I'm trying to get help."

"Coverage is spotty here, if there's any at all." He hit the steering wheel with the flat of his hand. "Let's go see what we've got. Maybe I can contain it."

"You've got firefighter stuff?"

"Some. In back." He gunned the engine, and the truck rocketed toward the smoke.

Misty's pulse accelerated along with the pickup. She took slow, deep breaths. Somehow, she would handle this fire situation. She simply had to do it.

Trey hit the brakes hard, threw open his door, leaped from the truck, and ran a short distance down the road. He looked to the left toward the smoke, put his hands on his hips as if considering the danger, and then jogged back. He jerked open the back door on his side of the truck.

"How bad?"

"Not good." He grabbed a yellow firefighter jacket and matching pants. He quickly pulled them on over his regular clothes. He gestured toward the left side of the road where the smoke spiraled higher. "Texas Timber is going to lose acreage, no doubt about it. We've just got to make sure that fire doesn't jump to the ranch."

She glanced across the road at his land. "Oh, Trey, I'm so sorry." She pointed toward the right. "Now I see smoke on your side, too."

"What!" He swung around to look in that direction, then he turned back to her. "You know what this means, don't you?"

"We've got to get help." She punched 9-1-1 again. Still nothing.

"Misty, it means somebody started those fires. Two at once can't be an accident of nature."

"Like the house?"

"Yes." He fixed her with hazel eyes gone dark. "But it also means we were together when those fires were set, even if they smoldered for a bit before they got going good."

"And if we're together—" She felt her breath catch at the enormity of what he was telling her.

"Somebody else—"

"Not us."

He smiled, laugh lines fanning out from the corners of his eyes. "Here's what we're going to do."

"Do you have an extra fire extinguisher?"

"Forget it." He picked up a large red fire extinguisher with a black shoulder strap and set it on the ground. He pulled out another extinguisher and slung it by its strap over his shoulder.

"I want to help."

"Good. Take my truck back to Wildcat Road and drive toward town till you get coverage. When you reach 9-1-1, tell them where we are and to alert Kent and Sydney."

"Okay." She opened the door, stepped carefully down, and ran around the front of the pickup to him.

"After that, please go back to Twin Oaks."

"What?"

"You're not trained for these blazes. And remember your fire phobia."

"I helped before."

He tugged her gently against his chest and held her close a moment. Then he set her back. "I don't want you in danger."

"But I can help."

"If anything happened to you—"

"Nothing will."

"That's right, because you're leaving here." He twirled her around and nudged her toward the front seat. "No time for sass. Get going."

"Okay. I'm going, but only because somebody's got to reach Hedy at the station."

"That's my Misty." He slammed the back door, picked up the fire extinguisher from the ground, and slung it by its strap over his shoulder. He gave her a quick nod, then jogged toward the smoke.

She got in the truck and revved the big engine. She'd quickly come to like the height and power of a pickup. She made sure Trey was at a safe distance, then turned around and headed out. She drove with one hand on the steering wheel and one hand on the phone. She hit speed dial for 9-1-1 as she hurried down the road, but she still couldn't get coverage.

When she came to Wildcat Road, she spun the wheel one-handed to make the left turn and skidded toward the shoulder. She dropped her phone as she overcorrected in the other direction. Finally, she got the truck safely stopped on the side of the road. Good thing she wasn't in Dallas with all that traffic.

She felt the fast thud of her heart from the adrenaline that had kicked in, so she took several calming breaths. She had to be careful because Trey was depending on her alone to get help. She reached down, felt around on the floorboard, and finally found her cell wedged in a corner. She grabbed it and set up straight.

She hit 9-1-1 again. Still no response. She gunned the engine and tore down the road toward town, dialing over and over.

"Wildcat Bluff Emergency. How may I help you?"

"Hedy! Is that you?" Misty pulled to the side of the road and stopped the pickup so she could safely talk.

"Yes. Who is this?"

"Misty Reynolds. We've got a fire out here on either side of the road between Wildcat Ranch and a Texas Timber Christmas tree farm."

"Say again?" Hedy spoke in a calm, professional voice. "Fire on both sides of the road?"

"Yes. Trey's there now fighting the fire. He needs help. Please alert Kent and Sydney, too."

"I know the area. Alarm's gone out."

"Thank you." Misty felt deep relief. "He's alone."

"Not for long."

"I'm going back."

"Misty, you get out of there." Hedy's voice was no longer professional but filled with emotional concern. "We can handle it."

"The fire's on *both* sides of the road."

"Understood. But—"

"Thanks!"

Misty slumped against the seat and rubbed her forehead. She'd done it. Help was on the way. But she needed to do a little more before she went back to lend her support to Trey.

She called Audrey. No answer. She was probably in a meeting. Misty sent a text. "Fire at Christmas tree farm opposite Wildcat Ranch. Fire trucks on way. I'm at fire. GTG."

Next she hit speed dial for Cindi Lou, who quickly picked up.

"Tell me you've got him tied to his bedposts and you're just taking a break to spill all," Cindi Lou said in a sultry voice.

Despite the situation, Misty couldn't help but chuckle. "I wish."

"Shoot. What gives?"

"We've got a fire on the Texas Timber Christmas tree farm across from Wildcat Ranch."

"How bad?"

"There'll be loss but not total. Fire trucks are on their way."

"The hunk?"

"He's there now with a couple of fire extinguishers." Misty felt renewed urgency to return to the fires.

"That's like whistling in the wind."

"I've got to get back to him."

"Misty, you two take care. Hear now?"

"I hear you. Later." She broke the connection.

Misty had done her civic duty. Help was on its way. She could go back to Twin Oaks and nobody would blame her. But Wildcat Bluff was personal now, as well as professional. And now Trey was her trusted friend, as well as so much more. She wouldn't rest easy till he was safe.

She turned the truck around and headed back to the fire. She gunned the engine and heard the pickup respond with a deep growl. Reminded her of Trey. If he thought she'd run to safety and leave him to face danger alone, he didn't know her very well.

In the distance, smoke billowed up into the sky over the Christmas tree farm. It looked much worse than when she'd left a short time ago. Drought, heat, and a slight breeze were fanning the flames. She could smell burning cedar. Panic started to well up, but she batted it down. She wouldn't allow old feelings to overwhelm her. Not when Trey needed her.

As she turned off Wildcat Road, she slowed and reached behind the seat to grab Trey's firefighter parka. Between the parka and her boots, she'd have some protection when she helped him.

In her mind's eye, she saw a lone man in a firefighter jacket, desperately fighting to save lives and land. He was a larger-than-life hero.

Her hero.

Chapter 25

TREY'S TEMPER WAS HOTTER THAN A FOURTH OF JULY firecracker. He was sweating under the sun—part heat, part fury—as he sprayed pressurized water from the extinguisher along the far edge of the blaze. He had to get out ahead of the flames before they leaped the fence and raced toward a herd of Angus in the bone-dry pasture of Wildcat Ranch.

If he could get his hands on the culprits who were trying to burn down his family's ranch, there'd be hell to pay. Bad enough they'd tried to torch the ranch again, but they'd targeted virgin acres of the nearby Texas Timber Christmas tree farm, too. Made him mad as a Comanche who'd had a string of horses stolen in the dark of night. There was no going back. Just like the warrior who'd hunt down those thieves to the ends of the Earth to get back his prize herd, Trey would stalk these arsonists till he made sure they were brought to justice.

After the side-by-side fires and the heart-to-heart with Misty, he had to wonder if he'd been wearing his thinking cap backward. What if Misty was here to help, not hurt? What if Texas Timber wasn't trying to burn him out so he'd sell to them? What if some folks—or a single person—he'd never considered before were the culprits?

Trust was a fragile thing, but once it took hold, trust was strong and tenacious as barbwire. Misty was earning his trust in a big way. He might be a tad slow, but once he got the bit between his teeth he was hot on the trail. Now he was looking at the arsonists and their motives in a whole new way.

He could hear the crack and pop of cedar oil as fire spread through the trees behind him. A breeze caught the smoke from burning trees and blew it over him in a gray fog. He coughed to clear his lungs. If that wind got any stronger, his ranch would be vulnerable to fire jumping the road. But he didn't have the time or means to deal with both blazes, not with only two fire extinguishers. The tree farm had to wait for the rigs while he did what he could to control the flames licking toward his ranch's fence line on this side of the road.

As luck would have it, the culprits had been too lazy, or too stupid, to cross the barbwire fence and start the fire where it could do real damage fast. They'd focused on the shoulder of the road where the grass was short, sparse, and filled with gravel. Trey could smell gasoline and see an oily residue where liquid had been dumped on the ground. If he hadn't been here, the blaze would've taken hold and spread fast with the added accelerant and drought conditions. He hated to think about the destruction that would have happened on Wildcat Ranch.

Between the water extinguisher and the ABC dry chemical extinguisher, he hoped he had enough power in the cans to put out the fire before it broke loose. Cattle were vulnerable, but wild animals, too. Plus all the small ground critters like toads and snakes that could easily get caught in a fast-moving fire and not be able to escape.

Still, he was lucky. He'd arrived in the nick of time and the available fuel was limited so the burn was slower. Once more, Misty had proven herself to be his Christmas angel. If she hadn't wanted to see the ranch, they wouldn't have been on this road at this time of day. And they wouldn't have seen the fires.

As he sprayed with water, a flame escaped, blazed, and tried to claw its way up his leg. He stomped on the fire with his thick leather boot sole and drove the blaze into the ground. He stopped spraying while he beat back the flames near him with his tough cowboy boots.

If the fire managed to jump this fence, he had another plus in his favor. He'd baled hay last summer, although there was precious little good grass with the heat and drought this year. He'd even had to buy hay to make sure his cattle had enough food to last through the winter. Short, dry grass wouldn't provide as much fuel, so it'd burn fast but not as hot.

He continued to spray around the edges of the fire, wetting down an outer area of containment. He let the gasoline-soaked center burn as he moved inward with a wide spray that extinguished flames. Heat buffeted him. Smoke stung his nose and burned his eyes, but he ignored the sensations as he continued to douse the fire.

He aimed at another spot, but nothing came out of the extinguisher. He tried to coax a little more from the can, but he'd emptied his first fire extinguisher. He set it down on the road and picked up the can he'd saved for the gasoline-soaked area. He only had a limited amount of chemical, so he had to be smart about its use. He sprayed fine yellow powder over the center of the containment area to put out the remaining red-orange flames now surrounded by a blackened area.

He had the fire on the run, but it kept clawing back.

He hit the blazes with chemical and snuffed them out with his boots till finally the last of the fire fizzled and went out, leaving an area of blackened grass highlighted with yellow powder. He sighed in relief. He'd had just enough in the two cans to handle the blaze. For now, Wildcat Ranch was safe.

But he could feel heat from the tree fire behind him. He turned to survey the other side of the road. Not good. White smoke billowed upward from the burning saplings. Crackling and spitting sounds filled the air. If the fire hadn't been so deadly, it'd look beautiful. The fire jumped from one cedar to another to create a patchwork quilt of blazing bonfires across the tree farm.

Trey's jacket was made to repel heat and wick away inside moisture, but he was still sweating from the fire and exertion. He hoped the rigs got there soon. They had to stop that blaze fast before it spread out into the county or across the road to his ranch.

When he heard the deep growl of a truck, he grinned. Help had arrived just in time. He hung the fire extinguisher from a strap over one shoulder, then walked over and picked up the other empty can and slung it by the strap over his other shoulder.

He glanced down the road and felt his gut flip-flop. Misty had come back. He didn't want her anywhere near this danger. Even worse, she'd stopped in the middle of the road. She needed to either get out or get his pickup off the lane so apparatus could move in close to the fire.

He jogged toward her, pointing toward the ditch by the side of the road. His truck had enough clearance so it'd be no problem, but did she realize that? He kept gesturing as he neared her, looking toward Wildcat Road as he ran. If the rigs came barreling down the road, Misty would be planted smack-dab in the way. Last thing they needed was a crash or an impediment to stopping the fire in its tracks.

Finally, he saw her nod in understanding. She steered off the road, bounced over the ditch, and took out a line of saplings before she came to a stop. She turned off the engine, stepped down from the truck, and ran toward him.

He stopped, transfixed by the sight. She'd pulled on his yellow and orange Hi-Vis parka. As she ran, his jacket flared out around her like the wings of an angel — his Christmas angel.

Even so, he still wished she wasn't here. Sap in the cedars was exploding and sending out sparks as the blaze raced toward the bigger trees. Dense smoke was spiraling up and spreading out from where it covered the ground. He coughed to clear his lungs.

When she reached him, Trey wrapped an arm around her, not feeling much of her body because of their firefighter gear. Still, she was safe.

"I got hold of Hedy. Kent and Sydney are on their way."

"Great." He gestured toward his ranch. "Got that fire put out, but the other is—"

"Huge!" She stepped away from him, walked toward the tree farm, and then turned back, shaking her head. "That's dangerous."

"With the right equipment, it's containable."

"Good. How can I help?"

"Volunteers will be here soon. We'll get it under control. You can go on back to Twin Oaks."

"I want to help." She raised a foot. "See. I've even got boots this time."

He smiled, but he still shook his head. "So much smoke and fire can't be good for you."

"I'm better about it now."

"I can see that." He cleared his throat. "About Texas Timber—"

"First thing, let's save what we can of this tree farm. Then we talk."

"Okay." He kept an eye on the fire, wishing the apparatus would arrive. "Not much we can do right now but let it burn. No people or homes are in danger. As long as the wind doesn't come up, the ranch is safe."

She turned to face the fire. "It doesn't seem right to just stand here and watch those little trees burn."

"Yeah. Tell that to the arsonists."

She jerked her head around to look at him.

"I found gasoline on the ground."

"We've got to stop these fires." She walked down the road, looking from ground to fire and back again. "Can you tell where the fire started?"

He followed her, checking the fire's progress. "I'd say about in there." He pointed to a blackened area. "No fence on this side of the road so they could walk into the trees to start the blaze."

Misty kept on walking, glancing up and down. "Trey, look here!" She suddenly knelt on the road, pointing at the shoulder almost directly across from the burned area near his fence.

He jogged a few steps and knelt beside her. He saw a white tissue with a red smear that'd been pressed into the ground by a boot or animal or something.

"Could it be evidence?" Misty asked.

"Maybe. But anybody could've dropped that or tossed it out a car window anytime."

"Still, it's something. I'd like to pick it up, but I don't want to cause problems with an investigation."

"Let me handle it." He pulled his cell phone out of his back pocket, placed his foot near the tissue to indicate size, and took several pictures. He stepped back and shot a wider angle to show location. She took photos with her phone, too. He gently dislodged the tissue from the dirt and held it up by one edge with two fingers so she could get a better look.

"That's lipstick!" She pointed at the crimson smear on the white tissue. "It looks fresh, not dried out by the sun." She glanced up at his face. "Do you think our arsonist is a woman?"

"Let's not jump to conclusions. This might not have anything to do with the fire."

"True. But it's something to check out."

"You bet." He carefully eased the tissue into a big pocket. "I'll transfer it to a baggie."

"You've got some in the truck?"

"Yep. All the volunteers carry them just in case."

"Good idea."

A gust of wind sent smoke wafting toward them. Trey put an arm around her shoulders. "Let's get back to the pickup."

"Okay by me." She coughed, covering her mouth with her hand.

He didn't know if the tissue was evidence, but it was the first thing they'd found that might relate to the arsonists. And Misty had found it. He wasn't even surprised by this fact. She'd been good luck from the first. But now he wanted her where she was safe. She didn't need to be inhaling the smoke or fighting a fire. If she was a trained volunteer, he wouldn't feel so protective. On the other hand, maybe he'd feel the same need to keep her safe.

When they reached his truck, he laid the empty fire extinguishers on the back floorboard. He rummaged in a tackle box where he kept supplies and found the right size baggie. He eased the tissue out of his pocket, gently enclosed the evidence in the plastic bag, then wrote the date, time, and place with an indelible marker on the outside. Last, he put the baggie in the tackle box and shut the lid.

Now he had to focus on fighting the fire. He took off his cowboy boots and tossed them in beside the cans. He quickly pulled on his yellow waterproof firefighting boots and set his yellow fire helmet on his head. He grabbed a face mask and thick leather gloves, then stuck them in the pocket of his yellow jacket.

About that time, he heard sirens out on Wildcat Road. Fire-rescue was here. Now they could get this blaze stopped in its tracks.

"Sounds like the cavalry!" Misty pumped a fist in the air.

"Might as well be blowing a big brass bugle."

"And just in the nick of time."

"Thanks again for sounding the alarm."

"Any time." She glanced up at him with a smile on her face.

She looked good in his too-big parka, but he'd never known her to look any other way. Talk about fires. She knew how to light one in him by a single glance. But he pushed that thought aside for another time and place.

With siren shrieking, the new bright red booster turned off Wildcat Road and rocketed toward them. Trey heard the piercing sirens of the big engine back on the main road and headed their way. He hoped that'd be enough rigs, but they could call in more if necessary.

He gave a thumbs-up as the booster came to an abrupt stop in front of him. He ran around to the driver's side, jerked open the door, and grinned up at Sydney.

"What took you so long?"

Chapter 26

"Couldn't abandon my mani-pedi, now could I?" Sydney joked as she stepped down from the booster in full firefighter gear.

"Nope," Trey agreed. "I wouldn't want you to fight fire without your nails done. What would folks think?" He quickly matched his cousin's humorous coping mechanism that they'd all developed to deal with the tension, stress, and heightened emotions of fighting fires.

"Heaven forbid." Sydney glanced at the blazing tree farm, shook her head at the sight, and then nodded at Misty. "Looks like Trey's showing you another good time in Wildcat Bluff."

"He's just that kind of guy."

"Yep. Guess he thinks firefighting is a way to a gal's heart."

"I can grill a mean steak, too." Trey defended his abilities as he tried to suppress a grin at their antics.

"No wonder he's on the shelf at a young age." Sydney winked at Misty. "Think you can help him out?"

"Think he's worth it?" Misty asked.

Sydney cocked her head to one side as if seriously considering the idea. "Might need him for firefighting."

"Looks that way." Misty hooked a hand around Trey's arm. "Guess I better drag him off the shelf."

"Too late," Trey said. "I already jumped down." And to make his point, he jerked off his helmet and tossed it to the ground. He pulled Misty into an embrace, leaned her backward over one arm as if dipping in a dance, and gave her a kiss hot enough to make her toes curl.

When he raised her back up, he heard the sound of applause and whistles as the big red engine came to a stop behind the booster. He heard Misty's laughter as he made a quick bow to the volunteers and she dipped in a curtsey.

"Ladies and gentlemen, that's your entertainment for the day." Trey picked up his helmet, held it aloft, and then put it on his head. He figured that little stunt ought to have eased tension for the entire afternoon.

Now they needed to make plans before they engaged the fire. They'd been trained to never rush into a dangerous situation without preparation. He looked for Granny and Aunt Maybelline, but they must not have made this run. Most likely they were back at the café with Slade.

Kent, Morning Glory, and six other volunteers leaped from the engine wearing firefighter gear. They crowded around Trey since he was the acknowledged fire captain—first on the scene and by rotation.

"Hedy radioed we had two fronts." Kent looked at the fire, gave a loud groan, then glanced back at Trey. "But I only see one."

"We got lucky," Trey explained. "Caught the smaller fire on the right side of the road by Wildcat Ranch before it had time to spread. My two cans were enough to put it out."

"Lucky is right," Kent agreed. "And two at once can't be an accident."

"Nope." Trey pointed toward the burned area beside the road. "They used gasoline to prime the pump."

"Like the house?" Sydney asked.

"Same accelerant," Trey agreed. "But we don't know if we're looking at the same culprits."

"We'll get them," Misty said with determination.

Trey nodded as he smiled at her before he looked around the group. "More good news. We're looking at a Class A fire size, little to no wind, except for a few gusts now and then."

"That's good," Sydney said.

"Anybody who hasn't met my dance partner," Trey said with a smile, "this is Misty Reynolds. She helped me put out that grass fire on my property."

"She's Wildcat Bluff's Christmas angel." Kent raised Misty's hand high as if she were competing in a boxing match.

"Go Misty!" Morning Glory called. "With her on our side, we'll get this fire licked in no time."

"That's what we want," Trey agreed. "Now, let's use this road as our anchor point for fire suppression activity."

"Works for me," Sydney agreed.

"Misty, I'll make this plain so you'll understand what's going on around you."

"Thanks."

"Anchor point means we'll work from here to contain our wildland fire without the fire outflanking us." Trey glanced around the group. "Let's make a direct attack. Misty, that means we'll be wetting and smothering the fire and physically separating burning fuel from unburned fuel."

Misty nodded in understanding.

"Our objective is to make a fire line around the fire

that's to be suppressed. Namely, all those seedlings," Trey continued. "Everything inside that line can—and will—burn."

"Texas Timber is going to lose a lot of Christmas trees, aren't they?" Misty asked, sounding resigned.

"Nothing like they'd lose if this fire size goes from Class A to Class B," Sydney explained. "So far we're lucky as all get-out."

"True," Trey agreed. "Let's focus on what we've got. As far as an escape route in case the fire outflanks us, let's use this road. Doubt we'll have a problem with containment, but let's make this road the safety zone, too." Trey glanced around at the firefighters, who all nodded in agreement. "Don't think we'll need support from Montague, Grayson, or Fannin Counties, but I'm sure Hedy's got their fire-rescue on alert."

"And we'll radio Hedy if it turns out we need more of our own rigs and volunteers," Kent added.

"Right," Trey agreed. "For now, let's keep it simple." He glanced out across the burning section of the tree farm. "Birds have flown to safety by now. Most animals are probably long gone, but remember to keep an eye out in case some of the smaller ones have hunkered down on the outer perimeter."

"Nobody wants a skunk or rabid rabbit running up their pant leg for safety," Kent said with a chuckle. "Or a snake."

"Has that ever happened?" Misty asked in concern.

Kent shrugged. "Pays to be on the lookout for whatever may have gone to ground."

Trey could hear Hedy's voice in the background coming over the apparatus radios as she kept updates flowing to all parties involved in the fire. Out in the field, communications were doubly vital.

"Okay, firefighters," Trey said. "Let's get this show on the road. Sydney, why don't you pick a partner and take the booster and get out ahead of the fire. We'll make a running attack from here."

"Okay, Cuz." Sydney gestured toward a tall, hulking firefighter. "Jim Bob, let's pump and roll."

"Misty, we need your help, but not in the field," Trey said. "Will you take my truck down to Wildcat Road and head off any looky-loos who want to drive up here and get a closer view? Volunteers get through, but nobody else."

"How will I know the difference?"

"Ask to see their firefighter gear. That'll cull the wheat from the chaff," Sydney said. "I'll get you a flag from the booster."

"I'm happy to do it." Misty smiled at Trey.

"Highway patrol or sheriff deputy ought to be here to take over, but if they're on the far side of the county no telling when they can make it."

"I'll watch for them," Misty said.

"Appreciate it." Trey smiled at her. This way she'd be helping but not directly confronting the fire.

"Morning Glory, will you go with Misty to the truck?" Trey nodded toward his pickup. "There's a baggie in my tackle box that might contain evidence."

"That's big news," Morning Glory said.

He shrugged. "Don't count on it. But on the off chance it might be worth something, I'd like you to secure it in the engine and take it back to Hedy."

"Will do."

"Thanks." Trey glanced at his cousin. "Kent, we need some large hose lays out there from the engine."

"I'm on it," Kent said.

Trey turned back to Morning Glory. "Picks and shovels ready to dig ditches for containment?"

"Let's hope water works. It's too easy for fire to jump a ditch and waste our hard work."

Trey nodded in agreement. "Visual, radio, or vocal communications. Everybody got their portable radio?" He made a visual check to make sure all radios were on shoulders at head height for optimal use.

The volunteers nodded approval, squared shoulders, and focused intently on him.

"Okay, firefighters. Initial attack. Let's engage."

They leaped into action—all play and banter left behind as they went willingly into danger.

Trey stood at the center of activity on the road with smoke rising high into the sky. Sydney and Jim Bob boarded the booster with four-wheel drive and tore out across the edge of the conflagration. Morning Glory walked with Misty to Trey's pickup and quickly returned with the baggie. Kent motioned toward where he wanted the hoses. The other volunteers started forward laying hoses—two firefighters per line. Morning Glory stood ready to charge the hoses—to make water pressure available—as soon as lines were deployed at the fire.

Trey glanced down the road and saw Misty maneuver his pickup across the entry point. Soon she walked out where she could easily be seen on the side of the road, holding a bright yellow flag.

All appeared to be in order, so he stepped up and

sat down in the big engine. He keyed the mic. "Hedy, it's Trey."

"Say again," Hedy replied in a clear, calm voice.

"Initial attack is underway."

"Do you need additional rigs and firefighters?"

"Not yet."

"Stay safe."

"Always."

And that was that. Trey stepped down from the engine to keep watch and alert any firefighter who might unknowingly be getting into danger. So far, all looked to be by the book. The booster was already in place. The engine's lines were deployed. Morning Glory had charged hoses. When the first water gushed out onto the parched ground from the booster and engine, Trey raised a fist to the sky in triumph. Now they'd save the land and animals.

Time passed as the sun baked the ground—adding heat to the fire—and slowly moved from overhead toward the west. Trey spelled the other firefighters on the hoses so they could take a break and get a drink of cold water. Slowly but surely, they relentlessly tightened the noose of water around the conflagration until the fire had no place to go except burn itself out in the center of the tree farm.

Feeling a surge of triumph, Trey traded places with Kent, took off his helmet, grabbed a bottle of water, and poured half of the liquid over his sweaty face before he poured the rest down his dry and dusty throat. He put his helmet back on and glanced down at the end of the road. His pickup had been replaced by a DPS—affectionately known by some folks as the Dr Pepper Squad or technically correct as the Department of Public Safety—black-and-white Dodge Charger.

Vehicles had parked along the side of Wildcat Road. Folks were out taking photographs with cameras and smartphones. Misty stood talking with the trooper in his spiffy uniform. Trey felt a spurt of jealousy, but he pushed it down. No matter how many guys Misty talked to out there, she was soon going to be eating steaks with him.

He turned and walked back toward the fire. It was dwindling fast now. Little smoke in the sky. Few red-orange flames. Less stench. They'd done it. He clapped Kent on the back, and then stepped up into the engine again.

He keyed the mic. "Hedy, it's Trey."

"All still good to go?"

"Winding down."

"What I like to hear."

"We'll retract lines on the engine and send it home." He looked out the open door and saw the booster headed toward them. "We'll leave the booster to watch for hot spots."

"Sounds like a plan."

"Later."

Trey stepped down, feeling a great sense of relief as tiredness washed over him. What he wouldn't give for a hefty hunk of buffalo steak right about now. But he could wait. He wanted to share it with Misty.

He heard vehicle engines turning over and the crunch of tires down at the end of the road. Folks were heading out. The DPS car wheeled out with the trooper holding out a hand in good-bye to Misty. She waved at him before she turned to look toward Trey. She grinned and gave a thumbs-up in triumph. He replied in kind, thinking she looked mighty fine.

The booster roared up but stopped well away from the hoses. Sydney and Jim Bob leaped out. Black soot streaked their gear and faces. Trey knew he looked about the same. He held up his palm and gave them both a high five.

"Good job," he said, grinning at them. "You two up for staying here with the booster and watching for hot spots?"

"I live to serve." Sydney jerked off her helmet and ran a hand through her damp hair. "Storm's with Granny so I'm good to go."

"If she's staying I'm staying," Jim Bob agreed. "But I expect somebody to deliver up barbeque and Dr Peppers."

"Yum." Sydney laughed. "I'm so hungry I could chase a horse—"

"You're too tired to chase a horse, so don't even go there." Jim Bob winked at her. "Now I'm still in my prime after fighting a fire."

"Hah!" Sydney laughed as she walked toward the engine with Jim Bob right on her heels. "Got any cold water left?" she called. "We're all out."

"Have at it," Trey said as he glanced at Kent, who was retracting the engine's hoses. He stepped up and sat down in the engine's cab. He keyed the mic. "Hedy, it's Trey again."

"What's up?"

"Jim Bob and Sydney need barbeque and Dr Peppers brought out here pronto to the booster."

"Got it. Anybody else?"

"They're going home or back to the station."

"Good job."

"Thanks. See you later."

He keyed off the mic and leaned back against the seat. Another win. He couldn't ask for more.

He jumped down from the engine and looked toward the end of the road. Misty stood there all alone beside his truck, waiting for him.

He felt warmth expand in his chest.

Chapter 27

MISTY SETTLED ONTO THE FRONT SEAT OF TREY'S pickup while he stripped off his firefighter gear and stuffed it behind the driver's seat. She took a deep breath, exploring her physical reaction in the aftermath of the fire. She felt some tightness in her chest but not too much. She'd come through another fire much better than she could've anticipated before arriving in Wildcat Bluff.

Trey sat down on the driver's seat, heaved a big sigh, and looked over at her. "You okay?"

"Better question. How're you doing?"

He grinned, looking happy. "We won!" He held up his hand for a high five.

She grinned back at him, feeling a sudden lightness of heart, and hit his hand with the flat of her palm. She glanced back up the road at the booster and the few tendrils of smoke rising into the air. "Feels good to win."

"You bet. Now let's go home." He started the engine of his truck, backed up, and turned onto Wildcat Road.

"Why don't you take me to Twin Oaks? I don't want to put you out after the day we've had so far."

He glanced over with a mischievous glint in his eyes. "Are you trying to take away my reward?"

"More work isn't much of a reward." She didn't want him to feel obligated to show her around the ranch and cook dinner after fighting a fire. If she were in his boots, she'd just want to clean up and relax.

He reached over and tweaked the tip of her nose. "Don't you get it? You're my reward."

She just rolled her eyes at him. He knew exactly how to get under her skin and get what he wanted from her.

"That is—unless you're too tired or something to go." He sounded concerned as he flicked his gaze from the road toward her.

"I'm good to go just so long as you don't have me riding horses or walking miles across pasture."

He chuckled. "How about we take it easy? You can take a gander out your window as we drive up to the old home place."

"Sounds like a plan." She gestured toward the pasture behind the barbwire fence that enclosed his ranch land across from the tree farm. "Anyway, I've already seen some of it. Nice looking black cattle."

"Thanks."

"If you don't mind, I need to make a couple of texts."

"Texas Timber?"

"Yes." She didn't want to get into a deep discussion about her job or how it affected them right now. She just wanted a little time between worlds to catch her breath.

"Go ahead. There's time to talk later."

She felt as if he'd read her mind, but maybe he wasn't any more anxious than she was to get immediately back into their major problem. They'd won against fire again. Now was the time to take a few moments to enjoy their win.

She pulled her phone out of her pocket. She didn't need to say much. She just needed to reassure Audrey and Cindi Lou until she had time for a conversation. She sent both of them the same text, short and sweet. "Fire out. All well. Talk later."

Now she could really relax. She put her cell back in her pocket and looked out the window.

"Wildcat Ranch." She read aloud from a black wrought-iron sign that arched high over a cattle-guard in a stretch of barbwire fence.

"Home sweet home." Trey turned off Wildcat Road, drove under the sign, and headed up the gravel road.

"Beautiful." Now that she was on Trey's home turf, she wanted more than ever to learn about him. At first, she'd wanted to know for professional reasons, but that desire was now personal. After all they'd been through together, she felt she could ask and her questions wouldn't be rejected outright as coming from a Nosy Nellie.

"We like it here."

"We?"

"My family."

"Do you have brothers or sisters?" He'd never mentioned them, but maybe they lived in Dallas or somewhere else.

"I'm the only chick."

"Me too." She liked the fact they had that in common.

"If you're wondering, my parents aren't here." He glanced at her. "I think I mentioned I live in their guesthouse."

She nodded, feeling pleased that he was opening up to her. "Do y'all run the ranch together?"

"Yep." He hesitated, as if contemplating, before he continued. "I think that's part of why they're on a cruise right now."

"Isn't Christmas really important to everyone around here?"

"It is." He ran a hand through his thick hair. "They're making a point. They've always wanted to travel more and they deserve this vacation, but it's the timing."

"I'm lost." She turned from looking at the ranch to looking at him.

"It's kinda embarrassing."

"That's okay. You don't need to explain if you don't want to."

He slowed the pickup to a crawl. "Mom and Dad picked out a hill with a view of the Red River. I'm supposed to build my house there."

"You don't like the location?"

"I like it fine. But what would I do knocking around in a big, empty home?" He stopped and motioned at the land around him. "I'm taking on more of the job all the time. Soon it'll be mine."

"And that's bad?"

"No, that's good, too."

"I don't understand the problem."

"There's no way around it. They want me to see how it feels to be alone on the ranch at Christmas." He glanced at her and shook his head. "That's the only reason it makes sense for them to take off during the holidays."

"They want you to be lonely?"

"That's just it. They ought to know better. I've got all kinds of kin and friends around here."

"I still don't get it."

"Can you imagine being treated like a kid by your parents when you're a grown man?"

"I don't know." She just couldn't agree with him on this point. "I think it's kind of sweet. They're thinking about you being alone when they're gone."

"They've been saying things like that." He looked into the distance as if seeing something that wasn't there. "But they're a matched pair. You know, that's not so easy to find."

"They could be gone in the blink of an eye." She interrupted him, needing to get her point across quickly while she could still speak as her chest tightened and tears stung her eyes.

"Doubt it. We're a long-lived family."

"Sometimes accidents happen."

"What I'm trying to say is—"

"Oh, Trey, look. Buffalo!" She pointed at an area not too far away. She didn't want to think a moment more about losing parents before their time. She could smell the acrid scent of smoke in the truck and on him. She flashed back to the red-orange flames of the tree fire and the dense smoke spiraling up into the sky. And that started to take her where she didn't want to go—not now, not ever. She gripped the seat with both hands and stared hard at the buffalo.

"They're descended from a small bison herd saved by the Comanche. Mary Ann and Charles Goodnight—they were ranchers—saved a remnant of the southern herd, too. They were friends with Quanah Parker."

"Quanah Parker was famous, wasn't he?" Misty turned her thoughts to Aunt Camilla. She'd been a historian through and through, so she'd have loved seeing the buffalo and hearing Trey talk about the past.

"He was a Comanche chief. He was friends with

Teddy Roosevelt and took him hunting on the plains."
Trey cleared his throat and clenched the steering wheel.
"Sad time. Quanah was a war chief. He lost no battles.
In the end, he was given a choice between life and death
for the people he'd sworn to protect. He led them out of
Texas onto a reservation in Oklahoma to keep them as
safe as possible."

Misty felt Trey's deep sadness as if it were her
own. "I'm sorry. But at least some of the buffalo are
still here."

"Yeah." He glanced at her, smiling with an ironic
twist of his lips. "And Quanah left plenty of descendants. The Comanche still ride the plains."

"I'm glad." She considered Trey's dark hair and
bronze skin. "If you don't mind me asking, are you—"

"Yes. I'm not full-blood, but I'm proud of my
Comanche heritage."

"I would be, too."

He pointed at the buffalo. "Bison were the lifeblood
of the Comanche and other nations. Millions once
roamed the plains. Now bison are being turned to as a
good alternative to beef. Leaner meat. And tasty."

"I've never eaten it."

"You're in for a treat." He pointed northwest.
"You can see descendants of the Goodnight herd on
seven hundred acres at Caprock Canyon State Park in
the Panhandle."

"I'd like to see that sometime."

He reached over and clasped her hand. "Let me
know when."

She chuckled. "First things first. You promised food."

"You're right. Let's get this show on the road." He

gave her hand a squeeze before he took hold of the steering wheel again.

As Trey drove up a rise in the land, Misty saw a large gray brick and pale stone contemporary house with large windows and multiple rooflines covered by a shiny silver metal roof that overhung balconies and patios. Three dramatic square columns reached to the second-story peak. She could also see many outbuildings, including a big red barn, horse stables, corrals, and other structures that left her clueless.

Trey followed a circle drive around a dry stone fountain with a bronze statue of a buffalo with a wildcat on its back. He stopped in front of a four-car garage at the side of the house and turned off the engine.

"Sorry you won't get to see the original 1880s farmhouse. Mom spent a lot of time updating the place."

"What happened to it?"

"Fire."

"Oh no!"

"That's what got all of us so determined to make sure nobody else lost so much of their heritage."

"I understand. I really do. You have my complete sympathy."

"Thanks." He pointed at the house. "Anyway, they rebuilt for comfort and convenience."

"Beauty, too."

"Mom's doing." He opened his door. "Come on. If you want, I'll show you the house later. Right now, I want to get my firefighter gear out of the truck and get cleaned up."

She nodded, but she hardly heard him. She felt as if she was reeling back in time. Trey had lost his family heritage in a house fire. Yet he was so very lucky that was all he'd lost.

He opened her door and looked at her, concern in his hazel eyes. "You okay?"

"Yes, of course." She snapped out of her reverie and stepped down to the cement drive.

"Hang on a sec." He opened the back door on the driver's side of the pickup, hauled out his firefighter gear and the empty fire extinguishers, and shut the door. "I'll set this stuff in the garage till I get it cleaned up."

She watched as he unlocked the garage door, set everything inside, and relocked the garage. All his movements were mundane, and yet she never tired of watching him do anything.

"I'm glad you're here." He reached into the truck, pulled his bluebird out of the console, and shut the door. "Don't want to forget my gift." He put an arm around Misty's shoulders and tugged her close as he led her around the side of the garage.

"I doubt your parents would approve of me being here."

"Why would you say that?" He stopped and looked at her.

"Don't they want you to be alone?"

He chuckled as he clasped her hand and led her forward again. "You're exactly what they'd like to see here."

"But why?"

He grinned, laugh lines fanning out from the corners of his eyes as he teased her. "You'll figure it out."

She just shrugged as she glanced around the back of the house. "This is gorgeous."

"Thanks. You won't see the cats here right now. They hightailed it to the barn in protest at parental desertion."

"I'm sure they'll be back soon." She chuckled at the image as she looked at the property.

"If the weather changes from hot to cold, they'll be back so quick your head will spin."

"I take it they're warm-weather felines."

"Pampered is more like it."

She laughed with him as they walked together as if they'd done it a million times before that moment.

Right in the center of wide open spaces that allowed someone to take deep breaths and feel free was a large modified courtyard. A swimming pool made of pale stone with deep blue water nestled between the patio at the back of the house and a small octagon house with a wraparound covered balcony on the second floor. A stone walkway connected a pool house on one side and an outdoor kitchen in a gazebo on the other side of the swimming pool. All the roofs were made of shiny silver metal. Wooden patio furniture with white, green, and blue cushions made the area a perfect destination point.

"You like?" Trey asked.

"I think I could live out here."

He chuckled. "It might get a bit chilly when real winter gets here."

"But it's perfect right now."

He put an arm around her waist. "Even if it gets cold, I know how to keep us warm."

She laughed as she leaned against him, already feeling hotter just because of his presence. But she wouldn't admit it, not when she could tease him. "I see a fire pit over there. Is that what you mean?"

"Not even close." He rubbed circles on her back with one hand. "I'd kiss you if I wasn't so dirty."

"What's a little dirt between friends?" She pushed her fingers into his thick hair and pulled his head down toward her.

"Misty, you're playing with fire."

"I hope so." She pressed her lips to his mouth, toyed with the tip of her tongue, but lost control when he jerked her against his warm, damp chest.

"You're driving me crazy." He deepened the kiss as he thrust into her mouth to tease and torment at his leisure.

Heat spiraled outward from her center, setting her ablaze. She felt languid, as if his body heat, his intense desire, the touch of his hands were turning her into a molten pool of desire—a wantonness that began and ended with him. How had she ever lived without him?

Abruptly, he stopped the kiss, put his hands on her shoulders, and stepped back. "You're making me forget my good intentions."

"And they are?" She felt bruised, as if she were so sensitive in every part of her body that the slightest touch, even a gentle breeze, would be too much to bear. She put a fingertip to her lips and felt the swelling that he'd caused with his tantalizing kiss. He'd marked her. That thought caused her to shiver with anticipation of what else he might do with her.

"I'm not even gonna talk about good or bad intentions. That could get us both into trouble."

"What kind of trouble?"

"Not another word." He grabbed her hand and started walking alongside the swimming pool.

He skirted a long planter with a row of evergreen shrubs that provided privacy for the guest residence made of brick and stone that matched the main house. He stopped in front of double pale oak doors with square, steel contemporary hinges and door handles set in the center of a wide swath of floor-to-ceiling windows. He threw open the doors.

"Welcome to my home." He gave her a mischievous look, tugged her inside, and planted a hot kiss on her lips.

"It's lovely here." She glanced around, then back at him. He'd become north on her personal compass, for her attention always strayed back to him.

"Make yourself at home. If you want to freshen up, there's a half bath over there." He gestured at a closed door. "I'll run upstairs, grab a shower, and be back real quick."

"Don't hurry on my account."

"That's exactly why I'll hurry." He headed for the oak staircase set against a wall of stone near the entrance, then turned back. "Almost forgot." He took long strides over to the bar in the kitchen, tugged the bluebird out of its sack, and proudly set it on the bar. He crushed the sack and tossed it in the trash.

She watched as he took the stairs two at a time with his long, strong legs. When he disappeared from sight, she turned to focus on the open floor plan of his beautiful home. She looked up at the high ceiling in the octagon shape of the outside. Wood slats filled the ceiling between exposed beams, and a contemporary steel ceiling fan hung from the center. The walls were gray brick with floor-to-ceiling windows framed with pale oak. A cordovan leather sectional couch sat on a colorful geometric pattern area rug that covered a wood floor in the center of the room.

Everything in the house looked so lovely that she decided to take off her dusty red boots and leave them by the front door so as not to track dirt into his home. She leaned against a wall, tugged off her boots and socks, and set them in a corner. Then she ventured deeper onto the house.

On one side was a kitchen fronted by a long wooden bar with a black-and-gray granite countertop and stainless bar stools covered with black-and-white cowhide. Oak cabinets and stainless steel appliances finished off the area. Across from the kitchen rose a large natural rock fireplace with a simple oak mantel. A single Christmas stocking that appeared to have been knitted by hand of red and green yarn hung by its lonesome in the center of the mantel. In one corner of the expanse of windows across the back wall rose a cedar tree trimmed with vintage glass ornaments and a blond angel on top.

Misty adored his home—classy and warm and inviting all at the same time. She decided to clean up a bit in the powder room. As she walked over to the door under the staircase, she decided she'd never again leave home without her handbag. Of all the times when she could have used so much that she normally carried, she had nothing except her lip gloss. It'd just have to do.

She opened the door and closed it behind her. Another beautiful room with oak cabinets and a black-and-gray granite countertop accented with a stainless steel sink, large mirror framed in oak, and a crystal and steel vanity light above the mirror. Red-and-green fingertip towels with Frosty the Snowman were laid out for seasonal fun.

She selected a cabinet and found an unopened tooth-brush and toothpaste, as well as a small comb and brush. Thank goodness for planning ahead for guests. She quickly took advantage of all the amenities, washing and brushing till she felt more her usual self. She glanced in the mirror and added a little lip gloss. She didn't need any color in her cheeks because they were pink from the exertions of the day or simply the nearness of Trey.

She walked out, feeling much more refreshed after everything. She could hear the shower running upstairs and knew Trey would soon be down to join her. She stopped in front of the wall of windows and looked out over the ranch. She could see a red ribbon in the distance that must surely be the Red River. It was a beautiful, peaceful sight.

She stepped from there to the Christmas tree. She reached out and touched one of the ornaments. The red-and-green swirls looked familiar. She looked closer and felt her breath catch in her throat as emotions started to rise. She'd had a Christmas ornament just like this one so very long ago. Tears stung her eyes. She felt her breath catch in her throat. She smelled smoke.

Misty whirled around and put her back to the tree. But it was too late. Everything had been too much for too long. And it'd finally caught up with her. She didn't want to be here, not now, not when she suddenly felt so fragile. She needed to be alone so she could recover in privacy. But it was too late.

She stumbled blindly to the couch with her eyes filled by tears, no longer seeing the room. Memories were crowding in on her, overwhelming the present. She'd held them so long at bay. She'd been so careful. She'd never allowed herself too much of anything. Aunt Cami had understood. They'd carefully negotiated the perils of Christmas.

But now Trey and Wildcat Bluff had pushed past her defenses, knocked down her carefully constructed walls, and lured her into wanting more than she ever had before.

Tears streamed down her cheeks as she curled into a small ball on the couch, hoping against hope that she could have her cry out before Trey came back downstairs. She desperately didn't want him to see her true self instead of the person she'd presented to him.

Above all, she wanted to flee.

Chapter 28

TREY BOUNDED DOWN THE STAIRS. HE'D SHOWERED OFF the stink and dirt of the fire. Fortunately, he hadn't sustained any injuries. He'd pulled on a Frosty the Snowman T-shirt, comfortable jeans, and leather loafers. He felt good. And he was all set to enjoy Misty's company.

"You ready for some good home cooking?" he called as he came down the stairs.

When she didn't respond, he chuckled. "Not afraid of my ability as a chef, are you?"

Still no response. His mood abruptly shifted. Had she left? She could've hiked down to Wildcat Road and walked or hitchhiked back to town. But why? Everything was good between them, as far as he knew. Maybe a few kinks to iron out, but he wanted to tackle Texas Timber on a full stomach. Maybe she was outside looking around the property or petting a horse down at the stables.

But he felt uneasy. Something wasn't right.

When he heard glass break near the Christmas tree, he glanced over there. Misty was by the tree, looking small and alone. Why wasn't she sitting on the comfortable couch or rooting around in his refrigerator looking for food and drink?

"Misty?" He quickly strode over to her.

"I'm sorry." She sat with her head bowed and legs crossed under her.

"Why are you sorry?" He knelt beside her.

"I smashed your tree ornament." She held out her hand, palm up where broken glass mixed with blood. Most of the ornament lay in pieces on the floor.

"Misty!" He reached for her hand, but she snatched it back.

"Not fair. It'd hung there, hadn't it? Christmas after Christmas after Christmas."

"Yes. It was a bit of our family heritage left. Our oldest ornaments were with Kent's parents when the fire broke out."

"I just couldn't stand the memories." She looked up, revealing tear-filled green eyes and moist cheeks.

He felt his breath catch at the pain etched on her face. He hurt for her, not only for her abused hand but for her obvious deep torment. This time he didn't take no for an answer. He raised her hand, turned it palm up, and flicked pieces of glass onto the floor beside the broken ornament. Fortunately, the cuts on her palm looked minor, but the glass was sharp and her injuries could've been worse.

"I'm so sorry to have caused you to lose more of your past."

"I don't care about the Christmas ornament. That's an old memory." He reached down and gently lifted her to her feet. "I care about you. We can make new memories."

"You'd better take me to Twin Oaks. I'm not fit company."

"I'll do no such thing."

"And I'll pay to replace what I broke."

"Forget it."

He led her over to the couch and set her gently down

in the corner near the fireplace. When she trembled, he pulled a Frosty the Snowman throw off one edge of the sofa and spread the soft cotton over her lap and legs.

"Stay right there."

He walked over to the kitchen and grabbed the small medical kit he kept handy near a fire extinguisher. He went back, set his kit on the large cedar coffee table, and sat down beside her.

"I'd like to clean your wounds now." He kept his voice soft and low so as to comfort her. "Is that okay with you?"

"If you'll take me to Twin Oaks, I'll be fine."

"Remember, I'm your personal paramedic. If you get an infection on my watch, you know I'll never hear the last of it from my cousins."

She sighed. "Okay, get it over with." She placed her hand, palm up, on his thigh.

He knew he had to go as gently with her psyche as with her hand. He couldn't help but think her reaction to the ornament was somehow related to her reaction to the first fire. "I'll use hydrogen peroxide to clean the wounds. If you feel any discomfort let me know."

She made an irritated sound in the back of her throat. "Pain. That's what you mean. I don't need to be mollycoddled with you substituting 'discomfort' for 'pain.'"

That was a good sign. He needed her strong to heal. But he still had to proceed with caution. "Misty, why don't you share what's troubling you while I see to your wounds?" He opened the medical kit, hoping his physical actions would distract her mind and free up the memories underneath.

"I'm not troubled."

He silently kicked himself. He knew better than to be so direct. He'd used the wrong word and lost her. He pretended like he hadn't heard her while he set out cotton swabs and the small bottle of peroxide.

"Anyway, you don't want to hear about me."

Good. She was reaching out to him. He'd learned that was the way it worked with folks. If you reached out, they pulled back. If you pulled back, they reached out. Automatic human reactions. "You were a good listener when I talked about my parents being gone for the holidays. Helped me see why they'd do it."

"They must love you a great deal."

"Yep." He gently cleaned her palm but remained quiet to draw her out.

"I'm already embarrassed enough. Everybody in Wildcat Bluff is so strong. And now—"

"You fit right in with us."

She wiped away moisture beneath her eyes with one hand, not agreeing or disagreeing.

He gave her time like he would any wounded one. He used tweezers to gently pull out several small glass shards in her skin, and then quickly finished with hydrogen peroxide to disinfect.

She hissed on a breath and winced at his touch.

"I'm being as gentle as I can." Fortunately, her cuts weren't deep, but they could be painful.

"It's okay."

"I hope you know you can trust me. Anything you say won't go beyond my ears."

"I'm usually fine." She clenched her injured hand, moaned, and quickly released her fist.

"Hurt?"

"Not bad."

"Good." He gently applied antibiotic cream over the cuts before he covered her palm with a bandage. "All done."

She withdrew her hand as she glanced out the windows. "Everything that's been going on in Wildcat Bluff since I got here has pushed all my buttons."

"It can happen."

"But not to me. I'm cautious."

"Sometimes cautious can set us up for a fall."

She looked back at him, a puzzled expression in her vivid green eyes. "Really?"

"Early on I learned that if I focused on something like 'I won't fall off the back of a horse' that'd be the first thing I did. 'Course I never thought that till I fell the first time. Hurt my pride more than my backside."

She smiled at him, a little twitch of one corner of her mouth.

"I know. Hard to believe a horse got the best of me." He returned her smile, feeling relieved she was listening to him. Now if he could find a way to put together the right words to help her.

"I'd like to meet that horse."

"My lips are sealed. So are the horse's." He was rewarded with a bigger smile. "Anyway, seems like the more I try to avoid something the more it comes after me."

"Maybe like attracts like?"

"Yeah. And maybe if you take your eye off the current ball to watch a past ball, you lose your focus."

"I see." She nodded as she stared at the Christmas tree. "When I was twelve, my family's house caught on fire." She wrapped both arms around her chest as she sat stiffly upright.

"Oh, Misty, no."

He couldn't stand to see her look so alone. She must have sealed off a part of herself a long time ago. He wouldn't let her stay that way, not when he could do something about it. He put an arm around her shoulders and pulled her against his chest, drawing the throw up over them both. He rubbed his palm up and down her back for comfort.

She remained stiff for a long moment, and then she snuggled against him and laid her head on his chest.

"It happened early one Christmas morning," she said in a soft, almost childlike voice. "Still dark out. I was sound asleep. I'd been awake late because I'd been too excited to sleep." She glanced up at Trey, as if making sure he was still with her.

"I'm here. You're safe." He spoke softly and gently as he watched tears spill from her too-bright eyes and roll down her too-pink cheeks. She seemed unaware, so he caught her tears with his fingertips as his heart went out to her.

"Safe and sound." She glanced around the room before she refocused on him. "Daddy woke me. I smelled smoke. It burned my eyes. He carried me out through the living room. Our Christmas tree was full of lights. I wondered why the pretty lights were on so early. That's when I realized the tree was on fire."

Trey held Misty tighter as she clung to him. He felt her tears hot and damp against his skin. All he could do was provide a safe place for her to share her grief, but he wanted to do so much more. He wanted to go back in time and stop the fire before it had caused so much damage.

"Daddy pushed me out the front door. I didn't want to leave him. I wanted Mommy. He told me to run next door. He'd get Mommy."

Misty suddenly shoved away from Trey, tossed aside the blanket, and stood up. She paced over to the Christmas tree, as if hardly able to contain her energy, and pointed at it. "You must be careful of the cords, the electrical outlets. You can't overload or anything that might cause a fire." She glanced back at him. "Did you check?"

"I'm careful."

"Good." She wrapped her arms around her chest once more and stood a little straighter. "I never saw my parents alive again. Firefighters tried hard to save them, but it was too late."

"Misty, I'm so sorry."

"Thank you." She dropped her hands to her sides and whirled to look out the window.

He couldn't have been more proud of her. She had the courage of a lioness to relive and overcome a terrible personal loss. He felt honored that she'd allowed him to be part of this moment in her life. He'd known she was smart and strong and beautiful from the first moment their lives had come together on Wildcat Road. Now he knew she'd captured his heart.

He got up and joined her at the window. He gently wrapped an arm around her shoulders. "What happened to you afterward?"

"Aunt Camilla took me in. She was single with no children, but she couldn't have been better. We did everything together. She was a history teacher. I know you two would've liked each other."

"She's gone?"

"Way too soon. Cancer."

"I'm sorry." He hesitated to push Misty's memories any more, but he figured there might be a little more for her to recognize and release. "How did you two handle Christmas?"

"You guessed, didn't you?"

"What do you mean?"

"We avoided it. She'd lost her brother. I'd lost my parents. Instead, we celebrated Winter Solstice."

"A good compromise. But—"

"Maybe not so healthy in the long run."

"I wouldn't say that. You both did what you needed to do. Never doubt it."

"You're right." Misty stepped away from him and put a hand against the window as she gazed out at the Red River. "So wonderful here." She turned back and looked him up and down. "Just like you."

He didn't know if he felt so wonderful. He felt like he'd roped a buffalo and been hanging on for dear life. One slip and he could've lost Misty.

She slowly lifted her macramé necklace, kissed the angel pendant, and took the few steps back to him.

He stood very still, not knowing what to expect.

She lifted the necklace, dropped it over his head, and let the angel nestle against his chest. She tapped it with the tip of one finger, and then glanced up at his face. "You're my Christmas angel."

He smiled, feeling a warm glow deep inside. She'd come out on the side of the angels, strong and whole and beautiful.

"And I want you. *Now*."

Chapter 29

When Trey gave Misty a tender kiss, she felt like Sleeping Beauty being awakened from a long sleep by Prince Charming. Perhaps she was romanticizing Trey, but when he swept her into his arms, she thought perhaps she was right.

He quickly carried her upstairs to his big, airy bedroom. A king-size bed with crimson bedspread and forest-green throw pillows dominated the room. Across from the bed, a huge flat-screen television hung from the brick wall between floor-to-ceiling windows with sheer white drapes that muted the afternoon sunlight. A contemporary steel ceiling fan lazily circulated cinnamon-scented air. Two partially open doors led to a bathroom and walk-in closet.

He gently set her down on the bench at the foot of his bed. He stepped back, cocked his head to one side, and looked at her.

She felt exposed to his scrutiny. After everything she'd revealed to him, she suddenly felt vulnerable. She crossed her legs.

"You've been through a lot." He put his hands on his narrow hips. "Tell you what." He walked over and pulled open the door to his bathroom. "A soothing bubble bath ought to be about right."

"But Trey—"

"That's only item number one on my list for you."

He grinned at her, a mischievous light in his eyes. "I'll run downstairs and open a bottle of Slade's muscadine wine."

"He makes wine, too?" Now that she thought about it, she could easily imagine the big cowboy making wine along with his chili.

"He's got a fine little vineyard on his ranch."

"I'd like to try his wine."

"It's good." He stepped into the bathroom and soon the sound of water gushing into a tub filled the bedroom.

Now that the euphoria of releasing so much so quickly was passing, Misty felt tiredness creeping up on her despite her desire for Trey. She wasn't used to being pampered, but for now everything about it felt exactly right.

He walked back into the bedroom. "You've got lavender bubble bath. Mom swears by it."

"I like it, too. But why does she keep it here?"

"Guess she anticipated you." He chuckled as he left the room.

Misty heard him head down the stairs. She felt as if her life had been turned upside down. Maybe she'd inadvertently stepped from contemporary Texas into the Comancheria. She rubbed her forehead at the fanciful thought. Maybe she'd better simply get a bath and go with the flow. Plenty of time to figure out the ins and outs of her situation later.

She pulled her cell phone out of her pocket and checked for messages. "Yay!" from Cindi Lou. "Good news," from Audrey. And that was that, at least for the moment.

Misty set her phone, keys, and lip gloss on Trey's

dresser. She quickly stripped, folded her clothes, and set them on the bench.

She looked at Trey's bathroom. It was just as luxurious as she would've imagined after seeing the rest of his home. Wood, marble, glass, mirror, and chrome in warm russet and cream colors. Two sinks, one shower, toilet, and a jetted tub. The sweet scent of lavender filled the air. She was truly in heaven—as only befitted a Christmas angel. She laughed at her own thought.

She stepped into the bathtub, parting thick, white bubbles as she sank into the water and sat down on the smooth surface. Fragrant bubbles soon covered her from chin to toes. She smiled as she leaned her head back against the tub. She didn't know when she'd felt so happy with anticipation. Yes, she did know. She hadn't felt this way since that early Christmas morning before the fire. She examined her feelings. She felt lighter—definitely lighter—as if she'd released a heavy burden that she hadn't known she'd carried with her all this time.

Trey's gift to her. Not just for Christmas, but forever. She felt her body fill with such raw emotion that it swept her breath away. Could Trey have so quickly and easily captured her heart? She blinked at the momentousness of the thought. If the answer turned out to be "yes," would he give his own heart in return?

She closed her eyes, letting thoughts of Trey wash over her. Cowboy and firefighter. Tough and tender. Naughty and nice. She couldn't imagine wanting anything more as she let images of Trey overtake her.

She didn't realize she'd drifted off to sleep till she heard a knock on the closed bathroom door. She blinked and glanced around in surprise. Everything came tumbling back. And she felt amazingly good. Good enough, in fact, to feel excited by Trey's presence while she wore nothing but her birthday suit.

"You decent?" Trey called.

"I'm wearing bubbles, if that's what you mean," she teased in a come-hither tone of voice.

"Something I've got to see." He opened the door and stepped inside, carrying a mug in each hand.

"Yum." And she didn't mean the drinks. He looked and smelled good enough to taste, what with all his rugged masculinity on display.

"Wait till you taste test."

"Can't wait." She stroked him with her gaze, from his still damp hair to his T-shirt to his tight jeans. Somewhere along the way, he'd kicked off his shoes. He had nice feet, long-toed and high-arched, although she'd probably never say that to his face unless she wanted to tease him.

He handed her a red mug imprinted with "Merry Christmas" in fancy gold lettering. He had another matching mug in green. He sat down and held his mug out to her. "Here's to my Christmas angel."

She clinked her mug against his own. "And here's to *my* Christmas angel."

They laughed together, and then each took a sip, watching the other over the rim of their mugs.

"Oh, that's wonderful. Sweet and tart." Misty smacked her lips and took another sip. "Slade can certainly cook and brew."

Trey chuckled. "That's how he gets all the girls."

"I thought that was bull riding."

"Thing of the past."

"I guess there are a lot of things that belong in the past." She gazed thoughtfully at the deep crimson color of her wine. "You're right."

"I am?"

She glanced up at him. "I needed to let go of my painful past. Maybe I was clinging to it because that was all I had left of my parents."

"You can still cherish their memory."

"Yes, I understand that now." She held out her mug toward him. "Thank you."

"Glad I could help." He gently touched her mug with his own. "Is this a promise to start anew?"

"Me? You?"

"Us."

"There's us?" She shivered in excitement at the thought, so she took a gulp of wine to warm her body.

"There better be." He put his hand in her bathwater. "Cold. You should've told me." He quickly set his mug on the countertop and stood up. "I don't want you to get a chill. That's speaking as a paramedic."

She chuckled as she set her mug on the corner ledge of the big bath, knowing he was making excuses now.

"Let me warm you." He grinned as he unfolded a big red bath towel with reindeer prancing along one edge. He held it up and out in front of his face and body. "Come on. Don't lollygag."

"You wouldn't take advantage, would you?"

"Me?"

"You're audacious." She quickly stepped from the tub before he decided to peek and grabbed for the towel.

"Did you say bodacious?" He wrapped the towel around her body as he pulled her against his hard chest.

"You want to give an audacious, bodacious cowboy plenty of time to take advantage."

She couldn't help but laugh at his teasing ways, but he'd sent her temperature soaring at the very touch of his hot body.

"Best dry you so you don't catch a cold." He held her still with one hand as he rubbed the towel up and down her back, moving lower and lower in an exaggerated erotic pattern.

"Little chance of that." She felt a sizzle all over as he sensitized her bare skin with the rough towel, setting her nerve endings on fire. He cupped her butt with both hands, pulled her forward, and pressed his hardness against the most sensitive part of her. She moaned, desperate for the feel of his hard hands on her soft skin. She struggled to get free of the towel so she could touch him, needing to feel his skin under her fingers.

"Not yet," he whispered with warm breath against her ear. He wrapped the towel tighter and pinned her arms to her sides. "You're all mine now." And he pressed a soft kiss to the corner of her mouth before he continued to tease with the tip of his hot, moist tongue before he nipped and sucked her lower lip till she struggled in mounting urgency and frustration.

She returned his kiss with a desperation that he stoked with each touch of his lips, his tongue, his breath. When he finally thrust into her mouth, she groaned and kissed him back with so much fervor that he pulled the towel tighter and tighter, as if binding her to him for all eternity. He kissed her long and hard and hot as if he could never get enough of her. And she caught his hunger like a fever.

When her lips felt so swollen and sensitive she

thought she might burst with longing, he moved slowly downward, licking beads of water and pressing molten kisses across her satiny skin until he reached the edge of the towel. He wove patterns of kisses till she felt inflamed from the inside out. Finally, he raised his head and looked at her with eyes darkened by desire.

"Please, don't stop now." She moaned as she threw back her head to give him unfettered access, aching for more of his touch.

He slowly lowered the towel, inch by inch, followed by heated kisses till he revealed the peaks of her round breasts. "You're as beautiful by daylight as you are by moonlight."

She felt even hotter at his suggestive words. Now she realized she'd never stopped burning for him since he'd set her on fire when he'd touched her so intimately by the spring in the gazebo. She'd thrilled to his touch then, but at this moment he drilled deeper with every single touch of lips and hands and body. Still she wanted more of what only he could give her.

He lowered his face and took his own sweet time teasing and tormenting the tips of her breasts till she felt an answering blaze deep in her molten core. She needed him. She yearned for him. And yet she wanted to touch him as he touched her. But he still bound her tightly with the towel.

"I've wanted to do this since the first moment I saw you." He lifted her into his arms still wrapped in the towel and strode into the bedroom. He set her on the edge of the bed. He threw the extra pillows on the floor before he tossed back the covers to reveal silky crimson sheets.

"And what do you think I've wanted to do with you?" She reached behind her back and slowly, suggestively pulled the towel away from her body till she sat naked before him. When she heard the sharp intake of his breath and saw the intensity in his eyes, she wantonly tossed the towel on the floor beside the pillows.

"I hope like hell you've wanted to have your way with me."

She laughed, a low, sultry sound, as she gave a little twist of her hand to indicate she wanted him to reveal all.

He slowly pulled the macramé necklace over his head and set it on the nightstand. Next, he tugged his T-shirt over his head, revealing tanned skin stretched tight across hard muscles with only a little dark chest hair. He tossed his tee beside her towel and watched her reaction.

"Come here." She heard the huskiness of her voice and felt the rush of heat over her body. She wanted to feast on him now.

He dropped to his knees in front of her and wrapped his arms around her waist, hugging her tight.

She felt like a powerful goddess—all raw hunger, blatant need, infinite desire—as she lay back and spread out on the bed, baring her body to him just as she'd earlier bared her soul to him.

He stood up, unzipped his jeans, then stopped and smiled seductively at her as he slowly lowered his pants till he was completely naked, too.

She licked her lower lip as she gazed at him just as he'd earlier looked upon her. He was big, bold, and so obviously ready to give her pleasure that she felt breathless with passion.

"Come here," she said again, only this time in a soft,

urgent purr, as she beckoned him closer with one languid hand.

He quickly opened a drawer in his nightstand, selected a condom, and slipped it on his long length.

When he joined her on the bed, she felt as if she'd truly come home. She kissed him, wrapping her arms around him and binding him to her as he'd earlier bound her to him.

Trey entered her—gently and tenderly—and then he moved urgently with strong thrusts until she wrapped her legs around him.

And they both cried out in pleasure.

Chapter 30

TREY LAY IN BED PROPPED UP ON PILLOWS WITH HIS hands clasped behind his head. He watched the scenic landscape of Wildcat Ranch through the sheer drapes over his bedroom windows. No place on Earth could be finer. He glanced down at a sleeping Misty. She lay with an arm thrown across his chest and a knee over his legs. She felt soft and warm and cuddly. He didn't know when he'd been so content or so satisfied.

Not completely satisfied. That never seemed to work out in life. They still had the issues of Texas Timber and the fires to discuss and work out. But that'd wait till later, maybe at dinner.

He stroked a strand of soft hair back from her face. She was more than he could've imagined when he'd first flagged her down on Wildcat Road. She had depths and passions and smarts that made her even more delectable than at first glance. And that was before they'd tumbled into his bed. She might not like to hear it, but she fit him like a favorite pair of well-worn boots.

If he'd found the woman for him after his parents had pulled their little stunt to leave him lonely at Christmas, he'd never hear the last of it. It'd be "I told you so" for the rest of his natural life. But if he had found his special gal, he'd be happy to pay that small price for happiness.

He checked Misty's hand. Somewhere between bath and bed, she'd lost the bandage. He'd take care of her injury again later. How he'd hated to see her by the Christmas tree, hurting physically and emotionally. He'd known then he'd protect her with everything in him till the cows came home.

Speaking of cows, he sat up a little straighter. Why were his prized Angus drinking from the swimming pool? He blinked to clear his eyes. No, he hadn't been mistaken. Not one dang bit. Black, four-legged animals were definitely spending a little quality time by the pool.

If Mom found out, she'd be all over him. Those critters would eat her carefully tended pansies and mums, and then leave cow pies everywhere. Cattle tended to take water in one end and empty it out the other end at the same time. The pool could be pea green real quick.

But that was the small problem. The bigger one was that some of his cattle were loose. How the hell had the critters gotten out of the strong fence in the first place? He rubbed his forehead in disgust. Sabotage. Somebody had been at Wildcat Ranch again. First the fire. Now cut fence. But this time somebody was making a definite point that his family was vulnerable. The culprits had snuck up close to the house when they knew he'd be at the fire to do their dirty work. It was getting personal or maybe it always had been that way.

"Misty, wake up." He gently shook her shoulder. "I've got a situation on my hands."

She opened one eye and looked sleepily at him.

He couldn't keep a smile from crossing his lips despite the outside problem. She looked delectable and he wanted to start where they'd left off. Instead he thrust his feet over the side of the bed and stood up. "Don't figure you can ride a horse."

"Not today."

"Drive a four-wheeler?"

"Not even on my to-do list."

"At least you can walk and run."

"Not on my current agenda." She stretched, pulled the sheet to her chin, and rolled over to present him with her back.

He patted her round butt under the red sheet. "It is now."

She looked over her shoulder and opened both eyes. "You're kidding."

"Take a look at the swimming pool." He grabbed his jeans, jerked them on, and zipped up.

"You just ruined my best view by covering up your body." She pouted as she sat up.

"You can have it back later." He chuckled as he stepped away from the windows and grabbed his T-shirt.

"Are you sure you want to get up so soon?"

"No choice. I'll make it up to you later." He anticipated making that promise last a long, long time. "Take a look outside." He quickly tugged his T-shirt over his head and tucked the tail into his jeans before he adjusted the belt.

She looked outside, squinted, and looked again. "Does your swimming pool serve as a pond in winter?"

"Not in any world I can imagine." He sat down on the bench, jerked on his socks, and then pulled up his boots.

"That's not good then."

"Nope, it surely isn't." He stood, picked up his cell phone, and tucked it in his back pocket.

"Do you want me to do something with the cattle?"

"Yes, I may need your help."

"But they're huge, dangerous beasts."

"That'd be Brahma or Longhorn or bison. These are Angus."

"Honestly, Trey, I'm willing, but I don't know how I can help." She yawned as she got out of bed and quickly started putting on her clothes. "Maybe you'd better call Slade or Kent. Even better, why don't you call a ranch hand to help?"

"It's late. Hands are gone. It's not that big a problem, but I might need help. Looks like about eight have wandered over here. I'm hoping the others haven't noticed their escape route yet."

"Okay. But I don't know what I can do."

"You can sing, can't you?" Somehow or other the situation was beginning to get funny or maybe he was just having fun with Misty when she was a little giddy.

"What?"

He stopped in the doorway and looked back at her. "Didn't you ever watch any of the old singing cowboy movies or TV shows like Gene Autry or Roy Rogers?"

"Not on my to-do list."

"Bet I can change your mind."

"Only if there's muscadine wine with it." She picked up her phone and slipped it into her pocket.

"That can be arranged." He pointed at her, chuckling at her reaction. "Git along lil dogie."

"What?"

"Old tradition. Cowboys sing to their cattle to keep them calm. On a long cattle drive, you had a thousand head and maybe a dozen or so cowboys to get them from Texas to Kansas. Last thing they needed was a stampede."

"And you want me to be a singing cowgirl?"

"Just if those Angus get spooked."

"How will I know?"

"You'll see the whites of their eyes."

"Trust me, I'll never be that close."

He laughed as he teased her. She was making a bad situation much better. "They can move faster than you'd think."

"You are so making this up. I'm not falling for it." She flounced past him and down the stairs.

He followed her, wishing Kent and Slade were there to enjoy a greenhorn's reaction to ranch reality and the time-honored teasing that went along with it. But Trey had better go easy on her if he was going to get any help. Still, to get her in the right mood, he whistled a few bars of Gene Autry's famous "Here Comes Santa Claus."

She chuckled as he joined her. "Guess I'm on a learning curve."

"Not too steep." He turned serious for a moment. "First, we're going to find the break in the fence line. The pasture is next to the house, so the break can't be far away."

"Okay." She sounded a little skeptical.

"After that, we'll herd the cows back to their pasture."

"And by herd, you mean?"

"Just shoo them in the right direction."

"And by shoo, you mean?"

He laughed and gave her a quick hug. "I'll do most of the shooing, or luring. I just need you to keep them from going in the wrong direction."

"That'd be toward me."

"Yep."

"You said they can move fast. Are they unpredictable, too?" She put her hands on her hips and gave him a slit-eyed look.

"On occasion."

"If I get run over or gored by a cow, you're going to regret you ever invited me to your ranch."

"Gored is not a problem. Angus are polled."

"Polled?"

"They're a breed of cattle without horns."

"I feel so much better." She gave him a quick kiss on his lips before she stepped back, looking at him with a twinkle in her eyes. "I'm not sure I believe a word you've been telling me." She picked up her red boots by the door, leaned against the wall, and tugged them on her feet. "On the other hand, I'm taking no chances where dangerous beasts are concerned."

He laughed at her good humor. "Just promise you won't scream and run if a few cattle amble toward you."

"I'm promising nothing where cows are concerned."

"Just sing and you'll be fine."

Chapter 31

"You don't need to sing yet." Trey opened the gate into the pasture near the barn. He'd stuffed leather gloves in a back pocket of his jeans. He carried a bucket by a handle. It was half full of pressed oat pellets with wire cutters and a length of rolled wire set on top. He always kept a few ranch items like those handy in the house.

"I'm getting in practice in case your little darlings have mad cow disease and go berserk when they see a stranger."

He chuckled at her humor. "They don't have mad cow disease. I think you'll like them, if you give them a chance."

She stopped, grinned, and tossed her hair. "Not necessary. I need them to like me, so I don't get eaten or something."

"You've been watching too many zombie movies." He laughed as he checked a metal fence post. He had to hand it to Misty. She was cleverly turning his whole tease-a-greenhorn banter on its head. "Let's rework your agenda and put cowgirl at the top."

"You're the one with cows in your swimming pool. Maybe you need to add cowboy-refresher-course to your agenda."

He laughed even harder.

She put her hands on her hips, grinning. "I don't

think you're taking this cow situation seriously enough. Shouldn't we have some sort of defense mechanism in our hands just in case of a stampede?"

"I've been at this rodeo a time or two before. But okay." He glanced around, walked over to an old oak tree, set down the bucket, and picked up a fallen branch. He stripped it down to a switch about three to four feet in length. He held it out to her.

"What's that?"

"Cow defense."

"You are so not taking me seriously."

"Want the switch or not?"

She winked at him as she grabbed the branch. "Between singing and switching, I'm a lethal force. Army Ranger recruiters will be pounding on my door at any moment."

He tried not to laugh, so he ended up snorting like a bull instead. He wished Kent and Slade were here. They'd be laughing so hard they'd be rolling on the ground. He'd had no idea Misty could be so funny. He needed to add that to her list of attributes.

"Go ahead and laugh. I can see you want to do it. Won't hurt my feelings in the least. I'm immune to your silly cow antics."

He took several deep breaths to control his laughter. "Let's just check the fence."

"Suits me fine." She set off at a quick pace, running her switch up and down the barbwire as she hummed "Here Comes Santa Claus."

He just stood there and watched her. He could do it all day. He didn't know how moving a few head of cattle back into their pasture had turned into so much fun. But that was Misty's doing. He chuckled as he watched her sassy sway. In bed or out of it, she was making his life so much better.

Still, his teasing and her antics brought home the fact that they stood on opposite sides of a fence. He'd been seeing her as the cowgirl next door. Not true. She'd been seeing him as a cowboy firefighter. Not completely true. They were both complex, with hopes and dreams, loves and hates, pasts and presents. He didn't know how the hell they would get the barbwire down from between them, but he was willing to give it a good shot.

He turned serious as he stepped back to look down the line of fence. He wanted to sort out what didn't fit in the picture. Didn't take him long to see the problem. In one section, barbwire strands curled outward and a post leaned out, too. Culprits had tried to take out a post. That was serious stuff. They must have given it up as too much work or too much time.

What concerned him more than anything else was the boldness. Like he'd been thinking all along, he figured more than one person had to be involved in the sabotage. This time they'd chosen to do their dirty work up close to the main house. That put them near the barn and horse stables, which were all vulnerable to fire. They must want to make a statement: "We can get you where you live. We can cut your fence. We can set your house on fire."

Trey felt chilled to the bone. The culprits targeting Wildcat Ranch had to know his parents were out of town and he was distracted with Christmas festivities. Work by the ranch hands was cut back, too. Some were gone visiting kinfolks. Others were working shorter hours.

From a saboteur's point of view, this had to be the perfect opportunity, so the attack's place and time wasn't an accident.

He hated to think it, but the culprits were somehow keeping tabs on him. That meant Misty was vulnerable, too. He needed to have a heart-to-heart talk with her real soon. First, he had to get his head out of the clouds and focus on safety. He would set up a watch with his ranch hands. He wanted somebody making the rounds at the house, barn, and stables at all times, day and night. The sabotage had cut way too close to the bone, and he had to take a strong defensive position.

"Misty, I see the break up ahead." He walked past her and pointed at the fence. "But don't come any closer. I want to examine the ground for prints."

"Good idea." She stopped beside him. "I'll help."

He checked the area, but he was disappointed when he didn't see anything out of the ordinary. "Ground's too churned up by the cattle to tell much."

"That's too bad." She made a wide circle around him before she walked out toward the road.

He stayed near the cut fence. "I doubt there's much to see out there."

She stopped and pointed at the ground. "Look here."

He walked over, still looking for anything that'd give them a clue as to the saboteurs. "Dirt's too dry to take much of a print."

She knelt and used the tip of her forefinger to indicate a spot. "Maybe I'm wrong, but couldn't that be the print of a high heel that sunk into the ground?"

He knelt beside her and looked closer. "Good work. I'd never have noticed it. See how the grass is crushed in front of the indentation? Looks like a shoe print to me. And it's not from Mom's shoes. She'd never be so foolish to walk around in the pasture wearing high heels."

"Someone else might have thought the ground was hard enough to hold up under heels."

"Ground's hard, but you can still punch into it."

Misty slipped her phone out of her pocket. "Just in case this is important, I think we ought to get photos."

"Can't hurt." He pulled out his cell phone, too. "As hard and dry as the ground is right now, those holes aren't going anyplace."

"Maybe we'll get rain." She snapped several shots from different angles.

"Where'd you ever get an outlandish idea like that?"

She laughed at his response. "I know. Seems like it's been forever since we got rain in North Texas."

"I keep hoping for snow." He took photographs, too. He snapped her feet near the holes to indicate size and long shots near the fence for position.

"Now you're really living in a dream world. At least I only suggested rain might fall."

"Afraid you're right." He glanced up at the sky. Not even a wispy cloud in sight. But the sun was lowering in the west. They'd better get a move on. Night came on early in the winter and he wanted the cows back in their pasture before it got too dark to see what he was doing.

Misty stood up, took a few more photos, and put her phone back in her pocket. She walked back along the fence, pointing at the ground. "I'm following the holes. They're evenly spaced, but by somebody with shorter legs than me."

He stuck his phone in his pocket, moved out around

her, and returned to the cut fence. "Where do the holes end?"

She took short steps as she followed the trail back to him. "They're lost in the cow tracks."

"That'd make sense, wouldn't it?"

"Right. Tracks end where the cattle cross."

He glanced back down the fence line, reconsidering their quick speculation about the holes in the ground. "Best not get ahead of ourselves. Those holes could've been made by critters. We've got snakes, spiders, possums, and armadillos out here. You name it, and it's living in the pasture or nearby."

"But holes in a long row along the fence line?"

"I know. Doesn't look like anything I've seen before. But you've got to admit a critter makes more sense than a woman in high heels walking across my pasture to cut fence."

"True." Misty sighed as she pushed back her hair. "I probably got excited over nothing."

"Not nothing. I just don't want to jump to conclusions without more proof. We'll keep it in mind."

"Sounds good." She pointed at the swimming pool. "Guess I can't put off singing to the cows any longer."

"Guess not." He chuckled as he glanced at her. "Come along, lil dogie."

"Lil dogie?" She laughed, shaking her head. "Just what I always yearned to be called."

"It's something like sweetheart."

"Sure it is."

He joined her laughter as he stepped through the open fence line. He made sure the strands couldn't cut the cattle on their way back.

Misty followed him to the other side of the fence and held up her switch. "I'm ready to give those cows what for."

"Got no doubt by the time you're done they'll know never to stray out of their pasture again."

"And never—and I mean never ever—turn into mutant, zombie, flesh-eating, ninja cows."

"That'd be good, too." But he almost didn't get the words out because he was laughing so hard his eyes were stinging with tears.

He walked side by side with Misty into the courtyard. The eight cows had been busy. They'd finished their illicit drinks, taken out a row of tasty petunias, and artistically decorated the flagstone with several greenish cow pies. They were now contentedly chewing their cuds in the shade of the gazebo.

"Whatever you do, don't step in one of those cow patties."

"I wasn't born yesterday." She gave a cow pie a closer look. "Doesn't some Texas company guild the dry ones in gold and sell them for big bucks?"

"Yeah, I heard about that. Not sure if they're still doing it."

"Texas chic." She gave him a mischievous glance. "Maybe you're missing out on a lucrative secondary market."

"Could be, but I think I'll pass on it."

"Faint of heart?"

"Faint of nose."

She laughed as she carefully avoided a particularly large greenish splat on the cement.

"Guess we better get this show on the road." He

walked toward the peaceful cows giving him thoughtful looks with their big brown eyes.

Misty edged behind him. "I suppose that placid attitude and gentle appearance is simply a precursor to cows going all ninja on us with red glowing eyes. I bet pretty quick they'll stand up on their back legs and give us the ole one-two with vicious hooves."

"Might be a little active for them, but maybe not for your overactive imagination." He tried not to laugh too loudly. He really didn't want to spook the cattle.

"Hah! Don't let their innocent appearance fool you." She held out her switch and whipped it back and forth in front of her. "I'm ready for them."

"Ladies," Trey called. "Time to go home." He raised the bucket of oats and shook it till the feed rattled inside.

Eight heads abruptly turned toward him. One cow stretched out her neck and lowed deep in her throat. She started a slow amble in his direction. The others followed her.

"That's Bessie." He shook the bucket again to make the enticing rattling sound that no cow could resist. "She's the lead cow."

"They're picking up speed and heading right for us."

"Sure they are. I've got the oats." He walked across the patio toward the cut fence with Misty as his shadow.

"I'm keeping a look behind us. I'll let you know if they start to stampede so we can get out of their way."

He walked back into the pasture, turned toward the cattle, and shook the bucket again. Bessie picked up speed, from slow to fast amble, with the others right behind her.

"Look!" Misty pointed with her switch. "I think Bessie's eyes are turning red."

"Sun's in her face."

"Maybe. Then again, she's a ninja cow and she may be building up steam to put on the afterburners."

Trey laughed again. Misty was too adorable for words. Not that he'd ever tell her that to her face. He just couldn't resist her any longer. To hell with the cows. He stepped in close, put an arm around her shoulders, and kissed her with all the heat and passion that'd been building up since they'd left his bed. She responded with as much fire and urgency as he could possibly want from the woman who was making all his dreams come true.

And then a loud moo sounded directly in his ear. Misty jumped back with a little shriek and held up her switch.

"Bessie, mind your manners." He put a hand on the cow's jaw and pushed her large head away. She licked her soft nose with her big tongue while she looked at him imploringly with brown eyes.

"Okay. I got it. You're hungry."

He looked around for a good place to spread the oats. He walked over to the oak tree, cleaned off a wide area of ground with the sole of his boot, and then dumped a row of oats in a long line.

"Ladies, come and get it." He walked back over to Misty, who watched as Bessie started toward the tree in a trot.

"We'd better get out of here," Misty said in a low voice. "Looks like they're about to break into a killer run."

"Yep. Those oats don't stand a chance," he agreed, chuckling. "Now is a good time to fix the fence."

Chapter 32

"This is delicious." Misty cut a piece of flaky catfish with her fork. She hadn't felt this lighthearted in ages. She'd been making mischief just to see Trey's eyes light up with humor. "I'm not convinced Bessie doesn't have superpowers. You saw the way the other cows hid behind her."

"They weren't hiding behind Bessie." Trey set down his salad fork and smiled at her. "They were walking single file behind their leader in their pecking order."

"You may think that's normal, but it sounds more like Wonder Woman to me."

"If so, why didn't she load 'em up in her invisible plane and fly them back to their pasture?'"

Misty smiled mischievously. "No doubt she's working undercover as Bessie the Ninja Cow."

"And that explains why we're not eating bison steak."

"Exactly. No red meat while she's lurking about. She might be a little sensitive on the subject."

Trey chuckled as he forked up another bite of salad.

"Here's a thought." Misty couldn't resist expanding on her premise. "If those shoe prints turn out to be a clue to our culprits, we'll have Bessie to thank. She's the one who called our attention to them."

"I wish Mom was home. She would totally get into this scenario with you. She's a huge Wonder Woman fan. She's got a big collection that takes up one wall in her office."

"Really?" Misty grinned in delight. "I can't wait to see it. We gals must stick together."

"That include Bessie?"

"She's the leader, isn't she?"

"True."

"And now that I've proved my absolute devotion to your adorable cows, you won't breathe a word to your cousins or friends about my first introduction to the big beasts." She could just imagine Slade's reaction, or maybe he'd get into it and suggest Superman and Batman be given roles in the cattle herds. Morning Glory would probably offer really good suggestions. She might like Spider-Woman or the Huntress.

"My lips are sealed." He squeezed them shut as if to prove his point.

"Cross your heart and hope to die?"

"I wouldn't go that far."

"I knew it! You're gonna blab the first minute you see them."

"You've got to admit, it's a pretty good story."

"Bessie's eyes did look red in the sunlight. And she was wearing a black ninja suit. I rest my case." Misty forked another bite of catfish into her mouth.

"She's a black Angus. That's her natural color."

"Not if she's undercover." Misty set down her fork and leaned forward. "I bet Morning Glory would recognize Bessie for who she truly is."

"No doubt." Trey chuckled, coughed, and took a quick sip of tea. "I'm not sure you've earned your cowgirl spurs yet."

"What makes you think I want them?"

"You've got the boots."

"I do like the boots." She gave that idea a little thought. "Fortunately, they're red, not black."

"There are red Angus in another pasture." He chuckled as he speared a bite of salad.

She mock pouted at him. "You're just determined to ruin my dinner."

"Not after I went to so much trouble to change the menu."

"Bessie and I do appreciate the thoughtfulness." She drummed her fingertips on the tabletop. "Maybe I'd better go back to Twin Oaks, where there are no judgmental cowboys."

"I wouldn't count on that being a cowboy-free space."

"Dallas then."

"Not before Christmas." He gave her a quelling look. "We've got too much to do."

"Guess I'm stuck." She smiled at him, watching him watch her with that light in his eyes. "Thanks again. This is tasty catfish. Great hush puppies, too."

"Least I could do for the cowgirl who helped me herd cattle."

She laughed. "As it turns out, there wasn't much to it—if you know what you're doing."

"I've had a little experience."

"Who knew oats were the way to a cow's heart?"

"You want dessert?" He grinned as he set down his fork.

"Is that a bribe?"

"If it'll get you back upstairs."

"Yum. Dessert in bed." She felt heat spiral through

her at just the thought of his big bed. And Trey would be the most delicious, most sinful, most decadent dessert she could possibly imagine. Yes, he was definitely her tasty Texas Millionaire candy.

"Later," he promised with a hot gleam in his eyes. "Right now we'd better put our cards on the table."

She nodded in understanding. "The sabotage is escalating, isn't it?"

"They're hitting me where it hurts. I'm going to set up 24/7 guards, and I'll update the sheriff on the situation here."

"It's terrible. What can I do to help?"

"Tell me Texas Timber isn't involved."

She felt a sense of relief that he'd believe her about the company. "They're not. And I'll tell you why. They sent me here to find out who is sabotaging their tree farms and by extension causing you problems."

"That's it? What about buying my timber?"

"Far as I know, that's a genuine offer. These fires have nothing to do with your ranch."

She pushed back her plate and leaned forward. "Trey, I'm here to help. I was warned not to trust anybody. The culprits are operating here, so Texas Timber figures the arsonists must be local."

"That's why you were leery of me at first?"

"Yes. But I wanted to trust you."

He nodded. "I felt the same about you."

She experienced that deep connection with him pull at her, as it had from the first. "So here we are. A tissue. Heel prints. Not much to go on and probably not even connected to the case."

"Even if we haven't caught the arsonists, we've

saved lives and property." He took a long drink of tea. "But one of these times we're not going to be so lucky."

"That's why we've got to catch him, her, or them. And soon."

"I'm concerned they'll take advantage of Christmas in the Country. Everybody will be busy, including law enforcement and fire-rescue. Can you think of a better time to burn down another Christmas tree farm?"

"I hate to say it, but no." She rested her chin on her fist a moment, thinking. "Any ideas about who it might be?"

"I've racked my brain trying to pin the fires, the cut fence, the trouble on somebody, but I can't do it."

"What about Bert and his son?"

"Maybe," Trey agreed. "But I don't see how the tree fires and the cut fence have anything to do with them."

"I admit it's a stretch."

Misty rubbed her hand up and down the condensation on her tea glass, hoping something—anything—helpful would come to mind.

"Guess we might as well table it for tonight."

She nodded in agreement. "I'm glad you're going to post guards here. I can't stand the idea of more trouble. There're these beautiful homes. And your wonderful cattle."

"You like the cows?"

She glanced up at his face, warming to his expectant expression. "You know I couldn't resist kidding you. Bessie and the Bessiettes are the greatest."

He threw back his head and laughed long and hard. "Now you've turned them into a rock band."

"I bet they could do it."

"Not another word about the cows. I can't take it."
He stood up, still chuckling at her words. "Let's carry
Slade's wine to the sofa. We can watch night fall over
the ranch."

"Perfect." She looked up at Trey, drinking in every
little thing about him. "Why don't I put the dishes in the
dishwasher while you pour our wine?"

"Deal."

A little later, she heard soft Christmas music as he
turned on his surround-sound system. She dried her
hands and swiveled to look. Only the Christmas tree
lights illuminated the room in soft colors. He'd set
two wineglasses on the coffee table. Now he stood
thoughtfully gazing out the windows, a long, tall Texan
surveying his expansive domain.

She felt her breath catch in her throat. When had he
come to mean so much to her? How could it have happened so fast? She hardly dared think "love." And yet,
that's where her heart was leading her.

Trey had everything he needed in life. What would
he want with a city gal who knew nothing about cattle
or horses or ranches? She had a pair of red cowgirl boots
as her one claim to that life. Yes, they could enjoy a
fling, but he was teaching her to want so much more
than she'd ever dared to hope for in life. And now she
wanted him. Forever and always.

She felt like she was wishing on a star. Sadness
washed over her. She wasn't in Wildcat Bluff to find
love. She was here to do a job—one that had turned out
to be more important to the locals than she could have
imagined when she'd arrived in town. She needed to

keep her mind on business. Yet Trey beckoned to her with wine and so much more.

"Penny for your thoughts." He glanced back at her as the last rays of the fading sun turned him into a dark silhouette.

She tried to plaster a smile on her face, but she wasn't sure how far she succeeded in looking happy again.

"Come over here." He held out a hand to her. "I'm lonely."

She didn't say it, but she was lonely for him before he was even gone from her life. They'd been born too far apart in too many ways to ever bridge the gap. Yet he'd made her giddy with happiness and she wanted to keep that feeling forever.

She walked over to him and he wrapped a warm arm around her waist, snuggling her against the length of him. He smelled of cinnamon, citrus, and his own unique compelling scent.

She laid her head against his broad shoulder and watched the sunset, savoring the specialness of the fleeting moment. Magenta, crimson, and orange streaked across the deep blue sky. Longing burned so brightly in her that she felt tears sting her eyes.

"Do you think you could be happy in a place like this? I mean, outside the city." He stroked her waist with long fingers.

She caught her breath. How could he tantalize her with fabulous sex, endearing family, fascinating friends, and a beautiful home? After Christmas, he'd snatch it all away. She'd be left with what would now seem like a lonely life in an uncaring city teeming with millions of strangers. Of course, she had plenty of friends and acquaintances in Dallas. Cindi Lou was there. Her business was there. Memories were there. But Trey wouldn't be there and that now made all the difference in the world.

"You don't have to answer. I know what you're going to say."

"Do you?"

"Yeah. You'd be bored here in five minutes flat."

She swallowed against the lump in her throat. "You're so wrong."

"Am I?"

"You're here."

"And?"

She hesitated—and took a chance on love. "What more could I possibly want?"

Chapter 33

TREY FELT A GREAT TENDERNESS WASH OVER HIM. HE crushed Misty against his chest, stroking down her back with hands gone hot. He molded her to the length of him as night slowly fell across the ranch and wrapped them in a soft cocoon of gray shadows. He felt as if no one else existed except the two of them in this time and place of new beginnings.

He pressed a soft kiss to her forehead before he tilted up her face so he could look into her luminous eyes. She glowed in the soft, colorful lights of the Christmas tree, as if she truly were an angel come to Earth.

"Do you know how happy you make me?" His voice sounded low and raspy as if he'd delved deep into his soul to bring this message to her.

"Tell me." She pressed a fingertip to the corner of his mouth as if to encourage him.

Yet no words came to him. Only feelings. He kissed her fingertips, and then placed her hand over his heart so she could feel the fast beat of his desire, the solid strength of his intent, the enduring quality of his love.

She answered him with no words. She clasped his hand and moved it from his heart to her heart. And he could feel the strong, steady beat beneath his palm—a heart that beat for him alone.

Still, he didn't want her here under false pretenses so that she grew disillusioned with him later. It'd been so fast—their coming together—that nothing seemed quite real and yet nothing had ever seemed so real. He forced words to form in his mind and he pushed them out through reluctant lips. "You know I'm tied to my ancestral land."

"Yes, I know."

"Do you truly like it here?"

She reached up and softly cradled his cheek with the soft palm of her hand. "I feel as if I've come home."

"But is this enough for you?"

She gazed at him with green eyes as bright as a Christmas ornament. "You're all I need, all I want, all I desire."

And her words were his undoing.

He kissed her, all gentleness gone in the sudden surge of heat and need that rocked him to his core. He nibbled her lips, feasting on her as he slipped inside her soft mouth to delve deep as she returned his kiss with her own urgent fervor. He couldn't get close enough even as he wrapped her in his arms and felt her hands clasp his neck, then his shoulders, her nails digging into his skin through his T-shirt. He growled deep in his throat as he stroked downward and grasped her butt in his hands and pulled her against his hardness.

Now that she'd unleashed him, he felt as wild as a rampaging bull. He wanted more—everything she could give him. He left her mouth to trail hot kisses across her jaw to the sensitive whorls of her ear, then down her long neck, stopping to feel the fast beat of her pulse. He growled in frustration when he reached her clothes, but he remembered she wore a Western shirt. He pulled, and—snap, snap, snap—the buttons came undone. He tossed the shirt aside and pressed hot kisses to her bare flesh made festive in the lights of the Christmas tree.

He grinned in pleasure at the sight, knowing he probably looked half feral, because she backed up several steps toward the sofa. Then again, she was giving him a come-hither look that made a blaze spread out from his chest and kick into an inferno that turned him even harder with desire.

He couldn't wait another second. He surged forward, grabbed her around the waist, and toppled her backward onto the sofa as he planted his legs between her spread thighs. Heat burst between them like a match set to kindling as he pressed her into the soft cushions.

She tugged on his T-shirt and he jerked it up, over his head, and threw it on the floor. She helped him get rid of her bra. And then they were flesh to flesh. He could feel her breasts against his chest. And still it wasn't enough. He lifted his torso and looked down at her. She lay bare to him, all satin and silken skin in the lights of the Christmas tree. He stroked her pink nipples into hard buds, and then followed his fingertips with his lips till she moaned and clasped his shoulders, drawing him closer to her.

He grew urgent as he pushed between her thighs, feeling desperate to join them by burying himself in her hot, moist core. But their jeans separated them and he groaned in frustration as he kissed and licked and nibbled down to her belly button, where he teased her sensitive flesh. She moaned again and clutched him closer, raising her hips so that she rubbed against his hardness.

He captured her lips again, feeling their plumpness, knowing they were swollen from their desperate kisses.

Once more he thrust deep into her mouth, teasing and tormenting, as he felt her naked breasts soft and plump against his chest. He raised his head and looked into her green eyes so he could watch her expression as he held her in a tight embrace and pushed against her, setting a rhythm that had her writhing up against him.

"Trey, I need you—now." She moaned as she closed her eyes and dug her fingernails into his naked back.

He gave her a quick kiss, then pushed back and stood up. He racked his brain for the location of the nearest condom. He might have left a box in the downstairs bath, but it'd been so long since he'd needed one that he wasn't sure anymore. He quickly walked into the bath, found a half-empty box in a drawer, pulled out several condoms, and hurried back.

When he reached the sofa, he stopped in surprise. She hadn't waited for him. She'd taken off her jeans, set them aside, and now sat on his Frosty the Snowman blanket like the most beautiful of models. If he'd been hot before, now he felt like a flaming torch.

She smiled up at him, glanced down at his jeans, and pursed her lips in disapproval, but still beckoned him closer.

He couldn't shuck his jeans fast enough. He kicked them aside, feeling hard as a rock, and quickly slipped on a condom.

And then he hesitated—watching her watch him with eyes darkened by desire—as he savored the sheer pleasure of the moment. Only a few days ago he'd been alone, not knowing that he was missing a big chunk of his life till he'd flagged down his Christmas angel on Wildcat Road. Now he couldn't imagine life without her.

With that thought, his control snapped. He dove for Misty, tumbled her onto her back, and ended up in the place he most wanted to be—wedged between her long, tantalizing legs.

"Oh, Trey," she moaned. "Please don't make me wait any longer."

He pressed a soft kiss to her lips as he held her close. When she lifted her hips, he pushed into her hot depths. And knew he'd come home.

Quickly, he set the ancient rhythm. She set the blazing fire. And they moved ever closer to ecstasy as they shared their spiraling passion together.

Then she was coming apart in his arms—and he eagerly joined her.

Chapter 34

"I DON'T LIKE LEAVING YOU HERE ALONE FOR THE night." Trey stopped his pickup in front of Twin Oaks under twinkling Christmas lights.

"I won't be alone and I'll be fine." She put her hand on his thigh and felt his hard muscles contract under her touch. She thrilled at his response. They'd shared so much only a few hours ago that she still felt slightly giddy.

"You could stay with me." His voice held more than a hint of stubbornness.

"My stuff's here."

"Stuff can be transferred."

"You want me to move in with you after only a few days together?" She chuckled to try and lighten the mood.

"I'm worried about you." He slanted a glance at her.

She felt captured by his gaze. She didn't want to leave him. Once separated, she feared they might lose the bridge they'd built between them. Still, she had to trust their connection was strong, not fragile.

"Misty, you've undone me." He ran a hand through his dark hair. "If anything happened to you—"

"I feel the same. But we've got a situation on our hands."

"Doesn't mean I have to like it," he grumbled.

When she felt her phone vibrate in her pocket, she

pulled it out and glanced at the caller ID. "It's important." She looked at Trey. "Texas Timber."

He nodded in understanding.

"Hey, Audrey. How are you?"

"I'm okay, but I've been better," Audrey said in a muted voice.

Misty sat up straighter. "What gives? Thought I'd call you first thing in the morning about the fire since there might be more news then. But I can talk now, too."

She glanced at Trey and held a fingertip to her lips to indicate for him to be quiet. She put her cell on speakerphone so he could listen in on the conversation.

"Misty, I'm sorry," Audrey said in her West Texas twang. "I called as soon as I found out."

"Bad news?"

"Yes. I swear I didn't know till a moment ago. And I only found out from a friend of mine, so I got it through the back door."

"What's the problem?"

"Texas Timber may not be the only player in Wildcat Bluff."

"And that means?" Misty kept her voice neutral, although she was getting a sinking sensation in the pit of her stomach.

"National Timber is trying to acquire Texas Timber. Hostile takeover isn't off the table."

"But that's vital information I should've had from the get-go."

"I agree," Audrey said. "Still, you can imagine how anxious they are not to have that information leaked by anyone."

"But they hired me as their troubleshooter. Why

wouldn't they give me all the facts?" Misty rolled her eyes in exasperation at Trey. "Guess that explains why they were so anxious to get me here before Christmas to solve this issue before they had bigger problems."

"You know corporate think," Audrey said. "Need-to-know basis."

"Bottom line." Misty clenched her fist. "Are we looking at two separate culprits? Even worse, can I trust Texas Timber now? Are they causing problems, or is it all National Timber?"

Audrey grew quiet a moment. "I don't think my company is at fault here. But I'm guessing they'd be real happy if you'd catch the corporate saboteurs and solve two problems at once. Sabotage would take National Timber's play permanently off the table."

"I see," Misty said. "They're counting on me to catch the arsonists and expose National Timber without knowing in advance the real situation."

"That's right," Audrey agreed. "And you'd better play your hand that way or you'll expose me."

"What if it isn't National Timber?" Misty glanced at Trey.

"Then we've got a big problem," Audrey said.

"We've already got one." Misty kept a lid on her temper, but it wasn't easy. "Maybe I ought to call Cindi Lou and ask her to break my contract with Texas Timber right this very minute."

"Please don't. It could cost me my job," Audrey pleaded. "I shouldn't have told you any of this, but I didn't want you in more danger than necessary."

Trey put a hand on Misty's arm and shook his head in the negative.

She nodded to let him know she wouldn't abandon Wildcat Bluff, but she was mad about not getting all the information she needed to do her job right. "Okay. I won't pull out yet."

"Thank you," Audrey said. "You're the best."

"I'll let Cindi Lou know. She's not going to be happy."

"Would you tell her it's not my fault?" Audrey asked.

"She won't hold it against you, but Texas Timber is another matter."

"Just find the saboteurs fast."

"I'll do my best."

"Thanks," Audrey said. "And good luck."

"Bye." Misty clicked off her phone and glanced at Trey.

He looked disgusted with the situation. "You think the whole ball of wax is as simple as National Timber?"

"If I'd only known from the first—"

"I figure if National Timber wants to buy Texas Timber, they likely want to buy my ranch, too. Sabotage. If it's good for the goose, it's good for the gander."

"Makes sense." She glanced out the window at Big John, letting her mind wander over possibilities, and then she looked back. "But what if it's not National Timber? And even if it is, how do we catch the corporate saboteurs? They've been one step ahead of us all the way."

"Not anymore," Trey said. "We're on to them now."

"You're right." She smiled, feeling her confidence soar. "We've got a leg up. We'll win. And when we do, I'll get my troubleshooter fee."

"With those big bucks, maybe you'll take me on an Alaskan cruise where I can see lots of snow."

"Hah! With those *little* bucks, maybe I'll take you to see the Goodnight buffalo herd in the Panhandle."

"That'll work, too."

As they laughed together, she felt most of her tension ease away. She'd try to get a line on the saboteurs before Christmas in the Country with the chili cook-off and all the other festivities.

"As long as we're here, why don't we slip up to your room?" Trey squeezed her hand. "Bet it's got a good bed."

"And shock Ruby?"

"I doubt anything'd shock her."

"Not when it comes to cowboys, right?"

"Something like that." He grinned as if remembering lots of things he wasn't ever going to tell.

"Guess we'd better get this show on the road." She picked up her phone and put it in her pocket. She reached behind the seat and got her Gene's Boot Hospital sack that held her athletic shoes and the small fire extinguisher she'd borrowed from Trey.

"Yep. Christmas won't wait."

She watched as Trey got out of the truck, walked around, and opened her door. She stepped down into his arms and he hugged her tight. She inhaled his scent and felt his strong body surround her. Images of him naked above her, bringing her to peak after peak of pleasure, filled her mind.

He kissed her earlobe. "Better be good while I'm gone."

She decided to tease him. "Can I only be bad with you?"

"Absolutely."

She chuckled as she walked over and patted Big John's trunk. "Hey there, you big, handsome boy."

Trey joined her laughter. "Now don't go making me jealous or I'll start thinking chain saw."

She quickly turned back. "Don't you dare think such a thing, particularly not in Big John's presence."

Trey laughed harder as he put an arm around her shoulders. "Okay. So long as he doesn't get any ideas about stealing my gal."

"'My gal'?"

"You know it."

"That'd make you 'my guy'."

"In a heartbeat." He gave her a hot look before he opened the sliding glass doors.

She stepped indoors, caught the scent of cinnamon, and trailed her fingers up and down the poinsettias wrapped around the swing's chain.

"Ruby knows how to make a place feel like home, doesn't she?" Trey said.

"She's not the only one." Misty tucked her hand around Trey's arm as they walked to the inside door.

She hesitated with her hand on the doorknob, savoring their last intimate moment for a while, before she opened the door and stepped inside. She walked into the living room, saw the beautiful peacock tree, and smelled spice cake.

"Hey, Ruby." Trey closed the door behind him.

"Welcome home," Ruby called. "We'd about given up on seeing you two ever again."

"Been a little busy," Trey said.

"Busy enough to keep you out of trouble?" Ruby grinned as she looked from Trey to Misty and back again.

"Never that busy." Trey chuckled as he walked deeper into the room.

Misty moved over to the tree, nodding in greeting to J.P. and Charlene, who were sitting together on the sofa. Ruby sat in a recliner near the fireplace with a Santa Claus mug in her hands.

"J.P. and Charlene have been asking after you," Ruby said.

"We'd hoped you'd join us for dinner." Charlene uncrossed her legs, drawing attention to her shapely legs—revealed by her short skirt—and her black-and-white spike heels, then crossed her legs again.

"Sorry we couldn't make it," Misty said.

"Ate a bite at the ranch," Trey added.

"If you grilled bison steaks and didn't bring me any, I'm gonna pout." Ruby took a sip from her mug.

"Catfish. Delicious, too." Misty smiled at the group. "Trey's a great cook."

"You didn't try to impress her with steak?" Ruby appeared puzzled.

"She wanted fish," Trey said in a neutral tone.

Ruby shrugged a shoulder. "Glad you're here. Time to touch base on the chili cook-off."

"We're so excited about the benefit. We wouldn't miss it." Charlene turned to J.P. "We like to help animals. Don't we, sugar?"

"Sure do, sweetkins. And I never turn down a good bowl of chili."

"That's great," Misty said.

"Let's see." Ruby set down her mug and held up a hand to count items off on her fingers. "Slade volunteered to oversee the chili entries. Teddie's putting your Wildcat

Bluff Chili Cook-Off announcement in tomorrow's paper. Notices are up in stores across town, not to mention word of mouth. Everybody's excited as all get-out."

"It's all coming together so fast." Misty realized the town had put on a lot of benefits so they had a system in place.

"You and Trey are judges," Ruby added. "That's important work, too."

"I'd sure like to be one," J.P. said.

"Misty?" Ruby asked.

"Why not?"

"Thanks," J.P. said, grinning. "That'll be fun."

"Guess you know I got the school cafeteria squared away," Trey added.

"Yep," Ruby agreed. "You won't need to do much there. Staff will take care of setting up, cleaning up, and taking down."

"Sounds perfect," Misty said. "Y'all are making this seem easy."

"That's what comes from experience." Ruby smiled as she glanced around at the group. "We've danced to this tune a time or two."

"What about decorations?" Misty asked, suddenly realizing she hadn't even thought about that important part of an event.

"No problem. Place is already decorated for the holidays." Ruby patted herself on the back. "And I even got my vendor to accept a special order and overnight trophies for the event. That took some doing, but Wildcat Bluff is a good customer."

"Is there anything else we need to do?" Misty asked.

"Think we've got it covered for the moment.

Last-minute foul-ups are bound to happen. If and when, you get to step up and solve problems."

"I'll be happy to do it," Misty said. "Thanks for all the help."

"Glad to assist our volunteer firefighters any way I can." Ruby stood up. "May I get you something to drink or eat?"

"Thanks, but no," Trey said. "I'm gonna run Misty up to her room and then go. Plenty to do tomorrow."

Ruby winked at him. "You do just that."

"Good night, everybody," Misty said.

She quickly headed up the stairs with Trey right behind her. After she entered her suite, she set her boot bag on the desk, then turned to watch Trey shut the door. He took her in his arms and held her tight for a long moment.

"Want to try out the bed?" he asked.

"Not with folks downstairs."

"Better let me check your room then."

"I doubt anybody got in here."

"Locks can be picked. No point taking chances." He quickly looked in the bathroom, under the bed, and then opened the closet door.

She glanced over his shoulder. "That's odd."

"What?"

"That towel shouldn't be on the floor. I used it to cover up a decoration."

He walked into the closet, picked up the towel, then reached up and pulled down the angel. "You didn't want to see this?"

"Too many memories."

"What about now?"

She smiled warmly. "Let's set her back on the desk. I'd like to share my room with a Christmas angel."

"I'd like to do the same." He grinned at her with a knowing glint in his eyes. He set the angel on the desk. He hit the button and played "Hark! The Herald Angels Sing."

"Beautiful." She looked down at the angel in her white satin gown playing a golden harp. Only good memories came now. "I'm so glad I can enjoy Christmas. Thank you again."

"Least I could do for my Christmas angel." He pressed a kiss to the tip of her nose, and then glanced around the room. "Would you look and see if anything else is disturbed? Maybe the towel fell when your room was cleaned today."

"Ruby and I agreed no cleaning till I asked for it." She walked back into her closet and reached behind her large suitcase for the small bag containing her laptop and handbag. She froze. The bag was there, but off to one side. She quickly pulled it out and set it on the bed to check the lock.

"What is it?" Trey walked over to her.

"Nothing, I guess. I put my laptop and purse in here and hid it behind my suitcase. This bag wasn't exactly where I thought I'd left it. But maybe I'm mistaken."

"Is it still locked?"

She quickly checked. "Yes."

"That's good. But I'd rest easier if you were with me."

"I'll be fine. I'm probably overthinking the situation." She hesitated and looked up at him. "And if somebody is watching us, we don't want to change our pattern."

He nodded thoughtfully. "If anything odd happens, call me. Day or night."

"Will do." She wound her arms around his neck and kissed him, languidly and indulgently, stoking the fire between them.

He finally lifted his head, eyes dark with banked desire. "Best I go before I can't go."

She stepped back, feeling cold without his warmth.

"Do me a favor. Lock your door and wedge a chair under the knob."

"I'll do it."

Then he was gone, taking all his energy, strength, and sensuality with him. And she felt lonely.

Yet she wouldn't let herself feel down in the dumps, not after her amazing day. She knew the best cure. She pulled her phone out of her pocket, sat down on the settee, and hit speed dial for her BFF.

"Tell me you've got the big guy wearing nothing but his cowboy hat," Cindi Lou said by way of greeting.

"I'm back at Twin Oaks and I just sent him on his way."

"Bless your heart, you don't know when you've got it good."

"Oh yes I do."

"Well now," Cindi Lou lowered her voice suggestively. "How many fires did he put out in your bed tonight?"

"Let's see—let me count the times and ways."

"Oh lordy! That calls for a celebration. Hang on." Cindi Lou set down her phone with a snap, then came back. "Found these adorable retro glass bottles with metal lids of the very best Dr Pepper. You know, it's got real cane sugar. Tiny bottles, mind you, but supreme taste."

"We ever get you up to Wildcat Bluff, maybe we'll get you hooked on cowboys instead of Dr Pepper."

"Doubt my heart could take it." Cindi Lou smacked her lips. "Now if one of those darlings knew how to wrangle me up a Dr Pepper float with just the right touch of vanilla bean ice cream, then I might follow him anywhere."

Misty chuckled. "To a rodeo?"

"Let's not get too wild here. You know I'm a city gal through and through." She made a loud slurp. "Your guy's hot stuff, isn't he?"

Misty felt a tingle all over. "I hate to say it, but you were right from the very first."

Cindi Lou guffawed loudly. "I knew it! He's the one, isn't he?"

"Yeah." Misty got up and looked out the window at Big John's dark silhouette. "This is the most amazing place."

"That's what I hear." Cindi Lou's voice changed from playful to serious. "I got a call from Audrey. She figured—and rightly so—that she'd better come clean with me. Who'd a thunk it? National Timber."

"Trey's working with me now."

"Good. He's an insider and that always helps."

"Now that we've got all the pieces in place, we'll catch those culprits." Misty paced across the room.

"Big business equals big money equals big trouble."

"I know."

"So, stay safe."

"I'm on it."

"And, darlin', don't do anything I wouldn't do."

Cindi Lou chuckled in her low, husky voice and cut the connection.

Misty walked over to the Christmas angel. She stroked a fingertip across the blond hair, down the satin gown, and pressed the button. Soon joyous music of the season filled the air.

And she felt at peace.

Chapter 35

On Christmas Eve, Misty rode beside Trey in his pickup down Wildcat Bluff's Main Street. Christmas in the Country was in full swing on a beautiful sunny day with bright blue skies. A horse-drawn carriage festooned with red and green ribbons and filled with a family of merrymakers clip-clopped its way along the redbrick lane. Gene Autry's melodious voice on the outdoor sound system filled the air, along with the scent of kettle corn. A proprietor stirred sugar into popcorn in a big kettle under a bright red awning. A row of folks waited in line to get the fresh-popped kettle corn.

Misty had plenty of time to look through her open window as traffic stalled in a long line while folks found parking places. The town teemed with people wearing holiday clothes. Adelia's Delights, Morning's Glory, Gene's Boot Hospital, and the Chuckwagon Café looked to be doing big business along with other establishments. A line of children waited with their parents to talk with a jolly-looking Santa Claus wearing a bright red suit and sporting a long white beard as he sat on a bench in the shade on the boardwalk.

"Guess I should've taken the back road," Trey said.

"Oh, no. I wanted to see Christmas in the Country."

"You couldn't believe we'd get this big a turnout, could you?"

"It's amazing."

"And a tradition for some families. They come with their kids, grandkids, and grandparents in tow."

"I'm so happy to be here."

He smiled at her. "And enjoying Christmas, too."

"Thanks to my Christmas angel." She smiled back at him as she touched the angel on the macramé cord around her neck.

"I'm not going to have to fight you for that necklace, am I?" he teased with a twinkle in his eyes.

She grasped the horse harness hardware and gave him a cautionary look. "You brought it back to me, so that means I get it."

He laughed. "Come to think of it, I don't want to get on Morning Glory's bad side, so you'd better keep it."

"Bet she'd make you one if I asked her nicely."

"Thanks but no thanks." He laughed. "I'm doing fine with my usual holiday clothes."

He looked heart-stoppingly handsome in a forest-green Western shirt, pressed jeans, and snake cowboy boots. He was wearing his big Santa Claus belt buckle on a brown leather belt. He'd set a dark brown felt cowboy hat with a snake hatband on the backseat.

She'd worn a simple short-sleeve, crimson cotton top, jeans, red boots, and a gift from Trey. He'd brought her a pin in the shape of three green Christmas trees with five dangling miniature sleigh bells that jingled every time she made a movement. Kitsch at its finest.

"Did I tell you Ruby gave me that shirt I borrowed from her?"

Trey cast Misty a sidelong glance with plenty of heat. "Maybe it wasn't in too good a shape after we got done with it."

She tossed him an even hotter look in return. "You mean, after you practically ripped it from my body."

"Now you know why cowboys are partial to snap shirts."

She ran her fingers down the pearl snap buttons on his shirt. "How fast do you think I could get this shirt off you?"

"Not fast enough."

She felt a sizzle of heat jump from his chest to her hand. She quickly patted him, then leaned primly back in her seat. "Better get our minds on something else."

"Nothing better."

"Appreciate you bringing my stuff over from your place."

"Hoped you'd come back to get it."

"If not for Christmas in the Country, I would've."

"I'd like to see your stuff all over my house," he said in a low, husky voice that carried the promise of hot nights and satin sheets.

She felt his words go straight to her heart. She wanted to be in his big bed—and not just for a few hours. But she had to see this job through first, as well as the chili cook-off, so she decided to lighten the moment. "That's what you say now, but I can be messy."

"No problem. We'll get you an apron from the Chuckwagon Café."

She laughed at the idea. "Not bad. Those are snazzy. Slade looks mighty good in ruffles."

Trey joined her laughter. "Don't let him hear you say that."

"I think he's big enough to take it."

"With a large helping of chili."

"Reminds me." She turned to Trey in concern. "We'd better get our minds on business."

"Chili, yeah. But I'd hoped like all get-out that we'd catch those culprits before Christmas in the Country."

"Me too. But there wasn't enough time."

"Or leads."

"I keep thinking something'll come to me."

He hit the steering wheel with the flat of his palm. "Maybe all that chili tasting will set fire to our brains."

"At the least it'll set fire to our tongues."

"Bet we could do that without the chili."

She waved her hand in front of her face as if trying to cool off. "If you make me any hotter, I'll never make it through the chili tasting."

"We could skip it and go back to my house."

She cast him a narrow-eyed look. "Trey Duval, just shut your mouth."

He threw back his head and laughed hard. "Guess that puts me in my place."

"Hope so or we'll be in so much trouble with the other volunteers we'll never hear the last of it."

"True enough."

She leaned back as he finally made it to the end of Main Street. He turned off the road and threaded his way to the school in back of Old Town.

Wildcat Bluff ISD was a collection of redbrick contemporary buildings nestled in a park-like setting. Strings of blue lights outlined the flat rooflines and filled the large oak trees. In front of a two-story building, a sign read "Go Wildcats!" in red letters on a white background. Another sign was posted in front of a smaller building and announced "Wildcat Bluff Chili Cook-Off Benefit."

Vehicles took up much of the parking area, mainly in the section close to Old Town, but Trey slipped into a spot near the front of the school and switched off the engine of his truck.

"Great." He pointed toward the building with the chili sign. "That's the cafeteria, and somebody's already got a sign up."

"I'm impressed. We've gotten such huge support for the benefit."

"That's Wildcat Bluff." He squeezed her hand. "Let's go. We've got a benefit to put on."

While he got out, she tugged her cell phone from a back pocket. Cindi Lou had texted "Break a Leg!" Misty chuckled at the old Broadway phrase for encouragement. She put her phone back and checked to make sure she had keys and lip gloss in her front pockets. Despite her earlier vow, she hadn't brought a purse since she doubted there'd be a place to put it during the chili cook-off.

Trey opened her door with a big smile on his face. She stepped down into the afternoon's hot sunshine and dry air. Country Christmas music, children's high-pitched voices, and the rumble of vehicles drifted over from Old Town.

"All set?" He gave her a quick hug, then gestured toward the school.

"Let's get this show on the road."

They walked hand in hand into the cafeteria, a large room filled with tables and chairs. In one corner students had decorated a Christmas tree with old-fashioned red-and-green construction paper chains, popcorn strings, and candy canes. Children's crayon drawings on construction paper of cows wearing green wreaths, horses decked out with red-and-green holly, and wildcats pulling Santa's sleigh piled high with colorful packages were attached to the walls.

Slade walked out of the kitchen area wearing a large white apron over ripped jeans, tie-dyed T-shirt, and black boots. He gestured them toward the back of the building.

Misty hurried forward, suddenly feeling anxious about the event. What if nobody brought chili entries or came to participate?

"Ran over after I finished up at the café," Slade said. "Looks like you've got a winner on your hands."

"Really?" She walked up to a row of tables near a wall. At least three dozen Crock-Pots in various shapes and sizes filled the tables. "Folks actually brought chili. What a relief."

"No way would folks miss out on chili," Trey said.

"That's the truth." Slade chuckled in his deep voice.

Trey cocked his head at Slade. "That Morning Glory's work?"

Slade glanced down at the red-and-green patterns on his T-shirt. "She swears she was inspired by the Ghosts of Christmas Past. And I had to wear it to ensure the success of our benefit."

"Pays to stay on Morning Glory's good side," Trey said. "She knows what she knows."

Misty held up her pendant. "She gave this Christmas angel to me."

"Good thing you're wearing it," Slade said, chuckling. "We ought to be in good shape now."

Trey smiled and nodded in agreement.

Misty walked down the line of entries. People had handwritten or printed out their names with the titles of their entries and taped them on the front of their Crock-Pots. She read aloud from a few of the entries. "Bison Bliss. Turkey Fire. Not-for-the-Faint-of-Heart Venison. Pseudo Possum Pleasure."

"That's vegan," Slade said. "Nobody in their right mind would eat possum."

"Yep," Trey agreed. "Nasty, greasy stuff."

"Sounds like you've eaten it," she teased.

"Word of mouth only," Trey quickly explained.

"Good entries." Slade gestured at the pots. "Looks like we've got chicken, beef, rabbit, quail, goat, and pork, too."

"That's amazing." She glanced from Trey to Slade. "And we're going to be tasting all these?"

"That's the plan," Trey said.

"Yum," Slade agreed.

"J.P. Gladstone is a judge," Misty said. "Slade, you met him at Twin Oaks, didn't you?"

"Yep. And the fancy wife, too."

"Hedy's our other judge." Misty glanced toward the front door. "I'm sure they'll be here soon."

"I checked the kitchen," Slade said. "Staff's got minced onions, grated cheddar cheese, sour cream, chopped tomatoes, and shredded iceberg lettuce in the coolers ready to go."

"That's great." Misty walked down the line of tables to the end, where a row of wooden trophies with gold trim sat waiting to be claimed by winners. She picked up one and read, "Wildcat Bluff Chili Cook-Off Winner."

"Nice job, huh?" Hedy called as she zoomed up to the tables, letting the front door slam behind her.

"Looks wonderful." Misty set down the trophy. "Everybody really pulled together to make this happen. I'm so appreciative."

"That's the way we roll in Wildcat Bluff." Hedy laughed as she rolled back and forth in her wheelchair to make her point.

Everybody joined her laughter.

"And I'd like to announce that some special someone anonymously donated six animal oxygen kits to fire-rescue," Hedy said.

Trey and Slade whistled while Misty clapped her hands.

"Misty, don't guess you'd know anything about that, would you?" Hedy raised an eyebrow in question.

"Only that I'm really happy about it."

Trey slanted a glance at Misty, and then he grinned big-time.

"Hey!" a deep male voice called as the front door opened and slammed shut. "You didn't start the chili judging without me, did you?"

Misty waved J.P. forward. "You're right on time. Where's Charlene?"

"Where else? Shopping on Main Street." He guffawed at his own joke as he joined them. He raised a lid, sniffed, and set it down again. "Smells good."

"Guess there's no reason not to get started judging, is there?" Misty glanced around the more experienced group.

"I'll get plastic spoons and small cups from the kitchen," Slade said.

"We'd better all get a bottle of water, too," Trey added. "It's gonna be hot."

"I'll get the water," Misty said. "I want to make sure we've got corn chips."

"Looks like the staff filled your list," Slade said. "But it's best to check yourself. There's still time to pick up any missing items."

As Misty started to enter the kitchen, she thought of the little kitten. While they were having fun and eating great food, he was struggling to stay alive. "Slade, I'll be there in a moment."

She pulled her phone out of her pocket and stepped to one side. She hit speed dial for the vet's office. When she heard Sue Ann's voice, she spoke in a low tone. "This is Misty Reynolds. I'm checking on the injured kitten I brought in with Trey Duval."

"Hi, Misty," Sue Ann said in a cheerful voice. "Thought you'd be at the chili cook-off. By the way, can't thank you enough for making this benefit possible so all the volunteers and rigs carry animal oxygen kits."

"I'm not doing much. Fire-rescue really stepped up to the plate."

"You're the motivating force."

"I'm doing my best. I'm getting ready to judge chili right now. First I wanted to check on the kitten."

"He's hanging in there. I think he's going to make it."

"Oh, that's wonderful news. I'm so relieved for him." Misty hesitated, and then just blurted out what she wanted to know. "Do you think there's a chance I could buy the kitten? I'd like to make him part of my life."

"That's so kind. I could tell you were attached to him. Tell you what, I'll check with Slim. I doubt he'd sell—"

"Oh no."

"But he might give you the kitten since you and Trey rescued the little tyke."

"Thanks. I'd appreciate it."

"Will do. You have a good event. Bye now."

Misty put her phone back in her pocket as she glanced up. Everyone was watching her. She smiled. "I was just checking up on the kitten hurt in the house fire."

"How's he doing?" J.P. asked with sympathy in his voice.

"He's getting better all the time." Misty gave everybody a big smile before she headed for the kitchen.

She glanced back over the empty cafeteria. Soon the place would fill with folks ready to eat chili and donate to the cause. She felt a little amazed that she'd been able to do something as important as helping save the lives of animals. And yet, she felt as if her own life had been—if not saved—certainly rescued in Wildcat Bluff. She was happy to give back to the community that had been so generous to her.

Chapter 36

MISTY HAD THOUGHT SLADE'S CHILI WAS EXTREME until she'd tasted the chili cook-off's entries. Wildcat Bluff's residents had outdone themselves in competing for the hottest of the hot. Not only that, but they'd been creative. She'd tasted chili seasoned with jalapeños, tomatillos, onions, garlic, chili powder, and who knew what else in the clear-your-sinuses arsenal of chili verde and five-alarm chili.

Now she felt like a fire-breathing dragon. A single burst of air and she'd probably melt everything in her path. She chuckled at the thought. She took a quick swig of cold water from the bottle she held in her hand. Not that it stopped the burn, but it eased the symptoms.

As the chili cook-off wound down, she stood at the end of the line where folks had helped themselves buffet style. Not much food was left. She'd replenished sweet tea, coffee, and water. Early on folks had swarmed over the chili like ants at a picnic. Now they sat contentedly at tables, eating, drinking, and chatting with each other.

Misty was reluctant to see the benefit end. She'd had a wonderful time. She glanced around the cafeteria. Slade was in the kitchen. Trey had carried out several bags of trash. J.P. had left to find Charlene. And Hedy was off fielding any issues that might arise. Kent, Sydney, Storm, Morning Glory, and Ruby were also working the room, picking up litter, pausing to chat, and making sure the event went as smoothly as possible.

She'd met new people and enjoyed being a chili judge. When she'd handed out the awards, folks had applauded with wild enthusiasm whether they'd won or lost. There'd be photographs of smiling winners in next week's newspaper. People were even talking about making the chili cook-off an annual event. No doubt about it, the benefit for the Wildcat Bluff Fire-Rescue animal oxygen kits was a success.

She felt humbled by the outpouring of support by local residents and businesses. Every last bite had been a donation. Large numbers of local folks, along with many out-of-towners, had turned out to pay their five dollars and scarf down the chili and fixings.

She didn't know how much money had been collected, but she thought there'd be enough to buy plenty of animal oxygen kits with some funds left over for other fire-rescue needs. She felt proud of her small part in making this event happen. Soon animals caught in dangerous situations would stand a much better chance of survival in this county.

All in all, she'd discovered she liked everything about Wildcat Bluff. She could never have imagined that change of heart back in Dallas. Small town. Country folks. Cowboy firefighters. Who knew they lived such wonderful, warm, fulfilling lives? And were such generous people? If she were stranded on a desert island, these were the folks she'd want with her—and in particular a cowboy named Trey.

She felt an itch between her shoulder blades that

meant somebody was watching her. She turned around, expecting to see Trey. Instead, J.P. and Charlene walked toward her. Both were turned out in their usual Texas chic. She'd yet to see Charlene in anything other than skirts and high heels. Most people at the event had dressed comfortably casual with cowboy boots.

"What a fabulous event." Charlene smiled with plump, crimson lips. "Just had to stop by and tell you so."

"Thank you. Glad you could join us." Misty glanced at J.P. "And you made a great judge. I needed your expertise in making decisions."

"I've whipped up a batch of chili or two in my time."

"He's being modest," Charlene said. "He's won numerous awards for his chili."

"Guess it's a good thing for the winners you didn't enter the contest," Misty teased with a smile.

"Lots of fine competition," J.P. said modestly.

"Well, we're heading out," Charlene added, "so just wanted to thank you."

"Appreciate your support." Misty wished she'd been able to warm to the couple, but there was just something about them that left her cold.

"Glad to help out." J.P. turned to go.

Charlene hesitated, then stepped closer. "I was just wondering. Did you ever hear how that fire got started?"

"The Texas Timber tree farm?"

"I guess that's the one."

"Doubt they'll ever know for sure." Misty glanced from one to the other, wondering at their interest. But the fire had probably been the talk of the town.

"That's the way of fires," J.P. said.

Misty nodded. "See you back at Twin Oaks."

As the couple walked away, Misty still felt as if she were missing something about them. She glanced down at Charlene's shoes. *High heels.* Misty felt her breath catch in her throat as she thought back to Trey's pasture and the heel imprints. What about the tissue with a smear of what she now realized looked like Charlene's shade of crimson lipstick? No, surely not. They were simply a nice couple on an antique buying trip. And then she had another thought. At Christmastime? Wouldn't they be selling, not buying? Now that she'd turned her mind in their direction, she realized somebody staying at the B&B could have easily picked the lock and searched her room. And they drove a van that could be used to haul accelerant instead of collectibles. She felt the hair on the back of her neck stand up.

Maybe she'd eaten too much chili to think straight, but she couldn't deny the long list of coincidences. Had the corporate saboteurs been right under her nose this entire time? Yet she had no actual proof and the official investigation could take weeks if not months to complete and then it might not help much. But she felt excited, as if she'd finally taken a major step in solving the crimes. First, she wanted to run her idea by Trey.

There wasn't much more she needed to do here. The cafeteria staff would finish up. She emptied her water bottle in one long gulp and tossed it in the trash. She glanced around for Trey. And there he was. She felt her heart speed up at the sight of her very own good-looking cowboy firefighter.

"Hey," Trey called. "You ready for our hayride?"

As she looked at him, she felt sudden longing in her heart for a little girl with long, dark hair dancing in cowgirl boots.

"I wouldn't miss it for the world."

Chapter 37

After they said their good-byes, Trey tucked Misty's hand into the crook of his arm and escorted her outside. Night had fallen and a big yellow moon rode across the heavens as if ready to illuminate the way for Santa Claus and his reindeer. Blue lights twinkled in the trees, country music drifted from Old Town, and the scent of evergreens filled the soft evening breeze.

Mystical and magical, as always. Yet Trey had never enjoyed the season more, despite the fires and cut fence. He glanced at Misty. He knew who'd made this Christmas special for him. He pulled her closer against his side as they walked down the sidewalk. She smelled like chili and hot peppers. He figured he smelled the same way. And it was a tantalizing aroma. He wondered if she'd taste as hot as she looked at this very moment. Later he'd find out.

He nodded to people heading to their cars, Old Town, or the waiting hayride vehicles. Folks were getting in and out of pickups in the parking lot. They talked and laughed as they enjoyed Christmas in the Country.

On the far side of the parking lot, a long line of two-wheel flatbed trailers hooked up to ATVs waited for hayriders. He and his friends had built wood fences with two-by-fours, painted them red and green, and attached them to the trailers. They'd placed sweet-smelling, square-baled hay along the interior sides.

Folks could sit on the hay bales, lean against the fence, and see everything along the hayride route. Christmas lights twinkled in sparkling red and green along the flatbed fences.

Trey could hardly wait to take Misty on a hayride. She'd love the special route and he'd love having her with him.

"Come over here," Misty whispered, tugging on his arm. "I want to tell you something."

Surprised, he let her lead him under an oak tree with spreading limbs that was away from the revelers.

"I had an idea about the saboteurs." She spoke softly so as not to be overheard by anyone.

He leaned closer, anxious to hear what she had to say.

"J.P. and Charlene Gladstone."

"What!" His initial surprise turned to the realization that her idea was a distinct possibility. "Why do you think it's them?"

She began ticking off the points on her fingers. "They drive a van that could hide any number of dangerous items like gasoline in cans. They're staying in a nearby location at Twin Oaks. They're buying instead of selling during the holidays. And Charlene wears red lipstick and high heels. Those heels may be a fashion choice, but some women wear heels so much their tendons become shortened so they can't wear a low heel."

"I didn't know that." He nodded thoughtfully as his mind raced down the possibilities.

"Sad fact about high heels. Still, it might explain why she'd wear them in a pasture, if she was there."

"Pretty slim evidence." He played devil's advocate to push her theory.

"I know. But tonight there was something smug about them that set off alarm bells."

"They'd have a reason to be smug if they were putting this whole shebang over on us." He glanced out into the parking lot, but didn't see the Gladstones' dirty white van. "Something else. I noticed a lot of back-road dust on their vehicle."

"Good point. What I want to do now is—"

"Let's not spook them. Plus, you're in Wildcat Bluff County, not Dallas County. If you agree, let me run this by our police chief. If need be, he'll alert the county sheriff."

"That'll take time."

"But if you go off half-cocked, we might lose them."

"I won't do that. But I bet there's incriminating evidence instead of collectibles in their van."

"Requires a search warrant."

"True."

"Our law is as frustrated and anxious to stop these fires and catch the culprits as we are."

"I wish we could put a police tail on that van."

"Maybe we can."

"Should we warn Ruby?"

"Not yet. J.P. and Charlene may be innocent. Let me make a call."

She nodded in agreement.

Trey wanted to run out and confront the Gladstones as much as Misty did, but they had to handle the situation intelligently. He pulled his cell out of his pocket. The entire police department, augmented by sheriff deputies, was on duty during Christmas in the Country. He'd try to get hold of the police chief first. Harry was an old friend, and Trey had his cell number.

He kept calling till he finally got through. "Harry, it's Trey."

"Trouble at the chili cook-off?"

"No. All's fine here. Look, I've had an idea about the arsonists."

"Now? In the middle of Christmas in the Country?"

"Timing's lousy, I know." Trey ran a hand through his thick hair. "But it's the perfect time to set another fire with everybody so distracted, isn't it?"

"Hell yeah."

"Could you spare somebody to put a tail on J.P. and Charlene Gladstone? They're staying at Twin Oaks. And they drive a white van."

Trey heard Harry clicking on his computer. "Okay, got a hit. Nothing stands out about them."

"They left the chili cook-off a bit ago."

Misty tugged on Trey's arm. "Just a hunch. See if he'll check for them at the tree farm where we put out the last fire."

The thought made Trey's blood run cold. It'd be right across from Wildcat Ranch again. And it'd be an arrogant, smug, in-your-face kind of thing to do.

"Who's that with you?" Harry asked.

"I'll introduce you later," Trey said. "Misty Reynolds. She's a troubleshooter for Texas Timber. She wants to stop the fires as much as we do."

"Is she our Christmas angel?"

"Yep. That's her."

"Okay. I'll pull Jeremy off downtown and send him to Ruby's. If the van's not there, he'll go on to the tree farm. If he doesn't get a hit there, I'll see if the sheriff can spare a deputy."

"Thanks, Harry. Stay in touch."

"Will do."

Trey put his phone back in his pocket. "Could you hear any of that?"

"Bits and pieces."

"Okay. Harry's our chief of police. He's going to send Jeremy over to Ruby's to check on the van. If it's not there, he'll go to the tree farm."

"That's a relief."

"We may be barking up the wrong tree."

"True. But we can't take a chance." She looked up at Trey with a determined glint in her eyes. "And if that fails, we can drive backcountry roads all night till we do find the Gladstones."

"I can think of better things to do."

"Not if we catch them in the act."

"True." He squeezed her hand. "Harry's on the ball now. Till we hear from him, we might as well enjoy the hayride. Want to try?"

"Let's do more than try."

He pointed toward the line of ATVs with their colorful trailers.

"I don't mean to be ungrateful, but where are the horses?" Misty asked.

Trey sighed. "Everybody wants horses. They used ponies back in the day, but we've opted to hayride the easy way. Less mess. Less fuss."

"It'll still be just as much fun."

"That's right."

"Are you driving one of those rigs?"

"Not tonight." He pointed at the front of the line. "Kent leads the pack in his ATV. I bring up the rear in mine. We don't haul hayriders. That way, if there's an emergency or something, we're free to run up and down the line or go for help. And we're connected with our cell phones."

"Are you sure you've got room for a passenger?"

"You'll be right beside me." He put an arm around her waist and turned her toward the end of the line. They saw Bert Two walking up to them.

"Evenin'," Trey said.

"Enjoyed the chili." Bert Two nodded at Misty. "Good to see you again. You had a fine idea to raise funds for animal oxygen kits."

"Thanks for your support," Misty said.

"Anything to help our fire-rescue." Bert Two glanced at Trey. "Dad and I depend on them to help us. And we appreciate all the effort."

"Regret we haven't been able to save your buildings," Trey said.

"Most you can do is try. And hope there's an end to the harassment." Bert Two gestured toward the hayride trailers where folks were stepping aboard. "Don't let me hold you up. Just wanted to stop by and say thanks."

"Appreciate it," Trey said.

Bert Two tipped his cowboy hat to Misty. "Now, don't go forgettin' my offer."

"I won't," she said.

"You two have a fine Christmas Eve, hear now?" And Bert Two sauntered out into the parking lot.

"What offer? And where did you meet him?" Trey felt a stab of jealousy that he pushed back down.

"Adelia's Delights. And he's just being neighborly like folks do in Wildcat Bluff."

"He and his dad don't have the best reputations in the county."

"I've wondered if their building fires might be tied in with the tree farm fires."

"Could be. But Bert's building fires started before the first tree farm fire or my troubles."

"Guess there's no way to know yet."

"Let it go for now. Engines are revving up for the hayride."

He clasped Misty's hand and led her to his big Ranger ATV that could seat four people. Red and black with open sides and roll bars, the four-wheeler was his baby. It'd take on cross-country or streets and roads with nary a whimper. It wasn't a speed demon, but it was a work-horse. He couldn't have managed the ranch without it or his other ATVs. Some days a horse was the way to go on the ranch, but other occasions required a four-wheeler.

He settled Misty onto the passenger black leather bucket seat in front before he walked around to the storage bed in back. He pulled two cold bottles of milk out of the strapped-on cooler. He walked around, sat down, and handed her a bottle.

"Thanks."

"Milk is the best cure for chili heat."

"Double thanks." She took a long drink of milk. "What a relief!"

"Know the feeling." He chuckled, and then took a hefty slug before he set the bottle in a cup holder.

When the ATVs in front started forward, Trey turned on his engine. As the hayriders moved away from the cafeteria, they started singing in front and others picked up the song in a rolling wave till it reached the back of the line.

"They're singing?" Misty glanced at Trey in surprise as she set her bottle in a cup holder.

He grinned. "Didn't I tell you? This isn't just a hayride. Wildcat Bluff is waiting to hear our Christmas caroling."

Chapter 38

MISTY LAUGHED OUT LOUD WITH DELIGHT AND clapped her hands. She'd never have dreamed she'd be having so much fun on Christmas Eve. She certainly wouldn't have thought of caroling. Trey raised his voice in a deep baritone. She joined him with her soprano as she tried to remember songs she hadn't sung since childhood such as "Silent Night" and "White Christmas."

How her parents would've loved Christmas in the Country. She waited for the usual pain at their memory to bring tears to her eyes. Instead, she felt tenderness and love for all they'd given her and all they'd shared before the fire. She wished they could be with her now. Aunt Camilla, too.

Misty took a deep breath, feeling her lungs easily expand in contrast to the contraction she'd felt for so long. She'd healed in an unlikely place called Wildcat Bluff—thanks to its wonderful people, enduring spirit, and a cowboy named Trey Duval.

Trey must have sensed her thinking about him, for he glanced over with a hot glint in his eyes that promised more sizzling nights in their future. He took his right hand off the steering wheel and held it out to her. When she clasped his long, strong fingers, she felt as if she were cementing the bond they'd forged from the first moment they'd met on Wildcat Road.

When their train of hayriders wound around to Old

Town, Misty was amazed to see folks standing outside on the boardwalk and waiting for Christmas caroling. Businesses were still open with inviting holiday lights glimmering in windows and along the roofline above the boardwalk. A country band of men dressed in plaid shirts with jeans and women in long, colorful skirts played mandolin, fiddle, banjo, guitar, harmonica, and squeeze box in front of Adelia's Delights.

Kent led them to the far end of Main Street where he stopped so the ATVs pulling colorful trailers with laughing and waving hayriders could line up behind him in front of the boardwalk. Trey brought up the rear and braked at the entrance to Gene's Boot Hospital.

Soon the band broke into a lively "Winter Wonderland." Folks on the boardwalk joined in the song, clapping their hands, and the Christmas carolers raised their voices to add to the fun. Their joyful singing filled the night and spread out over the town like the bright jewels of stars across the night sky.

Trey held Misty's hand as they sang together, easily transitioning from popular country songs to old standards. "Joy to the World," "The First Noel," and "Deck the Halls" were favorites.

She could easily see a scene like this played out over a hundred years ago. Only she would be sitting in a horse-drawn wagon wearing old-time clothes—long-skirt and stylish hat. She felt a deep sense of continuity, a way of passing time-honored traditions from one generation to the next. She imagined enjoying Christmas in the Country with her yet-to-be little girl. Misty knew her parents had loved being together as a family at Christmas. From now on, she would celebrate the season in their memory and carry forward this fine tradition.

As the music wound down, the ATVs came to life, the hayriders waved in farewell, and folks on the board-walk waved back. Soon the caravan set off down Main Street, turned onto Cougar Lane, and trailed through neighborhoods as the hayriders sang Christmas carols to people who came out of houses onto their front lawns.

"Are you having fun?" Trey asked, glancing over at Misty.

"Yes! So much to do and so much fun."

"That's Christmas in the Country."

"I can see why folks come here from all over."

"One of my favorite sections of the hayride is coming up."

"There's more? And better?"

"Just wait and see."

Soon Kent turned down a street and the ATVs pulling trailers with their twinkling Christmas lights and happy carolers followed, one after another, until they disappeared from Misty's view.

"Now watch closely when I turn down that street." Trey pointed ahead.

"Okay." But she doubted there was anything that could top what she'd already seen in Wildcat Bluff.

As he made the turn, he slowed to a near stop, letting the caravan move on ahead without them.

"Oh, Trey! It's gorgeous." A large cluster of red, green, orange, and purple giant lollipops wrapped in cellophane were spotlighted by a single bright lamp at the base of the display on one side of the entrance to the street.

"Thought you'd like it."

"Lollipop Lane." Misty read the sign below the lollipops made with a fancy, crimson script on a bright, white board. She clapped her hands in delight.

Trey turned onto Lollipop Lane, driving at a snail's pace behind the line of hayriders. On either side of the street in front of the sidewalks ran a long ribbon of multicolored lights that connected the lane like an undulating river with gentle twists and turns.

"Oh! I love Lollipop Lane." Misty pulled her phone out of her pocket and snapped a few photos. She quickly texted one to Cindi Lou, knowing her BFF would love the sight, too.

Misty glanced from side to side to make sure she missed nothing along the lane. The residents had gone all out for Christmas. She'd never seen such a wide variety of decorations in such a limited area. She admired traditional red and green balls hanging from trees, an inflatable Santa Claus with reindeer, shimmering blue and white icicles stretched along a roofline with an illuminated angel on top, an electronic light show timed to Christmas music, and hand-carved and painted gingerbread folk. The creativity went on and on.

She wondered how the ribbon of light was made, so she looked closely at the ground. Folks had cut the ends off plastic gallon milk jugs and placed a colored lightbulb inside each container before laying them end to end to form a continuous line of stunning color.

She turned to Trey and smiled in happiness. "It's all so beautiful. Everyone has gone to so much time and trouble. Thanks for bringing me here."

"My pleasure." He returned her smile. "I knew you'd like Lollipop Lane."

"How long have residents been doing this?"

"Years. It's a tradition."

"And a wonderful one."

As the hayriders made their way down Lollipop Lane, singing Christmas carols with gusto, residents came out of their homes to watch and listen. Families laughed, pointed at friends, and waved to the caravan. Many folks carried kids, cats, or dogs in their arms. They were all dressed in colorful holiday clothes, including most of the cats and dogs.

Misty waved back, joining in the caroling with Trey, as the line moved steadily forward. Ahead, she saw that Lollipop Lane came to an end at a cross street. She was disappointed she'd soon be leaving behind this special place.

When she felt her phone vibrate, she checked and saw a text from Cindi Lou. "Yowzer!" Misty chuckled at her friend's response.

"Important?" Trey glanced down at Misty's phone.

"No. I just couldn't keep from sharing Lollipop Lane with my BFF Cindi Lou."

"And?"

"She loved it."

"Good."

As the last of the ATVs pulling trailers turned off Lollipop Lane, Trey stopped his four-wheeler.

Spread out before Misty on the front lawn across the street was a large Nativity scene illuminated by floodlights. The figures were beautifully carved of wood and hand painted to look as real as possible. She felt deeply touched by the beautiful sight. And then she looked closer to make sure her eyes weren't deceiving her.

"Are those horses?"

Trey chuckled as he pointed at the Nativity scene. "That's Wildcat Bluff heritage at its finest. Our ancestors decided it'd be smart for Comanche ponies to watch over the Baby Jesus instead of camels. If you look to the side of the manger scene, you'll see a panther guarding them all. "

"Makes a Wildcat Bluff kind of sense, doesn't it?"

"Yep. Horses once meant the difference between life and death to a person in the West. And cats have long protected this area. First, actual wildcats like cougars. And now other cats. It suits Wildcat Bluff."

She nodded in agreement as she turned to him with a smile.

He leaned over and pressed a soft kiss to her lips. "Just like you."

Chapter 39

As Trey drove away from Lollipop Lane, his cell phone vibrated where he'd tucked it in his shirt pocket.

He jerked it out and slid it open. "Trey here."

"All hell broke loose," Harry said in a gruff voice.

"How bad?" Trey got a sick feeling in his belly.

"What is it?" Misty appeared alarmed in the yellow light of a street lamp as she leaned toward him.

Trey turned on the speakerphone so she could hear his conversation with the police chief.

"Fires all over the place. Looks like somebody's trying to burn down the county."

"That's crazy."

"You're telling me." Harry's voice took on a hard edge. "Sent out all the rigs. Not enough. We called in Montague, Cooke, and Grayson Counties for support. Fannin County is on alert. Troopers and sheriff are on the job, too. But we're still shorthanded."

"Better get Hedy to call out the ranchers and farmers," Trey said. "They know our country roads like the backs of their hands and I bet they can spot a fire as fast as anybody."

"Hedy's on it. Christmas in the Country slowed our efforts, but the event's winding down so folks are getting freed up."

"Perfect timing for the culprits, isn't it?" Trey pulled off to the side of the street, stopped his ATV, and watched the caravan go on without him. Kent could do without backup at this point in the route.

"Yep. Somebody's got it in for us."

"How many fires?"

"Not sure."

Trey groaned. "Okay. Hayride's over. Kent's leading the ATVs back to the school. Call him. Soon as they unload the passengers and unhook the trailers, they can scour the pastures on their four-wheelers."

"That'll work."

"I'm free now. What do you want me to do?"

"Find Jeremy. I can't spare anybody else."

"Jeremy!" Trey felt like he'd been broadsided.

"Yeah. He reported in at Twin Oaks. The Gladstones' van wasn't there. He alerted Ruby. She checked their room, but they'd cleaned out without telling her."

"Suspicious, huh?"

"Damn straight. Ruby's staying there in case they come back. She's waiting with her shotgun, but I sent a guy over to stay with her."

"Good." Trey tapped his fingertips against the steering wheel. "Where did you last hear from Jeremy?" Trey hated to think the young whippersnapper might be in trouble.

"Wildcat Road at the turnoff to that partially burned tree farm across from your ranch."

Trey groaned again. "Think they went back to finish the job?"

"Crossed my mind."

"And Jeremy got caught in the middle of it." Trey's mind leaped ahead as he tried to sort out possible dangers. "Okay. I'll call in the hands to patrol the ranch, but I'll go after Jeremy."

"Thanks," Harry said. "And Trey, watch your back and stay in touch."

"You too." Trey clicked off his phone.

"Now I really think it's the Gladstones," Misty said. "But I won't contact Audrey till we know how this plays out. No need to worry her."

"Sounds good." Trey punched speed dial and got his foreman on the phone. "Greg, we've got a situation. Firebugs are attacking the county. They may try for the ranch again. Get hold of as many hands as you can and send them out on patrol. Call Harry if you run into trouble."

"They're not getting Wildcat Ranch," Greg said in a gravelly voice. "I'm on it." And he clicked off.

"Good man." Trey dropped his phone back in his pocket.

Misty gave Trey a determined look. "I can't think of any reason for the Gladstones to set all these fires except to scatter resources. That'd leave their real goals vulnerable, wouldn't it?"

He nodded in agreement. "The Texas Timber Christmas tree farm and Wildcat Ranch."

"Right. Nobody'd be around to stop the fires this time."

"If that's right, they'd go there last, wouldn't they?"

"I'd think so. And it'd mean we still have a chance to get ahead of the fires."

Trey hesitated and looked over at her. "Maybe I'd better take you back to the cafeteria. My truck's there."

"Why?" She cocked her head in puzzlement.

"I want you safe."

She smiled, but shook her head. "I don't want you in danger either. But that's not an option. We're in this together. Thick or thin."

"Let's go get 'em." Trey gunned the engine.

He tore down the street, and then turned down one lane after another till he'd driven out of town. He headed across open pasture, knowing the owners and knowing the fence gates that'd let him come in the back way to his own property. It'd give him a chance to surprise anybody watching the main roads.

He bounced the ATV across dry grass, startling sleeping cattle, driving cottontail rabbits out of hiding places, and sending birds flying from low perches in trees. He was glad the full moon illuminated the countryside. He had the ATV's headlights on, but those provided limited coverage.

Trey braked in front of a gate in a barbwire fence. He stepped out of his four-wheeler, opened the gate, got back in his ATV, drove to the other side, got out, and closed the gate.

When he sat down again, he glanced at Misty. "Rough ride?"

She smiled as she shook her head. "All in a day's work. Maybe you ought to let me open and shut gates from now on."

"It'd sure save time."

He took off across the pasture, bumping over clumps of grass and weaving around bushes as he watched the land and skies for anything that didn't fit. He dreaded to see the telltale sign of smoke over his ranch, but so far the night appeared normal.

Misty helped at the next gate, opening and closing it like an old hand. He hit a little-used dirt road that skirted the back side of his ranch. He didn't want to spook his own hands by tearing across pastures. He knew the sound of the ATV would carry on the night air, so he could only drive in so close without alerting others. He pulled up under the low-hanging branches of a live oak tree. He cut the lights and engine.

He stepped out and transferred his phone to the back pocket of his jeans. He listened intently as he gave his eyes a chance to adapt to the moonlight. No sounds of vehicles or folks talking. He didn't hear anything that was cause for alarm, but he still had an uneasy feeling that something wasn't right. He glanced back at the sky. As far as he could tell, there was still no sign of smoke in the bright full moon's light.

Misty got out and walked around to him. "What now?"

"Let's go in on foot to the road between the ranch and tree farm. See what we can see." He held a fingertip up to his mouth to indicate quiet.

She nodded in acknowledgment.

Trey set off at a jog and she kept right up with him. He was glad the dirt road muffled their footsteps so they could make good time. When they got close to the asphalt road, he slowed and held up his hand. She dropped down to a walk with him.

He crept up to a corner of the ranch's barbwire fence. Misty moved quietly like his shadow in the silver moonlight. Finally, he got a good view of the road. A Wildcat Bluff police car was parked on the shoulder up from the entrance to Wildcat Road. The front door was open. Trey felt a chill run up his spine. Misty squeezed his hand, so he knew she was concerned at the sight, too.

Where was Jeremy? He was a professional. He'd never abandon his vehicle and leave the door open. Now Trey was truly worried about the young policeman.

Trey glanced around the area again, but he didn't see any sign of the Gladstones' van. Maybe they'd come and gone or Jeremy might've spooked them to run for cover. Still, he doubted it.

He leaned down to whisper in Misty's ear. "Got to check on Jeremy. Stay off the road and in the shadow of the fence line."

She nodded in agreement.

He stepped onto the dry grass in front of the fence and started toward the police car. He kept his ears open and his eyes wide for any disturbance. One thing for sure, it was too quiet. Animals had gone to cover. That couldn't bode well.

They hadn't gone far when he heard the muted crackle of fire and caught a whiff of smoke. He looked in the direction beyond the burned area of the tree farm, but couldn't see anything. Still, he trusted his instincts.

When Misty clutched his hand, he glanced down at her. She pointed toward an area on the tree farm. She'd affirmed his suspicions. He glanced back at the police car. He was torn between going after Jeremy or seeing about the fire. Misty didn't give him a choice. She tugged hard on his hand, pulling him back toward the ATV. She was right. Jeremy was safer if they stopped the fire.

But where did that leave the Gladstones? Maybe they'd set the fire and used a back road to get out of there or maybe they were still lurking on the other side of the tree farm. Trey tugged his phone out of his pocket and tried to reach Hedy at the station. He hadn't expected coverage and he didn't get it. Even if he had gotten through, everybody was already out on calls. Bottom line, no backup. Whatever happened now, it was up to Misty and him.

He squeezed her hand and ran with her back to the four-wheeler. He leaped into the driver's seat and she jumped in the other side. He started the engine, turned on the headlights, and tore out down the dirt road. No time for stealth now. They were racing against time.

As Trey passed the asphalt road between his ranch and the tree farm, he glanced down it. Jeremy's police car hadn't moved an inch. He wanted to go down there, but it had to wait. He kept going so he could come up on the backside of the tree farm. Ahead, he finally saw the Gladstones' white van. He pointed for Misty to notice it, too. She nodded that she'd been proven right.

He cut left into the tree farm and kept going fast, dodging in between small cedars, smelling their pungent aroma, feeling the sharp limbs scrape across his bare arm through the open roll bars. He glanced to see if Misty was okay. She was leaning forward and toward the center of the ATV as she searched for the fire.

When he saw a flash of orange-red cut into the darkness, he aimed the ATV straight for the blaze. On the other side of the burning tree, J.P. and Charlene stood frozen with horrified expressions on their faces. They might as well be two deer caught in the headlights. He realized all they saw was a big four-wheeler barreling down on them. They couldn't see who drove the vehicle or the intent of the driver. Finally, J.P. grabbed Charlene's arm and started pulling her in the direction of their van, but she kept stumbling because of her high heels and impeding their progress.

Trey decided they weren't armed or they wouldn't be running away. He needed to stop them, but he had no way of subduing them. And then he had an idea that might work.

"Misty, take over driving, will you? No matter what happens, keep on their tail." He hollered above the sound of the engine and the scrape of the cedars against the ATV.

"I've never driven a four-wheeler before."

"You watched me. That's good enough."

He let go of the wheel and she caught it. He twisted around, grabbed the roll bar above his head, levered his body up and over the front seats, then landed on the backseat. He checked on Misty. She'd changed seats and was driving like a pro, staying right on the Gladstones as they tried to make it to their van.

He tossed a couple of old towels and a fire extinguisher into the front passenger seat. And he found what he was looking for on the floorboard. A rope. He grabbed it, made sure there was already a loop in place, and then stood up on the backseat.

With his head and chest above the open metal frame, he balanced against the swaying of the ATV with both feet, not unlike riding a bucking bronc. He raised his lasso over his head and started spinning it—waiting for just the right moment to rope two at once.

Trey watched as Misty kept after the Gladstones, but

they weren't an easy target. They were weaving between saplings, sometimes together, other times apart. Maybe this wasn't going to work after all. And then Charlene turned an ankle and went down. J.P. helped her up and kept an arm around her waist as they headed toward the van again. Just the opportunity Trey needed. He had one shot and it'd better work. He judged distance and forward momentum. And let the rope fly up—out, over— and the big loop of rope settled around the shoulders of J.P. and Charlene. Trey jerked hard and they went down in a heap with the rope binding their arms against their bodies.

"Stop!" Trey hollered to Misty. "I've got them. You get the fire."

As she slowed down, he leaped out of the ATV, keeping the rope tight in his hands. He heard Misty turn the four-wheeler around and head back toward the fire.

He ran over to the couple struggling to untangle from each other and remove the rope, but he'd been to this rodeo a few times before. He knew how to truss up a calf. He jerked hard, pinning their arms to their sides, then dropped to his knees and wound the rope around their ankles, back up to tie their wrists together, and tied off the rope. He'd been quick, just like he always was in an arena. Now they were hog-tied good and proper. They weren't hurt, except for their pride.

He hurried back to Misty, listening to Charlene's screams and curses as she struggled to get free. Guess she wasn't much of a lady when things didn't go her way.

Misty was beating at the fire with two towels, but trees with sap were hard to put out. He ran to the ATV, grabbed the fire extinguisher, came back, and doused the small tree as well as several saplings near it since he figured the Gladstones had poured gasoline over a wide area. Finally the blaze went out and the moonlit night again returned to silver and gray.

He hugged Misty close. "Got 'em."

"I've never seen anything to match you riding that ATV like the back of a horse and whirling that rope above your head. I'm so proud of you."

"Thanks. Got lucky."

They walked over to check on the Gladstones. J.P. and Charlene were struggling to get free of the rope that bound them.

"Hate to tell you," Trey said, "but the more you worry those knots, the tighter they'll get."

"How dare you truss us up like animals," Charlene complained as she gave Misty and Trey angry looks.

"How dare you burn down Texas Timber tree farms and cut Wildcat Ranch fence," Misty shot back at her.

"We don't know anything about that," J.P. said. "We saw a fire and were trying to put it out. Weren't we, my dear?"

"Yes, that's exactly right," Charlene agreed.

"Hope somebody is paying you a lot, 'cause you're in serious hot water." Misty put her hands on her hips and looked down at them.

"Don't know what you're talking about," J.P. said. "We were just taking a little drive after the chili cook-off."

"And helping out the community by trying to put out that fire," Charlene added.

"Guess the authorities will find a lot of collectibles in

your van," Misty said. "Then again, maybe they'll find something a lot more incriminating."

"Look, we're all professionals here," J.P. said in a voice that had taken on a wheedling tone. "Texas Timber has its goals, as you well know. Other folks have other goals. Why don't you untie us, send us on our way, and that's it. No harm. No foul."

"And there might even be a nice, fat bonus in it for both of you," Charlene added.

"Not gonna happen," Trey said in disgust.

"And I hope you broke all your fake, red nails," Misty bit out. "Petty of me, maybe, but there it is."

"Would a sprained ankle satisfy you?" Charlene asked in a snide tone.

"You'll answer to the law," Trey said. "Now, what did you do to Jeremy? And you'd better hope he's okay."

"Who?" J.P. asked.

"Wildcat Bluff Police."

"I can answer that." A shadow loomed up out of the darkness as a tall, lanky shape in a Wildcat Bluff Police uniform walked up to them.

"Jeremy!" Trey said in relief. "What happened to you?"

"I got out of my vehicle to help a lady in distress— namely that one on the ground," Jeremy said. "And I got bushwhacked by her partner. Knocked me out cold. I just came to. I've got a knot on the back of my head the size of an egg."

"I suppose we're going to have to go through all the legal formalities," J.P. said. "For the record, we want to file a complaint against these two vigilantes. We were innocently trying to put out a fire when they attacked us. And who knows what they might have put in our unlocked van to make us look guilty."

"News flash," Jeremy said. "You're in Wildcat Bluff County and we don't cotton to strangers trying to burn us down."

"No idea what you're talking about," J.P. said. "But if you don't get us untied soon, your city and county are going to be looking at a big lawsuit."

"Why didn't you gag them why you were trussing them up?" Jeremy complained.

"Didn't have my bandannas handy." Trey was shaking his head at the Gladstones' audacity when he heard sirens out on Wildcat Road. "You call in the cavalry?"

"Yep," Jeremy agreed. "Heard good news while I was at it. Fires all over the county were caught in time and put out. Thanks to our volunteers and friends in nearby counties."

"That's a relief," Misty said.

"Good," J.P. said. "Maybe we can deal with rational human beings, not Barney Fife here."

"And we want our lawyer now," Charlene added.

Trey glanced up when he saw several sets of blinking lights turn off Wildcat Road and drive up the asphalt road and stop across from their position. Soon Harry, with a trooper and a sheriff's deputy, tromped up to the Gladstones. They looked down and started laughing at the sight.

Harry glanced at Trey. "New rodeo event I didn't know about?"

"Got to keep in practice," Trey said.

"We demand to be released and to see our attorney," J.P. said.

"All in good time." Harry looked around the area. "Fire's out?"

"Misty took care of that." Trey pointed toward the dirt road. "The Gladstones' van is back there. Figure you'll find plenty of evidence in it."

Harry rubbed his chin. "We sent that tissue to forensics. Might be something interesting there, too." He looked at J.P. and Charlene. "You two ready to cool your heels in my fine jail?"

"Dinner and shower would be good," Charlene said, suddenly sounding pleasant. "I'm sure you'll see this is all a big misunderstanding."

Harry turned to Trey. "Thanks. All's well that ends well."

Trey nodded and put an arm around Misty's shoulders. "Figure you'll want a report, but we'd like to go home first."

"Later's fine." Harry tipped his cowboy hat to Misty. "Thanks. We've got this under control. It's Christmas Eve. Time for you to celebrate."

"Will you please contact Texas Timber and give them an official statement?" Misty asked.

"Sure will. We've been in touch with them since the first fire burned down their Christmas tree farm."

"Thanks." Misty smiled at the law officers. "And Merry Christmas to all of you."

They nodded and touched the brims of their hats.

Trey walked Misty back to his ATV, settled her inside, and joined her. He gave her a warm smile, then revved the engine and took off for home.

Chapter 40

MISTY AWOKE EARLY CHRISTMAS MORNING WITH A smile on her lips. She stretched in the soft cocoon of Trey's big bed. She felt completely content and satisfied with life. She'd talked with Audrey and Cindi Lou last night. Audrey had praised her work and promised a bonus. Cindi Lou had suggested she lasso Trey when she'd heard their story. One thing Misty knew for sure. She'd never have completed the Texas Timber job without Trey's help. They made a good team—in bed and out of it.

She smelled the tantalizing aroma of fresh-brewed coffee wafting upstairs from the kitchen. She doubted Trey knew her favorite coffee was Texas Pecan, but any dark rich brew would be good right about now. And she figured he knew exactly how to make it since he did everything so well.

When she heard his footsteps on the staircase, she just knew he was greeting her with a mug of delicious coffee first thing on Christmas. She loved the idea, particularly because he'd be holding the mug in his big strong hand and looking better than any fancy wrapped package.

She tried to hide her disappointment when he arrived in the bedroom carrying only a yellow sticky note.

"Merry Christmas." He wore nothing but a big grin on his face, an expanse of bronze, muscular chest, and reindeer sleep pants slung low on his narrow hips.

"Merry Christmas to you, too." She forgot all about the coffee. He looked good enough to be a luscious, satisfying breakfast all by his own self. She licked her lower lip in anticipation and patted the crimson sheet beside her. "Why don't you come back to bed?"

"Plenty of time for that later."

Again, he surprised her. Maybe he needed more enticement. She gave him a hot look and a suggestive smile.

He sat down on the edge of the bed with a mischievous grin. He shook the yellow sticky note as if to get her attention, then held the piece of paper out to her. "I want you to see my Christmas list."

"Okay." She took the note from him, deciding they could make up for lost time in bed soon. For now he wanted to share something with her and she was happy to do it. "Only two items?"

"That's right. But they're all I wanted for Christmas."

She set up to take a better look, wearing only his soft, cotton T-shirt in a rich lapis color. "Brrrr." She shivered. "Did you turn up the AC?"

He grinned even bigger. "Why don't you look at my list?"

"Number One," she read aloud. "Misty Reynolds."

"Notice that wish is checked off."

She cocked her head, trying to decide whether to laugh at his audacity or not. "When did you add my name?"

"First day I met you."

She did laugh then. "Cocky cowboy."

"Hopeful, that was it."

"I'm glad you got your wish."

He gave her a searing look with his hazel eyes, then glanced at the yellow note. "Notice I checked off my second wish, too."

"But Trey, you wrote down 'snow.' Did you decide to fudge this morning just so you could check off both items?"

"Fudge on a Christmas list?" He sounded horrified at the sacrilege. He walked over to the windows and snapped open the thick drapes.

Misty gasped, dropped the note, jumped off the bed, and rushed over to the sliding glass door. "Snow!" She slid open the door and stepped outside onto the cold, white, fluffy stuff. "I can hardly believe it." Bright sunlight sparkling across a blanket of snow had turned the ranch into a winter wonderland.

He followed her outside. "Blue Norther came through last night."

"And we didn't hear it?"

He wrapped his arms around her and pulled her back against the furnace of his body. "We were making plenty of noise of our own."

"I wouldn't have noticed anything but you." She snuggled back against him, enjoying the cold on one side of her body and the heat on the other. "Crazy Blue Northers. Sleet first. Then snow. If the temperature stays cold, no telling how long it'll take that snow to melt."

"Could be we're snowed in all day. Good thing Greg already volunteered to make sure the herds had food and water."

"Generous of him."

"He might've thought I'd be a tad distracted today."

Misty chuckled. "Can't imagine why." She snuggled her bottom against Trey and felt a satisfying hardness in response.

He wrapped his hands around her stomach, cradling her against him. "No telling what kind of fun we can get up to in the snow."

She spun around and thrust her hands into his thick hair. "Why don't we find out right now?"

He gave her a quick, hot kiss. "I've got a better surprise downstairs."

"Better?" She didn't know that could be possible, but Trey's surprises were usually wonderful.

"Yep. And this one won't wait."

He grasped her hand, led her back inside, and closed the door behind them. He rummaged around in a drawer and pulled out a pair of cotton sweatpants. "These are too big, but I don't want you catching cold."

"Thanks." She pulled them up under the big T-shirt and rolled them around her waist. She loved being wrapped in his clothes and his scent.

"Don't forget this." He picked up the macramé necklace from the nightstand and held it out to her.

"You're right." She slipped the necklace over her head and centered the angel pendant near her heart.

"Looks perfect." He grinned at her, excitement shining in his eyes like a little kid on Christmas morning. "Let's go."

She led the way downstairs, a little excited, a little apprehensive. At the bottom of the stairs, she turned around to look at him. "If you got me a Christmas gift, I didn't get you one. I'm sorry."

"Misty, you're all the gift I could ever want."

"But—"

"Come on." And he walked with a determined stride toward the Christmas tree.

She hesitated as she took in the wonderful scene. Colorful lights glowed in the deep green of the fragrant cedar. A roaring fire of red-orange flames danced in the fireplace and sent out delicious warmth. The Bluebird of Happiness gleamed on the coffee table. A pristine white landscape stretched to the Red River on the outside of the windows. But nothing was as fine as Trey Duval.

As she walked over, she saw that he'd knelt in front of the Christmas tree. He pulled a cardboard box with holes in its sides from under the tree. He reached inside, murmured something, and looked up at her.

"What have you got there?" She leaned down to get a closer look.

He raised a small bundle of black and white fur up to her. "Merry Christmas."

"Oh, Trey!" She sat down beside him, took the kitten into her hands, and nestled the little one in the crook of her arm. She kissed the top of the kitty's head and he gave a soft, contented meow in response. "Slim decided I could raise this kitten?"

"Yes. Sue Ann told Slim about your request. He's more than happy for you to enjoy the kitten you saved."

"You saved this little one, too."

Trey nodded. "We'll need to bottle-feed him since he was separated from his mother too early. Sue Ann will know what to do, so we can ask her about it."

"I'll be happy to do whatever is necessary to help this kitty."

"Me too. Now, what are you going to name him?"

"That's a big responsibility. But there's really only one name that suits this kitten. *Noel*."

"That's just right." Trey hesitated, as if not quite sure. "Misty, I know we haven't known each other long, but I've got no doubt. Will you look at Noel's collar?"

Puzzled, she stroked the green-and-white Christmas collar. "Pretty."

"There's something on it."

She looked closer and tugged loose a beautiful ring. Sparkling diamonds surrounded a large oval emerald set in rose gold. She glanced up at his face in confusion— but also hope.

"Will you marry me? I'm totally in love with you."

She gasped, feeling her heart race with excitement.

"That's my great-grandmother's wedding ring." His hazel eyes—ringed with gold, brown, and green—grew dark with concern. "If you don't like it, we can get something new."

"Not like it?" She felt tears of happiness fill her eyes. "I love it." She quickly set Noel gently on her lap, where he snuggled into the soft fabric. Then she threw her arms around Trey's neck. "I love you. Yes, oh yes, I'll marry you."

He pressed fervent kisses across her face, lingering on her lips, before he looked deep into her eyes. "We'll figure out your job, my ranch, everything later. So long as we're together, we can work out the rest."

She smiled as she held out the ring to him, wanting him to be the one to first place her engagement ring on her finger.

He solemnly slipped the ring onto the third finger of her left hand, and then he gave her a tender kiss.

She cupped his beloved face with her palm, watching her wonderful ring sparkle in the light of the Christmas tree. "I'm happy to make any plans you like—just so long as we have a cowboy wedding."

Acknowledgments

Support, encouragement, advice, and laughter got me on down the road in writing *A Cowboy Firefighter for Christmas*, so thanks go to C. Dean Andersson, Elaine English, Elisabeth Fairchild, and Deb Werksman for always being there.

A very special shout-out goes to the Clayton Volunteer Fire Department for saving the real Twin Oaks from a wind-whipped wildfire.

About the Author

Kim Redford draws her inspiration from a Texas life-style of cowboys, cowgirls, horses, cattle, rodeos, and small towns to create her bestselling novels. When she's not writing steamy romances, she's a rescue cat wrangler and a horseback rider. She divides her time between Texas and Oklahoma. *A Cowboy Firefighter for Christmas* is first in her Smokin' Hot Cowboys series with *Blazing Hot Cowboy* coming soon. Visit her at www.kimredford.com.

The Trouble with Texas Cowboys

by Carolyn Brown

New York Times and *USA Today* Bestselling Author

Can a girl ever have too many cowboys?

No sooner does pint-sized spitfire Jill Cleary set foot on Fiddle Creek Ranch than she finds herself in the middle of a hundred-year-old feud. Quaid Brennan and Tyrell Gallagher are both tall, handsome, and rich, and both are courting Jill to within an inch of her life. She's doing her best to give these feuding ranchers equal time—too bad it's dark-eyed Sawyer O'Donnell who makes her blood boil and her hormones hum...

"Brown's modern storytelling is humorous, heartwarming, and full of sass and spunk. The banter between Jill and Sawyer is infectious, and the chemistry between them sizzles. Add a solid, well-crafted plot filled with distinctive characters, and readers will be left with one entertaining read." —*RT Book Reviews*, 4 Stars

For more Carolyn Brown, visit:

www.sourcebooks.com

How to Kiss a Cowboy

Cowboys of Decker Ranch series

by Joanne Kennedy

—✸—

This cowboy is living a charmed life

Winning comes naturally to bronc rider Brady Caine. Ruggedly handsome, careless, and charismatic, the rodeo fans adore him and the buckle bunnies are his for the taking. He's riding high when he lands an endorsement deal with Lariat Western Wear that pairs him up with champion barrel racer Suze Carlyle.

Until one wrong move changes everything

A stupid move on Brady's part lands Suze in the hospital, her career in tatters. Now it's a whole new game for both of them. Brady is desperate to help Suze rebuild her life, but he's the last person she wants around now. Suze's got plenty of grit and determination—learning to trust Brady again is a very different matter.

—✸—

Praise for Joanne Kennedy:

"Joanne Kennedy's heroes are strong, honest, down-to-earth, and sexy as all get out." —*New York Journal of Books*

For more Joanne Kennedy, visit:

www.sourcebooks.com

Rough Rider

Hot Cowboy Nights Series
by Victoria Vane

—◦◦◦—

Old flames burn the hottest…

Janice Combes has adored Dirk Knowlton from the rodeo sidelines for years. She knows she'll never be able to compete with the dazzling all-American rodeo queen who's set her sights on Dirk. Playful banter is all Janice and Dirk will ever have…

Until the stormy night when he shows up at her door, injured and alone. Dirk's dripping wet, needs a place to stay, and Janice remembers why she could never settle for any other cowboy…

—◦◦◦—

Praise for Victoria Vane:

For more Victoria Vane, visit:

www.sourcebooks.com